THE
SELF-MADE
WIDOW

The
SELF-MADE
Widow

FABIAN NICIEZA

G. P. PUTNAM'S SONS
NEW YORK

PUTNAM
— EST. 1838 —

G. P. Putnam's Sons
Publishers Since 1838
An imprint of Penguin Random House LLC
penguinrandomhouse.com

Hardcover ISBN: 9780593191293
Ebook ISBN: 9780593191309

Printed in the United States of America
1st Printing

Interior illustrations by Jim Tierney

BOOK DESIGN BY KRISTIN DEL ROSARIO

To Tracey, my Sisyphus of patience,
along with Mariano and Marie, Steve and Stacie, Steve
and Nina, John and Karen, Rick and Francesca,
Bill and Mary, Laura and Mike, Thea and Reynold,
Lorie and Jeff, Kim and R.J., one and all shining
examples of suburban marriages done right!

THE
SELF-MADE
WIDOW

PART ONE

Only the Goode Dies Young

1

DEREK Goode rarely had pleasant dreams anymore. Between stress at work, stress at home, and stress about stress, he had been very stressed. His partnership track at the firm had been derailed. Even though his side project had generated much more revenue than he'd expected, now he was worried it would all blow up on him. Molly had been mad at him all summer, but he'd been too afraid to ask why. Henry hadn't made the premier soccer team, and Brett had started to display blatantly effeminate inclinations. For Derek, surprisingly, that had become a source of tremendous pride, though for Molly, unsurprisingly, a source of tremendous anxiety.

All things considered, when Derek went to sleep that night, it was understandable that his subconscious would be working overtime. His dream started off in quite a pleasant manner. It was a perfectly crisp summer day. No kids in the house. He wondered if it was even his house, since there were empty glasses left on the kitchen island and one couch pillow seemed slightly askew, which Molly would never allow.

He opened the stainless-steel refrigerator to find it completely filled with Kentucky Bourbon Barrel Ale. He grabbed one, then a second, and strolled into the backyard. Curiously, Molly was digging a hole in the walking garden. More curiously, she was wearing a black string bikini. She hadn't worn a bikini since she'd gotten pregnant with their oldest, Henry.

Thirty-eight and after two kids, in a dream or out, she looked great. Runner's body, flat abs, and her breasts were pre-kids. It was his dream, so he rolled with it. Her body glistened with sweat and her lean, tight legs were smeared with topsoil. She looked incredibly sexy. That was the thing about Molly: cold as ice, but hot as hell.

Derek shielded his eyes from the strong sun. The light was ridiculously bright.

He asked, "What are you doing?"

"Digging a hole," she said.

"What for?"

She didn't respond, but when she thrust the spade into the ground again, Derek clutched at his chest.

Molly dug into the ground again and he collapsed to his knees. He tried to get her to stop, but the words came out garbled.

She looked at him.

She smiled.

She went in for a third shovelful. He gasped for breath, but none came.

Did people breathe in dreams? Derek wondered.

Molly dug the shovel one more time, with greater force. She slowly twisted the shaft so that the blade ground into the dirt with a sickening scrape. To Derek, it felt like her every move was twisting his chest into knots.

He thought about the boys and how unfair this would be to them.

He wished he could see them again, but the sun was too blinding.

"Wow," he muttered. "That light is really bright."

And then Derek Goode died.

. . .

IT WAS 7:20 a.m. when West Windsor Police Department patrol officers Michelle Wu and Niket Patel pulled into the Windsor Ridge complex to address the 911 call. The paramedics had arrived moments before them. Emily and Ethan Phillips were entering the house. The twins had been born and raised in town and had joined the coincidentally named Twin W First Aid Squad while they were in college.

There was a third car in the driveway that led to a three-bay garage. Michelle assumed the husband and wife kept their cars inside, and their children weren't old enough to drive. Had Molly Goode called someone before she called the paramedics? More people in the house meant more emotion to deal with, and Officer Wu despised human emotion.

"I hope I don't have to string up a perimeter," muttered Niket, a joke between them alluding to the murder of a gas station attendant last year in which he had spectacularly lost a wrestling match with a roll of crime-scene tape.

"Pretty sure it'll be natural causes," Michelle replied, to Niket's great relief.

They were greeted at the front door by a woman with a Cheshire smile. It looked sincere but also entirely inappropriate for the moment. She had shellacked blond hair, with large, inviting eyes. Michelle was unnerved, less because of the woman's warmth and more because the officer recognized her. But from where?

"I'm Crystal Burns," she said. "I'm Molly's best friend. She's upstairs with the paramedics."

Officer Wu noted that Molly Goode's two sons were sitting in the kitchen. The younger boy cried as his older brother consoled him. The house was immaculate. Practically sterile. As she mounted the half-turn stairs, Michelle caught a ray of sunshine coming through the foyer window and couldn't see a single particle of dust floating in the air.

They stepped past Molly, who stood by the entrance to the master bedroom, tissue in hand but not a tear in her eye. Michelle noted a flash of tentative recognition in Niket's eyes. Molly looked as familiar to the two patrol officers as Crystal had.

The paramedics were inspecting Derek Goode's body. He lay in his bed, his hands frozen where he had clutched at his chest. His eyes remained wide open, staring to the ceiling. Heart attack was Michelle's first thought. He wore a faded Creed T-shirt from their 1999 *Human Clay* tour, which Michelle assumed he would never have worn had he known he'd be dying in it. Plaid boxer shorts and white ankle socks completed the regrettable shroud ensemble.

He had been a handsome man, tall with brushed-back brown hair that was graying at the temples. He was in good shape. Both of the Goodes were.

Michelle eyed Molly, who wore an Alala Essential long-sleeve workout shirt and Vuori Performance jogging pants. That was almost two hundred bucks' worth of workout clothes just to greet the paramedics. That was on the high end of unnecessary, even by the standards of West Windsor, New Jersey.

Molly Goode was pristine. Loose auburn hair, uncolored, bounced in a bob at her shoulder. She still had freckles, which gave her features a youthful glow that contrasted with her stern demeanor. She was five feet seven, thin and taut. It was clear Molly exercised quite a lot. Michelle thought, No hidden bag of Reese's Peanut Butter Cups in this one's night table drawer.

"I'm sorry for your loss," Michelle said.

Ethan Phillips said, "Patient is nonviable. We have to call the medical examiner."

"I didn't hear anything," Molly said. "I woke up at six forty-five to get the kids ready for school and I thought he was still sleeping. I heard his alarm go off from the kitchen at seven. When it didn't stop, I came up to see why and—and he was . . . he was . . ." She hesitated.

When Emily Phillips caught Michelle's glance, the paramedic said, "Rigidity has set in. I'd estimate time of death was about"—she looked to her brother—"four hours ago?"

"Give or take thirty minutes," her brother confirmed.

"Give or take," Emily agreed.

The doorbell rang. Crystal's loud voice echoed from the foyer as she let someone in. Michelle peeked out from the bedroom over the foyer railing. Another woman had arrived. Short, thin, with tightly cropped wavy brown hair and a raspy voice. Michelle recognized her, too.

And then she remembered where she knew these women from.

Shit, she thought.

"Molly, Bri is here," Crystal called out, her voice echoing.

"Excuse me," said Molly as she went downstairs to greet Brianne Singer.

Niket had also come to the same realization as Michelle, saying, "Those three women . . . ?"

"Yes," Michelle replied with dread in her voice.

The doorbell rang again.

With unintentionally synchronized timing, Michelle and Niket turned to look at each other.

Incapable of ignoring the bug-eyed fear on the cops' faces, Ethan asked, "What's wrong?"

The front door opened to the piercing wails of a crying baby. Lungs capable of rattling the three-thousand-dollar foyer chandelier blasted their noise through the house.

"Veshya kee santaan," Patel cursed in Hindi.

They could see her downstairs.

Her.

Andrea Stern.

She held her eleven-month-old baby and a diaper bag with her right arm. Completely indifferent to the child's howling, she hugged Molly with her free arm. Her curly dark hair was shorter and less enraged than the last time Michelle and Niket had seen her. From a circumference standpoint, Andrea had deflated about 85 percent from the size she had been during her pregnancy. Michelle quickly did the math and couldn't reconcile how the woman had given birth to a fifty-pound baby.

Andrea whispered something into Molly's ear. Molly nodded.

Michelle Wu took a step back as Andrea, still carrying the fleshy foghorn, made her way up the stairs. She entered the bedroom, nodding politely—no, sarcastically—at Wu and Patel.

"Officers," Andrea said in a sweet, lilting voice that fought against its native Queens accent.

Remaining indifferent to the child's incessant wailing, Andrea stopped just inside the door frame and scanned the room. She absorbed every detail. The position of the covers. Derek's frozen posture. The alarm clock on his side of the bed. The master bathroom door was open, so she could see the double-sink counter, where everything was arranged in a strict, regimented manner.

The baby kept crying. Michelle noted it was another girl. That made four girls and one very outnumbered boy.

The paramedic siblings looked uncertain as to what was going on. By now, nearly everyone in the sister towns of West Windsor–Plainsboro knew who Andrea Stern was. Besides having solved the murder of Satku Sasmal and having severely damaged the reputations of the West Windsor Police Department and township administration, she also had become a monthlong global viral sensation. A video of her water breaking in the middle of the heavily attended news conference last fall had made the rounds, exploding on Twitter before going through several TikTok variations. It had been entertaining though hollow revenge for those who had blamed Andrea for shattering the illusion of their storybook suburban lives.

Andrea was an investigative savant who should have been an FBI profiler but had ended up becoming a baby-making machine. While still in high school, she had solved the case of Emily Browning, missing in South Brunswick for twenty years. In college, Andrea had cracked New York City's notorious Morana serial killer case. She had also gotten pregnant before graduating, which had derailed her goal of working for the FBI.

Over the past year, she had become a semi-regular fixture at police headquarters as Detectives Rossi and Garmin had taken to requesting her advice on several cases. Even the mayor, who happened to be Officer Michelle Wu's mother, had asked for Andrea's input on administrative matters a few times.

Now, just as she had the first time the officers had met her, Andrea Stern was performing what the media had come to call "panoramic immersion." The small, annoying woman visualized the moment of Derek's death, capturing a mental image of the events as they had unfolded while retaining a photographic memory of the most minute details in the room.

The first time Michelle had seen Andrea do this—at the gas station where Satku had been killed—had unnerved her. This time, the officer was thankful as Andrea snapped out of it quickly and looked at her baby with a bemused, gentle smile.

"Hey, JoJo," she cooed. "You smell like fifty pounds of shit in a five-pound bag."

She spun the crying baby onto the bed right next to Derek's body. She slung the diaper bag so that it practically landed on the supine corpse. She removed the baby's diaper, which smelled like a Taco Bell had relieved its bowels in the middle of another Taco Bell. She removed wipes and a fresh diaper. Then, as if by prestidigitation, she cleaned and changed the baby with such speed that Michelle needed a slow-motion replay to confirm it had actually happened.

"That was a super-stinky poop," Andrea baby-talked.

The baby stopped crying.

Stern slid her arm through the diaper bag strap and, in a pirouetting motion, scooped up the baby with the same arm. JoJo giggled. Michelle guessed that by the fifth child, spastic grace just became muscle memory.

Andrea looked at Wu and Patel.

"Has anyone been in the bedroom since you arrived?"

They shook their heads in unison.

"Did you touch anything on either of their nightstands or in the bathroom?"

They shook their heads again.

"Did you call the medical examiner?"

They nodded.

She smiled at the cops. "Look how much better you guys are getting at this."

2

TWELVE minutes later, the Mercer County medical examiner's van arrived. Two men from the coroner's office spoke briefly with Molly. Pretending to be engaged with Brianne and Crystal in an effort to keep Henry and Brett distracted, Andrea had one eye on Molly the entire time. Andrea could tell that not a tear had been shed, but that was to be expected. Molly was rigidly, almost pathologically in control of everything in her life, especially her emotions. Andrea noted a small sore on her friend's lip, which hadn't been there when she'd last seen her, the previous week. Had Molly bitten her lip? A concession to the anxiety she must be internalizing?

Andrea had been friends with the other members of the club she secretly called the Cellulitists for about three years. She still thought it was very pithy to combine the word *cellulite* with *elitists* to come up with her private hashtag. She wasn't sure how to properly pronounce the composite word and rarely said it aloud. They had all met because their lives overlapped due to their children's school or recreational activities. None of the three women were the types Andrea normally would have befriended; then again, she had never really befriended any types throughout her entire life.

Crystal Burns was the gossip of the group, perpetually working her phone like an old line operator from a 1920s movie. She lived by the adage that knowledge is power, but in her case, it was the power to validate her self-worth. She was indescribably insecure, but also incredibly competent. Wanting to know something about everything meant she rarely knew much about anything, so the gossip too often amounted to ephemeral suburban hot air. And yet Crystal was also genuinely warm and caring, and would do anything for anyone anytime they needed it. Andrea sometimes suspected that she was kind for selfish reasons, but the fact remained that Crystal was the glue that held the group together.

Brianne Singer was the closest thing Andrea had to a real friend among the group. She was an interesting contradiction: feisty but timid, nurturing but selfish. Brianne was smart, but she was intellectually lazy, mostly as a result of all the years spent being intellectually lazy. She was selectively fierce and passionate about certain topics, but rarely informed enough to hold her own in an argument.

And then there was Molly Goode. The woman all other women were jealous of. Always put together, but never in a way that flaunted it. Molly was in better shape than you and better dressed than you, her hair was better than yours, and so were her manners. Even her grace in knowing she was better than you was better than the grace you tried to show in knowing she was better than you.

This morning, on what Andrea had to assume was one of the worst of Molly Goode's life, she looked as upset by her husband's death as she might have been by running late for a class at YogaSoul.

The doorbell rang again. Molly greeted Detectives Vince Rossi and Charlie Garmin. They saw Andrea over Molly's shoulder and nodded politely.

With Garmin supervising, the coroner's assistants bagged Derek's body upstairs. Rossi walked over to Andrea. She didn't need eyes in the back of her head to know her friends were all watching the exchange.

Her relationship with the Cellulitists, never warm and fuzzy to begin with, had become more distant since the revelation of her notorious past. Friends, apparently, aren't supposed to keep it a secret that they have a Wikipedia page under their maiden name. But at least that cat was now out of the bag, since someone had edited her entry and added her married name.

"Please don't tell me you have a theory?" Rossi smiled grimly.

She smiled. "Not yet."

Andrea knew that Rossi liked her, but he was also wary of her, as any cop a few years short of their full pension would be. She looked at the glimmer of tension behind his eyes. Andrea knew he was weighing if even she could find a way to turn a heart attack into a murder investigation.

She watched as the ME and the twin paramedics came down the stairs first, trailed by the coroner's assistants bringing Derek down in a body bag strapped to a stretcher. Patrol Officers Wu and Patel left the house with the paramedics. Andrea glanced over her shoulder at her friends. Crystal buried Brett's face to her chest to shield him. Brianne placed a comforting hand on Henry's shoulder as he watched his father being taken away forever. He was in middle school and was trying hard not to break down, but he looked like he'd been hollowed out from the inside.

Molly took it all in with icy detachment.

"You are kidding, right?" said Rossi softly. "About the theory?"

"Sure," Andrea replied. "I'm just kidding."

The ME, an Asian woman who worked out of Trenton, signed a form on a clipboard for the surly, burly Garmin, who then went over to his partner. "She thinks it was a heart attack."

"Damn young for that," muttered Rossi.

"According to the wife and the meds in the bathroom cabinet, he had a heart condition," said Garmin, looking at the clipboard. "Atrio-ventricular septal defect. Congenital."

Rossi cast a glance at Andrea, waiting for her to drop a bomb on that conclusion.

She said, "I didn't know about it."

Rossi nodded, thankful for the limited drama. Unexpected deaths tended to drag a lot of uncontrollable crying out of the families and friends, but this one had almost been downright convivial. The detectives spoke briefly to Molly, explaining to her what the next steps would be, and then they left.

The front door closed.

Andrea wondered for a moment: What would this feel like if it happened to her? After all she had been through in her marriage, what would she do if Jeff died on the way home from work?

Molly came to her and spoke in a soft voice so the others wouldn't hear. "Can you prevent them from performing an autopsy?"

"Why would they want to?" asked Andrea, but her brain said, *Why wouldn't you want them to?*

"Because of his age, I gather," Molly said. "The men who took him said the medical examiner would talk to Derek's doctors and confirm his prescriptions before making a decision."

"If he had a heart condition, then his doctors will confirm it, so I doubt they'd do an autopsy," Andrea said.

Molly hesitated, biting her lip so that her teeth scraped the edge of the cold sore. With a slight choke, she said, "The thought of him being cut apart just to find what we already know."

Andrea put a gentle hand on her friend's shoulder, sensing a vulnerability Molly rarely showed. She said, "I'll see what I can do."

BY TEN A.M., Andrea had lugged a fidgeting Josephine into the West Windsor Police Station. The kid was trying hard to walk these days, which meant she was getting impossible to carry. Each of Andrea's children had started walking earlier in progression than the previous model, and JoJo was keeping that streak alive.

Ruth, the oldest, hadn't walked until she was sixteen months. They thought she had motor-neural paralysis, but it turned out she just knew that the second she started walking her responsibilities in life would increase.

Elijah started at thirteen months, but then he'd mostly sat down for the next ten years.

Sarah began at eleven months and was running at a full sprint about a week later.

Sadie at ten months, but that was just to reach the stroller so her mother could push her around.

JoJo began a standing furniture shuffle at nine months and Andrea had mostly spent the past four weeks trying to keep her from hurting herself while she stumbled about like a rubber-suited monster from a *Power Rangers* episode.

She greeted Tom Templeton, the desk sergeant. After months of visits, he still glared at Andrea like she was a live virus. If she had asked for Garmin and Rossi, he likely would have begrudgingly buzzed her in, but because she asked to see Preet Anand, the new chief of police, he made her wait for clearance.

A minute later, she was walking through the station house. Garmin and Rossi nodded to her as she approached them. Hoping Garmin might have a piece of bagel for her to teethe on, JoJo fussed when Andrea whisked her by. Frustrated, JoJo started her warm-up in anticipation of an Olympic gold-medal meltdown.

Garmin stretched out his massive paws and said, "Hand her over before she forces us to draw our weapons."

Andrea smiled, always astounded how such a social lout could be so sweet with her baby. Charlie always said JoJo was good practice for when either of his two kids finally gave him grandkids.

JoJo was thrilled to play with the big teddy bear of a man. Rossi, as usual, was happy with whatever kept his partner quiet and kept Andrea moving along, which this did.

She walked toward Anand's office. Though Mayor Wu had settled on Anand months earlier, the chief hadn't been officially hired until August. He was young, in his early forties, forceful, commanding, and completely prepared for the job. Born and raised in Illinois, he had a master's in criminology and had served in the military for five years and then with the Michigan State Police for almost ten. He was no stranger to systemic prejudice and consistently overcame it through sheer hard work and competence.

He checked all the boxes the mayor had needed to fill for a town that was 70 percent Asian and had been underrepresented on the police force for years.

Andrea had been impressed by Anand during the interview process. He might not have small town community policing experience, but he was an agile administrator, smoothly political when necessary, and a truthful boss, and he seemed a sincere family man, all qualities that played in West Windsor.

He greeted her at the entrance to his office and invited her in. She apologized for not having made an appointment.

"This is about the death this morning?" he asked. "Garmin said you were a friend of the family. Heart attack?"

"Looks that way," she replied.

"But . . . ?"

"No buts." She smiled. "Just asking for the family if there will be an autopsy."

"That's up to the ME," said Anand, eyeing her with growing suspicion. "You know that."

"I do," she said. "It's just . . . Molly is wound pretty tight."

"I get that, but it's still up to the ME."

"I know," she said. "Maybe I'll call Jiaying to take the pressure off you."

Name-dropping the mayor by first name might have worked on the usual rubes, but Andrea realized she had made a mistake when Anand handed her his phone.

"If you don't know her cell number from memory, it's 609-555-1414," he said.

"That won't be necessary," she said.

"I know Derek Goode donated five thousand dollars to Wu's re-election last year," he said. "And four the time before that. And three before that."

She put her hands up in surrender with a smile. "Okay, I hear you. Subtlety didn't work."

"It might have, if you'd tried it." He smiled as his phone vibrated. "Excuse me."

He listened more than he spoke. When he hung up, Anand said, "And look at that, it was a card you didn't even need to play. Medical examiner spoke to Goode's doctor and cardiologist. His heart condition was legitimate. Described as 'a ticking time bomb.' She's calling it natural causes. No autopsy."

"Thank you," Andrea said.

She started to walk away when he said, "Andrea, since we're still getting to know each other, for the record, I've watched IEDs blow up my friends and I've been shot five times, with my vest stopping only three of those."

He let that sink in for a second.

"You have to come at me with something much better than veiled threats to my job."

"Filed for future reference, Chief," she said. "Threats to your wife and kids it is, then. . . ."

"Worth a shot," he said.

She smiled.

"But one shot is all you would get," he said.

Then he smiled.

She thought two things: this one might not be a pushover, and he had really nice teeth.

3

ON Friday morning, Derek's memorial service was held at the First Presbyterian Church of Dutch Neck, where the Goodes had worshipped. The old white building had been certified by the Presbytery of New Brunswick in 1816. Though Andrea certainly wasn't one for organized religion, she found a feeling of comfort inside the church, like the first sip of homemade soup.

The walls were cast in soft yellow and white, the pews mahogany. Very modest decorations made sitting in this church feel less uncomfortable for her than sitting in the synagogue when Jeff dragged the family there for show. Maybe because she felt no pressure here? Though she was a very sporadic attendee, the members of Beth El knew that Andrea frowned on religion. The truth was, she just wanted the right to judge everything and everyone around her without fear of being judged herself.

The pastor wore a black gown with a yellow-and-white-striped stole. He was tall, with white hair, and spoke in a soft voice that still managed to resonate throughout the hall as he extolled the virtues of Derek Goode.

Andrea wished she could see more than the back of Molly's head in order to gauge her reactions to the proceedings. Then she wondered why she had thought that. Molly was sitting in the front row next to her kids. Her brother-in-law, David, sat to her right with his wife, Deirdre, and their two children. Molly's brother and sister sat in a different row.

"Derek was a lawyer who worked with the elderly, managing their estates and helping them navigate the challenges of age and family security. An avid golfer who claimed a fifteen handicap," the pastor said to polite laughter from several people in the audience, including Jeff. "An active member of the community, a recreation league soccer coach, and a parishioner in good standing of this church."

He went on for a few more minutes, all of which Andrea knew was mostly horseshit. Derek hadn't been a dutiful husband to Molly, because Crystal had long ago gossiped about his affairs; he had been a soccer coach for one year; and most heinous of all, since Jeff always bragged about kicking Derek's ass on the green, he wasn't much of a golfer either.

Andrea just chalked it up to the platitudes necessary to ease people through the trauma of death. She saw death as a puzzle to solve rather than a life to celebrate, but the willful sugarcoating annoyed her. Derek and Molly didn't have a fantasy marriage with wind chimes resonating as they pranced about a grassy field like a pharmaceutical commercial distracting you while the rapid-fire voiceover warned you about side effects like rectal bleeding. Their marriage had gone through the same daily shit as anyone else's. Derek had been a party boy at work and a softy at home, but Molly made up for any softness on his part by being a hard-ass 24/7.

Maybe that's what had originally attracted them to each other.

Derek had been a successful lawyer, but he was childish, which was ironic considering his clientele were all elderly. He had been knowingly imposing and forceful in that handsome white-privileged way that most tall, handsome frat bros had. But he was funny and charming, and he had always doted on his children.

On the other hand, Molly was as spontaneous as a cabinet. And ultimately, that's what she was on the inside as well, a perfectly organized cabinet. Everything in its place and a place for everything. She had been a systems analyst for Wells Fargo before she gave birth to Henry. She was aware of her rigidity, and would joke about it with the Cellulitists but also casually dismiss it as a requirement of her upbringing.

Molly made monthly meal plans. She scheduled all her personal and social activities weeks in advance. She had six-month schedule organizers for her children, but assured everyone she was open to unexpected changes. Molly probably planned the days she would have sex and even the positions they would choose on those days.

Andrea realized she wasn't judging Molly for that so much as herself. For someone whose mind was so keenly attentive, Andrea's home life was a haphazard storm of daily drama over where to be, what not to forget, what had been forgotten, and where eggshells needed to be walked on.

Chaos had been her upbringing, but not her preferred default. Andrea's calmness while standing in the middle of any storm was what had originally attracted Jeff to her. They both had analytical minds, he for numbers, she for people, but Andrea processed information with a studied reserve, while he tended to process in rushed bursts of accelerated activity.

She now studied Crystal Burns, who sat two pews in front of her. Her husband, Wendell, sat at her right, their kids, Malcolm and Brittany, to her left. All were the very model of proper decorum. Crystal had her children well trained, not through a regimen of stern repression, like Molly, but because her kids knew from a very early age that if they didn't comport themselves, they'd be harangued about it for a never-ending span of time. And not never-ending in kid terms, but literally; Crystal's ability to fixate never ended.

Wendell looked bored, but then he always looked that way: tired of life and tired of trying not to look tired. Andrea liked him well enough, but as he had worked for the same accounting company since he'd graduated college, drudgery had become embedded into every pore of his skin. Commute to New York, work, commute home, hear about the kids' boring day at school, hear the same boring complaints from Crystal about the same boring things, rinse and repeat. But he maintained a stiff upper lip about it all, a by-product, she figured, of his New England upbringing.

Andrea turned her attention to Brianne and Martin Singer, who sat in the same row to her right. Their triplets had gone to school for the day so as to protect them from the ugly reality of death. Brianne was more fun than the others, with a crackling, self-deprecating sense of humor, and—kudos to her—she was someone who actively avoided whining about the same things everyone else whined about.

Her marriage to Martin was strained, Andrea knew. Brianne wanted more excitement than he was able to provide her. He had wanted to work in sports management, but ended up managing four assisted-living facilities in New Jersey that were owned by his family. As a result of forsaking passion in his work, Martin had forsaken passion in his life. He was quiet to the point of simulating plaster. Brianne complained that he was barely present for her or the triplets, but Andrea chalked that up to not even being present in his own life.

The Cellulitist husbands, Jeff included, weren't bad men, just worn down from the burden of the financial responsibilities their zip code demanded of them and terrified of a future that would include nothing but greater financial responsibilities. Ever-rising property taxes, car payments, mortgages, utilities, kids' activities, and in a few years, third and fourth cars and college tuition.

College. Tuition.

Amazing how one word—*greed*—could turn those two words into curse words.

Maybe Derek had gotten out while the getting was good, Andrea mused.

She noticed that Josephine, who had been sleeping in Jeff's arms, had started to rustle. She had sent their four other kids to school because wrestling all of them during a memorial service had not been an option. With all of them in full-day school sessions, life had become a lot easier for Andrea. Even though she still had to pick up Sadie from Montessori preschool at three, Ruth, Eli, and Sarah all took the bus, which meant less running around for her.

Andrea reached for the sippy cup in the diaper bag. Though the hall was warm, the formula didn't feel too bad. JoJo would likely survive. As the fifth—and absolutely the last—child Andrea would ever spawn, Josephine Esther Stern was already a hardscrabble survivor. Andrea hated Josephine as the choice of name, but since she'd picked three of the four previous ones, she had begrudgingly let Jeff have this one. Josephine had been named after his maternal grandmother.

She never called the baby Josephine, which she knew bothered Jeff. Andrea doubted his grandmother had ever been called JoJo, except possibly a time or two in the backseat of a '65 Impala, but she liked the nickname because it had a strong Queens vibe to it.

JoJo rubbed her closed eyes with her meaty little fists. The air-conditioning in the hall hadn't been turned on and the weather had remained in the seventies throughout the week. Andrea hoped the stale air wasn't going to set the baby off.

JoJo opened one eye. Seeing Andrea looking down at her, she smiled. Her front baby teeth made her look like Bugs Bunny. She was adorable.

"Want me to take her?" she whispered to Jeff.

He handed JoJo to Andrea, who gave the baby her sippy cup.

Finally, the pastor's eulogy ended. He called Molly to the altar to say a few words.

Molly went up with Henry and Brett on either side. The boys were in nice gray suits, which, considering how quickly they had been growing, seemed to have been tailored for the occasion. She wore a black skirt suit with a gray blouse whose color matched the boys' suits. Andrea mused that Molly looked as impeccable in mourning as she did on any given morning.

Her friend stepped to the microphone and thanked everyone for coming.

"Though this is a tragic shock for many of you, Derek and I had faced the possibility of this happening for years. We knew he had a heart condition, but he preferred we not speak of it. I apologize to all of you for that."

Andrea glanced toward Jeff. "Did you know?" she whispered.

He sheepishly shrugged his shoulders, which meant he had.

Molly spoke a bit more about the charitable work Derek had done for the church and his unflagging support in helping the elderly as a result of having lost his parents at a young age. She talked about his love for his sons. It was all perfunctory and lacking any real commitment.

Andrea glanced at Molly's older brother and sister, Jack and Maureen Parker, recognizing them from the lone photo Molly had of them at the house, taken during her wedding to Derek. They were stone-faced in the picture and stone-faced now. But not in sadness, Andrea thought. They looked . . . she hesitated, trying to pin down the right word.

They looked punctured.

Sagging. Deflated. Defeated. Molly's brother and sister had clearly traveled a different road than she had. Their lower-middle-class

Pennsylvania pedigrees were everything Molly had always sought to run away from.

Henry and Brett both spoke next, talking about how their dad had called himself "the human pillow" because he was the one they went to for hugs. Henry's voice cracked as he fought back tears. The entire hall was silent save for soft sobbing. Molly awkwardly hugged her oldest as Brett quickly joined in, and then together, they stepped off the altar.

The pastor returned to the podium and said, "Thank you for coming to the memorial service. There will be a light lunch and beverages in the fellowship hall. The Goode family welcomes all to attend."

With that, the service ended. The funeral was planned for Saturday and would be for family and invited guests only. So, small talk aside, that was that. Save for the hushed personal condolences and the sad shaking of heads over a tragic loss, Derek Goode was done.

Life seen through a windshield on Wednesday and in a rearview mirror by Friday.

Andrea picked up JoJo and slung the diaper bag over her free arm.

"I can carry that," Jeff said.

"It's okay, I got it," she replied. "Thanks."

She wanted to use the baby as her excuse to escape any conversations she didn't feel like having, which meant any conversations at all.

Over a hundred people had come to the memorial and half of them shuffled to the fellowship hall as the other half slid out of the church to escape. The Burnses came over to Andrea. An overwrought Crystal dramatically dabbed her blue eyes with a tissue that was already smeared by her running mascara. Jeff and Wendell sheepishly shook hands, both feeling some measure of silent guilt for still being alive. Malcolm and Brittany looked mortified by their mother's drama.

Brianne and Martin came over next.

"You sent your kids to school?" asked Crystal.

"I didn't want to have to wrangle them during the ceremony," said Andrea.

"I think it's important they understand the process of death now that they're old enough," said Crystal, adding her usual twist. "And Ruth *is* older than Malcolm."

"Ruth helped me investigate a double homicide last summer, so that's practically like having her mortician's license," replied Andrea. Malcolm and Brittany laughed, but were stifled when their mother gave them the stink eye.

The men grunted their way through the small talk while the women waited for an opening to visit Molly, who held court with her boys alongside the pastor and her siblings. Henry and Brett tugged at Molly's suit coat, wanting to see their cousins and Uncle David.

Flustered by their annoying antics, Molly eventually let the boys go and they rushed to see their uncle. He gave them a huge group hug, but it was the casual glance Molly tossed their way that Andrea noticed. A shade of envy that rarely darkened her eyes. Brianne trailed Crystal, who trailed her kids to the buffet. The men continued their caveman conversation. None of them had noticed the look that Andrea had seen.

She kept her attention firmly focused on Molly.

There was a strain between Molly and her siblings as they chatted. The pastor clearly sensed it, but tried to ignore it while consoling them. The three grew more agitated and the pastor's overtures became more emphatic. The siblings abruptly left the conversation and actually stormed out of the hall.

The pastor tried to comfort Molly, though she clearly didn't need it. Even when angry, she remained stoic. Andrea was curious what that encounter had been all about. She knew Molly's parents had died in a car accident when she was in college and that she didn't have a close relationship with her siblings. Jack was divorced and childless, while Maureen had never married, so there weren't nieces and nephews to generate the facile reasons for family gatherings. The excuse Molly always gave was that they lived three hours away in Quaker country. Molly said she had spent too much time and energy trying to get away from there to expend either going back.

Andrea realized she was starting to sweat. She reached around JoJo to get a cloth wipe out of the diaper bag to dab her forehead. As a direct result of JoJo's fascination with pulling at her curls, Andrea's mop of hair was now shorter than it had been since high school.

The hall was getting stiflingly hot. How Molly could be wearing a suit jacket and not have a drop of perspiration on her was unfathomable to Andrea. Others noticed her discomfort. Or were they just noticing her? Andrea's weight loss after JoJo's birth and the haircut had gone a long way toward alleviating the stares of recognition she'd received around town.

Those first six months after the embarrassing press conference and viral video had been torture for her. Almost a year out, maybe people had just moved on. She hoped so, but the glances now made her question it. Her preference leaned toward being the world's best but least recognizable crime solver.

Finally, Molly peeled away from the pastor and headed toward Andrea. Her friend was interrupted twice along the way by condolences from other people.

When Molly reached her, Andrea said, "Enough with the condolences."

"I was tired of them before I heard the first one," Molly replied. She did appreciate Andrea's complete absence of bullshit. "This is for everyone else as much as it is for me and the boys, right?"

"I think," Andrea said. "I don't have a lot of experience, to tell you the truth. But I know I wouldn't be able to endure it as well as you have."

Molly nodded, liking the choice of "endure" to describe it. She looked around the room. "A buffet?" she said. "I mean, it's just so . . . pedestrian."

"Hearing Derek had a heart condition was a surprise," Andrea said.

"It was . . ." She hesitated. "It was something that was always just there. Since he was young. Certainly a part of our lives since I met him. He was embarrassed by it. It was possible he would die from it, but at a certain point, when you *haven't* died yet, then it just stops feeling real. Does that make sense? It became no more of a concern than one might have about getting hit by a bus on any given day."

After a moment, Andrea said, "Have you had time to think about what you'll do next?"

"Think? I think I will put my husband in the ground tomorrow," she replied. "And then, I imagine, we'll all just go on living. What else are we supposed to do?"

She excused herself to greet some people from the church who had been waiting to offer their condolences. Andrea wondered if Molly's clinical assessment was logic, denial, or willful indifference. When does a naturally reserved and rational disposition step over the line and become pathologically unemotional?

Andrea stopped herself. She was in a bad mood and looking to turn a bad day into something worse than it already was. Molly's request that she try to bypass an autopsy had begun to rankle Andrea and had her looking for underlying reasons why someone would die of a heart attack. Absurd, but her inclinations always led her to look for a culprit even when there wasn't one to be found.

She needed to leave. Her habit of dissecting people through observation wasn't serving her—or her friends—well in this situation. She looked around for Jeff. When some children ran by them, JoJo fussed, wanting to join in. The baby blurted out a frustrated squawk that drew the attention of everyone around them.

Then JoJo decided to double down and let loose with a piercing scream. Her sudden outburst froze the entire hall. Everyone stared with the usual mix of admonition, compassion, and humor.

But it was one look in particular that caught Andrea's attention. Molly had turned from her conversation to watch an embarrassed Andrea wrestle with JoJo. A look in her eyes hit Andrea like a punch to the stomach. Not annoyance or frustration, not surprise or concern, not sympathy or support.

A look of . . . victory.

It was a look that combined judgment and gloating at the same time. A superior sympathy that the winners of a game always gave to the losers.

Jeff came over. "Time to go," he stated as much as asked.

"Please," she said as she handed the baby to her husband. He had a way of calming JoJo down that Andrea currently lacked. She had expected to be impatient with the baby, because honestly, she had never wanted a fifth child. Or a fourth, third, second, or, as much as she couldn't imagine her life without Ruth, even a first.

Maybe Andrea was unfairly placing the burden of all the opportunities she had lost in life on the baby because she had just gotten a taste of the life she could have had. The previous summer had been the most alive Andrea had felt since college. Which happened to be the last time she had been in pursuit of a killer.

"Should we say goodbye to Molly?" asked Jeff.

"No," Andrea said, abruptly enough that it caught him off guard. She softened. "She has enough on her plate. Speaking of . . . I can't eat that buffet. Let's get Shanghai Bun on the way home."

As they walked outside to their car, Jeff saw him before Andrea did. *Him.*

Kenny Lee.

The intrepid boy reporter, who had been Andrea's childhood friend and had worked with her to solve the Sasmal murder.

Kenneth Lee, Pulitzer Prize–winning journalist in college, perpetual screwup through his twenties, and now, having turned thirty, an unrelenting self-promotion machine. He had parlayed the murder investigation and the turmoil it had caused to the sister towns of West Windsor and Plainsboro into a book deal with Penguin Putnam, a Netflix documentary, and consistent appearances on conservative stations like Fox and Trust News as, of all things, an expert on crime and prejudice.

Kenny Lee, whom Andrea hadn't seen in three months, since the sentencing hearing for Satkunananthan Sasmal's killer.

Kenny Lee, wearing a Tommy Bahama black polo shirt with gray slacks and new black Ecco slip-ons. He casually leaned against his eighty-thousand-dollar metallic gray 2021 BMW 7 series and waved to them. She already missed his old Prius.

"What is he doing here?" Jeff asked.

"I don't know," she said. "Get JoJo in. I'll be with you in a second."

"Hey, Jeff," Kenny said.

Jeff released some kind of primordial grunt that might have meant "Hey" in Cro-Magnon.

Andrea strolled over to Kenny.

He hitched a thumb at JoJo, whose stubby arms reached over Jeff's shoulder, clutching air in a futile attempt to reach Kenny. "That one is a lot quieter than the others."

"You didn't hear her inside," Andrea said. She wasn't interested in banter with him. Their relationship had become strained. In some ways, she wasn't being fair to him, since her overwhelming desire to avoid publicity was in direct opposition to his desperation in seeking it out.

In his defense, she had read a proof of his manuscript over the summer and he had stayed true to his word and included Andrea more in the book than he ever had in his television appearances. She would always play second fiddle to Kenny when he was the one telling the story, and she knew she had no one to blame for that but herself.

"Why are you here?" she asked.

"Heart attack is what I heard," he replied by not replying.

"Looks that way," she said.

They watched Jeff finish up with JoJo. He closed the back door to the Odyssey and then scooted to the driver's side, keeping a suspicious eye on them the entire time.

Kenny and Andrea looked at each other for an awkward amount of time.

Then, at the same time, they both said, "I think Molly killed her husband."

4

ON Wednesday morning, while Andrea and the Cellulitists had gathered in Molly Goode's house to watch Derek removed in a body bag, Kenny Lee's day had started as most had over the past few months. He caught the 8:25 a.m. New Jersey Transit express train from Princeton Junction to Manhattan, then walked downtown twenty blocks to Union Square and the offices of Muckrakers Productions, the company that had optioned his book for a Netflix documentary.

He had everything he had wanted for the past several years.

Opportunity. Achievement. Respect.

Kenny had come to enjoy the sights, sounds, and yes, even the smells of the city in a way he hadn't when he had first worked in Manhattan, after college. For the brief period of time he'd been with the *Daily News* years earlier, Kenny hadn't appreciated what the city had to offer. Now fulfilling work with a group of people he actually liked being around had opened his eyes to a lot of things.

Once he had finished the first draft of the *Suburban Secrets* manuscript in March, Kenny had shifted his focus to the documentary. He had juggled both the book rewrites and the production needs of the documentary 24/7. Though his plate was full, his appetite had only grown. He'd become the Joey Chestnut of typing, a yawning maw that no amount of work could fill.

He stopped at the Starbucks on Broadway and Sixteenth and got coffee for everyone. He liked this Starbucks more than the one on Fourteenth or the one on Park and Seventeenth and definitely more than the one on Twelfth. He smiled as he paid for the drinks. Imagine Kenny Lee buying coffee for his crew, much less Kenny Lee having a crew. And most unbelievable of all, Kenny Lee remembering what his crew's regular Starbucks orders were.

New Kenny would have broken into a spontaneous Gene Kelly sidewalk dance if Old Kenny wasn't keenly aware that he'd trip and drop the coffee tray.

Kenny passed the Staples office supply store and entered the small, nondescript lobby at 9 Union Square West. He nodded good morning to Carlos at the small security desk and lucked into an elevator waiting for him on the ground floor. He walked through a large open office space on the fourth floor to the back, where the Muckrakers sublet from the computer-analyst-software-developers-who-knows-what-the-hell-they-do company that leased the floor. It was an open L-shaped floor plan and their production company leased the back of the L between the kitchen area and a large conference room.

Kenny couldn't wait for them to have their own floor, then their own building. He chided himself for thinking that way, since he had no ownership stake in the production company. He'd been without a sense of purpose for so long that he craved the friendships and mutual goals, but he had to constantly remind himself to keep it at arm's length. He was a contract player, and when the job was done, Muckrakers Productions could just walk away from him.

Business hours were technically ten to six, though as with everything in the digital age, work was expected out of you seven days a week with an extra dollop of guilt thrown at you by your corporate masters for not defying time and inventing an eighth day. Even getting to the office twenty minutes early, Kenny was the last to arrive. Jimmy Chaney, his friend from West Windsor, greeted him. Jimmy rode in from the same station as Kenny, but he usually took an earlier train. The Kenny Lee of a year ago would have been insecure about that. The Kenny Lee of today was glad to be a part of such a motivated group.

"What's the day looking like?" he asked as he put the cardboard tray down on a counter across from the desks. The counter ran underneath a row of windows that looked out over an alley between the backs of buildings and had become piled with excess office crap.

Jimmy grabbed the closest cup. The athletic African American had been, until a few months ago, a cable-line operator for Xfinity in Mercer County. He had helped Kenny and Andrea on the murder investigation the previous summer. When Kenny signed the Netflix deal, he had brought Jimmy along as his jack-of-all-trades, assistant, and cameraman.

Jimmy handed the cup he'd grabbed to Shelby. The fifty-one-year-old Shelby Taylor had served in the City of Charleston Police Department and was now a private investigator, kept on retainer by Muckrakers' parent company, the WWF Group. Wolfe-Weber-Fischer was considered a small multimedia conglomerate and had established Muckrakers, among dozens of other similar entities, as a production-specific LLC for *Suburban Secrets*.

Wearing a tight dark blue T-shirt and tight faded jeans, and with blond hair she assured everyone was natural, Shelby looked more like a former surfer than a former cop. But she was in better shape than Kenny and Jimmy combined. And Kenny conceded Jimmy accounted for 86 percent of that group total.

Jimmy passed a chai to Sitara Sengupta, their boss and supervising producer for the *Suburban Secrets* documentary. She thanked him and took a sip from her tea before running down the day's agenda. The thirty-one-year-old Indian American had thick black hair that was tied back in a hair band. She wore a loose-fitting Muckrakers T-shirt and casual brown linen pants with vintage beige suede ankle boots. She was an organizational savant who also had the ability to recognize the emotional core of any moment captured on camera. She was also Kenny's girlfriend. He was afraid that even thinking of that word might make it fall apart in the real world, but after a few months of active dating, this was as close as Kenny had come to a girlfriend in years. And years would be measured by the thirty he had existed on the surface of the planet.

As Sitara talked about administrative details that didn't interest him much, Kenny was distracted by a notification on his phone. The West Windsor Police Department had responded to a 911 call. He recognized it as the address of Andrea's friend, Molly Goode. Kenny noted that the medical examiner had been called in, which meant someone there was dead. He smiled when he saw that Officers Wu and Patel had been dispatched. He hoped for their sake it was death by natural causes. He had interviewed Molly for the documentary, but she'd been so stiff on camera that Sitara had cut all of her footage.

Pretty early in production on the documentary series, Kenny found the interview process to be his favorite part. He liked the Q&A. He liked the opportunity to hold people accountable for their mistakes on camera and he liked giving the people who had helped in the investigation their due. Building the story visually was quite a different experience from how he'd wrestled his newspaper articles and his book manuscript into shape. Ultimately, though, it was all storytelling, and *Suburban Secrets* had a great story to tell.

But something had been nagging Kenny for weeks and he had refused to listen to its whining chirp. He had ignored it not because of the workload of the documentary, or the book's impending release, or because his relationship with Sitara had entered new territory for him. He ignored the annoying pull because giving it voice might ruin the streak he'd been on.

Snapping himself out of his reverie, Kenny abruptly said, "I need to drag Jimmy to a meeting."

"Book meeting?" Sitara asked.

"Yeah," he said.

"I do need him here," she said.

Willingly entering into the passive-aggressive tug-of-war, Kenny said, "I'm paying half of Jimmy's salary out of my own pocket, so half of his time is mine."

"I'll give you the top half 'cause my face is so pretty," Jimmy said to Kenny, then turned to the women. "But I'll save the lower half for the ladies, because, based on all my Yelp reviews, that's the part most people prefer."

Shelby bounced her empty cup off Jimmy's head. Any potential argument between Kenny and Sitara had been thwarted.

"That's the way the day shapes up, then," said Sitara. "I'm editing. Shelby will do whatever Shelby does, which in my experience has been . . . whatever Shelby wants to do."

"Today I'll be pounding the pavement far and wide for a slice of authentic New York Sbarro's pizza," Shelby interrupted.

"You've lived in Brooklyn for three years. The hillbilly act doesn't work." Sitara continued, "And . . . Jimmy and Kenny are off to ensure Kenny's ego remains well fed."

Grabbing the four-thousand-dollar Sony PXW-FS5M2 4K XD-CAM camera that Kenny had paid for, Jimmy tapped Kenny on the shoulder and said, "We all know how hungry that beast is. Where we going first?"

THEY WENT UPTOWN to the offices of United Talent Agency to visit Kenny's book agent. They met Albert Lǔ for an update on the book's preorders and the cities that Putnam had finalized for the publicity tour. Though Albert hated it, Jimmy filmed the meeting for Kenny's

YouTube channel. Kenny was torn between promoting his own brand and still needing platforms like Putnam and Netflix to make him legitimate to a wider audience. And, gun to his head, Kenny couldn't verbalize what the end goal of all his self-promotion truly was, since he didn't have a personal agenda other than wealth and fame, and maybe not even so much wealth.

But still . . . the nagging buzz in the back of his mind wouldn't go away.

Their next meeting was with Digital Partners, the publicity agency Kenny had hired to help separate his own interests from those of his corporate partners. They were all about clicks and likes and views as if they were tangible things, but those meant significantly less to Kenny than things of substance, like wealth and fame, and maybe not even so much wealth.

Afterward, they returned to the Muckrakers office so that Jimmy could lock up the camera. Jimmy hadn't trusted Kenny even with the combination to the safe lock, much less with carrying the expensive equipment around the city. He said his goodbyes and left for the day, heading back to Penn Station to take a train home to West Windsor. Most nights, Kenny would have gone home with Jimmy, but since he'd started seeing Sitara, he often stayed and ate dinner with her.

An hour later, the young couple went to E.A.K. Ramen on Eleventh for dinner. They ordered water, since Sitara didn't drink and she was never thrilled when Kenny did. He figured if he was going to be in a mature, respectful adult relationship, he should probably get used to unequivocally submitting to her demands now.

"Can we talk about Thanksgiving?" she asked.

He was caught so off guard that an udon noodle almost came out his nose. "It's September, Tar. I can't tell you what I'm doing for dinner tomorrow night much less two months from now."

"Well, my family is in Boston and I figured it might be the perfect time for you to get to meet them," she replied.

"I guess," he said hesitantly, trying to figure out where the land mines were hidden in this conversation. "I'd have to make sure my mom is pawned off on my brother."

"Speaking of which, they're both in Jersey," she said. "So, when am I going to meet them?"

Before he could answer, *After I've been dead for five years*, Kenny's phone rang.

He didn't want to be rude, but he also didn't want to be engaged in this conversation, so he looked at the screen.

Unknown name. Unknown number.

Well, Sitara didn't know that, he reasoned, so he answered the phone.

"I have to take this," he lied, then quickly said, "Hello?"

"Is this Kenny Lee?" asked a woman's voice, purposefully muffled to such an exaggerated degree that she sounded like Charlie Brown's teacher doing Christian Bale doing Batman.

"Yes. Who's this?"

"Molly Goode killed her husband," said the voice. "He didn't die of natural causes. She killed him."

The caller hung up.

Sitara asked who it was. Without hesitation, and knowing his answer was the correct one, Kenny said, "Just someone helping me figure out what it is that's been nagging me for the last few weeks."

He smiled. He had a new story to tell.

5

As Andrea and Jeff drove from the memorial service, Jeff realized that his excitement for pork soup dumplings had been ruined by the unexpected appearance of Kenny Lee. From his perspective, the reporter was an existential threat to his marriage. On the other hand, Andrea had offered to take JoJo with her when she met Kenny later, so that meant he'd have an hour of bliss to himself. But the existential threat was there. Jeff worried that there could be another investigation right around the corner that would generate more problems between them. How intractable would Andrea become later if he came on too strong now? He decided to acquiesce for the time being.

"It's probably stuff about the documentary," Andrea lied. "And I think his book is coming out soon, so he needs to talk about the publicity that's going to come out of it."

Jeff grunted as he pulled into the cramped Ellsworth Center parking lot. He went into the restaurant and came out minutes later with a takeout bag. He said nothing as they drove home. She didn't push it.

Last year, when the shit hit the fan between them about her investigation, Andrea said she would never again be anyone but who she was. She had consulted with the police and the mayor a few times during the past year and Jeff had said little about it, though it had annoyed him.

She had granted Kenny an interview for his book, and then allowed the production company for the documentary to do the same. She had even agreed to be a paid editorial consultant on the first draft of the book manuscript. All of that had been done, she knew, so Kenny could cement her tacit acceptance of his version of events. Jeff had encouraged her to do it, because he knew the alternative of Andrea not participating would have bothered her even more. And, she suspected, because Jeff wanted her voice diminished in the telling of the story.

But now the reality of who Andrea was had resurfaced, and in her first opportunity to either placate Jeff with a lie or openly state her intentions, she had chosen the former.

After having promised herself she wouldn't deny or excuse her motivations ever again, she had done just that. Her anger at her weakness was sudden—but it was also fleeting, because making the right choice proved to be nowhere near as difficult a decision as she had feared it might.

"I'm not sure Derek's death was from natural causes," she blurted out.

"What?"

"Kenny got an anonymous phone call Wednesday night," she said. "We have to talk about it."

"He died of a heart attack in his sleep, Andie," Jeff said. "Molly said so."

"I know," she replied. "I still want to talk to Kenny about it."

"You think Molly killed her husband?" he asked incredulously. "She's your friend!"

Andrea winced, knowing she really didn't feel that Molly was her friend. At that moment, she wasn't certain she knew what Molly was at all, but she felt certain she wanted to find out.

THE SELF-MADE WIDOW   41

She said nothing. He hissed air, but also didn't say anything. For now.

They pulled into the driveway on Abbington Lane. The front bumper scraped the apron because Jeff took it too quickly. He opened the garage door. She wondered how he never struggled to do that, considering she hadn't changed the batteries in forever.

"I'll save you a chive bun," he said as he walked into the garage with a wave.

She got behind the wheel and drove to the MarketFair mall on Route 1 to meet Kenny.

He sat at a small table outside the entrance to Starbucks. He had already bought her an iced mocha. She was determined never to get pregnant again if only so she could keep drinking coffee.

"So, did you tell Jeff?" he said with a smile.

"I actually did," she said. "The new and improved Andie. No more hiding major murder investigations from my husband."

"That'll make for a healthy relationship, I'm sure," he muttered.

"Speaking of which, how is it going with your producer?"

"Wait, how did you know?" he asked, surprised, but realizing who he was dealing with, he shrugged. "Don't tell me."

"No, let me." She raised a thumb. "When you were filming my interview, you looked to her for approval seven times. I've never seen you look to anyone for approval but me, and then you would do the opposite of what I'd say anyway. In this case, you did everything she asked."

She raised her index finger. "You glanced at her ass four times, and you're not an ass-glancer. In fact, until I saw you look at her, I honestly didn't know if you were gay, bi, or an asexual plant."

"She does have a great ass."

"Goes well with you being one," she said, raising her middle finger. "During a break, you were getting tea and you grabbed a handful of M&M's. But you didn't have any; you gave them all to her."

"She likes M&M's. As far as vices go, it's pretty cute."

Fourth finger went up.

"Okay, enough already," he begged. "Fine. The world is your Dick and Jane book. We've been going out for a few months. So far, so good."

"That long?"

"I know, a new world record," Kenny replied.

"So, the call?" Andrea asked. The banter she felt compelled to conduct in order to keep Kenny from seeing how angry she still was with him had come to a comfortable conclusion.

"Eight twenty p.m. Unknown name, unknown number. Female voice. Muffled. All she said was, 'Molly Goode killed her husband. He didn't die of natural causes. She killed him.' Then she hung up."

Andrea considered it for a moment. Even with someone else's suspicion to go along with hers, she wasn't sure if it was true. Certainly, there had been something so condescending in the look Molly had cast at her at the service that it had infuriated her. But Andrea was above that level of pettiness for it to be her sole motivating force. *A motivating source,* sure, but not the *sole* one. She relied as much on instinct as she did on evidence, and in this instance, she wasn't sure she had either.

"I don't know," Andrea admitted. "There's just a level of uncertainty I'm feeling."

"I spent some time yesterday looking into it," he said. "The doctors confirmed his heart condition."

"Yes, which makes me feel like less of a chump for asking them to forgo the autopsy," Andrea said. "They said his heart could have killed him twenty years ago, or on Wednesday. But why that day? Did she do anything that might have led to his heart attack?"

"Would she have had any reason to?" Kenny asked.

Andrea said nothing.

Kenny was curious about her lack of commitment. "What are Molly's motives? Money? House is one-point-two mil on the market. He's making, I assume, low-to-mid six figures at his law firm. Life insurance policy? One million? Two? Was he having an affair? Was she being physically abused? Is her personality profile inclined to murdering her husband?"

Without missing a beat, Andrea answered in rapid succession, "They have money, or enough that money wouldn't be my first instinct. House is one-point-*three* on the market. Derek was making two hundred seventy-five thousand a year. I'm sure they have an insurance policy and it's two million at a minimum. Maybe more. I suspect he's had affairs, but I don't know if he was currently having one. Molly never indicated she was in an abusive relationship, but who knows for sure? If she was being abused, she's covered it well, and considering she never shows skin from the waist up, it's worth pursuing."

She thought some more. "Molly is president of the PTA at Millstone Upper Elementary School and has been for five years running, spanning both her kids attending it. In her real life, she was a systems analyst for Wells Fargo. She's organized and exacting to a terrifying degree. She can probably tell you how many freckles she has on her left cheek and provide you the most efficient path to connecting them all."

"Well, she sure sounds like a catch, but none of that says she's a murderer," Kenny responded.

"No, it doesn't," Andrea reluctantly agreed. "But whoever called you thinks that Molly is, so I have that person on my side."

"And just for the record, the person making that call wasn't you?"

She laughed at his audacity. He laughed in response, thinking that gave his audacity a pass.

"Fuck you," she said. "Fuck you twice. What do you think? I need to fabricate a murder investigation because that's the only way I can be happy? Or you're arrogant enough to think I couldn't handle an investigation without you? Fuck you a third time, Kenny."

"Whoa, wait a minute," he said, no longer interested in kowtowing to her. "I said it was just for the record. I didn't think it was you."

"Fine," she said. "It wasn't me. And I wouldn't have called you for help anyway."

"Well, that's good to know, because if you had, I don't know that I would have had the time to help you. I got enough going on that a privileged white suburban wife killing her privileged white suburban husband isn't enough of a blip to show up on my radar."

They sat in silence for several seconds. He sipped his chai. She sipped her iced mocha.

Kenny was indifferent to Andrea's insecurity. Her neediness. Her failure. Her hesitancy to accept and embrace how much smarter she was than everyone else around her. She exhausted every instinct he had and every amorally ambitious cell in his body.

Andrea was furious at Kenny's conceit and his presumption. At his newfound success that he owed to her. At his vapidity for considering his shallow accomplishments as a mark of success. He exhausted every instinct she had and every morally righteous cell in her body.

They sat in silence for several more seconds.

"I can start digging into Derek's work and finances," Kenny said.

"I can start digging into Molly's personal life," Andrea said.

6

THE morning of the funeral, Andrea wondered why the death of her friend's husband had caused such malignant thoughts to settle inside her brain. Why did she want to think Molly had done something wrong? Was it exactly what she had denied to Kenny? Could her own insecurities have led her to think the worst of Molly? Since childhood Andrea had shunned close relationships, and living in a state of arrogant superiority to others while being so insecure about herself had remained an entertaining contradiction for her.

Until middle school, Andrea had been a child grifter and part of an organized gang that ran scams throughout Queens. That had been the result of nurture as much as nature. Her parents claimed to be salespeople, but mostly what they had sold were black-market goods funneled to them by her father's friends, who were the kind of people who always knew someone who knew someone who saw some things fall off the back of a truck. Andrea now thought of it as disorganized crime, because people like her parents were too stupid to be organized about it.

Their apartment never saw a shortage of boxes filled with microwave ovens, DVDs, CDs, and cell phones. At the least, she had hoped all that cardboard would have dulled the sound of the constant arguing and yelling, but it hadn't. And the strife only got worse after her brother was killed.

*"**IT'S YOUR FAULT,** Andrea Esther Abelman!" her mother had shouted when they had come home from Isaac's funeral.*

"And that hoodlum trash you hang around with!" her father added for emphasis. "Bunch of con artists and thieves! Starting trouble with the gangs, for what?"

"Think you're so much smarter than everyone else," her mother added, "then why couldn't you figure out they would make you pay for what your gang did?"

Andie didn't cry as her parents berated her. She hadn't cried during the funeral. She hadn't cried two days earlier when Isaac had been stabbed in the chest right in front of her.

Eight years old and harder than a city sidewalk, Andie Abelman knew that tears wouldn't bring her brother back.

Nothing would. There was nothing Bernice and Jacob Abelman could say that would make her feel worse and nothing she would ever be able to do to unburden herself of the responsibility for Isaac's death.

ANDREA DIDN'T LIKE reminiscing about her childhood before moving to New Jersey when she was twelve, but the self-flagellation gave her the angle she needed to work Molly Goode.

Throughout history, wives had killed their husbands for plenty of reasons—and based on Andrea's personal experience, plenty of valid reasons. But she wasn't sure any of those played to Molly's situation or her sensibilities.

For money?

Because of sex?

To avoid physical abuse?

Any of those seemed possible, but none of them seemed plausible.

But what if Molly thought she could outsmart the planet?

That seemed plausible.

So, now all she had to do was prove it was possible.

She would have preferred dreary weather for Derek's funeral. In every comic book she'd read or movie she'd watched growing up, funerals were held in torrential downpours. That Saturday morning had turned out to be another sunny, hot September day with temperatures in the low eighties, but no humidity, which her hair was thankful for.

The Sterns had brought their entire brood to the church, except for JoJo, who was being watched by Andrea's friend Sathwika Duvvuri.

Ruth, her oldest, was somber. She knew Henry well and, at eleven, she was fully aware of the hole this would leave in his life moving forward. She was an intuitively aware preteen, in many ways like Andrea, though lacking her mother's cynicism.

Elijah was in a far better mood than he should have been considering the circumstances, but Andrea suspected it was because the funeral had given him an excuse not to attend his travel soccer game. After coming to the realization that the cool cred travel soccer offered wasn't worth the hard work it required, he had wanted to quit the team. Because their commitment to the season had already been made, Andrea and Jeff were forcing Eli to ride it out.

On the other hand, Sarah was furious she'd be missing the opportunity to steamroll her physically and mentally deficient opposition as clueless parents cheered her dozen breakaway goals during her G1 rec soccer game. Andrea had never been much for sports, but watching Sarah pummel anyone and everyone who got in her way, teammates included, in soccer, basketball, and lacrosse had her considering exploring the availability of D1 scholarship opportunities for six-year-olds.

Sadie, now her second youngest—and still pretty perturbed about having had no say in abdicating the crown—had seen a play set behind the nursery school adjoining the church and wanted to go to it. When the answer was the obvious no that even a soon-to-be-four-year-old should have seen coming a mile away, Sadie had angrily declared, "Funerals suck my foot!" Andrea commended her deft navigation around owing money to the swear jar.

The funeral was for close friends and family only, so there were far fewer cars in the lot than had been for the memorial service. Andrea felt a pang of guilt at wishing she hadn't qualified. Then again, maybe Jeff's friendship with Derek was the real reason they were there. Blaming him worked better for Andrea.

The Singers were getting out of their car. Brianne wore a black dress that was too short by four inches. Her legs were wiry, but toned enough to carry her sagging spirit for miles. Years of scattershot diets after the birth of her triplets a decade ago had somehow managed to work for her.

The triplets looked, as they always did, like an infinite mirror reflection. Clearly, Brianne had gone to Forever 21 yesterday after the service. Morgan, Madison, and Mary wore floral lace dresses with short sleeves and pleated skirts. They looked appropriately attired for grieving, but a few accents would turn those dresses into perfect mitzvah outfits. In contrast to Molly's impeccable dressing of Henry and Brett for the memorial and again today in different suits, Brianne didn't have the luxury of hand-me-downs and had to stretch a fashion dollar.

Martin wore a dark gray suit, and having lost thirty pounds in the past year, he looked like he was modeling for the Joseph Abboud scarecrow collection. But it was his eyes that caught Andrea's attention. More so than yesterday, when Martin had looked tired, now he looked . . . nervous. That meant a subconscious file for Martin Singer had just been opened in Andrea's mind.

The Burnses were mingling with several people outside the doors of the church. Crystal always arrived fifteen minutes early to gatherings in order to gossip. The narrow width of the sidewalk in front of the old entrance made the crowd spill out onto South Mill Road as they talked. Crystal waved Andrea over. The kids stood awkwardly around each other, unsure if it was inappropriate to talk or laugh or play. Ruth ordered them inside and for a change, they were glad to follow her commands.

"She is getting so bossy, I love it," said Crystal. Then, continuing without waiting for Andrea's answer: "How are you? This is awful. It just gets sadder, doesn't it? It's tragic. So young. The news about the heart condition, that was something, wasn't it? She hadn't told many people. I knew, she had told me, but still, you never expect it. It's so tragic. You think she's going to handle this? I don't know if she's going to handle it."

As Crystal drew in some oxygen, Andrea took advantage of the opportunity and replied, "Molly seems to be handling it just fine, doesn't she?"

The sarcasm edging Andrea's tone drew the curiosity of the small group of people around them, but they couldn't necessarily disagree with her. Molly, who was calmly engaged with the pastor and her older siblings, looked Audrey Hepburn–elegant in a Tifa stretch crepe long-sleeve belted dress that had to run at least seven hundred bucks. Considering the temperature, no one else had long sleeves, but Andrea could easily explain it away because of the circumstances.

Henry and Brett asked for Ruth and Eli. When Andrea told them they'd gone inside, Brett asked, "Can we go in, too?"

Taking advantage of the opportunity, Andrea held Brett's hand and said, "Let's go ask your mother."

She started walking them over to Molly, but the boys protested. "She's not going to let us," said Henry. "Can we just go hang with Uncle Dave?"

Andrea saw Derek's brother milling with his family several feet away from Molly. Guilty that she'd basically wanted to use the kids to access the conversation Molly was having, she said, "Sure, boys, go ahead. I'll just go tell your mom."

Henry and Brett scampered to Uncle Dave, who greeted them warmly. Andrea hovered near the Parker siblings and the pastor until Molly reluctantly said, "Andrea, you may not know Pastor John de Graaf, and my brother and sister, Jack and Maureen Parker? This is my friend Andrea Stern."

Recognition flashed in the eyes of the pastor. Andrea had become accustomed to the look. It was the combination of fascination, curiosity, and repulsion that most locals showed upon recognizing her.

"Yes, that one," Andrea responded, trying, in her stilted manner, to dispel the unease. She quickly turned to the siblings. "Jack, Maureen, it's good to meet you. We all knew you existed but Molly has been very secretive about you two."

Andrea could see Molly tense up beside her. She pasted a frozen smile for the pastor and through clenched teeth said, "I'm too private a person, even with my friends, I admit."

"So much to be private about," Maureen said, so softly that Andrea barely heard her.

"Our whole family has always been a bit close-lipped," Jack interjected quickly. "Maybe growing up so close to Quaker country. Hope it won't be that way for Henry and Brett now."

Andrea noted all the inflections, tics, and emotional shadings of the three siblings at the same time. Her initial impressions were exactly what she had expected. The older brother and sister had a bond that alienated them from Molly but seemed to protect them from her, as well. They were intimidated by her, but whatever anger they had toward her provided them some measure of defiance. The line about the distance to Quaker country justifying their lack of contact had been established long ago as a convenient rationalization to cover for something else.

Molly, the perfectly bitchy younger sister, must have made their lives miserable growing up. Manicured, cultured, and wealthy by their standards, she had done everything she could to separate herself from her Pennsyltucky roots. It showed in the way she dressed, talked, stood, moved, and breathed.

Hoping to steer the exchange, the pastor said, "Let's proceed inside for the service." He didn't wait for them. He practically skipped up the small steps and into the church.

Molly politely gestured to her siblings to go first and they did. Her hand gently guided Maureen along. It might as well have been a shove off a cliff, Andrea thought.

"I'll see you after the service," Molly said to her.

Crystal made her way toward them with Jeff and Wendell in tow. "Everything okay?" she asked.

"Sure," Andrea said.

Andrea entered the church.

Thankfully, the ceremony was short. Andrea hadn't been to many funerals in her life: Isaac's, which, to this day, she remembered to the minute. Zhi Ruo Gwan, her college roommate at Columbia, whose death had also been Andrea's fault. Jeff's grandparents. And now Derek Goode.

The cemetery was to the side and behind the church. The graves closest to the church and the roadway all dated back as far as the early 1800s, while the ones to the rear were more recent. The names on the worn, weathered stones of the larger family plots read like a history book of West Windsor: Appelget, Conover, Dey, Grover, Hawk, Tindall, Van Nest, Wycoff; all were among the architects of the town, their names now borne on housing developments, fields, parks, streets, and schools. As they walked along the gravel drive to the rear of the church, the kids pointed out the names they recognized.

Brianne was dabbing her eyes with a tissue. Martin was walking several feet in front of her, so Andrea sidled over. "You doing okay?" she asked.

Her friend nodded too vigorously and then started crying more forcefully. Andrea gently guided Brianne off the gravel path to allow others to walk by. She let her cry for a bit, then hugged her softly.

"What is it?" she asked, with an edge that implied there had to be something.

For a moment, Andrea sensed Brianne was going to say something— divulge something—but the moment passed.

"I'm just sad," Brianne muttered, nervously patting Andrea's hand, then quickly walking away.

Andrea watched the crowd of people numbly shuffle their way to the burial plot. They gathered where a hearse had driven the coffin the hundred yards to the open hole in the ground. She thought about the plans she'd had for her life, solving the most heinous and complex murders. She thought of the victims.

Andrea had once been quite emotionless in her consideration of the victim's place in their own murder, opting to focus on her role in trying to catch the murderer. But now, with a husband, kids, and a community that could be affected by all of it, she understood the tangled threads between crime and justice.

She looked at Jeff and the kids. She took in her friends, with their husbands and children, as well as Derek's brother and sister. She noted with curiosity that Henry and Brett were by them and not their mother. Maureen and Jack Parker stood off to the side of Derek's plot.

A warm breeze blew Molly's auburn hair delicately across her face. She peeled a strand away, tucking it curtly behind an ear. She looked like someone who felt that they had performed enough already and wanted the crowd to go home. Andrea could see no real sadness in her eyes, no subtle clenching of her jaw from stress or slouching of her perfect posture. Mostly, she looked a little bored.

The coffin was lowered into the ground. Molly tossed flowers, followed by Henry and Brett, and then members of Derek's family. Andrea stayed a distance away, scanning everyone's actions and reactions.

She didn't see enough to convince her that her paranoia was justified, but she also couldn't let go of the call Kenny had received. She had to reconcile her inclination that a dead body meant a crime had been committed with the off chance that a dead body just meant someone had died.

People died. It happened.

But people were also murdered. That happened, too.

AN HOUR LATER, Andrea drank iced tea on Sathwika Duvvuri's patio while JoJo crawled around Aditya, her friend's still mostly planked eight-month-old son. Though Sathwika said the pediatrician had assured her the infant was fine, Andrea wasn't sure if he would ever move. JoJo rolled over Aditya with the delicacy of a newly licensed teenager getting to drive the big rig at a monster truck rally.

As they sat on the very uncomfortable cushions over the wrought-iron patio chairs, Sathwika's in-laws, Samar and Esha, brought them plates with sambharo and cauliflower gashi. Andrea sampled the hot curry first, knowing if it was too spicy for her, the cold carrot and coleslaw salad would ease the burn. As usual, eating with Sathwika reminded Andrea of how mundane her food choices had been throughout her entire life.

"Thank you, it's delicious," she said to the in-laws. They were nice, if too chatty for Andrea's tastes. They wanted her to bring them a new episode of *Delhi Crime* every time she came over. And on this day, when she possibly had the makings of an episode, she wasn't in the mood to talk with them about it.

They sat down on the empty chairs around the table and waited to join in the discussion.

Sathwika, deliciously blunt as usual, said, "Sasu ji, Sasu ma, if you don't mind, Andie and I were just going to talk about our lactating cycles and nipple abrasion."

The in-laws quickly rose and excused themselves.

Andrea stifled her laugh by raising her glass to her mouth. "You are my sister from another mister," she whispered.

They ate in silence for a few seconds, watching their babies on the play mat.

As Andrea's rug rat came dangerously close to wandering off into the landscape bed, she chirped, "JoJo! No!"

JoJo stopped and looked at her mother.

Then she climbed into the raised landscape bed.

"Little shit!" Andrea exclaimed, but didn't move to stop her child's explorations.

Surprised, Sathwika said, "You're not going to get her?"

"Let her go," Andrea said. "If I stop her now, then it's something she'll want to do twice as badly tomorrow."

"When did you get so relaxed with them?" asked Sathwika. "I mean, at which point?"

"Probably with Sarah," Andrea replied. "She was an absolute monster. She climbed everything, threw tantrums, she had breath-holding spells. At some point, I just realized that they tend to survive."

Sathwika looked at Aditya, lying on his stomach and struggling just to crane his neck. Andrea knew Sathwika was worried about her baby, but respected her right to talk about it when she was ready.

After a few minutes, Sathwika said, "Your friend's husband? How hard has it been?"

"A lot harder for him than the rest of us," Andrea replied, giggling in her characteristically high pitch, which only made her giggle more. Reluctantly, Sathwika joined her. They stopped when JoJo tumbled off the other side of the landscape bed and down to the grass.

"JoJo, are you okay?"

No response. Then JoJo's head popped up over the raised pavers and she cooed.

"So . . . something is bothering you," Sathwika said. They had met during the Sasmal investigation and had become close over the past year. With JoJo and Aditya born three months apart, they had scheduled a lot of the usual baby activities together.

If Andrea could tell anyone about her current conflicted feelings, it would be Sathwika.

"I'm fine," she lied.

A gust of wind blew Andrea's curly hair in front of her eyes. She pushed it back. Compared to how Molly had smoothly done the same at the funeral, Andrea might as well have been fighting a mop in a hurricane.

"You're not going to stop JoJo?" Sathwika asked.

Andrea thought of Molly and her condescending look. Arrogant and smug and victorious.

"I like to give them a head start," she said. "But they never get away."

7

AT seven in the morning on Monday, Kenny sat in a makeup chair before his segment on *Fox & Friends*. He had been on the network often enough that he'd lost any sense of the jitters. The segment went smoothly. The negative was that clearly none of them had read the advance galley of his book, but the positive was that they let him do the bulk of the talking during his segment.

As he left the studio on Sixth Avenue, Kenny got a text from Albert congratulating him on a job well done. He pocketed the phone and entered the subway station. He didn't really care. Insofar as it would help the book sell, he was satisfied, but Kenny had gotten to the point where appearing on other people's shows wasn't enough. He wanted his own show.

Not on a stupid cable news channel talking about the hot air of the day. Something more. A Vice meets adorable but serious Jacob Soboroff meets *Columbo* magazine type of thing. But for a streaming platform, with episodic storytelling, blowing the lid off unsolved murders, corporate crimes, political scandal.

He didn't want to wait any longer. He felt he had been waiting his whole life.

Kenny Lee had always wanted more even when he had more than enough.

Book publicity, store signings, documentary editing, final follow-up interviews for any pickup shots they'd need after the initial edit—all of those things were currently on his plate, and all he could do was look at the dessert menu.

All he could think about was whether Molly Goode had killed her husband and who had called him to say that she had.

He decided to ride the F train down to Fourteenth and walk a block to Union Square rather than switch lines at Herald Square. The N and Q would drop him off right in front of the office, but he wanted to delay his return by as much time as he could steal.

He thought about the call. The options for who had made it broke down pretty simply into three categories. It had to be:

a) someone who knew Andie and the Goodes and knew of Kenny's involvement with Andie;

b) someone who knew Kenny and the Goodes; or

c) someone who knew Kenny was a dashing suburban muckraker and called to offer a tip.

As he emerged from the platform to the corner of Fourteenth and Avenue of the Americas, Kenny passed on options two and three. They were possible, but not probable. Which led him to suspect it was either one of Andrea's friends, or someone who worked closely with Derek and knew of the *Suburban Secrets* story from the news.

It wasn't likely he could dig into the Cellulitists the way Andrea could, but he had the resources to dig into Derek's work life. A game plan started coming together in his mind.

He walked to the back of their sublet space. Jimmy was hunched over Sitara's shoulder, editing footage with her. Shelby was painstakingly scanning her files and notes into a shareable PDF. How they picked up on Monday was pretty much how they had ended on Friday.

Maybe that was part of the problem for Kenny. This new work environment had come together quickly, within just the past six months, but it still felt too slow for him.

"How'd the interview go?" asked Sitara.

"You guys didn't watch it live?" he asked, a bit disappointed.

They were silent for a few seconds, then Jimmy said, "You picked your nose."

"I did not!" he replied.

"You did," Shelby said.

Kenny looked to Sitara for some kind of support. She nodded, slowly and with great empathy in her brown eyes.

He was crestfallen. Had he actually picked his nose on live TV? He did remember an itch. Had he just scratched it and it looked like a pick?

Everyone started laughing and he knew he'd been pranked.

Jimmy raised his fist and Kenny didn't want to leave him hanging, so he bumped it.

"Assholes," he muttered.

He dropped his backpack on his chair and emptied it. Casually, he said, "I was hoping to pull Shelby and Jimmy for some legwork today."

Sitara knew that was intended for her, phrased like a request but in actuality more of a benign order. She stopped editing and spun her chair around. "Legwork?"

"About that thing from Wednesday night," he said. "The call I got."

"Yeah?"

"I just wanted to dig into it a little bit," he said. "I thought about it over the weekend, did some research on Derek Goode. Maybe there's something there."

"Maybe there is," she said, returning her attention to her edit bay. "But I know there is something here."

"I delivered the new script you wanted, so can I just sniff around this a little?" he said, frustrated both that she expected him to ask permission and that he knew he had to ask for it.

"What's up?" asked Jimmy.

"Lawyer in West Windsor died last Wednesday of a heart attack," Kenny said. "Friend of Andie's. He had a preexisting heart condition, but I also got an anonymous call saying his wife killed him."

"What does Andie think?" asked Jimmy, trusting her instincts far more than Kenny's.

"She's got her radar up, too," Kenny said. Then off Sitara's look: "I talked to her on Friday about it. Her instincts have her curious about the possibility, at the very least."

"And any of this should involve us, why?" asked Shelby.

"My hometown," said Kenny. "Could be a good follow-up to *Suburban Secrets*. A different kind of sequel, but maybe expose a different kind of rot in the underbelly of suburbia?"

Shelby shrugged. Good enough for her. She liked rot.

"What do you need us to do?" asked Jimmy.

That got Sitara out of her chair in a jump. "Can we talk for a minute?" she said to Kenny.

They couldn't go to the large conference room behind them, since the wall facing their work area was floor-to-ceiling glass and you could see anything happening inside.

And in this case, "anything" meant Sitara yelling at Kenny.

She led him into the unisex bathroom, where she could vent without everyone hearing.

"Did you bring me here for office sex?" he asked.

"We haven't had *sex* sex yet—why would our first time be office sex?" she said.

"It's hot?" Kenny answered in the form of a question, because frankly, he had very little comparative data to go by.

"First of all," she started.

"There's more than one thing?" he interrupted.

"What?" she said, confused.

"You said, first of all," he said. "That implies a second of all, and probably a third, too. Too meaning also, not two, which was covered by second of all."

She ignored him. "First of all, we never said we would take time from our schedule to work on a new case. *Second of all*, we're contracted to work on *Suburban Secrets*, not *Suburban Secrets Two*. And I mean the number two, not also. And yes, there is a third of all: third of all, you don't set the schedule, I do. Oh, and look, holy shit, there is a fourth of all, too! Half of Jimmy works for you, but all of Shelby works for me. You can't order her around."

He waited a few seconds. The newly mature Kenny Lee bit his tongue on the fifty comebacks he'd already formulated. He breathed slowly and deeply. Considering the smell of urinal cakes cohabiting in sin with the floral air freshener, he regretted it immediately.

"I'm sorry," he said. "You're right on all counts. I would like to use Jimmy and Shelby for the afternoon, but if you need either or both, I understand. If you let me use them, I promise a dinner for two at Bengal Tiger."

Now it was Sitara's turn to take a breath. She regretted it, too. She crinkled her nose, which Kenny found to be cute, but he tried to maintain his aura of immovable machismo. She grabbed his hand and said, "Let's get out of this bathroom."

"Good idea," he said. "But do you honestly believe Shelby works for anyone?"

"No," Sitara replied. "I was just trying to sound commanding."

They walked back to their desk area. Sitara said, "Everyone in the conference room. Quick talk about Kenny's exciting new case."

Jimmy and Shelby exchanged glances, feeling awkward about Kenny and Sitara's relationship interfering with their work environment. Also feeling uncomfortable with the thought of either Kenny or Sitara in a romantic relationship, much less with each other.

In the conference room, Sitara tossed Kenny a whiteboard marker, which he fumbled to catch.

"The floor is yours," she said.

Kenny picked the marker up and wrote Derek Goode's name at the top of the board. To the left he drew a connecting line and wrote Molly's name, then beneath that Andrea's name. Below them he wrote "The Cellulitists" and admitted he'd forgotten all their names.

Shelby said, "Crystal Burns. Brianne Singer. Andrea Stern."

"The last one I remembered," Kenny said.

To the right, he wrote down "FCS," for Finch, Conover & Stanton, the name of the law firm where Derek worked in Manhattan. Beneath that he wrote a question mark.

Kenny explained that Andrea was going to poke into the details of Molly's marriage, family, and friendships. He wanted to explore Derek's professional world.

"Why?" asked Sitara.

"I told you why," he replied. "It could make for a really interesting sequel."

"Why now?" she asked.

"Because we all get in on it from the ground floor," Kenny said.

"But we're not all getting paid to get in on it from the ground floor because we don't have a landing spot for whatever this is or will be," she argued.

"I just want to take a peek under the hood. Maybe kick the tires," he said. "You're making it sound like I already bought the car and I'm cruising down the turnpike."

"No one cruises down the turnpike," Sitara replied.

"Can I please just have Jimmy and Shelby for the afternoon?" he asked, giving her his best innocent-boy puppy eyes.

"Fine," she relented. Kenny jumped several times in the air in a very poor display of cheerleading as she left saying, "I'm going back to editing the assignment we're actually being paid to do."

Shelby smiled and shook her head. "You push to the point of exhaustion."

Kenny smiled. "I know, but it's everyone else's exhaustion, not mine, so it's okay."

"What do you want us to do?" asked Jimmy.

Kenny asked Shelby to look into FCS while Jimmy went there posed as a messenger sent to clear out Derek's office.

"What if they don't let me in?" Jimmy asked.

"Who wouldn't be charmed by your six-foot-five-inch splendor, sculpted Black biceps, and megawatt smile?" Kenny said.

"You raise a valid point," Jimmy said.

"No, he doesn't," said Shelby. "He's as much of an idiot as you are. Give me half an hour to mock up a delivery service ID badge for you."

"I'll find a few empty banker boxes," Jimmy said.

"What are you going to do?" Shelby asked Kenny.

"I have to meet a reporter for coffee at Starbucks in twenty minutes," he replied. "We have to promote *Suburban Secrets*, right? I can't be wasting time on work we're not being paid to do. . . ."

KENNY SAT AT an outdoor table in front of the Starbucks on Sixteenth and Union Square West, wondering why he couldn't be content with what he had.

Pulitzer Prize at twenty-two, laid off from the *Daily News* at twenty-five, fired in disgrace from the *Star-Ledger* at twenty-seven, and reborn at thirty. His transgressions, his perpetual arrogance, all forgiven—or at least rationalized—because he had nailed a story that had resonated across the country. The one thing Americans liked more than seeing someone fall from grace was watching their redemption tour. But Kenny was so preoccupied with climbing higher that he hadn't found the time to enjoy the view from the vantage point he had regained.

The reporter from *Vanity Fair* showed up.

She didn't pose any questions he hadn't already been asked and he didn't provide any answers that he hadn't already given. It would be that kind of a nothing-burger sidebar piece alongside a review of his book.

Once she left, his phone vibrated. He looked at the screen. It was a text from Jimmy: in cab on way back got some good stuff

Though he hated that Jimmy never used punctuation in his text messages, Kenny was glad to hear the news. Thankfully, he thought, the amount of time he had spent chasing his own tail had been minimal. It was time to chase Molly Goode's tail.

He made a mental note not to phrase it that way when talking to Sitara.

For the moment, he was satisfied, which was twice as long as Kenny usually spent being satisfied. He knew, deep down, that no matter whom he decided to chase, he'd never be able to run fast enough to escape himself.

KENNY LEFT HIS brother Cary's room and sat down on the hall landing, slipping his legs between the rails to let his feet dangle over the foyer. He could hear his parents in the kitchen below, their voices getting louder.

His parents had been arguing with greater frequency over the past year. His father was soft, his mother was hard. Instead of finding a good balance in the middle, his mother thought that gave her the right to be relentless and punishing and, ultimately, victorious. Though Kenny wasn't sure what she would be winning. He looked to his brother for comfort, but as usual found none.

Even at eight years old, Kenny knew he loved his mother but didn't like her.

And he liked his father, but Kenny wasn't really sure he loved him.

Li Jun "William for the real estate placards" Lee had left his modest but steady job at GEO Specialty Chemicals in East Windsor to join his mother's growing real estate practice. Financially, the decision had been rewarding for them. A bigger house, new furniture, and more toys had surrounded Kenny over the past three years, but so had an increase in tension between his parents.

Finally, his father said, "Do what you want, Blaire. It's what you always do."

Kenny watched his dejected, defeated father stroll into the office/library at the front of the house. He closed the door behind him. Kenny didn't know who was right or wrong; he didn't know how he could help or if he should try. He only knew for sure that his mother would win this fight like she won them all.

The strong win out over the weak.

It was no different around a kitchen table than it was on the playground. His mother had taught him that already. Be ruthless and you'll get what you want.

KENNY WALKED THROUGH KASH's main office space. The acronym stood for Knowledge Acumen Scope Hope. It was as pretentious a name as they were useless a company. Everyone was mummified at their desks, staring at their screens and dutifully coding software for financial business solutions. He approached the Muckrakers corner space and was thankful Sitara was the only one there. If his macho tactic failed, he wouldn't want to be embarrassed in front of the others.

Again.

She looked up.

Be strong like your mother, he thought.

With virile determination, Kenny said, "No matter what you say, we're going to chase Molly Goode's tail."

She looked at him quizzically.

That hadn't gone the way he'd planned.

8

CARRYING JoJo in her portable car seat, Andrea met Crystal Burns and Brianne Singer for lunch at Panera Bread in Plainsboro. They had asked Molly to join them, but she had declined. Andrea was glad she'd have the opportunity to see what her friends knew of Molly's home life.

They were already seated with their food. Andrea placed the car seat on the empty chair, running its straps through the backrest to secure it. Crystal and Brianne ogled the sleeping baby as Andrea went to order food. She bought a strawberry poppyseed salad with chicken, just like Crystal and Brianne had.

She had been dieting and exercising for nearly a year since Josephine was born. Although she was exhausted by it and, in an odd way, resentful of becoming the very essence of the Cellulitists she secretly mocked, Andrea had to admit she felt in better shape than she had since Ruth was born. She'd lost the baby weight she'd gained from JoJo and most of what she had gained from Sadie. The first three might stay with her forever.

Andrea set her tray on the table and JoJo opened her eyes. It would be another one-handed meal. She undid the seat restraints before JoJo could have a conniption and Crystal interjected, "I'm almost done, let me hold her so you can eat."

"You sure?"

"Please," said Brianne. "It's the main reason she came to lunch."

The baby cooed at Crystal's enormous blue eyes and whiter-than-a-toothpaste-commercial smile. "Hello, Josephine. Hello." Andrea suspected getting Crystal to call the baby JoJo would be a forever problem. "You are so beautiful. Yes, you are."

Andrea ate a forkful of salad, wishing it were a plate of loaded fries from the Bel Aire Diner in Queens. Then she jumped right to the point and said, "So, did both of you know about Derek's heart condition?"

They glanced at each other uncomfortably, indicating they both had known. A part of that annoyed Andrea, but since she was the last one to have been folded into the group, it stood to reason there were things they had discussed among themselves that she wouldn't have been privy to. By the same token, it wasn't her imagination that they had all become more discreet around her after her past had been revealed.

"Molly told me after Wendell had that scare with the neurofibromatosis," Crystal said.

"Martin told me after Derek told him when they were golfing last year," Brianne said. "When I asked Molly about it, she said Derek went to bed every night thinking he might not wake up in the morning."

"Oh, that's awful," said Crystal, but she said it in a sweet, playful manner to keep JoJo's attention.

"It's why he said he did some of the things he did," Brianne said absently. "Live for the day kind of things."

"I understand that," said Crystal. "Don't you understand that, Josephine? Yes, you do!"

"What things?" asked Andrea before sliding in another forkful of salad. She hoped eating would give them time to talk and her to listen.

"What?" replied Brianne.

"You said it's why Derek did some of the things he did," prodded Andrea through a mouthful of food. She had the table manners of a bear. "Like, what things?"

"Oh, I don't know," Brianne said. "I mean, that's just what he said to Martin. That's what Martin told me he said."

She wasn't a good liar. She never had been. But what was she lying about exactly?

Andrea turned her attention to Crystal, understanding that one question could lead to a twenty-minute jag, so she had to phrase it just right in order to limit her friend to ten minutes.

"What exactly did Molly have to say about it when she told you, Crystal?" Andrea asked.

"Oh, you remember Wendell's chest pains he was having a few years ago?" she started. With that, Andrea knew her attempt had been futile and she would have plenty of time to finish her salad. Crystal spent five minutes talking about Wendell's neurofibromatosis before she even got to Derek and Molly. "So, one morning after it flared up again, I was having a Zumba class with Molly and that's when she told me about Derek. She said she didn't expect he would survive to see the boys graduate high school. Then she said it's why Derek was always so lenient with the kids and that she was always so guilty for making him feel guilty about it."

Crystal finished, looking like she was going to cry, but JoJo's giggle quickly brought her out of that Emmy-worthy moment. Andrea also couldn't imagine Molly feeling guilty about much. How much more did each of them know? Crystal talked a lot and usually said little, while Brianne said little but the things she *didn't* say spoke volumes.

"You think they were having problems?" Andrea asked.

"Molly and Derek?" said Crystal. Andrea wanted to smack her a hundred times on top of her head in quick succession like on the old Benny Hill VHS tapes her father would watch.

Andrea prompted, "We all have to deal with different shit, right?"

"I guess," Crystal said. "Derek was a bit of a loose cannon, handsome as he was."

Brianne nodded and quickly averted her eyes, so Andrea said, "He was handsome."

"He was," reiterated Crystal, with her habit of agreeing with you for having agreed with her. "Bit too much of a party boy. He would call Wendell to go out for drinks after work in the city, but Wendell wouldn't. That just seems like the kind of thing you do before you have kids, not afterwards, right?"

"Jeff goes out for beers after work sometimes," Andrea said. "I mean, if he did it every night, I guess that would bother me."

"Oh, absolutely," Crystal agreed.

"Did Derek do that?" Andrea poked. "Every night?"

Conspiratorially, Crystal looked left and right, then spoke directly to JoJo as if that would absolve her of guilt for gossiping. "More than Molly would have preferred. Oh, yes, he did. Yeah."

JoJo squawked loud enough to disrupt the surrounding tables. Luckily people preferred loud babies laughing to loud babies crying.

"He was trying to make partner," Brianne chimed in. "That takes a lot of schmoozing."

"Yeah, it must," said Andrea.

"You're asking a lot of questions," said Brianne.

"Am I?" Andrea responded. "I guess I am, I'm sorry. I was curious."

"Curious?" said Brianne.

"One of our friends dies at forty-three years old in the middle of the night, I don't see how I wouldn't be curious about it," Andrea said. "If I'd known about his condition, I probably wouldn't have as many questions."

Brianne wasn't buying it.

Andrea decided to confront it directly. "I'm not interrogating anyone, Bri," she said with a smile.

Flustered, Brianne backed down. She laughed and waved absently. "I know. I'm sorry. It's just . . ." She let it trail off, the answer inherent in her silence: *It's just that I think you are.*

"If I were interrogating you, I'd ask, 'Did you know of any specific problems in Molly and Derek's marriage?'"

Brianne could tell her friend wasn't joking now. Timidity lost out to defiance and she held her ground. "And if I were being interrogated, I'd say, 'You have to define the word *problem.*'"

Crystal, who had pretended to ignore most of that exchange, kept bouncing JoJo on her knees. Then the baby barfed up the formula she'd drunk earlier all over Crystal's floral-print blouse.

Andrea apologized profusely. As she helped Crystal clean up, all she could think was that her friends knew more than they were saying, but did that indicate they thought Molly could have murdered Derek? No. They all hid secrets of their marriages, from each other and even from themselves.

All that meant was that she had to keep digging.

9

AFTER getting a good look at what Jimmy had brought back from Derek Goode's office, Sitara backed down. Just like that. She had told Kenny to outline how he wanted to approach the investigation and she would build a schedule to accommodate it while they also worked to finish the documentary.

Kenny walked home from the Princeton Junction train station to his condo at Canal Pointe thinking about Jimmy's haul. The fact he did that while casually walking two and half miles from the station would have boggled old Kenny. He could pretend it was because he didn't want to pay the daily rates for parking at the train station, much less the king's ransom required for a yearly pass. Or that he didn't want to risk his new car getting stolen. But the truth was, he now loved to walk. The traffic from Route 1 buzzed below him as he walked the overpass. He pictured Jimmy returning to the office a few hours earlier, dropping the banker's box on the conference room table.

THE MUCKRAKERS REMOVED the odd assortment of items Jimmy had taken from Derek Goode's office. Folders, pictures, loose receipts, autographed baseballs. It almost looked as if Jimmy had just swiped an arm across the top of Goode's desk and whatever fell in was good enough for him. When asked if the drawers had been locked, Jimmy smiled and flexed his biceps.

"Everything you have here was illegally obtained," said a frustrated Sitara.

"Maybe not," Shelby said. "He was willingly let into the office."

"On false pretenses," said Sitara.

"What did you say when you got there?" Shelby asked Jimmy.

"What you wrote out for me to say," he replied. "I was there to get some personal belongings from Derek's office."

"You gave them a fake ID badge," Sitara countered.

"They didn't ask for my name, or even if I was from a messenger service," Jimmy said. "Nothing. Didn't even ask who had sent me. I didn't have to lie once."

"Can we just see what Jimmy got?" Kenny interjected. "Anything we find is going to need second-source corroboration anyway."

They skimmed through several files, a desk calendar that had a few scattered notes on its pages, a black satchel zipper-lock money bag, personal framed pictures, a few autographed baseballs, and a framed autographed photo of Derek with Barack Obama.

"What the hell?" Sitara said, already tired of the role she'd assumed. She was too rebellious by nature to be the kvetching contrarian. "You took his picture with Obama? And how the hell did he get an autographed picture with Obama?"

"We'll figure out a way to return the important stuff if we have to," Kenny muttered, looking at the baseballs. What he could make out of the chicken-scratch autographs included Barry Bonds, Mark McGwire, and Sammy Sosa. Someone was a fan during the steroid era.

As Shelby rifled through the manila folders, Kenny said, "The bag."

"It's locked," said Sitara.

Jimmy got his Swiss Army knife out. He used the pliers to break apart the small lock attached to the zipper on the pouch. He took items out of the bag.

"Gold Amex card in Derek's name. Receipts to restaurants and hotels in Manhattan. Five . . . ten . . . wow, twenty one-hundred-dollar bills. Did I say twenty? I meant six. Three flip phones. They look like burners. Amex statements for the last year. The billing address for the credit card is the lawyer's office."

"Corporate card?" asked Kenny.

Shelby, who had already plucked it from the pile Jimmy had been forming, said, "No corporate ID on the card. Just his name. Member since 2014."

"The expenses Derek didn't want Molly to see," Kenny said.

They looked at Sitara.

All she said was, "Keep digging."

KENNY REACHED HIS condo. Some of the neighbor kids were kicking a soccer ball in the courtyard. It was almost eight at night. They should be in bed, or something, he thought. His old Prius had gotten two dents from those fucking kids, diminishing its trade-in value when he bought the new car. Then again, what kind of a trade-in value did the Prius have by that point? New Kenny had shrugged it off.

"Hi, Mr. Kenny," said one of the Indian girls, whose name Kenny couldn't remember.

New Kenny could still be Old Kenny when it suited him.

"Hey," he muttered, walking up the steps to his second-floor unit.

His one-bedroom condo was neat and organized now. He'd hired a cleaning person to come twice a month. Since he'd also been going into the city regularly, he hadn't been around enough to turn the place into a sty.

He hung his jacket on the hook behind the door instead of tossing it on the floor. He separated the mail, putting the fliers into a recycling container on the floor and the bills into the wall organizer he'd put up with his own two hands. And by that, he meant that after having missed the studs with the drill he had bought at Lowe's and poking six holes into the wallboard, Kenny hired a handyman, whom he paid with his own two hands.

In Kenny's defense, the handyman took care of a few things besides just the wall organizer, but that was so Kenny could rationalize his humiliation.

New Kenny Lee still had some room for improvement, which made his confusion over his situation with Sitara all the more frustrating. He was having conflicted feelings, and other than adrenalized arrogance, he preferred not having any feelings at all.

He'd never had anything even remotely resembling a steady girlfriend. Junior year in high school, he had gone out with Lisa Kwan for three months. She had broken up with him because she had decided to stop lying to her parents about being lesbian.

In college, he had always been too busy trying to be the youngest person ever to win a Pulitzer for journalism to worry about hooking up. Sure, that part had worked out, but it had been at the expense of experiencing a normal intimate relationship—or even a deviant intimate relationship.

Kenny had been indifferent to the entire concept of mating. He didn't have a particularly high sex drive, but the few times he had engaged in sexual activities, they had been a perfectly pleasant, if temporary, distraction from whatever perceived injustice or slight he'd been stewing on.

Now he wondered if he was just looking for ways to sabotage his relationship with Sitara before it got too serious. Pushing buttons is what had attracted them to each other, but was he doing it now to push her away? He knew if Derek Goode's death turned out hinky, he'd obsess over it to the detriment of the documentary, and as a result, to the detriment of his relationship with Sitara. And he really didn't want that. She was smart as hell, funny, complex in her thinking, passionate, and accomplished. For all those reasons, he liked being with her, and for all the same reasons he was terrified of being with her.

His phone rang. His laptop followed suit a second later. The ringtone was Old Car Horn, which meant it was a FaceTime call. It also placed a comedic cap on his ruminations, but not before a thought lightning-whipped through his mind: he was scared of being hurt.

Shaking it off, Kenny answered the call on his laptop.

"Hey," he said to Jimmy, whose beaming face appeared on his screen. The guy was never not in a good mood. How exhausting, Kenny thought. Jimmy angled the phone to reveal Shelby seated next to him.

"We spent the last couple hours digging a little more into Goode," said Shelby. Kenny loved the experience she brought to their group. He knew she barely tolerated their millennial self-aggrandizing, but by the same token, their righteous indignation about everything fueled in her a passion she had abandoned long ago.

Shelby had been a cop in Charleston, South Carolina, for almost fifteen years. At thirty-eight, after several miscarriages, her latest pregnancy had made it into the fourth month and she had shifted to desk sergeant duties.

Three weeks into that safe gig, a bipolar homeless man they all knew named Donny Madigan had been brought in to cool off after he'd had an episode on East Bay Street. The times he had acted up before had all been peaceful, but they intimidated the tourists, which was the city's lifeblood. So, they brought Donny in to cool off.

Everyone had the complacency of routine about them that day and Shelby would admit she did, as well. They were understandably surprised when Donny grabbed an officer's gun and started firing wildly throughout the squad room.

Before Donny Madigan was shot to death, the wild spray of bullets had killed one officer and wounded three others, including Shelby Taylor.

Technically, the official report should have been two dead, since Shelby's wound had been a bullet to the abdomen that had gone through her five-month baby boy's head.

It took her six months to physically recover.

She never recovered mentally.

She was divorced within two years.

On her forty-second birthday, she left South Carolina and moved to Boston to start a new life. She became a private investigator and did some work for WHDH TV news. By age forty-five, she had become an in-demand PI helping news organizations and documentarians throughout the Northeast.

On her fiftieth birthday, needing better health insurance for her recurring gastrointestinal issues and perpetual therapy bills, she accepted an offer from Netflix as their director of internal investigations. Basically, she worked with whichever production company they assigned her to on whichever project required either a helping hand, a mommy, or a snitch.

Shelby said, "We used the loose notes on Derek's calendar and the receipts from the credit card to create a timeline and map for all of his activities that we could account for."

Jimmy added, "He didn't use the card every day, so there are a lot of blanks."

"Assume those are just days he went home to his loving wife and children like a good suburban husband," Kenny said. "What's the picture?"

"Derek is having a lot of fun, spending a lot of money, but depending on the clients he's entertaining—or at least claiming to entertain— they're not unreasonable expenses," Shelby said.

"But they're places we may not be able to afford to check out in the pursuit of an unfunded investigation," Jimmy said, smiling. "Gramercy Tavern, Sushi Yasuda, and Uncle Boons for dinners, never lunches, and the Elegance Gentlemen's Club for only the highest-quality entertainment that money can legally buy."

"Wow, just sitting at the bar to take a look around is going to bankrupt me," Kenny muttered. Then he added hesitantly, "Did you run this by Sitara?"

"Tried to," Shelby said, "but she waved it off. Not angry or anything. She's focused on editing. She said she'll look at it when we have a story worth looking at and a plan of action to look into it."

"You think we have either of those?" asked Kenny.

Shelby and Jimmy exchanged reluctant glances.

Kenny could tell they wanted to say yes, but they could only muster, "Not yet."

"That's okay," he replied. "First day and we already have a credit card he hid from his wife and regular visits to a strip club. I call those reasons to have a second day."

10

WHILE Kenny was riding the 6:32 New Jersey Transit train home from New York Penn Station to Princeton Junction, New Jersey, Andrea Stern was storing the remains of another indescribably poorly received dinner in a container, knowing the leftovers would likely sit in the fridge. The blackened tempeh bowl had gone over as she'd expected.

Trying to eat healthier meant she was making worse meals than she usually did. Sathwika had shared two dozen vegan dishes for her to try, so she'd been slowly going through her list. Ruth was loving it, since she had strongly lobbied for the family to try eating fewer animals, whereas Jeff, Sarah, and Eli would eat any and all animals placed on a plate in front of them, dead or alive.

After dinner, Andrea asked Jeff to take Sarah to the office in the basement to help her with her homework. She balanced Jeff's lingering sadness over Derek's death against Sarah's inability to sit still for ten minutes and decided the chance to talk to Ruth was worth the risk of either—or both—of them having a meltdown.

Sadie sat with JoJo in the playpen they'd set up in the family room. As much as their formerly youngest daughter hadn't been thrilled with

JoJo sucking all the oxygen out of the room that had previously belonged to her, Sadie did like playing with the baby when no one was watching.

Andrea asked her oldest to help with the dishes.

"I have homework to do, too," Ruth said as a blatant ploy to avoid helping with the chores.

That changed when her mother said, "I need to run something by you."

Andrea rinsed and passed the plates along to Ruth, who loaded the dishwasher. She had a "math mind" that Andrea lacked and understood geometric spacing in a way that would meet with Jeff's stringent expectations for proper dishwasher loading.

"How do you feel about Mr. Goode passing away?" she asked.

"It sucks," Ruth replied. "It's scary—I mean, he wasn't much older than you and Dad."

"Not much."

"But it makes you think that, I don't know, we can die just like that."

"We all can," Andrea said. "Did Henry go to school today?"

"Yeah," she replied. "He looked like a ghost. You know, he's kind of really pale to begin with—"

"Molly says it's her fair Irish skin," Andrea interrupted.

Ruth gave her a "whatever" shake of her head.

"Did you talk to him?"

"A little," she replied. "I told him again I was sorry and I'd help him out if he needed to catch up on any work he missed."

"That was nice of you," Andrea said. "Did Henry ever mention any problems between his parents?"

"Problems?"

"Arguing about anything," Andrea said. "Money, work, things like that."

"No," Ruth said. "I mean, we don't talk about that kind of stuff, Mom. *Gross.* No one talks about that."

"Think you could try?" Andrea asked.

Ruth's confused look quickly shifted as the lightbulb went on in her head. Andrea hated her daughter's increasing hormonal annoyance, but she loved her mental quickness.

"You think something happened?" Ruth asked.

"I do," Andrea replied. She learned last year that not only could Ruth handle the truth about her mother's past, but that it excited her daughter, who had taken to reading and watching more true crime mysteries as a result. "But it's just a hunch right now. That means I have to look for evidence."

"You don't think Henry would have—"

"No, not at all, honey," Andrea interrupted her. "It's not Henry. But before I can think it's anybody, I have to confirm a few things."

"Motive, opportunity, evidence of a crime, or evidence of a cover-up," Ruth rattled off.

Andrea laughed. "Ruth Knows the Truth. That could be the name of your crime diary."

"My what?"

"Nothing, never mind," said Andrea. "By the time I got to ninth grade, I had started recording diaries of all of my investigations. Every cell phone I'd found for people who lost them, a couple teachers and a school janitor who were causing trouble, things like that."

"Do you still have them?" Ruth asked.

"I don't know," said Andrea. "Probably, though I doubt the Sony cassette recorder I used still works."

"You stopped doing it?"

"Doing what?"

"Recording a diary of an investigation," Ruth said. "I mean, you didn't do that last year."

"Yeah, I stopped," Andrea said. "Some things happened during the Emily Browning case. The recordings I made ended up hurting some people even though I hadn't meant them to."

Ruth nodded, accepting that answer, for now, but Andrea knew her daughter was already performing the mental excavation of figuring out where in the basement her tapes might be hiding.

"Anyway, I need you to—really discreetly—find out what's been happening in Henry's house," Andrea said. "See if he can tell you if his parents were fighting, having money or health problems."

"I can do that," said Ruth. "But I don't want to hurt him."

"I appreciate that, honey," said Andrea. "It's not a matter of hurting him or forcing him to talk. Most people reveal a lot of interesting things just through casual conversation. So, just talk to him like a friend, okay?"

Ruth nodded.

"Go do your homework before Sadie tries to pawn JoJo off on you," said Andrea.

"I heard that!" Sadie called out from the family room.

Andrea and her daughter giggled. Ruth went upstairs with a bounce that froze her in Andrea's eyes, forever trapped between being a child and a teenager.

The moment of bliss was broken when she heard Jeff yelling from the basement. She went to the steps and called out, "Is everything okay?"

"Stupid new math!" he called back.

"We've been doing it for six years now, I don't think we can call it new anymore," she replied.

He came to the steps. "You don't have to call it anything since you never help them with their math homework."

"When it involves numbers, you're the go-to," she said. "When they have to solve a murder, I'll be there for them."

"Very funny," he said.

"We need to talk after they go to bed," she said. "Some tea for two and one of those cups will have a shot of whiskey in it?"

He slumped, acknowledging his mood and, in his own meager

way, apologizing for it, all with one hound dog slouch. He nodded and went back to Sarah.

JoJo cried out loudly.

Sadie shouted, "I didn't do anything!"

Which, of course, meant she had done something.

Sadie's defense was called into question by the sight of JoJo perched halfway over the playpen guardrail, on the brink of falling face-forward onto the area rug.

"She climbed up all by herself," said Sadie. "She's worse than Sarah."

"God, let's hope not," said Andrea.

"I heard that!" shouted Sarah from the basement.

"Sorry, honey, we were just joking," Andrea said, hoping Sarah's payback wouldn't involve climbing one of the town's recently added six-story cell towers.

Andrea scooped JoJo into her arms before the baby could fall and warmed up a bottle. She sat on the sofa chair in the family room, fed JoJo, and watched Sadie play with two American Girl dolls. The dolls belonged to her older sisters. Ruth had outgrown hers a while ago, but Sarah's was new. Two days after getting it for her sixth birthday in February, Sarah had chopped all the hair off the doll and dressed it in a Mets baseball jersey and jean shorts. She had tried playing rookie softball last spring, but the game had moved too slowly for her. She still watched games on TV with Jeff, and he was happy that his pitiful love of the Mets was being passed down to at least one of his kids.

Andrea suspected there was more bubbling under Sarah's surface. She worried that as the middle child, Sarah would endure the Jan Brady syndrome, and she didn't want that for the child.

Mostly because Jan Brady had been an asswipe.

As Andrea fed JoJo, the garage door opened and the door chime went off. Eli had come home from soccer practice.

"Cleats in the laundry room," she called out. "And your socks and shin guards, too."

"I know, I know," she heard him respond. Lately, his equipment and clothes had started to smell like the exposed insides of a roadkill raccoon. He bounced into the kitchen, liberated from the drudgery and embarrassment he felt during every practice.

Both financially and logistically, Andrea was thrilled that he didn't want to play travel soccer anymore. But by next year, Sarah would be making up for that exponentially. Andrea feared travel soccer, basketball, and lacrosse in her middle child's future, because it promised exhausted and expensive misery in theirs.

"You hungry?" she asked. "We have cereal."

"Eggos with vanilla ice cream," he said as he started to get the items out.

She liked that Ruth, Elijah, and, to a surprising extent, Sarah had become much more self-sufficient in the past year. Helping to care for JoJo was a part of that, and the responsibility had been good for them. The real reason for it was that JoJo and Sadie demanded so much of Andrea's attention that the older siblings had little choice but to fend for themselves. That triggered the part of Andrea— probably of every mother—that felt guilty for not giving them enough individual attention. But how could any given day be divided equally by five?

Eli got a scoop of ice cream for Sadie and then put sprinkles on it. They ate together at the kitchen table as Andrea sat on the couch and made small talk with them about school and Eli's practice. Things within the family had gone far more smoothly than she'd thought they would since JoJo had popped out. There had been a release of air from the tires, Andrea thought. A lot of the tension and resentment she'd been carrying for years—against Jeff, against herself, and even against the children—had hissed out of her coiled body.

Solving the murders last fall had solved the riddle of her life. It had put everything into perspective. It hadn't solved the main problem—that Andrea Stern wasn't living the life she should be—but it had gone a long way toward easing the doubt she had felt for so many years. She knew who she was. Maybe she wasn't in a place where she could fully be that person just yet, but the insecurities she had long felt, like winter ice on a windshield slowly losing its fight against the defroster, had melted enough to give her a clear view of the road ahead.

Jeff came upstairs with Sarah straddling his back, strangling him from behind. "The monkey is done with her homework!"

"Let her run around the backyard a few dozen times," Andrea said. "I can keep an eye on her from the sunroom."

Jeff opened the sliding door leading to the deck and Sarah vaulted like a dog that had waited all day to be let out. He watched for a minute as she ran circles around the property. Once he was sure she wouldn't run into the pond, and once he stopped thinking about how much goose shit she was stepping on in her bare feet, he turned away.

"I'm going to give Sadie her bath and get her ready for bed," he said.

"I'll bring Sarah up as soon as she's exhausted herself," said Andrea.

"That could take hours," he said. Then he added with a smile, "That tea with whiskey you mentioned? I'll have it without the tea."

Sadie complained as Jeff plucked her out of the baby's playpen and took her upstairs. JoJo finished the bottle and wanted to get down. Andrea wanted to burp her first, so they wrestled for a bit until the baby let out a wet gurgle.

"Close enough," Andrea said. She set JoJo down so she could stand propped against the couch. A wobbly JoJo started inching her way down the couch.

Andrea looked outside and didn't see Sarah. That flash of anxiety eased when she saw her daughter perched *atop* the play set. Should have been the first place she looked. Which was a remarkable testament to

Sarah's exhaustive physicality, that Andrea's anxiety could be allayed by finding her on top of a play set.

After the kids had all been put to bed, Andrea wondered for the millionth time during the past year how they were going to juggle five kids in three bedrooms for much longer. Ruth was now sharing a room with Sarah and neither was thrilled about it. Eli, as the only boy, still had his own room, and he remained thrilled about that. Sadie and JoJo shared a room, but because the baby hadn't slept through the night until recently, neither had Sadie. Maybe they could turn part of the finished basement into a bedroom for Ruth.

After Jeff's plea agreement a few years ago, they'd "downsized" into a four-bedroom house. She wished they still lived in their previous home. It had six bedrooms, five full baths, and a fully finished basement. Life had been more spacious before federal securities fraud.

She sighed and opened up the liquor cabinet. Once Ruth hit puberty, Andrea would have to consider putting a lock on it. If only her oldest knew how many liquor cabinet locks Andrea had picked by that age. She poured Jeff a whiskey and put some ice in it. She made herself a tea. He had a Mets game on. They were going to miss the playoffs by just *this much*. Again. And Jeff knew it, so this was just a form of self-flagellation.

She handed the glass to him. "Thanks," he said.

"Wanna turn that off and talk about what's bothering you?" she asked.

"I didn't think it was that obvious." He sipped his drink, turned the TV off, and tossed the remote aside.

"Is it just Derek?"

He nodded. "I mean, I can't believe he just died like that. Gone. We knew it was a possibility."

"When did he tell you about his heart condition?" she asked.

"A couple years ago."

"But you didn't tell me?"

"He asked us not to, Andie," Jeff said. "I mean, c'mon, guys are always getting stuck between a rock and a hard place when it comes to telling our wives stuff, right?"

"I guess," she agreed. "But Martin told Brianne."

"Brianne would've found out anyway, I'm sure," he said.

"So what else is on your mind? Work?"

"Yeah," he said. "I'm playing the game, but they still won't let me trade, just advise."

"The sanctions against you don't come up for a hearing until next year," she said.

"I know, but they can expedite that; they're choosing not to," he said.

"Did they give you a reason?"

"No. They don't have to. And I can't make real money until they do," he said, quickly adding, "Listen, I know it's my own fault and I know I'm lucky I didn't go to jail, but it's still frustrating."

"I know," she said.

"I got a secondary assignment," he said. "It's the good team. It's generated more money than I expected, but it's probably going to be over pretty soon."

"Why?"

"The project hit a dead end," he said.

She held his hand. "Listen, we've had our problems, and you've made mistakes, but there's one thing on this planet I have no doubt about, and that's your ability to earn."

He smiled. He didn't smile too often. She didn't give him much reason to, she knew. Her words meant so much more to him than she thought they should have. She wondered, and not for the one thousandth time, much less the first, how much love she really had left in her heart for him.

"Once the sanctions are lifted on your ability to trade, you'll make back anything we lost, anything you owed," she said.

He finished his whiskey. "Thanks for pushing me to talk about it. You know, getting it out really helped."

"Thank the whiskey."

"Thank you," he said to the empty glass. "I'm going up to bed."

"I'll be up in a while," she replied. She had taken to waiting until midnight to go to bed, because JoJo had shown a penchant for waking up between eleven and twelve with residual hunger. Andrea didn't want to always placate her, but that extra half bottle usually kept her sleeping through the night. Mostly.

No more kids, ever, ever, ever, no matter what. *Ever.*

She had turned thirty-four years old on April 27 and she'd been pregnant or caring for newborns for more than ten years.

Jeff had known about Derek's condition. Andrea wondered which bothered her more, that he hadn't told her, that her friends hadn't told her, or that Molly hadn't told her. Husbands rarely had the fortitude to keep secrets like that from their wives, and the wives generally were incapable of keeping them from their friends.

But all of them had managed to keep it from Andrea.

At 11:50, she heard JoJo through the monitor, rustling. Andrea went upstairs before the baby could awaken Sadie. She brought JoJo downstairs and warmed up half a bottle. She cradled the groggy baby in one arm and propped the bottle with her free hand.

After a few minutes, the bottle was empty and the baby was sucking herself back to sleep on it. Andrea left it on the kitchen counter and gingerly brought JoJo back to her crib. Closing the door, she was ready to go to bed. The lights in her bedroom were off. She had asked Jeff to leave her night table light on countless times if he was going to sleep first, so she wouldn't have to change in the dark.

She decided not to go to bed yet. She knew she'd probably pay for it tomorrow if she stayed up too late, but something was bothering her. If she didn't process it, she'd toss in bed until sunrise.

Andrea went down to the basement. She removed a whiteboard

from the toy closet. She had bought it several months ago. After getting called in by then–acting chief Rossi and Detective Garmin to consult on two cases in a one-month span last winter, she had abandoned the rolled-up old rug with sticky notes clinging to it and decided to go high-tech with a washable-marker board.

She propped the board vertically against the back of the couch and knelt down into a catcher's position. It had been the first time in years she had felt healthy enough to do that without the fear of becoming permanently locked in a squat or the need to spit a baby out on the ground.

She wrote Derek's and Molly's names at the top. She continued to fill out a flow chart of relatives and friends on Molly's side and question marks on the left for Derek's work life. There was some crossover. She knew Derek's firm had represented the assisted living homes that Martin Singer's family owned. She knew that a few years ago Jeff had recommended Derek for estate planning to some of his clients. Well, former clients.

There didn't seem to be enough, but that's not what nagged her. It wasn't what wasn't on the board, it was what she didn't know that should be on the board.

Her eyes ran past Brianne's name on the chart.

What had Jeff said?

Brianne would've found out anyway, I'm sure.

What did her friends know that they were afraid to tell her?

11

*T*UESDAY morning meant baby swim class with Sathwika and Aditya. Andrea had come to loathe the class, not because changing in the locker room was a logistical nightmare. Or because the option of going to the car in wet bathing suits was worse. Or because the amount of chlorine they pumped into the pool to kill the urine made her smell like a mothball all day long. Or because the teacher demanded far more effort from babies than babies could realistically be expected to expend.

It was because JoJo had an outboard motor for legs, while Aditya lounged about in his life jacket like a floating Zagnut bar.

So, while Sathwika fretted in mounting ways about her son's delayed physical maturation, Andrea had to deal with the second coming of Michael Phelps. Nothing could likely ever match the effort it had taken to corral Sarah on a daily basis, but in the pool, JoJo gave her older sister a run for her money. On the plus side, Coach McMurty never had anything but praise for the 150 percent effort JoJo dedicated to every class.

Teacher's pet.

Usually, after about twenty minutes of chasing her, Andrea would give up and just talk to Sathwika in a corner while the Zagnut lolled on the waves generated by his more motivated classmates. Since she hadn't slept well, today it only took Andrea five minutes.

Sathwika took note of her friend's frustrated state.

"Slept for shit," Andrea said.

Sathwika nodded. "If you think Molly killed her husband, I won't judge you. I'll just make sure I don't kill my husband around you."

"I think Molly killed her husband," Andrea said, and with it came a sigh of relief. For days, she had felt guilty for nursing that thought.

"Glad you got that out in the open?" Sathwika said.

"Is it strange to say I feel better because I think my friend killed her husband?"

"By normal standards, pretty strange," Sathwika responded. "By yours? Typical Tuesday."

Their conversation was interrupted by Coach McMurty's blistering whistle. Andrea swam to retrieve JoJo, who had kicked her way to the deep end.

"Why do you have these suspicions?" asked Sathwika when they returned. When Andrea hesitated to answer, she continued, "Gut feeling? That's okay. Based on your history, that just means there is something to be found. So, find it."

"I mentioned it to Kenny already," Andrea said. "He's poking around a bit. I guess I've started, too, but it's dicey."

"Because you're investigating your friend, which means interrogating your friends," Sathwika said. "In order to get the truth, are you prepared to lose your friends? Because chances are pretty good that's where this road will take you."

In her real life, as they liked to call their lives before children, Sathwika had been a crisis management specialist. She could read a person's road map like no one Andrea had ever met. She could predict where their roads would take them or plan a route that would get them to a safer destination. It was a skill set that overlapped nicely with

Andrea's, who was better suited to reading where a person had been and what they had done. More than once, Andrea thought they would have made a kick-ass TV detective team: *The Tandoori Knishes.*

"If lies and secrets form the foundation of our friendship, then it wasn't much of one to begin with," Andrea said. "So, lunch after this?"

"Can't," Sathwika said. "Pediatrician."

"Is Aditya okay?"

"Yeah," replied Sathwika, pushing her son gently like a bathtub toy. "This is for Shreya. She stayed home from school. I'm worried about strep."

"Geez, they've been back to school for three weeks and it's already starting," Andrea said.

"I'm allergic to penicillin, and so is Divam, but we don't know about Shreya yet, so I have to worry about that, too," Sathwika said. Something about that tugged at Andrea's memory, but she wasn't placing it. Her friend continued, "I'm doing great passing along my genes, aren't I?"

"I blame all the bad ones on Jeff," Andrea said.

"Clearly, then, this is all Rehaan's fault," Sathwika said.

"The bastard."

"I probably should kill him," said Sathwika, her large brown eyes slyly cast toward her friend, with puppy dog innocence.

"I promise to look the other way," replied Andrea.

"You're full of shit," laughed Sathwika.

"And you of all people should have known where the road would lead before you killed Rehaan," Andrea said.

"So, why didn't Molly?" asked Sathwika.

Through the guilt she had felt thinking Molly had killed Derek, that was a question Andrea hadn't thought to ask. As smart as Molly was—as highly organized and highly detailed a person as she was—on top of knowing she had a friend like Andrea, why would she think she could get away with it?

"Good question," Andrea muttered.

12

KENNY spent Wednesday morning with Sitara, ostensibly editing down several interviews before they had to be delivered to the editors to edit them down for the director, who would then ask for edits. But as they sat in the conference room, the samurai sushi boat, nigiri, and edamame he'd bought proved up to the challenge of greasing Sitara into approving the plan of attack he'd formulated to take on Derek Goode.

Shelby and Jimmy had generated a map they could call up on their iPads with the locations Goode had visited in Manhattan over the past few months. Shelby needed more data to discern deeper patterns, but it was a good start. Jimmy had also made a PDF file that contained photos and summaries of the team members Derek had worked with at his law firm, including two associates, three secretaries, and a paralegal. It also included information on the three partners, though Shelby stressed, based on her experience, that anything illicit or extracurricular Derek might have been involved in likely trickled down to his subordinates, rather than reaching up to his bosses.

Kenny scrolled through the file and smiled. For him, this was target practice.

TWO HOURS LATER, Kenny exited the elevator and entered the lobby of FCS. He was impressed by its style. Not a stodgy conservative mausoleum, but not painfully Brooklyn-hipster either. The receptionist was Latina, in her forties, and he could tell she'd put in hard time kicking pests like Kenny out of her lobbies.

"I'm a reporter with the *Princeton Post*, and I'm doing a story on the passing of Derek Goode," he said, using the name of the paper he no longer had filing privileges with.

"Did you call for an appointment?" asked the receptionist.

"No, I'm sorry," said Kenny. "I was nearby in the city for something else and I thought I'd take a chance and pop by to see if I could get a few quotes from Mr. Goode's coworkers."

The receptionist relented and said, "Let me call his executive assistant Camille."

A large African American woman in her fifties approached the reception area. Camille introduced herself and led Kenny to the area where Derek's team was situated. His office was unoccupied, but most of his things were still inside. Kenny noted immediately that it wasn't particularly large, nor was it along the row overlooking Fifth Avenue. Camille led him to a small conference room. He sat at a round table with six chairs. It was cramped, and the room was lined on all sides by solid walls.

"I'll round up anyone from the team who would like to say something," she said. "A few of them are still very upset."

"I understand. Thank you for doing this on such short notice, Camille," Kenny said. Then, "If possible, I'd prefer to see them one at a time."

Off Camille's curious look, he added, "People tend to be more reserved in a group setting and I want to honor Derek with as much honesty as I can."

A few minutes later, a short woman walked into the office. She had thick dyed curly blond hair, from a perm that had seemingly become permanent sometime in the late eighties. She introduced herself as Gloria Haber, Derek's executive assistant since he joined the firm fifteen years earlier. Kenny asked her permission to record, which he had been doing before he'd even walked into the office. He ran through some general questions about when she had first met Derek, what he was like when he was younger, what she knew of his home life, and how he was around the office.

He wrote down notes as she talked, which he liked to do when specific things jumped out, but also because it made his subjects feel like he was validating what they were saying.

For Gloria, he wrote:

He initiated all the social activities, then I would have to organize them.

That slowed down once he had kids. (makes sour face)

All the women here loved him. (sad eyes)

We used to have so much fun, I ended up getting a divorce because of it! (???)

The next person up was Derek's junior associate, Bill Winthrop. He was twenty-eight, out, loud, and proud in a way that no law firm that grosses half a billion annually would have accepted twenty years ago or tolerated ten years ago, but touted on their websites today. He was handsome, rail thin, whip smart, and with enough product in his hair that his head could be used as a ski jump.

Kenny's notes, culled from what Bill said, included:

The most bi-cis-boss I've ever worked with. (laughs)

He didn't care about rules, he cared about results. (real respect)

Molly never knew how good she had it. (jealous?)

When Camille brought in the team's paralegal, Skylar Lawford, Kenny thought she would hide in a corner if he said boo. She was in her midtwenties, petite, and beautiful in an elfin way. She had enormous brilliant blue eyes that were as stoked from the inside by intelligence as they were dulled on the outside by insecurity. She had only been at FCS for a year, but her youth and inexperience hadn't yet led her to say too much or say the wrong thing.

Kenny's notes included:

Derek asked me to go out after work a lot, but I didn't feel comfortable. (grooming?)

Derek told me the firm could help me pay for law school. (grooming?)

Derek helped me when I had to get out of a bad relationship. (grooming!)

The last person Camille brought in was Derek's senior associate, Darrah Smalls. She was put together like she could handle a fight in a boardroom or a back alley with equal measure. Kenny decided to play her very slowly because he feared she would eat him alive and then use his bones as toothpicks. Darrah seemed wary of him, or at the least, wary of talking about Derek. He tried to keep it light.

"How long have you worked here?"

"How long have you worked with Derek?"

"What kind of a boss was he?"

"I heard he brought this firm together on a social level?"

"How well did you know his family?"

She kept all her answers terse, guarded, and frigid.

Then, at one point, Darrah asked, "You said this was for the local paper in West Windsor?"

Kenny said, "Yes, the *Princeton Post*."

She nodded. "That was the paper that broke the story about the Black man who'd been killed fifty years ago?"

"Yes," he replied.

"And you were that reporter, weren't you?"

"Yes." Kenny smiled, thinking this might break the ice a little.

Instead, it was the iceberg the *Titanic* had run into.

She abruptly stood up, straightened her suit skirt. Calmly, she said, "Thank you, Mr. Lee."

Darrah Smalls left.

Camille popped her head into the office and said that the last executive assistant on the team, Francine Esposito, had begged off providing any quotes other than to relay through Camille that they all loved Derek and would miss him.

Kenny asked if he could stand in Derek's office for a moment, just to absorb its ambience. She explained a messenger had already cleared out some of his personal effects. She took him to Derek's office, and when her back was turned, he slipped the Obama picture out of his backpack and propped it on a shelf that still had a few other pictures on it.

Camille led him to the lobby. Kenny thanked the receptionist, being exceedingly polite in case he needed to come back. He waited for the elevator. His story-dar kept sweeping in a circle, pulsing with blips of light at every hidden mine he had found buried under the surface of Derek's sudden death. It probably didn't help—or did, depending on your point of view—that the story-dar was filtered through Kenny's perpetually cynical view of people:

Gloria had been Derek's older lover when he was younger.

Bill had experimented with his boss or had definitely been led to believe it was a possibility.

Skylar had been the timid woman Derek had tried—and failed?—to have an affair with.

Francine was afraid to talk to him, which meant she had something to hide.

Darrah refused to talk, which meant there was something worth hearing.

Based on the dinner receipts and regular visits to high-end strip clubs, the question had changed from "Was Derek Goode having an affair?" to "Was there anyone in his office Derek hadn't had an affair with?"

13

WHILE Kenny was finding out what a swinger Derek was, Molly was getting back into the swing of things. She invited the Cellulitists to her house for lunch. Even in mourning, Molly managed to lay out a delightful assortment of healthy lite options that greeted them on their arrival. The kitchen island had a meticulously arranged platter of arugula beet salad, various fruit, Greek yogurt, and a bowl of almonds.

Crystal, Brianne, Andrea, and Molly sat down at the large round table on the deck. The houses in Windsor Ridge were set back into a heavily wooded stretch, so Molly had been unable to place a pool in her backyard. Lacking that as a showcase, she had done the next best thing and turned her backyard into a mini-arboretum, with pavers leading off the deck in a winding trail down her inclined property to the trickling creek that divided her from her neighbor.

Azaleas, astilbe, hostas, and hyacinths lined the path. It was lovely to look at, but a bitch to maintain. Molly had once expressed tremendous respect for the "hardworking little brown people" she hired to keep her property luscious.

She placed a pitcher of mint water with glasses in front of them.

Andrea listened to Crystal and Brianne force small talk, but she kept her eyes on Molly. She searched for a tell, a sign of impatience, agitation, guilt, *something*, but she couldn't spot a speck of difference between today and Molly at the funeral or Molly the day Derek died or Molly on any other day. The only break she had shown Andrea was the single look of gloating she had cast at the memorial service.

After Crystal's third helping of mentioning how beautiful the yard looked, Andrea decided to cut to the chase. "Since I was late to the truth about Derek's condition, please tell me you had planned in advance?"

Molly gave Andrea an almost thankful look. Crystal would have danced around it for two hours and Brianne would have bitten her tongue to the point of needing stitches.

"Since we've known about his condition for so long and Derek's practice specializes in elder care and estate planning, yes, we were prepared," she replied.

"You could get life insurance with a preexisting condition?" asked Crystal.

"If you're willing to pay the premiums, you can get it for anything," Molly said.

"Three million," said Brianne abruptly.

Molly seemed a bit—Andrea considered the reaction carefully before coming to any conclusion—unfazed that Brianne knew the amount. But within that casual acceptance, Andrea saw something, a hint of . . . disappointment.

Brianne shrugged. "Derek told Martin and Martin told me."

Crystal said, "Three million is a lot!"

"Not if you consider what Derek's income would have generated over the course of twenty more years," said Andrea, alleviating Molly's discomfort.

Casting a glance at Andrea, Molly said, "Jeff helped us when we redid the policy last year."

Andrea hadn't known, and Molly suspected as much, but she refused to take the bait. "That was smart," she agreed with a nod. "Jeff's great with that sort of thing."

JoJo fussed in her carrier. Of course, she would wake up the second Andrea started to eat. Crystal shushed everyone and motioned them to look at the baby so that when JoJo woke up, she would awaken to a fish-eye lens of the Cellulitists gawking at her. JoJo rustled but didn't wake up, disappointing Crystal, but giving Andrea a chance to dig into the beet salad.

"You look tired," said Crystal. "I mean, it's totally understandable, of course, I would be exhausted, who wouldn't be, but are you having trouble sleeping?"

Molly had barely put any food on her plate but had taken a very small bite just as Crystal finished her question. Her delayed response was due less to the food in her mouth than to the painful reaction of having bitten into the cold sore she still had on her lip. It had faded since last week, but it was still there. She swallowed, tugging politely at the cuffs of her long-sleeve blouse—never mind that the rest of them were in short sleeves—and said, "I thought I had been sick. I've been tired and my throat was swollen last week, but maybe it's just from stress."

"It's been such a horrible week," Crystal said. "And I know that's not a lot of time, but have you thought about what you're going to do?"

"I don't understand," Molly said, fully understanding.

"Are you going to stay in the house? Stay in West Windsor?" Crystal prodded. "If something like this happened to Wendell, I can't imagine leaving with the children still in school, and my friends all here. But on the other hand, staying in the same house would be so scary. All the reminders, every day . . ."

Molly said, "I don't plan on going anywhere. Derek worked very hard to create this life for us. Leaving it would seem like . . ."

She paused.

"A betrayal," said Brianne softly.

"Yes." Molly smiled in the same way a shark would when considering the remora. "I discussed it with Henry and Brett in a very reasonable manner. They also preferred not to move. This is the only home they have ever known, after all."

"Well, I for one am very happy you're not leaving," said Crystal. "Where else could I get a homemade roasted beet salad like this?"

"Exactly where she got it," said Andrea. "Witherspoon Grill."

"*Noooo*," Crystal moaned as Molly smiled. Then Molly actually laughed.

Then they all laughed. And for just a second, they were all just friends, laughing.

But JoJo killed the mood by waking up and crying. Andrea got her out of the carrier. After pushing Crystal's clawing fingers off her chubby little hands, JoJo stopped crying and got her bearings. She rubbed her face after Andrea kissed her.

"Are you hungry, spud?" Andrea asked. "I have some Cheerios for you."

Brianne excused herself to use the bathroom.

Andrea followed her inside the house to get the cereal and bottle out of her diaper bag. As they walked, she asked her friend, "Are you okay?"

"Yeah," Brianne stammered. "Yeah, just sad."

Brianne entered the powder room on the first floor. Andrea looked out the kitchen window to see Crystal talking Molly's ear off. She realized this would probably be her best opportunity.

"Oh, Josephine Esther Stern, this is one of the most horrific poopies ever unleashed on human civilization," she said in a singsong that was louder than it needed to be—loud enough for Brianne to hear over the bathroom fan.

She grabbed JoJo and the diaper bag, walking past the powder room. "I have to take the baby to the upstairs bathroom to change her."

"I'll be out in a second," Brianne said through the door.

"It's okay," Andrea replied, hopefully not too abruptly, as she reached the foyer stairs. "This is a bad one and I need . . ." What did she need, a fire extinguisher? "More elbow room."

She climbed the stairs quickly and walked into Molly's master bedroom. The door was open and the room was immaculate. There were no signs of Derek left exposed, no clothes left out and nothing on his night table. Andrea placed JoJo and her bag in the middle of the king-size bed, right where Derek had died.

Hoping JoJo wouldn't crawl off the edge, Andrea stepped into the bathroom. The hand and shower towel racks that had held two towels now each held one. All of Derek's toiletries were gone. His toothbrush: gone. In the shower, any men's shampoo, shaving cream, or grooming products: gone.

It wasn't normal in the grieving process, Andrea thought. Textbook guidelines didn't anticipate the entire removal of all traces of a loved one after their sudden passing. If they truly were a loved one, Andrea thought. Then the guilt coursed through her. She had just laughed and eaten with the woman she was now trying to find party to the murder of her husband. But why should Andrea doubt herself when Molly had methodically scrubbed her husband's presence from the place where they had been the most intimate?

She looked at Molly's night table, quickly opening the two drawers to find them filled. She went to the night table on Derek's side. His drawers had been emptied.

In the master closet, which was the size of the one Andrea used to have, basically the size of the apartment she had grown up in, Andrea saw that all of Derek's clothes—his suits, pants, and shirts—were hung in several vacuum bags that had been appropriately labeled. His shoes were all in their original boxes and stored in four large labeled packing boxes to be donated.

Molly was erasing all traces of him from her private sanctuary.

Was that putting the pain behind you or was it an attack on what had caused you that pain?

There was a large silver suitcase in the corner of the closet. She tried to open it, but it was locked. Andrea noticed that one pile of perfectly folded shirts on the closet rack was of a slightly greater height than the others. At the bottom of the taller pile, with clothes as camouflage, was a metallic gray Pelican Protector double pistol case.

They owned guns. Not a big deal to Andrea, who had two herself, of which one was even legally registered. Derek hadn't been shot, so she dismissed it.

She went into the bathroom next and opened the medicine cabinets. They contained various hair and skin products. Some Zyrtec, Motrin, Tylenol, and Aldara cream.

She turned the prescription bottles to get better looks at them. Ortho. Diflucan.

Andrea paused.

There was a bottle of ceftriaxone with pills still in it. The date on the prescription was from early September.

Before she could get a better look at it, Brianne called out from downstairs. "Everything okay?"

"Yeah," she said, frustrated. She put the pill bottle back and quickly left the bedroom.

As she walked downstairs with JoJo, it clicked into place.

The fatigue. The cold sore. The lack of appetite. The sore throat . . . or swollen lymph nodes?

Aldara cream was used for genital warts.

That was the tug Andrea had felt yesterday when she was talking to Sathwika about taking Shreya to the pediatrician.

Molly was the only other person she knew who was allergic to penicillin.

Molly was taking ceftriaxone as an antibiotic.

Because all signs pointed to Molly having syphilis.

And it was fair to assume that she had caught it from Derek.

Because Derek was having an affair.

Which gave Molly Goode motive to kill her husband.

ANDREA and Sathwika sat at a sidewalk table in front of Small Bites on Nassau Street. The women had their babies in their arms, feeding them bottles. Aditya seemed far more animated now that he was eating. They had ordered an assortment of breakfast pastries and four Greek coffees in anticipation of Kenny and Sitara's arrival.

Sitara could have taken the short Dinky train that connected the Princeton campus to the Northeast Corridor line at Princeton Junction train station, then walked a quarter mile to Nassau Street, but Kenny had picked her up at the main station and was driving over.

When Andrea had called Kenny the previous night to tell him what she'd seen in Molly's medicine cabinet, she asked to officially fold Sitara into the investigation. Though Kenny was hesitant, Andrea thought a face-to-face meeting would do them all good. When they had met during the documentary filming, the producer had struck Andrea as a no-nonsense person. She expected that having her production process interrupted by Kenny's quixotic quest for a new story would likely perturb Sitara.

The pastry platter Andrea had ordered was specifically designed to sway Sitara to the cause. Who could resist a sixty-dollar assortment of galaktoboureko, bougatsa, baklava, kataifi, loukoumades, and Portioli coffee?

She saw Kenny's fancy new car make a right onto Nassau Street and drive past them. She missed his Prius. His old car was *so* much more him. He found an open parking space a block away and, after feeding the meter on his parking app, crossed the street with Sitara. He seemed far more relaxed than she'd expected, but Sitara seemed tentative and frustrated. Train face, Jeff had always called it. Anyone who rode New Jersey Transit between NJ and NY had that beaten-down look about them, even if they only did it one time.

Andrea and Sathwika stood up, and with unplanned synchronized switching of the babies to their opposite arms, they exchanged handshakes as Kenny made introductions. Kenny had met Sathwika after Andrea's water had broken all over his face at the press conference last year. Sathwika thought he wouldn't remember she had been the one who wiped his face clean, but he did. That surprised her, considering his eyes had been closed and he had been shrieking like a constipated blue jay at the time.

Andrea gestured for them to sit as Sathwika offered the platter to them.

"These look great," Sitara said. "Thank you."

"Try the galaktoboureko," said Sathwika.

"Which ones are those?" asked Kenny as Sathwika cut a pastry into quarters.

"I love the loukoumades," said Andrea.

"Which ones are those?" asked Kenny as Andrea cut one into quarters.

Chewing, Kenny nodded in appreciation and said, "This is how Andrea says thank you for coming all the way out here."

Sitara said, "And it's a very good way, but you have no reason to. I wouldn't have come unless I thought there was something worth discussing."

Hoping to prevent Sitara from taking over the flow of conversation, Andrea said, "As an impartial, and from what Kenny says, a disinterested observer, what do you think we have here?"

That caught Sitara both off guard and mid-bite. She chewed, all eyes on her. Then she did something that drew Andrea's admiration: she didn't rush. She slowed down, and then took a casual sip of coffee. She said, "You might not like what I have to say. Dead lawyer, wealthy by most people's standards. A wife who may or may not have murdered him. So what? It's not enough for me, for what I do, anyway. It's missing the kind of hook that *Suburban Secrets* had: juicy complications. Deeply rooted racism in a small town, police cover-up, yesterday's sins connecting to today. That gets you to binge eight episodes in one night. That isn't here."

Andrea nodded and smiled, soaking it all in and making a joke in her own mind that she murmured aloud without realizing it. "Now I see why he likes you."

Kenny quickly moved the conversation past that. "The story isn't baked yet, but the ingredients are here to make the cake. White privilege, secrets behind closed doors, unfulfilled suburban housewives. Has feminism failed to fulfill women? All that fun stuff."

"It's not a story," Andrea said calmly. "It is a possible homicide."

"Now comes the clarion call for justice," interrupted Kenny. "She's good at selling this."

"If I'm good at 'selling it,' it's only because I believe it," Andrea replied. "I don't care if it's a stranger or a friend, we look for evidence and we follow that evidence to whatever the truth bears out."

Sathwika jumped in. "If you liked Kenny's book enough to make a documentary series out of it, that's because the book fairly and accurately told the truth of what happened. He didn't need to fit the theme into the truth because the theme came out of the truth all along."

"You're saying I should be patient?" said Sitara.

"I am," replied Sathwika.

Speaking to Sitara, Kenny chimed, "Sathwika worked in crisis management for—"

"I did my oppo research," interrupted Sitara. Then, immediately realizing how that sounded, she added, "Not that either one of you are the opposition."

"But we are," said Andrea matter-of-factly.

No one said anything for a few seconds until Kenny broke the uncomfortable silence: "How about some of that baklava? Wow, that's sticky."

The women glanced at him in mutual exasperation, which actually helped to break the ice.

"Listen, I tend to be pretty straightforward. I think both of you are as well," said Sitara. "Within the understanding that, of course, every death is a tragedy, which I don't believe for one second is our objective reality, I honestly don't care if Molly Goode killed her husband. I'm not being paid to care."

Straightforward it would be, thought Andrea and Sathwika.

"My job is to wrangle a very acerbic and very talented moth and keep it focused," Sitara continued, hitching a thumb at Kenny. "You are a very bright light to him and have been for over twenty years. I only worry about this wild goose chase insomuch as it distracts this moth from the rough cut of the documentary series I have to put to bed by Thanksgiving."

"Fair enough," said Andrea. "And I really do appreciate the honesty. So, from my position, I don't want to speak for Sathwika, but insomuch as I respect you have a job to do, I don't care about your documentary. I don't care about glorifying murder, I despise giving killers the kind of adulation your programming generates for them, and I especially don't care about the attention it might bring on me. I care about people who did bad things not being allowed to get away with the bad things they have done. Period."

Sensing her path had just presented itself, Sathwika jumped in. "And that's where we meet in the middle. Sitara, you can't do what you do without people like Andrea doing what she does. That you're here means Kenny convinced you that—at the very least—the possibility exists for this investigation to generate the kind of narrative that interests you. And Andrea, borderline spectrum murder savant, can't do what she wants to do without help."

"The Suburban Dicks are becoming a franchise!" Kenny said.

Off their looks, he added, "Oh yeah, I never told any of you. That's what I originally wanted to call the book. I changed it to *Suburban Secrets* because the publisher didn't get it."

"*Suburban Dicks* is really a gross title," said Sathwika.

"'Dicks' is old slang for private detectives," added Andrea. "But it's too cute by half."

"Okay, insomuch as we've established I'm always going to be the cranky thumbtack in the shoes of our intrepid heroes," said Sitara, "can we review why we think there might or might not be something substantive here?"

Both babies fell asleep for a late-morning nap and were placed in their carriers. Kenny ran through his impressions about Derek's legal team, then his suspicions based on the information Jimmy and Shelby had gathered. Ultimately, Kenny thought there was something skeevy about the lawyer.

Andrea ran through her impressions of Molly's borderline pathological erasure of her husband and the fleeting glimpse of her ceftriaxone prescription, which was used, if you were allergic to penicillin, for treatment of bacterial infections linked to sexually transmitted diseases.

"And we're sure Molly didn't give it to Derek as opposed to the other way around?" asked Sitara.

"Can't rule it out, but Derek had more opportunity than she did," said Andrea.

"How so?" Sitara nudged.

"It might look like Molly's opportunity is a pretty big window between seven thirty a.m. and three thirty p.m. Monday through Friday," replied Andrea. "But if you saw her calendar schedule for yoga, Zumba, weight training at the gym, treadmilling, shopping, and social lunches, you'd wonder how she fits breathing in there, much less an affair. Plus, if you knew her, you couldn't imagine Molly introducing outside fluids into her hermetically sealed household, much less going to a hotel to engage in sex."

"That painted so many pictures I'm uncomfortable with," said Sitara.

"Tell us about it," said Sathwika. "I have to get the baby to a mommy and me fitness class in an hour, then I have to run over to the Comfort Inn to have sex with my lover before the kids come home from school."

"Okay, we get the point," said Kenny. "Women are wonderful, men are scum."

"Yeah, that's the takeaway," said Sitara. "Buying into this, Andrea, do you think Derek having an affair was enough of a motive for Molly?"

"My gut is, no, it's not," said Andrea. "But it could be as part of a bigger picture. Love, money, and self-protection are the three most common motives in any marital homicide."

"We're looking at money and love," said Kenny. "Just from the receipts on his secret credit card, it appears Derek was accessing accounts outside of his personal and business ones. It's the kind of spiderweb that inevitably tangles coworkers and friends."

"Let's break it down," said Sathwika. "I like to predict the path so we know the narrative signs to look for. The Muckrakers are asking: Was Derek involved in financial malfeasance? If so, how would that impact Molly? Was Derek having any affairs? If so, why, who with, and did Molly find out? Andrea and I are looking to see what factors in their relationship might have led Molly to murder. Was Molly in an abusive relationship? How much did her friends know about it?"

"Fair enough," said Sitara. "How much time are you giving yourselves to see if any of this is plausible?"

Andrea and Kenny shrugged and, at the same time, both said, "Two weeks?"

They agreed. Andrea told them she'd taken care of the bill. Kenny laughed and said, "I finally have enough money that I can pay for something and I can't even show off."

They said their goodbyes. Kenny and Sitara planned to work from Kenny's apartment for the rest of the day before she returned to New York. Sathwika gave Andrea a hug and lugged the sleeping Aditya off to another function he would lie prone for.

Andrea sat alone at the table for a moment, absorbing the passing of cars, the movement of the people on the sidewalk and the students shuffling about the fringes of the campus. For all its stodginess and self-righteous privilege, she loved Princeton. For three blocks it felt like a small city in the shadow of aristocratic majesty.

JoJo woke up. She grunted. Her face turned red. She was taking a poop. So much for majesty. The noise and smell drew discomfited stares. She changed the baby right in the carrier chair, deciding to put the diaper into her own bag and spare the people outside rather than leaving it in the sidewalk trash receptacle.

Andrea's mind was back in Molly's bathroom. She couldn't make out the label on the prescription bottle clearly. It was just out of focus.

And what Kenny had said nagged at her.

It's the kind of spiderweb that inevitably tangles coworkers and friends.

If Derek was engaged in illicit activities, how much did his friends know? Or how much were they a part of it? But an even more nagging irritant had crept into her thoughts and refused to get out: If Derek was engaged in illicit activities, how much did her own husband know?

And . . . how much was Jeff a part of it?

PART TWO

An Affair to Dismember

15

ON the drive to his condo after brunch at Small Bites with Sath-wika and Andrea, Kenny said, "That could have gone worse."

Sitara eyed him. "Just be aware that the second I closed the car door, the time I had allotted today for riding your unicorn ended. Now we focus on cleaning the script for the recording session, and we continue to pare down the interviews in episodes four and five."

"Understood, boss," said Kenny as he drove past McCarter Theatre and the Dinky train station. Crossing the Delaware and Raritan Canal, he weighed what he would say to Sitara for the next few hours. A real girlfriend was new to him, but between his parents and his brother's high school romance with Andrea, Kenny had understood since he was a kid what a dangerous minefield relationships are.

"WHAT DO YOU *mean you're breaking up with Andie?" Kenny asked his brother.*

"You say you want to be a reporter, but you don't hear too good," Cary grunted between reps.

"Hearing is for sound," Kenny replied. "Listening is for context. I heard you, I just don't understand."

"I broke up with her, that's all."

"You guys have been going out for years," Kenny said, feeling tired just from watching Cary bench-press in rapid succession. They were in the unfinished basement, where Cary had set up free weights. "I mean, you guys going out is all I know."

"Maybe it's time you stopped crushing on a girl who is three years older than you and only knows you exist because of me," Cary said. He started doing arm curls. "Listen, I loved her, I can admit that, but this whole thing has gotten nuts."

Cary bared the depths of his soul the way rice paper bared its thickness.

"The Emily Browning case?" Kenny asked.

"You say it like she's a cop," Cary chided. "She's a high school sophomore—"

"Who found the body of a missing girl and then found out who killed her!" Kenny jumped in, defending her. He had helped Andie a little while she investigated the cold-case disappearance of Emily Browning. His inside access had led to several stories published in the Panther Press middle school newspaper.

Cary had been uncomfortable with all of it. There was no doubt Andie had become darker and moodier, but even Kenny knew that was just the part of the process that got her to the answers.

"Listen, I already had the conversation with her, I don't need to have it with you, too," Cary said. "She was my girlfriend, not yours. And now she's my ex-girlfriend. Simple."

"How can it be simple?" asked Kenny. "Didn't any of that matter?"

"All of it mattered, Kenny, but I'm in tenth grade," said Cary. "Listen, she is who she is. I get that. But it doesn't mean that's who I have to be with."

After that, Kenny didn't see Andie Abelman for two years. Losing her *from his life was as close to heartache as Kenny Lee had ever felt. He could only imagine what it would have been like if the relationship had been more than just the creation of a boy's overactive imagination.*

One way or the other, someone gets hurt.

How could love be worth having, if that kind of pain was the price you had to pay?

KENNY TURNED IN to his condo development. He watched Sitara emerge from his car and walk up the stairs to his second-floor unit. He really did like her, but in his heart, he already knew their relationship was destined to end. He didn't know if the journey counted more than the destination. The journey was where everything happened, good and bad, happy and sad. The final destination was . . . what? Divorce or death? How could "happily ever after" be happy if death is what it took to part you? Or was "ever after" meant to imply the afterlife? Yeah, Kenny thought, that was something to bank on.

All of the sayings were total bullshit.

At his condo, Kenny and Sitara worked all day. They had developed a fluid rhythm between them. She had an intuitive grasp of the voice and tone he strove toward and consistently made smart edits to his work. The highest compliment Kenny could have paid her was that in days gone by, she would have made a great newspaper editor. Not that he had paid her that compliment yet.

He knocked out several pages of script and several more rewrites, and they reviewed her first-pass edits on three interviews. Through it all, Kenny couldn't stop wondering if he should make a move on her. This was the first time she'd been to his condo. The first time they'd really had a chance to have sex. Or make love. He wasn't sure which one it was supposed to be.

Sitara hadn't given Kenny any kind of signal that he should initiate what he imagined would be an hour of wall-shaking lovemaking but expected would be thirty-five seconds of torturous embarrassment. Then he spent several minutes worried that he'd likely not even recognize a signal were she to send it. Then he worried that he wouldn't even make it to thirty-five seconds. Was Kenny expected to perform like a porn star?

His mother's voice wormed its way into his head. Blaire barked at him to stay focused on work. Why would Kenny ever think he'd be a capable lover when he took so much after his father? In his imagination, his mother lauded Cary's sexual prowess while scoffing at his.

It all made for a very tense afternoon inside Kenny's head.

At 5:20, Sitara started wrapping up her electronics and asked if Kenny could drive her back to the train so she could make the 5:44 express back to Manhattan. She still had more work to do at the office.

He stammered. Should he ask her to stay the night and they could go into the city together in the morning, or should he just nod numbly and let her go?

He nodded numbly and let her go.

They reached the train station with a few minutes to spare. She said, "Your condo is really nice. And Princeton's campus looked gorgeous. I'd love to spend a weekend and you could show it to me."

He should have made a move, he thought. Or was she indicating that today wouldn't have been the right time? In that moment, he hated life.

Sitara kissed him lightly on the lips. He thought he kissed back, but he wasn't sure. She smiled, her eyes alight with a fire he knew was not for him, but for the work ahead of her. But he understood, since it was the way his eyes lit up when he had work ahead of him, too.

Sitara disappeared down the concrete stairs to the tunnel under the tracks and emerged on the New York–bound platform.

She waved and gave a big smile.

She was beautiful in a brainy way. And beautiful in a beautiful way, too.

He waved back. He worried that he had waved like a dork.

Kenny drove back to his condo, determined to do whatever was necessary to make sure he never fell in love with her.

16

WHILE her mom was preordering the pastries for her morning meeting, Ruth Stern rode the bus to school, nervous about her plans to interrogate Henry Goode. She didn't want to trick her friend into saying anything, but she also wanted to help her mother. Over the past year, she had gained an understanding of—and an unexpected respect for—her mother.

She had binged five books about the Morana serial murders, which her mother had solved while in college. She'd also dug up what little information she could find from old local newspapers about the Emily Browning missing-person case she had solved in high school. Ruth hadn't told her mom because the last thing any sixth-grade girl wanted was for her mother to know that her daughter thought she was cool as shit.

Ruth's stomach was in knots as she got off the bus. Thinking about Henry had led to restless sleep. Or maybe it was because she had Chinese class first period, and less than one month into the school year, she knew she would never figure out the differences between *wo*, *ni*, *nin*, and *ta*.

On her way to her locker, she played the part of the cheerful morning student, saying hello to friends and laughing at some of the antics in the hallway. Ruth was well liked. Everyone had thought she was cool even before her mom had made her cooler. The teachers liked her because she was one of the few Caucasian students who had a clue about what was going on academically, and the cultural jambalaya of students that comprised the West Windsor–Plainsboro student body liked her because she couldn't be pigeonholed. She was brainy but not a nerd, sarcastic but not mean, and independent but not a loner.

She wondered if they would all still like her if they knew she was going to give a boy whose father had just died the third degree. Ruth wasn't quite sure what the third degree was, or what the other two degrees were. How had her mother ever maintained a normal relationship? Maybe she hadn't. Ruth had never seen her interact with anyone in any kind of a comfortable way. In the past year, she'd paid closer attention.

Her mom's eyes were always the tell. Always . . . doubting.

Ruth didn't think she wanted to live like that.

Then she rounded a hallway corner and bumped into Henry.

"Hey," he said. He looked sad and very aware of the stares and whispers that trailed him.

"How're you doing?" Ruth asked, then, not waiting for an answer, continued, "Meet at lunch and I'll go over the stuff you missed? We have a quiz tomorrow in Algebra."

"Okay," he said, not offering an ounce of enthusiasm. It was only his second day back at school and he looked exhausted.

Henry walked away. Ruth watched the whispering heads turn in his wake. Once he was out of range, she loudly snapped, "Just tell him you're sorry for his loss instead of gossiping behind his back. Have a fucking clue!"

She took in their collective looks of astonishment. Having struggled with her mom's notoriety through fifth grade with prepubescent mortification and an undercurrent of pride, Ruth had seen the old

Tank Girl movie over the summer and decided on a give-no-fucks attitude moving forward. She wore a black Community Middle School Panthers T-shirt with long gray shorts and clunky black Doc Martens. She hadn't dared buzz her hair down to stubble, or even her mother, who had been a fan of the original comic, would have killed her.

"Kèfú zìjǐ," she snapped, telling them to get over themselves in Chinese, knowing she had butchered the pronunciation and the pronouns. She turned and stomped upstairs to language class. The sound of the boots really echoed nicely in the stairwell. Tank Girl fucking rocked.

LATER, RUTH WALKED into the lunchroom and spotted Henry sitting with a few of his friends. She made her way over to them. Amy Xu, the smartest kid on the planet, who Ruth liked even though she pretty much existed on a plane removed from reality, shyly motioned for Ruth to join her for lunch. "Sorry, Amy, I have to help Henry catch up on work he missed."

"See you in bio," Amy said, unable to hide her disappointment over having to eat lunch alone again.

"You can join us," Ruth said.

Amy shook her head vigorously. Too many boys at one time for her to handle.

With a sympathetic smile, Ruth moved on. Henry Goode was a handsome kid who was born-on-third-base popular. Guys liked him because he was athletic and smart; girls liked him because he looked like he could have fronted a boy band. He forced smiles at his friends' banter, but she could tell how hard this was for him.

"Hey," she said. "You want to go over stuff first or after we eat?"

"Eat first," Henry said as he elbowed Cade Nolan to his left. Cade elbowed Akush Modhi to his left, who elbowed Jagdish Reddy to his left. All the boys slid down the bench. A little awkward being the only girl in the group, and hesitant because it wasn't how she'd planned this out, Ruth sat down.

A good investigator had to roll with the punches. She didn't understand why she would be getting punched, but like the third-degree thing, it sounded right. She took a Tupperware container and can of flavored seltzer from her lunch bag.

"Whatcha got?" asked Akush.

"Blackened tempeh," she said almost apologetically. "I asked my mom to try more vegan meals and every one she makes is worse than the one she made before."

"Yeah, that looks . . . interesting," muttered Cade.

"Interesting food for an interesting girl," Ruth said with a cocky smile.

The boys laughed. They talked a bit about this and that. Ruth looked for an opening to ask about Henry's mom, but couldn't find one. After fifteen minutes, she pulled her algebra book and notes out. The other boys took that as their cue to scatter.

Cade slapped Henry's back. "Sucks to be you, man."

They laughed as they left, but Ruth could tell the comment hit Henry harder than he wanted to let on. She waited until the boys had cleared the area and said, "I don't think he meant anything by that."

"Cade never means anything by anything," Henry muttered.

"How are you and Brett holding up?"

"He's a mess," Henry replied. "You know he's a drama queen, so I guess he has a reason for going over the top, but it just . . . I don't know. . . . It doesn't help. . . ."

"Sucks up all the oxygen," Ruth said. "Doesn't give you a chance to be you."

"Yeah, exactly," he said. "How did you—"

He stopped himself when he saw Ruth's smile.

"I guess your mom is sort of that way?"

"She definitely doesn't mean to be."

"And look at your back-to-school outfit," Henry said. "Hasn't stopped you from being you."

"I'm pretty sure she dressed exactly like this when she was in sixth grade," said Ruth. "Worse, probably."

Henry grunted. Ruth thought he must have been picturing her mom in a Tank Girl outfit, which was kind of gross. Ruth had her opportunity, and in that moment, she hesitated. She felt so sorry for Henry that the thought of making him feel worse bothered her. But the thought of Henry's mother getting away with murder bothered her more.

"We don't really know our parents, do we?" she said softly.

"Your mom and that whole thing last year was something," he said.

"My dad, too," she said, unsure how much Henry knew of her father's crimes. "He probably should have gone to jail a few years ago. He's lucky he didn't."

"I heard, but I don't know much about it," he said.

"What about your dad?" she asked. "How much did you know about his heart?"

"He told us a couple years ago," he said. "My mom was pissed at him, but I have to be honest, I didn't think about it much. I mean, he seemed fine. It's not like he was in a wheelchair, or couldn't breathe, or something."

He hesitated, biting back tears.

"I just ignored it because I couldn't think about anything bad happening to him," he said. "I couldn't think about not having him around and it just being my mom. . . ."

He let that hang. Ruth wasn't sure if she should hug him or if he'd think that was lame, so she just put a hand on his shoulder. Would he think she was coming on to him? Boys were naturally idiots, and middle school boys were even bigger idiots. He didn't react one way or another, which was a relief, but she still needed to push a bit more.

Henry, do you think your dad had a heart attack because your mom poisoned him?

Maybe not that direct.

"Did he have a lot of stress?" she asked. "Like work stuff or problems with your mom?"

He shrugged. "He came home late all the time, so I guess he was working hard. I don't know. Do you know anything about your dad's work?"

"Only that he's always complaining about it," she replied.

"Not my dad," Henry said. "He seemed to like it. Or the people he worked with, anyway. He'd been there since I was born."

"What about your mom?" she asked.

"What about my mom?" he said, a bit more sharply than he might have intended.

"She's always so put together," said Ruth, realizing she'd found the sore spot.

"Yeah," he mumbled.

"I don't know, I thought maybe she's a bit of a perfectionist and that's kind of hard to live up to all the time."

He laughed, but there was no humor behind it. "She'd be pretty pissed about being called 'a bit of a perfectionist.' One hundred ten percent perfect isn't good enough in her book." He pulled his phone out of his pocket. He showed her the GeoLocator app on his screen. "You want strict? I can't go to the bathroom without her knowing it."

"A lot of parents have trackers on their kids' phones," she said.

"Do you?"

"No," admitted Ruth. "But I'm sure the minute I get caught doing something wrong, I will."

"Yeah, well, I didn't do anything wrong, so I guess she didn't need a reason to be an ass," he said. She lost her opportunity to probe any further when he opened up his notebook and said, "Can we run through the work?"

. . .

THAT NIGHT, ANDREA had to get Eli from soccer practice and asked Ruth to join her. Getting to sit in the front seat since the summer, Ruth felt more mature now. Certainly, the topic of conversation was more mature than those of the past. Ruth remained torn about how to categorize it to her mother, worried that any particular word would trigger something in her, but not knowing which words those might be. She decided not to include her own opinions, and tried to just re-peat what Henry had said.

"Did you record it?" asked Andrea.

"Mom, no!" Ruth exclaimed. "Don't be weird."

"Inflection over recollection," Andrea said. "His actual words tell his actual story more truthfully than your recollections do. It's as much for his protection as yours, in a way."

"In a way, sure," Ruth said. "In a way that lets you spy on him. That's sick."

"It's all a little sick, Ruth," Andrea said. "The thought of Molly killing Derek is sick, or the thought of me looking into it and asking you to help me. What did your dad always say when he taught all of you how to swim?"

"If you're in up to your knees, then you might as well go underwa-ter," Ruth recited. "But isn't underwater the only way you can drown?"

"Smart-ass," Andrea said gently. She really did love her daughter.

They pulled into the parking lot at the Duck Pond soccer fields. Ruth replayed her conversation with Henry as they strolled the hun-dred yards to where Eli's team was practicing. The lights were on, and fading remnants of sunset colored the horizon orange and purple. An-drea never stopped marveling at the thought of raising her kids in a town that had fields for every major sport across several parks, much less with lighting. When she was little, if the streetlight on the corner of Sixty-fourth Road and Booth Street worked, it became a block party.

"Okay, you described what he said, and your memory was really strong, now tell me what you thought," Andrea said.

"He's scared. More than just because his dad died, I think," Ruth said.

"Keep working it."

"He's sad in a bit of a selfish way, because of how this is all going to affect him. And Brett. Because of how difficult things are with his mom. . . ."

"Difficult how?"

"He didn't exactly say, but I could tell he's angry at her," Ruth said. "I don't know if she did anything, or just, like, regular angry at her."

"Molly is tough on them," Andrea said.

"Yeah, I know," Ruth said. "But something more."

"Go with it," Andrea encouraged her. "Follow it, voice it out loud. If your instincts are there, when it feels right, it usually is right."

"He's tired of . . . the weight."

"The weight of what?"

"Expectations," Ruth said quickly, knowingly. "What everyone expects out of him." They stopped at the field. Eli was dogging his way through the flying sprint drills that ended the practices.

"You have to go with that," Andrea said. "Keep talking to Henry."

"Mom, it really doesn't feel good to do this," said Ruth.

"No, it feels like shit," Andrea said strongly. "Guess what? Have you ever seen a happy investigator on TV? It's not a happy job. So, if you want to do it, if you want to help me, then you have to understand that and accept it."

Ruth nodded, thankful for her mother's bluntness, and for her not treating her like a baby.

"You don't have to answer now and you absolutely, totally *don't* have to do it if you don't want to, Ruth. Honest," Andrea said. "The line between personal discomfort and moral distaste is different for everyone and only you can judge for yourself where that line is for you. So, just think about it."

AT ELEVEN THAT night, Andrea saw light peeking under Ruth and Sarah's bedroom door. She opened it softly, hoping they might be asleep. Sarah was, but Ruth was wide awake and listening to music on her headphones.

Andrea whispered, "Lights out, okay?"

Ruth pulled out an earbud and said, "I'll talk to Henry again, Mom."

"Okay, hon," Andrea replied. "Lights out, good night."

She went into Sadie and JoJo's room. Both were asleep. She'd likely regret not waking the baby for a pre-midnight feeding but decided to roll the dice.

She went to her bedroom. Jeff was in bed, reading *The Wall Street Journal* on his iPad. He looked up. Almost too innocuously, he asked, "Anything happen with that whole Molly thing?"

"Just poking and seeing if there's anything there."

"Is there?" he asked.

She shrugged, noncommittal.

"I have to tell you, I think it all sounds a little bit crazy," Jeff said. "You really think Molly is capable of doing something like that?"

Andrea got into bed, thinking about what he had said.

After a few minutes, she said, "I think people are capable of anything."

17

ANDREA couldn't sleep. Jeff was sawing bones, and she was digging them up. Her past, buried for a reason, continued to insinuate itself into her thoughts. She hadn't thought about Isaac as often over the past few years. Raising a family in a struggling marriage had made it easier to ignore her guilt over her brother's death. Made it easy for her to ignore the fact she could amputate a few fingers and still count on two hands how many times her children had seen their grandparents. Her parents hadn't even met JoJo yet. She could use the excuse that they had moved to Florida, but the truth, Andrea knew, was that her parents had always been scared of her and they had never stopped blaming her for Isaac's death.

"YOU ARE NOT going to court to see that man again," Bernice Abelman shouted as Andie, just shy of turning twelve, got dressed in full preparation of defying her mother's edict.

"Tito is being sentenced today," she said. "It's the last time I'll see him."

"That man is the reason your brother was killed!"

"You don't know that," Andie said. "He said—"

"*Tito Envaquera is a convicted felon!*" her father shouted from the kitchen.

"*He is a con man,*" Bernice added. "*And he tricked you and all those other children into stealing for him.*"

"*The Fagin of Forest Hills, the newspapers call him. You were all a bunch of lemmings and he was the Pied Piper!*" said Jacob. "*Led you all right off a cliff!*"

"*The Pied Piper led rats,*" Andrea muttered, more out of embarrassment over their stupidity than out of any desire to educate them.

"*You might as well take off that fancy dress,*" shouted Jacob. "*You're not going anywhere and that's final!*"

An hour later, Andrea Abelman walked through the metal detectors at the Queens County Criminal Court entrance. She found the room where Tito's sentencing hearing was being held. Three of her former club members were there, Caveat, Romeo, and Juliet. She had never learned their real names, just as they had never learned hers. Tito had said, "*Who you are out there is not who you are in here.*"

"*In here*" was not a gang, exactly, but more like an exclusive club whose admittance required you to be a child of extraordinary intelligence who was morally comfortable with liberating the worldly possessions from those of ordinary intelligence. It was a fancy way to describe a group of pickpockets, scam artists, and thieves. But to pull off their largest scores had required intensive training, rigid preparation, and coordinated teamwork.

Maybe one out of a million kids, ten million, would have been intelligent enough—and indifferent enough to the concepts of right and wrong—to be adopted by the Fagin of Forest Hills.

Insight, the name Tito had given Andrea, had been one of those kids.

The back doors to the hearing room opened. Tito Envaquera was escorted in by two courthouse officers. He stood next to his lawyer. He didn't acknowledge the children, but Andie saw him tap his right thigh with one finger to acknowledge her, and then three times on his left to acknowledge the others.

The door to the back of the room opened and the judge entered. Andrea slouched in her chair slightly and covered half her face with her hand. She recognized the judge as a mark whose purse she had lifted two years earlier at the Rego Center.

This wasn't going to go well for Tito.

When she got back to the apartment, Andrea's parents read her the riot act for having snuck out. But through the numbing din of their escalating caterwauling, very jarring words came out of Jacob's mouth: "You're making us have to leave the city!"

"What?" she asked.

"Your father and I can't expose you to this any longer," said Bernice. "You can't control yourself. Look what happened to Isaac because of you."

"That was three years ago!" she said. "Where are we going?"

The next day, all her belongings packed into two large green contractor garbage bags, Andie Abelman left Queens, New York, and moved to West Windsor, New Jersey.

ANDREA HADN'T THOUGHT of Tito's sentencing or her last day in Queens in a long time.

That her parents had left Isaac's bed in the bedroom she had shared with him for years after he had died had been a daily reminder of his death. But moving to New Jersey had alleviated some of the guilt brought by that constant reminder and had helped her to focus more on herself. She'd been raised in a household where she'd been lied to every day of her life, and she had been part of a gang where she'd been rewarded for lying to others. On the day they had left Queens, Andie had promised herself that all she would ever care about from that point on was the truth. It was a promise she had broken time and time again. But not anymore. No matter what it might cost her.

After all, how could the truth ever hurt as much as the lies had?

O N Friday morning, Kenny and Jimmy rode an early train into the
city together. They arrived at the Muckrakers office by eight and
had finished most of what they needed to get done for the day by noon.
Sitara had morning meetings at Netflix, so Kenny wanted to be gone
before she showed up at the office.

Shelby had been making calls since the previous night. Between
the information gleaned from the Finch, Conover & Stanton website
and an "acquaintance" who worked at the New York City Bar Associa-
tion, she had gotten a solid handle on Derek's client list dating back
several years.

She had checked their names against any outstanding criminal
warrants and talked directly to much of his client list, but so far she
hadn't turned any dirt that would have lent itself as motive for murder
from that side of his life.

Though Shelby remained skeptical that Derek Goode had died
from anything other than natural causes, to her credit she had put the
work in to try and dispel that notion. And that was when she was willing to turn it over to Kenny and Jimmy.

She watched with her usual bemusement at their stupid energy as they packed up to leave for their planned assault.

"My MetroCard is out of swipes," Jimmy said.

"Your card is always out of swipes!" Kenny whined.

"Which makes me super grateful that yours never is," Jimmy replied as he retrieved his mock messenger bag from the small coat closet.

The plan was simple: wait outside the FCS building to see if anyone from Derek's team went out for lunch, then basically accost them. They struck pay dirt within five minutes of arriving as Derek's associates, Darrah Smalls and Bill Winthrop, emerged onto the street together. She went uptown. He went downtown.

"Dibs on the Nubian goddess," said Jimmy, not even waiting for Kenny's response.

"Shit," he muttered. And to Jimmy's back, added, "Focus on Derek and not your groin!"

"I can do both!" Jimmy shouted back as he jogged through traffic to cross the street.

Kenny stayed several yards behind Bill, who walked two blocks to a Cava. Kenny hated Cava. Now he'd have to go inside and pretend it was an amazing coincidence he had bumped into Bill at a fast-food place he hated. He approached the entrance, then waited. He hadn't really made a run at anyone in months. Stoked, he waited impatiently for someone else to go in before him to put some space between himself and Bill. A homeless man bugged him for change. Kenny shooed him away just as a Brooklyn hipster, who must have had Raynaud's phenomenon because he was wearing a wool cap in seventy-degree weather, entered the Cava.

Kenny followed. Bill stood with his back to him, looking at the menu board. There were about eight people in line in front of Bill. Kenny would wait until the lawyer turned around, then feign a spontaneously accidental meeting. He was fairly confident that it was at a Cava on Pennsylvania Avenue that Woodward and Bernstein had gotten Deep Throat to spill on Watergate.

JIMMY CAUGHT UP to Darrah on the corner of Fifty-fourth Street and Avenue of the Americas. He decided to go full-on annoying wannabe player, because what savvy city woman wouldn't be attracted to a loud, obnoxious messenger? His usual tactic was to let women come to him. That method had worked since he was in middle school. He found that being ridiculously handsome, tall, and buff, combined with a general indifference to the attentions thrown his way, usually made him irresistible to the opposite sex.

Though Darrah was gorgeous, Jimmy wasn't looking for a date, or even a hookup. For that matter, he didn't care much whether she knew anything, or even whether Molly had murdered her husband. Jimmy just wanted to have fun, and his life had certainly become a lot more fun since he had used his cable locator to find buried body parts for Kenny a year ago.

"Hey, beautiful! You work at FCS, don't you?" Jimmy said, loudly enough to cut through the noise of the city.

Darrah turned, offering over the course of one second exactly the reaction Jimmy had expected: disdain at the disrespectful approach, followed by appreciative curiosity at his good looks, culminating in self-recrimination for having expressed any interest at all. To a climber like Darrah Smalls, Jimmy's gorgeous-ocity could never win out over his being a messenger. Maybe she'd be willing to go for a roll after four drinks, but he certainly wasn't someone to be considered as relationship material.

"I saw you at the office last week," Jimmy said. "You are one totally fine Perry Mason package, lady."

"Yeah, that might play with the bar trash who frequent your corner dive, but it won't work on me," she said.

"You like 'em white, rich, and married, I'm guessing," Jimmy said, figuring he should go for the fences with the first swing. Kenny might have danced a bit, but Jimmy lacked that kind of patience. Plus, he'd passed a gyro food cart on the corner of Fifty-third and he was starving for lunch.

"What the fuck did you say?" she snapped.

Jimmy smiled. He had a beautiful smile that said "I love you" and "Fuck you" at the exact same time. "I figure, law firm, white boss, climbing the ladder? I mean, no judgment."

"What the hell is your problem?" she said.

"My momma says I got hit too much playing football, but I don't think so, since no one could ever touch me," he replied.

"I must have missed you catching a corner route from Mahomes on Fifty-second Street," she said.

Jimmy laughed. He could really like this woman if his job wasn't to make her hate him.

"Listen, sorry, I'm coming on strong, but I'm not a messenger. I was hired by an insurance company to find out if Derek Goode's death was on the up-and-up," Jimmy said. "His wife stands to cash in on a pretty sweet policy."

She took a moment to let that sink in, for the first time looking directly into Jimmy's eyes to try and gain a measure of him. He backed up from her just a bit, sensing his bombshell hadn't landed in the way he had hoped it would.

"So, you want to know if Derek was having an affair?" she asked. "Or if he was doing drugs, or anything that might have exacerbated his heart condition and violated the policy?"

"Yeah, I don't know what exacerbated means, but yeah, like that." He smiled. Charming Jimmy now.

"That's odd, since right before I left for lunch and before you rudely got all up in my face, I had two men in my office who were representatives of Derek's insurance company and they were asking me those same exact questions," Darrah said.

Jimmy stood, flummoxed.

"So . . . who the hell are you?" Darrah snarled, her face inches from his chest. She needed to crane her neck to look him in the eyes, but she still totally dominated their space.

Jimmy paused, unsure of what to say. This hadn't been in any of the scenarios he had discussed with Kenny. It was a situation that required quick thinking.

He turned and ran at a full sprint in the opposite direction.

He made his getaway, deftly weaving through the lunchtime pedestrian traffic.

Looking over his shoulder to make sure Darrah hadn't chased after him, Jimmy stopped at the food cart and got two gyros.

KENNY'S ENCOUNTER WITH Bill Winthrop went smoothly. The lawyer had casually turned and been the one to initiate enthusiastic conversation.

"What a surprise!"

"I can't believe it!"

"What are the odds?"

Bill was so naturally loud that, to avoid being trapped in the middle of their conversation, Brooklyn SkiCap ManBoy offered to switch places with Kenny. Much to the man's discomfort, Kenny politely declined, but continued his conversation with Bill.

"Did you write up the piece?" Bill asked.

"I did," Kenny lied. "Might run this Wednesday, but likely next week."

"Oh, I'd love to see a copy."

"You really liked Derek?" asked Kenny. "I mean, out of everyone I talked to, you really seemed to like him the most."

Flattered, Bill touched his hand to his heart and bit back tears. "We all loved him in different ways. He hired me out of law school. He encouraged me to be me." Then, conspiratorially whispering, even though it was all traveling through the ears of Brooklyn SkiCap ManBoy between them, he added, "Even when being me is being a really bad boy!"

Kenny laughed. "You guys caused a lot of trouble, I hear. I mean, some other people I talked to, his friends, they all said having kids didn't really stop Derek from having a good time."

"Oh, it slowed him down some," Bill laughed, with a wink. "He started driving the speed limit, but trust me, that car still drove!"

"I heard a lot of gossip—none of it went into my story, but they said Derek fooled around behind his wife's back, partied too much," said Kenny. "In all honesty, you're kind of confirming it for me."

"Yeah, he did," said Bill. "He's been gone over a week, so the statute of limitations on decorum be damned! But listen, in his defense, you think you might die tomorrow, is it wrong to live for the day?"

"I thought it was statue of limitations," said Brooklyn SkiCap ManBoy.

Bill and Kenny both stared at him for a moment, then Kenny said, "No judgment from me, but Molly might have had some opinions on that if she'd known."

"Oh, she knew, honey," Bill said.

"She did?"

"Totally," he said. "Derek invited her along for the ride before they had kids."

"And she went? On this metaphorical ride?"

"Live in your twenties, Kenny," Bill said as he stepped up to the counter to order. "Because after that, lunch at Cava is your thrill for the day."

Bill was in his late twenties, so that sounded even sadder than it should have. Molly had been a party girl, too? He wondered if Andrea knew that. Could you really be two different people before and after you got married and had kids?

While Kenny waited for SkiCap ManBoy to order, Bill's food order came up and he started to leave, waving goodbye.

"Wait, Bill," Kenny said. Bill turned, clearly hoping an offer to meet for coffee or drinks might be in the offing. "What did Derek think of Molly?"

"He thought she was an unhappy, controlling, bitter, rigid pain in his ass," Bill said without a moment's hesitation. "But he loved her. Married couples, right?"

"Considering his heart condition, Derek had quite a hefty insurance policy," Kenny said.

"And you think Molly . . . ?" Bill smiled conspiratorially. "I loooove it! But, I don't know."

"You don't think she would be capable of that?"

"For money? Anyone is capable of anything," said Bill. "But that's not my point. Why kill him for money when he was the only means she had of making money?"

"The insurance policy?"

"Peanuts over the long haul compared to what he was making," Bill said.

The girl behind the counter asked Kenny what he wanted. "One second," he said, frustrated. He turned back to Bill. "He's not even a partner at the firm."

"Derek hit that wall a yearish ago," Bill said. "He was making extra money on the side."

"Doing what?"

"Sir, can you order please?" she interrupted again.

"Um, a grain bowl," Kenny said, which surprised him because he'd intended to say, *Can you please shut the fuck up?*

Back to Bill: "You mean outside the law firm?"

"Sir, your dips and spreads?" said the counter girl.

"What?" asked Kenny.

"You have a choice of three dips or spreads," she replied.

To Bill: "Wait one second."

"I have to get back," Bill said.

"Wait," said Kenny.

"Can you choose three, please?" said the counter girl.

"I really don't care, pick for me," said Kenny.

"I can't do that, sir."

Bill had almost reached the door.

"Everything in this place tastes like shredded cardboard, just pick three fucking sides for me!" Kenny snapped at the counter girl. Back to Bill: "What did you mean?"

Bill turned. With a smile, he said, "Ask his golfing buddies."

Bill left.

"Anything to drink?" the counter girl asked.

"A bourbon," Kenny said. "What's my total?"

He paid and threw the bag with his food into the garbage can by the exit.

He came back inside two seconds later, reaching into the trash bin to pull his bag back out. He gave the entire unopened bag to the homeless man still sitting outside the door.

Several paces down the block, he heard the homeless man shout, "You forgot to get a fork!"

KENNY SAW JIMMY waiting for him by the entrance to the subway. It had been their prearranged rendezvous. Jimmy was finishing a chicken gyro and had a second one in his other hand.

"You got that for me?" asked Kenny.

"No," said Jimmy, opening up the second one and taking a big bite out of it.

"What did you find out?" asked Kenny.

"Derek's life insurance company is sniffing around looking for something that might void his policy," Jimmy said.

Kenny nodded. That was interesting. He hadn't expected that result. "Nothing on whether Darrah might have been having an affair with him?"

"She didn't say," Jimmy replied absently as he started toward the steps to the platform. "Didn't say no, either. Got mad when I suggested it, though. What did you get?"

"Derek had something on the side going on," Kenny said, but kept it at that.

What were the odds of one of his "golfing buddies" including Jeff Stern? he thought.

"Hey, can you swipe for me?" asked Jimmy as he waited by the turnstile.

Kenny didn't like where this was going. He swiped, his stomach grumbling, as Jimmy took another bite of his second gyro.

19

SARAH Stern tensed in a slight crouch, a hawk ready to pounce. A group of players swarmed around the ball in front of her. She didn't join the scrum because she knew the ball would pop out. Within seconds, it did. Sarah nudged the soccer ball away from the pileup. Keeping it close to her feet with soft taps, she smoothly dribbled into a controlled breakaway.

She approached the open mini-goal and didn't try to blast it, or kick it with her toe, she just casually used her instep to finish the play and strike the ball into the net. There wasn't another six-year-old girl within twenty yards of her. It was the fifth time she had done that. Not that Andrea was counting.

As he did every week, the coach for the under-eight, second-grade travel team strolled over to remind Andrea that travel tryouts for next year's team were in May. Andrea, as she did every week, smiled politely and nodded.

"Doesn't seem like fair competition," said a voice behind her.

She turned to see West Windsor detective Vince Rossi walking toward her. He was dressed for the midseventies September Saturday morning in a white polo shirt and khaki shorts. She wasn't used to seeing him in such casual attire.

"She should be playing with the boys," Vince said. Then, immediately realizing it was a dumb thing to say, he added, "I mean, maybe with older kids? Or some competition."

"Eli was really good in first grade, too," Andrea said. "Now he's the lowest-ranked player on his travel team, so these things have a way of evening themselves out."

"You're saying that to be diplomatic," said Rossi. "Which you don't need to be with me. The kid's a beast."

"She pretty much is," said Andrea. "You should see her play basketball."

She got off her high-end Eno Lounger DL camping chair, which had been a godsend while she had been perpetually pregnant, but now seemed a bit extravagant for rec soccer. Sadie and JoJo were behind them, playing with blocks on a large blanket spread. JoJo was teething on a plastic block, which had led Sadie to chew hers, too. Her second-youngest had taken to acting like a baby just for the negative attention. Eli was kicking a ball around with some of his friends in one of the empty fields at the Zaitz Farm complex. Ruth had stayed home to read, which Andrea took to mean TikTok with her friends.

"You didn't ask me here to impress me with your future Olympian?" Rossi said.

Andrea gently walked the detective a few feet back from the row of seated parents, but not so far that she couldn't keep an eye on Sadie and JoJo.

He laughed, a knowing, weary snort.

"What?" she asked.

"You think Molly Goode had something to do with her husband's death?" he said, then added, "You're not always ten steps ahead of everyone else, you know."

Andrea explained what they had learned to that point. She was interrupted when Sadie started pummeling JoJo with the plastic blocks. Andrea lifted the baby, who cried out, not because she'd been hurt, but because she wanted to get down to fight back. Sadie danced around them, holding blocks in each hand and taunting her little sister, which only made the baby cry more.

"You're such an incredible masochist," Rossi said.

"Don't I know it," Andrea replied. Through JoJo's crying, she continued relating what Kenny and his team had learned so far, or at least what they suspected, plus their strategy to press forward. She was interrupted twice by the polite but jealous applause of the parents. Sarah had scored two more goals.

The whistle blew. It was halftime.

The kids rushed for the most important part of the game: the orange slices, whose sugar rush wouldn't kick in until twenty minutes after the game ended.

Sarah came running over to say hi with an orange rind in her mouth covering her teeth.

She mumbled, "Hi, Detective Rossi. Did you see my goals?"

"Not a single one, sweetie," he replied. "But that was a sweet instep on that breakaway."

Sarah giggled and it made the rind pop out of her mouth. JoJo screamed to get down so she could retrieve it. Sadie started complaining that she wanted an orange slice, too.

"I'll get you one," said Sarah. She dashed off like the Flash and returned with a slice for Sadie and one for JoJo. The referee blew the whistle and the players made their way back for the second half, most of them begrudgingly. Sarah was the first one at the center line, ready for the tap-off. The strategy they'd perfected early into this young season had been to tap the ball to Sarah and then get the hell out of her way. Ruth called it the "Give the ball to the Italians" strategy from the *Kicking & Screaming* movie, which they'd watched a thousand times already in the Stern household.

The referee, a pimply kid barely older than Ruth, blew the whistle to open the second half.

After Sarah scored, Andrea noticed the parents' applause had grown noticeably wearier.

"You think you have a motive?" said Rossi.

"More than one," said Andrea. "Besides the likelihood Derek Goode was having an affair, I suspect there may have been physical abuse as well."

"Based on . . . ?"

"Molly Goode only wears long-sleeve shirts," said Andrea. "Even at the community pool. Even at the service and funeral when everyone else was wearing short sleeves. When she exercises. When we have lunch. Always."

"You think she's covering up bruises?"

"She claims it's her fair Irish skin."

He said nothing.

"You think I'm wasting my time," she said.

"No," Rossi replied. "I think you're wasting *my* time."

Even though his tone was playful, that frustrated her. She wanted to snap back at him, but knew that wouldn't help her case.

"Listen, Andie, you know how much I respect you," he said. "And I know you can handle my blunt honesty in a mature manner."

"You're worried I'm going to go Queens Karen on you?" she said.

"I have to admit, I am." He smiled with relief. "Okay, here we go. Andie, you need drama in your life. Because you weren't able to find it through a career, you're looking to manufacture it whether it's there or not."

"Really?" she said, trying to sound bemused, but knowing he had hit a target she'd long pretended hadn't even existed.

"I'm sorry, I don't want to offend you," he said. "You're standing here telling me you think your friend murdered her husband and I'm standing here wondering why you think that. You have threadbare motives, you have no proof, and worst of all, you have medical documentation that the 'victim' had a preexisting condition and that his heart was a ticking time bomb. So, give me something beyond a hunch—because as much as I respect the ones you have, right now, this one is lacking."

Andrea said nothing for several seconds. She knew her prolonged silences made Rossi uncomfortable. He was wondering if he'd gone too far. Nothing he had said wasn't true, and they were things she had already dismissed, but not because he was wrong, rather because she was worried he was right.

Finally, she said, "I'm not disagreeing with you, though I might take umbrage with the level of spite."

"First of all, there was no level of spite at all," he said, smiling. "And second of all, I know you're full of shit when you say things like 'umbrage.'"

"The truth is, it's all stuff I've wrestled with the last few days," she said.

"Andie, you're like the daughter I never had because I was smart enough not to have kids," said Rossi, "but if you want some fatherly advice, I would say get your PI license or apply for a job at a police department or call your friend Mercado for a consulting contract with the FBI. Make who you are a job and not a hobby."

"And if I did that, Vince, then you'd be okay with me proving Molly killed her husband?" she said coyly.

"*Proving* is the key word in all of this."

The whistle blew, ending the game. All the kids skipped and cartwheeled off the field, indifferent to the score everyone said they weren't keeping track of. It was 16–8. Sarah had twelve goals and three assists. First grade and she actually knew to pass the ball to open players. But again, Andrea wasn't keeping track.

"We good?" asked Rossi.

Andrea held one finger up as she called up a contact on her phone.

She cupped the phone to her chin, trying to screen some of the noise from all the kids running around and parents chatting.

"Molly? Hi. Monday is our mutual free morning, right?" Andrea said. "Can you show me the path you take at Plainsboro Preserve?"

She waited.

"No, I know you go into the woods," Andrea responded. "I think I have to scale up my workout and I was hoping you could help."

She waited.

"Great! I'll meet you in the parking lot at nine."

Andrea hung up and pocketed the phone.

"You're just going to come right out and ask her if she killed her husband, aren't you?" Rossi said.

Andrea smiled. "A confession counts as proof, right?"

20

WHILE Andrea was at Sarah's game, Ruth was not home TikTok-ing with her friends, she was texting with them. Specifically, one of them: Henry Goode. She had reached out to him, using the algebra work as her ruse for trying to continue probing into his home life.

It had taken Ruth some heavy thinking and even heavier rationalizing to come to terms with what her mother had asked of her. She understood why her part was necessary, and as importantly, she understood why she might be the only person who could pull it off. But based on what she had learned of her mother's history—and seen of her methods—Ruth refused to hit Henry like a hurricane, without any concern for the damage she'd leave behind.

So, she went in soft, and threw herself into the fire before she was willing to burn him.

> **RUTH:** You said something that worried me.
>
> **HENRY:** what
>
> **RUTH:** About how strict your mom was. I felt bad, I know what thats like.

HENRY: ur mom doesnt seem so bad

RUTH: No, not my mom being strict. But its hard cos shes got eyes on everything. You feel like your caught before you even do anything.

HENRY: i get that sucks you got supercopmom and i probly got cameras hidden all over the house

RUTH: Are you joking?

HENRY: lol probly not feels that way tho

Ruth paused, knowing this was her opportunity but that she'd have to word it accurately. She noted the inconsistency of her punctuation in her texts and Henry's total indifference. She was channeling *some* of her mother's aggressive energy, and Henry was defying what Ruth was sure would be his mother's stern disapproval of his shoddy writing.

There was her angle. Her fingers flew over the keys:

RUTH: I can ask my mom if ur mom is legally allowed to record you guys

HENRY: lol i don't think shes doing that I was kidding

RUTH: oh

HENRY: but she might as well be she watches everything we do like a hawk

RUTH: you told me about your phone. Im sorry that's not fair

HENRY: fair doesn't matter fair means my dad would still be alive

RUTH: I know.

HENRY: i don't know what were gonna do he was the only thing that kept this house sane

RUTH: how?

HENRY: ah, forget it

RUTH: no, Henry, you have to talk about it. You can't keep it all bottled up. I'm here for you

HENRY: thanks its just my mom is always so tense she makes me n brett feel tense all the time

RUTH: ugh are all our parents like that?

HENRY: no my dad wasn't he was always stuck in the middle between us n my mom he was really chill about the stupid little stuff that always drives my mom up the wall

RUTH: your dad takes the hit?

HENRY: every time stuck up for us told brett its ok if he wants to dress well u no how he likes to dress

RUTH: colorfully

HENRY: LOL nice way of putting it

RUTH: does she have a problem with brett?

HENRY: OH HELLS YEAH but i think even she knows she doesnt have much of a choice u r what u r

RUTH: yeah your dad is cool with all that

HENRY: brett told me that dad told him to stand tall

and proud and be whatever he wants to be. i mean, he's only 10 but brett said dad made him feel safe

RUTH: you don't feel safe with your mom?

HENRY: not that, just brett gives her another reason to complain about somethin judge us like she always does

RUTH: like what?

HENRY: EVERYTHING :(grades clothes chores manners how we talk what we say how we say it how we p

RUTH: WHAT?!

HENRY: no seriously this is gross i cant tell you about it

RUTH: missing the toilet?

HENRY: YES how did you no

RUTH: a stupid little brother and a lazy father!

HENRY: does your mom go crazy about it?

RUTH: nah

HENRY: mine does stupid nuts all the time every day always finding something to be angry about every single fucking day

HENRY: sorry I cursed

RUTH: no fucking worries

RUTH: ;)

HENRY: lol your cool, ruth

RUTH: I am

After several seconds of silence from his end, Ruth realized she had to keep it going just a little bit longer.

RUTH: so what now?

HENRY: zero clue mom asked if we wanted to leave the house and we didn't

RUTH: that's hard. I mean its where your dad died, but the house is all you know. I've moved twice in my life, so that part I think I could deal with

HENRY: the house is part of it but I don't want to leave school and my friends

RUTH: totally would suck

HENRY: yeah I mean it all sucks either way staying without my dad is going to suck so wud leaving

RUTH: you think your mom is going to get worse?

HENRY: ha cud she get any worse? yeah i think she can n i think she will

RUTH: whatre you going to do

HENRY: cry

HENRY: lol

HENRY: no just gonna do what ive always done put up with it an pretend its all cool

RUTH: you don't have to pretend with me

HENRY: thanks

HENRY: gtg

RUTH: me 2

HENRY: homework

RUTH: tiktok

HENRY: i wish. Molly wont let me dwnld it

RUTH: suckage its fun

HENRY: i remember fun

HENRY: not

HENRY: thnx for talking

RUTH: anytime

HENRY: CUNS

RUTH: CUNS

Ruth opened her TikTok app and randomly scrolled through videos she didn't even pay attention to. Such an innocuously stupid way to spend your time. It was all a distraction from anything that was important in life, she knew, but often necessary. Even at her young age, Ruth had come to understand that a distraction was good as long as it was just a distraction rather than your reality. She already knew too many peers who couldn't distinguish between the two.

She thought about her mother in comparison with Molly Goode. It gave her an anxious knot in the pit of her stomach to realize that she wasn't sure if she could differentiate between their respective pathologies. Not to say they were the same, but could Ruth really exonerate her mom from her single-mindedness when she was locked on a case? Was Andrea's indifference to anyone she drove over or left behind on the road to solving a crime all that different from Molly's rigid determination that people and places and things be what she demanded of them no matter the consequences?

No matter the consequences.

Ruth couldn't accept that, certainly not when people—when her friends—were those consequences.

But she also couldn't accept someone getting away with murder.

Her first thought was: How does Mom do this?

But Ruth's next thought, immediately coming after the first one, and bringing both excitement and trepidation in its wake, was: How do I do it better?

21

O**N** Monday, Kenny Lee had to sprint to make the 6:14 a.m. New Jersey Transit train to New York before the doors closed. He was pretty sure that having to run through a tunnel and up two flights of stairs to catch a train that early qualified as a crime against humanity.

He chided himself that he hadn't reached the platform in time to spot his target. It meant he would have to go car by car in search of Wendell Burns. Kenny had entered in the middle of the train, so it was a fifty-fifty choice to go forward or back. He surmised that since Wendell worked uptown in Manhattan, if he walked to the office or rode the 1/2/3 subway line, he'd be more likely to sit at the front of the train.

He found Wendell sitting in the second car from the front. He was thankful it wasn't the first car, which was a Quiet Commute car, since Kenny fully intended to not be quiet. Wendell was in a two-seater by himself, reading *The New York Times* on his iPad.

Kenny pointed to the empty window seat and asked, "Can I sit in there?"

Wendell gave the cursory frustrated glance all commuters used when losing an open seat next to them for even a small part of the slog into the city. As he stood, Wendell added a discreet grinding of the teeth after seeing other empty seats Kenny could have chosen. It wasn't until Kenny settled into the seat that Wendell recognized him.

"And here I thought we all looked alike," Kenny said. "Yes, it's me. How have you been, Wendell? Haven't seen you since we interviewed your wife for the documentary, right?"

Wendell failed to stammer out a response.

"You're frustrated you had to move your backpack to the floor, right? I'm sorry. God knows what's really on these floors. They say they clean them every night, but I don't know. How do you do this every day? This early, anyway. I mean, I'm going into the city several days a week now to work, which I haven't done since after college. I'm working on a Netflix docuseries. Commuting used to suck then, but it's okay now. Probably because I'm excited about the show. The Netflix show, like I mentioned. But you knew that, on account of the interview with Crystal."

"And you just mentioning it several times," muttered Wendell.

Kenny continued, "Yeah, I feel it's worth several mentions a minute. About the docuseries, listen, don't get mad at me, though seriously, by now, you probably have a bit of a clue, but your wife talks a lot. I mean, prescription-ad-telling-you-all-the-side-effects fast. We're probably going to cut her out of the final edit. She just wouldn't take a breath in between her run-on sentences. I hate that, don't you? Who am I asking? Just look at your face, of course you do."

Kenny took a breath, appreciating the deer-in-the-headlights look from Wendell.

"We need to talk," Kenny said with malignant weight.

Wendell didn't say anything.

"You used to golf with the Cellulitist husbands, didn't you?"

Wendell seemed confused. Kenny put his fingers to his lips in an exaggerated "whoops" mea culpa. "I'm sorry, you didn't know that was their nickname? Cat's out of the bag. Andrea calls her friends the Cellulitists, and now I can't think of them any other way."

Since Wendell didn't appear any less confused, Kenny added, "Cellulite plus elitists equals Cellulitists. She pronounces it with a long *e* and I think it should be pronounced with a long *i* but it's a made-up word, so what difference does it make? Anyway, you played golf with Derek Goode, right?"

Wendell nodded, having meekly chosen to surrender to the moment.

"But you haven't over the last year," Kenny said.

"Done what?"

"Played golf with them. Don't deny it, I checked the playbooks at the Mercer Oaks and Cranbury courses. Derek is logged in with Martin Singer and Jeff Stern at least once a month, but your name hasn't been in the books for a while. What happened?"

"Nothing," said Wendell.

"You stopped liking their company?"

"No."

"You stopped enjoying the game?"

"No, it's fine."

"The ball and chain got pissy about you disappearing for most of Saturday?"

"No, no, Crystal was okay with it."

"No, she wasn't."

That mustered a soft chuckle out of Wendell. "No, she wasn't, but that's not why I stopped."

The express train blew past the New Brunswick station and over the Raritan River. Kenny cast a reflexive glance to his left at the Rutgers dorms lining the riverbank. The farthest one, Campbell, was where he had lived when he broke the story that toppled the administration of former New Jersey governor Walter O'Malley. He used to think of that time with bitterness and regret, but now, on top of the world again, he had reclaimed some pride in his accomplishments.

Kenny waited a few minutes, letting Wendell suffer the uncertainty of where the conversation was headed. As they passed the crowded Metropark station, he said, "You stopped playing because they were getting involved in things you didn't want to get involved in."

Wendell fumbled with his iPad and then made a show of putting it away in his backpack. It was awkward, since he was tall and his knees pressed against the back of the seat in front of them. New Jersey Transit train seats were made for people the average height of Danny DeVito, who happened to be a New Jersey native but likely didn't appreciate that the seats had been designed for him.

"I need to know what they're doing," Kenny said.

"I don't know. I haven't played with them in a while," Wendell said. "You said it yourself."

"Touché, Wendell," Kenny said. "Let me refine that: I need you to tell me the original discussions they were having that generated enough discomfort in you that you stopped playing with them."

Wendell said nothing.

"I can follow the trail without you," Kenny pushed.

"Trail?" Wendell asked. "What trail? Why?"

Kenny weighed how much he should tell him. It was too early to tip their hand about Molly, but he hadn't really prepared a cover story. He quickly came up with a good one.

"I think Jeff Stern is involved in improper financial operations," Kenny said. "You can't tell Crystal because I haven't told Andie yet. As we were preparing to vet the documentary for oppo research—that's when we plan for what other people might use to—"

"I know what it is, Mr. Lee," said Wendell.

"Okay, sure, anyway, Jeff's history came up," Kenny said.

"Of course," said Wendell. He'd had some money invested with Jeff's wealth management company when it collapsed a few years ago, but it hadn't been affected by Jeff's illegalities. It had been concerning enough to make Wendell very wary of Jeff's business choices.

The train pulled into Newark Penn Station. Kenny gave it a rest as half the car filed out. It quickly filled up with new people boarding. It would become standing room only into Manhattan once they stopped at Secaucus Junction. Commuting was fun, he thought.

"I don't want to get anyone in trouble," Wendell said.

"I'm trying to protect Andrea, but I don't know if I can until I know what it is."

Wendell hemmed and hawed.

"If they're doing something wrong, but it doesn't have anything to do with the documentary, I don't have to report it to the police," Kenny said. "Or worse, your wife."

"It was something Derek came up with," said Wendell. "He'd clearly discussed it with Martin, because I remember they brought it up to Jeff and me in unison."

"Like a sales pitch?"

"I guess, yes," Wendell said, avoiding eye contact at all costs.

"So, the bullet points?" Kenny prodded.

"I don't know the details, so I can't really bullet-point it," Wendell replied.

Kenny wasn't sure how far he could push, then reminded himself he would push someone off the edge of the Grand Canyon if it meant getting the story.

"I can turn around at Penn Station, take the next train back home, go knock on your door, and ask Crystal what she knows."

"I'm not scared of Crystal," Wendell said.

"Dude, you're *terrified* of her," Kenny replied. "No judgment, I'm terrified of her, too."

It became standing room only at Secaucus. People wedged into the aisle and center vestibule. Wendell said nothing until the train miraculously made it through the tunnel without any delays and pulled into the platform at New York Penn Station.

The passengers slowly shuffled their way out of the car. Wendell said, "They wanted me to manage a set of books. I didn't want to hear it. Any of it."

"But it involved something they had in common, right?" Kenny said as Wendell stood up. "Derek does wills and estates for the elderly; Martin runs senior care facilities. And Jeff does asset management."

"But he can't authorize trades because of the penalties against him," Wendell said.

"There it is," Kenny said. "They needed you to make the trades Jeff recommended and manage the account."

Wendell shrugged. On the platform, he started to walk away from Kenny to the steps leading up to Penn. He wanted to get away as quickly as possible.

Kenny let a throng of people get between him and Wendell, but once the frightened man reached the steps, Kenny loudly called out, "Oh, Wendell, one more thing."

Wendell stopped, flustered because that delayed the march up the steps for everyone behind him. Frustrated commuters tried to go around him, like a river circumventing a rock that had been dropped into it. Kenny prolonged the discomfort longer than he needed to by a purposeful count of three Mississippis.

Kenny smiled. "How much do the wives know?"

22

B<small>Y</small> nine o'clock, while Kenny Lee downed his third macchiato at the Muckrakers office in Manhattan in a valiant struggle to stay awake, Andrea Stern pulled into the Plainsboro Preserve gravel parking lot to meet Molly Goode. She didn't see Molly's car, though there were several others already there. The morning walkers who used the trails around the abandoned quarry were out in force.

Close to one thousand acres of habitat, the property had once been owned by Walker-Gordon for their dairy farms and labs. McCormack Sand and Gravel Company had stopped mining the site in the seventies, but left behind a beautiful quarry lake that formed the centerpiece of the preserved tract. The land was purchased between 1999 and 2003 by Plainsboro Township, Middlesex County, and New Jersey Audubon, who jointly turned it into a wildlife refuge.

Andrea and Jeff had gone to the preserve only once. He didn't like nature unless it came with a nineteenth hole, and she didn't like it without concrete sidewalks and blaring taxi horns. She also didn't like entering unfamiliar terrain to accuse someone of murder, but she knew the location would lure her friend. Andrea doubted Molly would be packing a pistol, since it would kill the clean lines of her yoga pants. If it came down to a titanic hand-to-hand struggle at the tip of the peninsula that jutted out into the lake, Andrea remained confident she could kick the shit out of Molly.

JoJo had fallen asleep in the car. Andrea unlatched the car seat and gently lifted her out. She stirred as she was transferred to the Osprey Poco child carrier pack. Before Andrea could run JoJo's chubby little arms through the shoulder harness, she woke up. She smiled. Andrea smiled back at her and playfully pinched her nose.

"Hey, JoJo girl, ready to catch a killer with Mommy? Yes, you are."

Andrea thought that in case she was wrong and Molly was packing heat, she could always use JoJo as a shield.

She hoisted the carrier onto her back and tightened the straps. It was really comfortable and airy, which, at a cost of three hundred bucks, it damn well better have been. Andrea was five foot three and the harness was practically half her height. Her Yeti water bottle was holstered in the left holder and JoJo's formula bottle in the right, like suburban pistols ready for a quick draw.

She felt comforted spotting the familiar black Lexus SUV parked ten yards away, just as Molly's silver Mercedes-Benz GLE pulled into the lot. It gracefully rolled over the gravel with a dignity Andrea's Odyssey couldn't pull off. Molly parked right next to the minivan.

Molly emerged, perfectly prepped from head to toe. Rust-brown Cloudrock mid-cut hiking boots, beige Bridgedale StormSocks, taupe Arc'teryx Gamma LT pants, and a blood red Melody hybrid half-zip top comprised the six-hundred-dollar outfit she wore for a casual walk through the woods. Her hair was pulled back in a ponytail.

"Thanks for meeting me," said Andrea. "You look great."

"I want to break out the fall outfits, but Democrats with their global warming are purposefully trying to vex me," she said with a smile that Andrea knew was only half self-deprecating. Molly was comfortably and slyly conservative in a town that tended to shy away from any overt declarations that weren't kumbaya progressive.

"The kids are all calling it climate change now," Andrea responded.

"Speaking of kids, I hope it doesn't sound tacky, but I loved the suits the boys wore. I have to get Eli one soon."

"Jos. A. Bank Clothiers in MarketFair," Molly replied. "Their tailor is wonderful."

Their shoes crunched over the gravel as they walked past the environmental education center, a brown wood-and-stone building that housed several exhibits featuring the flora and fauna found in the preserve. They reached the start of the entrance trail, JoJo kicking her legs in excitement at the sight of a cardinal flying by. Andrea noted that twenty yards into their walk, Molly hadn't even acknowledged the baby, the way any typical warm-blooded organism would.

"Let's follow the White Trail to the end before deciding how much further you can go," Molly said.

"I don't know the trail names," Andrea replied. "I just want to go to the end of the peninsula so that JoJo can see it."

"The White Trail leads us to Maggie's Trail," said Molly. "That'll take us where you want to go."

"That sounds like a plan, then."

"It's only a mile each way," said Molly.

"Two total? Is that too little or too much?"

Molly laughed. "You're so coy. I usually do six when I come here."

"I'll die before that, so please just take good care of JoJo. Preferably an Ivy League college." Andrea nodded. "Lead on."

Molly led on. Even while attempting a casual stroll, she walked faster than Andrea.

"I love this preserve," said Molly. "Its stillness is so elegant. There is too little civility around here."

"How do you mean?" asked Andrea.

"Places that aspire to what's best in us, rather than what is worst," said Molly. "To be something more than malls and highways, mortgages and property values. Places that help us think about who we could be and what our perspective should be."

"I love walking around Princeton campus," said Andrea. "The architecture is beautiful."

"It is, but for me, too great a reminder of our place in a class structure," Molly replied. "My favorite is the Grounds for Sculpture."

"Never been," said Andrea.

"In Hamilton? Really?" Andrea was tsked by Molly with unfettered reprobation. "To me, it is a place that speaks to . , . freedom . . . from so much that binds us, physically and spiritually, even morally."

Molly's excitement about the conversation had generated an even faster pace. Andrea struggled to keep up.

"I'm lugging an extra twenty pounds here," Andrea said.

"Oh, even giving you the credit due for the work you've done to lose so much weight, Andie, I'm sure you're lugging a little more than twenty."

So, that's how it was going to be, Andrea thought.

JoJo yapped when she saw a herd of deer munching on the remnants of the soybean subsidy growth in the farm field to their left. They walked a little farther up the trail until McCormack Lake was clearly visible through the heavy growth to their right.

Andrea's and Molly's phone notifications pinged at the same time. They looked at each other and knew: Crystal.

"If we don't respond, she won't stop," said Molly.

"If we do respond, she won't stop," Andrea said, smiling.

They bit the bullet and looked at their screens.

Crystal's texts came, as all her texts did, in short rapid bursts, but this was made worse by multiple alerts with different ringtones pinging out of sync on two different phones.

> Are you guys out yet?
>
> Is it nice?
>
> Does Josephine like it?

"You answer," said Molly.

Andrea sighed. She responded:

Just started walking

All good

They waited for the inevitable response, but it didn't come, which meant Crystal was spinning multiple text threads at the same time.

"How are the boys?" Andrea asked, trying to slowly slide into the conversation.

"They're quite devastated, as you might imagine," Molly replied. "It's hitting Brett more than Henry. He is very sensitive."

"Ruth talked to Henry at school last week," Andrea said. "She said he was angry."

"Angry? Perhaps. That might serve to strengthen him," said Molly. "It's tragic, of course, but I've found it all a bit . . . futile, as well."

Andrea huffed a bit. An excited JoJo dug her heels into Andrea's ribs like she was pushing a horse down the home stretch to win the Triple Crown.

"You've dealt with death, Andrea," Molly continued. "From the perspective of those who were killed and those who would commit murder. From your viewpoint, doesn't there have to be a purpose to life and death? If it can be viewed as an equation . . . then I can understand it."

"How so?"

"Motivations, desire, planning, opportunity, committing the very act itself, covering it up, dealing with its ramifications for both the killer and the loved ones . . . those are all things that one should be able to quantify in some manner, because in nearly all ways they can be qualified," Molly said. She looked up at the trees as she talked. Was this a philosophical discussion, or was Molly pushing Andrea's buttons?

A male jogger approached them on the trail. They moved to the right as he ran by.

"You feel the math doesn't work in Derek's death?" Andrea asked.

Molly laughed. It had an undercurrent of mocking that made Andrea's teeth grind.

"No, actually, just the opposite, Andie," she said. "The math works perfectly. Heart disease plus heart attack equals death. No, my disgust about it"—she spat those words out—"is how sadly simple an equation that turned out to be. I would have hoped it might have been more complicated."

They walked another hundred yards, catching up to a woman pushing a jogging stroller. She was very thin, with dark hair and dark skin. And she didn't seem to be putting much effort into the jogging aspect of the jogging stroller.

Molly and Andrea walked past her. Molly said, "Good morning."

JoJo got very excited, reaching toward the woman and almost blowing their cover.

With Aditya in the stroller, Sathwika blithely pulled one earbud out and said, "Good morning."

Andrea said nothing.

They kept walking.

Sathwika kept a slower pace behind them.

After several more yards, Andrea said, "Let me see if I have this right. You wanted Derek to have a more dramatic death?"

"Or perhaps a less mundane one," Molly said. "I don't know. After all these years of living under the shadow of this possibility, it felt very anticlimactic."

"It's the dramatic deaths that tend to draw the wrong attention," Andrea said.

Molly smiled. "Are you saying if Derek had died choking on anti-freeze, it would have piqued your curiosity?"

"A little," Andrea said. After a few seconds, she added, "Your lip looks better."

Molly seemed temporarily thrown by the non sequitur.

"The cold sore?" Andrea added.

Molly absently touched her lip. "I had hoped it wasn't noticeable."

"It wasn't a big deal either way," Andrea said. "Just a cold sore."

A shadow passed over Molly's eyes; she was irritated but feigning indifference. Her friend was so guarded with her feelings that Andrea's skills at reading people needed to be hyperfocused, as she looked for a slight tightening of an eyelid, a tic of a finger, or a clenching of the jaw.

"You know how I hate to mar my fair Irish skin," Molly replied.

Andrea's suspicions that they were playing a passive-aggressive game were confirmed. Her probe about the cold sore had brought the game out into the open.

"Always have to worry about sunburn, right?" said Andrea.

Molly didn't respond as they reached the end of the White Trail. They took the spur to the right. A small wooden bridge crossed a narrow brook that ran from the edge of the lake and into a patch of wetlands to their left. They walked the narrow trail that bisected the peninsula. JoJo made happy noises as the swallows poked their heads out of the wooden birdhouse posts that lined the trail. The birds flew out of their houses, one after another, as they passed by.

The trio reached the stone bench at the end of the peninsula. From that vantage point, they had a full view of the lake. They took a minute to soak in the relative peace. Andrea looked out across the quarry lake. The sun's rays sparked off the surface.

"Perfect place to bury a body," she said.

The tranquility was marred not only by Andrea's cynicism, but by the sound of a horn as a New Jersey Transit train rolled along the

Northeast Corridor line that ran at the perimeter of the preserve. Andrea smiled. Even here, the frigging train found a way to spoil her fun.

She unslung the harness and settled the carrier on a bench. She removed JoJo from the carrier. The baby kicked her legs in anticipation of being fed. Andrea uncapped the bottle and JoJo sucked as if she hadn't eaten in three days.

Molly was bathed in sunlight. She really was everything Andrea wasn't. Tall, graceful, cultured, and cautiously controlled. She was a beautiful woman, but she came across as harsh, not because of the way she looked, but because of the way she was.

"You should really come right out and ask," Molly said unexpectedly.

Or, maybe, exactly as Andrea had expected.

Andrea looked up to her friend, squinting slightly as the sunlight silhouetted Molly.

Without a hint of hesitation or intimidation, Andrea said, "Did you kill Derek?"

Molly chortled, a loud nasal snort, not at all in keeping with her dignified self. It felt like a purposeful admission of her original Pennsyltucky upbringing, no different than when Andrea exaggerated her Queens accent. Molly composed herself, brushed imaginary woodland debris off her shoulder. "One of my best friends has hunted murderers as a hobby since she was in high school. Would I risk that kind of a challenge?"

"The math wouldn't add up, if you looked at it as a simple equation," Andrea admitted. "But murder is rarely that easy."

"I imagine its many variables should be taken into account before committing the act," said Molly. "In that regard, it does sound like an exciting challenge for someone like me."

"It does, doesn't it?" said Andrea. "A life, a career, devoted to the structure of probabilities."

"But let me ask the ace investigator," Molly parried. "Why kill someone who was going to die eventually anyway?"

"That word, *eventually*, is quite the complex variable, Molly. Wouldn't you agree?" Andrea responded.

"That is a valid point," said Molly. "Eventually could seem like an eternity to some."

"And eternity sure is a long time to wait," said Andrea.

"Far too long," said Molly. She watched a gray egret rise from the shallow edge and cross the lake. Its dangling feet brushed the surface, causing a slight ripple in its wake.

"You never answered my question," Andrea said.

Molly turned, looking her friend directly, firmly, and coldly in the eye. "Didn't I?"

She adjusted her clothing and tightened her hairband. "I am going to run through the trails in the woods. It's better exercise. And far more challenging than this."

She let that hang in the air.

Fighting every confrontational instinct she had, Andrea let it hang as well.

Molly jogged back along Maggie's Trail to the mainland.

JoJo finished her formula until she was only sucking air. Too apt a metaphor, Andrea thought.

Her phone chime went off.

Crystal: Are you guys having fun?

Having a blast, Andrea responded.

Chime. Wish I could be there.

That would be swell, Andrea thought.

Chime. Where are you guys?

That was Brianne.

Chime. They went to Plainsboro Preserve to walk.

Crystal had answered, not even considering it was probably

Andrea's or Molly's place to respond, since they were actually the ones at the preserve.

Chime. That sounds like fun!

Chime. Bugs!

Chime. Oh yeah. I forgot about the bugs.

Chime. Don't want to cook. Pick up Chinese on the way home?

Crystal, Andrea, and even Molly, currently somewhere in the woods, simultaneously responded to Brianne: You texted the group by mistake!

Chime. Sorry!

Andrea turned off her text notifications, knowing it could go on for hours.

She maneuvered JoJo back into the harness and walked back quickly, working up a sweat.

Sathwika was waiting for her in the gravel lot. Aditya was asleep.

"How did it go?"

"I didn't get a confession, if that's what you mean," said Andrea.

"And you didn't get a dramatic fight at the tip of the peninsula, which is probably what you were hoping for," Sathwika said.

Andrea smiled softly. Her friend knew her too well already, and was trying to lighten her obviously flustered mood. As she removed JoJo from the harness, she said, "Either Molly didn't do it and I'm an idiot, or she did it and she thinks I'm an idiot."

"What now?" Sathwika asked.

Andrea's phone rang. It was Kenny.

"I'm in the city, but I'm coming home in the afternoon," he said. "Can we meet around four thirty?"

"What do you have?" she asked, a part of her not wanting to know.

Kenny said, "Derek Goode was definitely involved in some shady side business."

"Can you just tell me over the phone?" she asked.

"Your husband may have been a part of it," he said.

"I'll pick you up at the station," Andrea replied.

She hung up. As she was securing the belts of JoJo's seat, the baby regurgitated a splash of formula on the back of Andrea's neck.

"How is this fucking day going to get worse?" she asked out loud.

JoJo laughed.

ANDREA picked Kenny up at the train station at 4:23. He was annoyed she had JoJo, Sarah, and Sadie with her. He was more annoyed when Sarah and Sadie started up their oldie but goodie, the "Kenny-Kenny-bo-benny" song. And then extremely annoyed when they wouldn't stop for the five minutes it took them to drive to the Delaware and Raritan Canal lot on Alexander Road.

"You don't mind walking the canal?" Andrea asked. "It keeps the two of them where I can see them."

"I'm surprised they don't dive right into the water," Kenny said. "And no, I don't mind. The new me walks a lot more."

"The new you?" she said with a smile. He no longer saw coy, knowing brilliance in her soft smiles. He saw judging arrogance. Was that on him or her? He wasn't really sure. For a few years, since his fall from grace, he had defaulted to blaming everything on his own insecurity, but now he wondered how much of Andrea's know-it-allness was her problem.

"It's the old me, for the most part, just with a tighter ass," he said.

The girls laughed in the back. "He said ass!"

At least it got them to stop singing the fucking song.

They pulled into the D&R Canal State Park lot. JoJo grew hyper when she saw her sisters running around and wasn't able to join in. Andrea moved the car seat onto the stroller. Sarah wanted to push and Sadie whined until she was allowed to help.

They made their way down to the walking path that ran along the canal. It was a beautiful late-September afternoon. The kids pushed JoJo ahead of them as Andrea and Kenny walked.

"You brought the kids so you could control yourself depending on what I have to say?" he mused.

"I brought the kids because that's called parenting," she said. "I'm just in a not-horrible place where Ruth and Eli have enough school and sport activities that I don't usually have to handle all five at once."

Kenny watched Sarah and Sadie swerve the stroller so forcefully that they almost toppled the baby over. "Yeah, seems like a piece of cake now," he muttered.

They walked for a few steps.

"How bad is it?" she asked.

"I don't know," he said.

"What do you know?"

"Not enough to accuse Jeff of anything," he replied.

"But enough to arouse suspicion?" she said.

"I could walk away right now," Kenny said. "I could have not said anything to you at all."

"But?"

"If he is involved in another dirty scheme, I thought you would want to know," he said.

Andrea thought about Jeff's financial indiscretions from a few years ago and what it had cost them. "Indiscretions," she thought, knowing that even now she tiptoed around the truth. He had taken money from his clients without their knowledge. He had made them more money as a result, but it was still unethical and illegal.

They walked a little farther in silence. The kids continued to treat the stroller like it was their own demolition derby. JoJo was giggling loudly the entire time.

"Sarah, take it down a couple notches," Andrea said.

Kenny took her lack of response as tacit approval to continue. "Derek wasn't on the partner track anymore, so he was working an outside opportunity."

"What happened to him at work?"

"Best guesses?" Kenny said. "He was frivolous. He was a party boy. That made him popular in the office, but probably not with the partners. He was also an HR jacket waiting to explode."

"Harassment?"

"I'd lean consensual, but I think if you're sleeping your way around the office for years, eventually it's going to cost you," Kenny said.

"Only when the higher-ups want it to," she muttered. "You have proof on any of this?"

"Lot of smoke," he said. "Opening some doors and we found some fires."

"Hey, Sarah, slow down," Andrea called out.

Sadie had stepped onto the stroller's standing board, leaving all the pushing to Sarah, who was perfectly fine with that, since it meant she could go full throttle. They were twenty yards farther along the path; her middle child either hadn't heard or had conveniently ignored her.

Andrea said, "Run it through for me."

Kenny explained the potential health care insurance scheme and how Wendell had all but confirmed it.

"Should I go through Crystal to get Wendell to break?" she asked.

"No, Wendell is out of the loop. He refused to get involved from the beginning," he said. With no hesitation, he followed it with, "I think you should go through Jeff."

"Yeah," she replied, drawing the word out, exhausted already at the very thought.

They watched Sarah hit a rut in the towpath. The stroller toppled over. Sadie got tangled up in the wheel base and JoJo fell out the side, landing in the grass right along the incline to the unprotected canal.

Andrea screamed and ran to them. Kenny, normally slow to respond to such things, sprinted ahead of her. By the time he had reached JoJo, Sarah had already picked the baby up and carried her away from the embankment.

Sadie was crying, JoJo was laughing, and Sarah knew she was about to get in trouble.

"I know!" she shouted before Andrea could say anything.

"You know *what?*" snapped Andrea.

"I know that you warned me to slow down and I didn't listen and I was wrong and now Sadie got hurt and JoJo would have sunk to the bottom of the canal and died," Sarah responded in a breathless rush.

Andrea and Kenny looked at each other. That had pretty much summed it up.

Except for . . .

"And . . . ?" asked Andrea.

"And if JoJo had drowned, all those swimming lessons were really a waste of money," Sarah said.

Andrea wanted to laugh and punt her child at the same time.

Kenny just laughed.

"Pick up the stroller," Andrea said, moving over to Sadie.

"I got JoJo," Sarah protested.

"Give JoJo to Uncle Kenny and pick up the stroller!"

"Uncle Kenny doesn't want JoJo," Kenny said.

Andrea turned on Kenny, ready to punt him, too.

"Uncle Kenny is going to hold JoJo while Sarah straightens out the stroller," Andrea said through gritted teeth.

"Fine," Kenny and Sarah said at the same time. Sarah handed JoJo to Kenny, who took her as if she were an oozing bag of toxic sludge.

"She's not gonna bite, Uncle Kenny," Sarah said.

"I'm not worried about the puppy teeth," he said as he tried to properly hold her. "I'm worried about dropping her."

Sarah struggled to get the stroller upright, saying, "She'll be fine. We drop her all the time."

"No we don't," Andrea said quickly, as she tried to help the crying Sadie come down from the terrible trauma of a scrape on her knee.

"We do," Sarah laughed. "Like, *all* the time."

"We don't," Andrea said, then, looking at Kenny, she softly repeated, "We don't."

JoJo grabbed Kenny's mouth. She had a surprisingly firm grip on his lower teeth and lip.

"What do I do?" he garbled.

"You bite down really hard and she'll let go," said Sarah, as she extricated the stroller from the rut.

"No, you don't!" snapped Andrea, unsure if Kenny would have taken the advice.

"I wasn't going to do that," he said.

Andrea patted Sadie on the butt. "Sarah, let your sister push the empty stroller. Kenny, hand me the baby."

Playing a teething game with her meaty little fist, Kenny said, "No, it's okay. She's tasty."

Sarah laughed. That made Sadie laugh and that made JoJo laugh. Sadie pushed the empty stroller slowly enough that it gave Sarah the bright idea to run circles around her while chanting, "Slowpoke!"

Sadie shrieked at Sarah to stop, which only made Sarah run faster and chant louder.

"Sarah, give your sister a break, will you!" Andrea shouted angrily, her patience expired.

Sarah turned on her mother and with explosive anger screamed, "I can never do anything!"

She suddenly seized. Her eyes rolled up. Her head pitched

backward, craning her neck in an awkward arc, and her arms froze spastically. Sarah collapsed to the dirt.

Sadie pushed the stroller past her unconscious sister, muttering, "There she goes again."

As Andrea casually walked toward her prostrate child, Kenny said, "*What* the fuck was that?"

From several yards ahead, Sadie said, "Quarter in the swear jar!"

"What the fuck *was* that?" Kenny repeated.

Andrea cradled Sarah in her arms as the six-year-old slowly opened her eyes.

"Breath-holding spell," Andrea said calmly.

"What the fuck is *that*?" Kenny continued.

"Quarter! Quarter! Quarter!" called out Sadie.

Kenny removed his wallet from his back pocket and threw it at Sadie. It fell a few feet short of its intended target, which had been her head.

"Take my fucking Amex card!" he snapped. As Sarah was getting to her feet, he again said, "What the fuck is that?"

"Sarah has breath-holding spells," Andrea said.

"She stopped breathing!" Kenny said.

"Yeah."

"She passed out!"

"Yeah."

"But she's fine now, thirty seconds later?"

"Pretty much," said Andrea. "It's a reaction to anger or shock."

"Why not just get angry or shocked like a normal person?"

"I am normal!" Sarah said, groggy but with defiance.

"Yeah, sure you are, kid," Kenny replied as he picked up his wallet. JoJo laughed. "Glad you think this is funny," he said to the baby. Then, realizing the ticking time bomb he might be holding, he panicked. "Wait, it's not going to happen to this one, too, is it?"

"Probably not," Andrea said with a smile. She kissed Sarah on the forehead. "You okay?" Sarah nodded. "What have we talked about?"

"I gotta try not to get so angry about things that don't deserve getting so angry about," Sarah said, by rote. She'd clearly been through this drill before.

"And how do we do that?"

"Count down from five when I think I'm getting super mad," she said. "Step back and away from my anger."

"Okay," Andrea said, mussing Sarah's perpetually mussed hair. "Sadie, climb up on the standing board and let Sarah break the speed limit."

Sadie cheered. Sarah ran ahead and started pushing the stroller as fast as she could, with Sadie squealing in delight.

"You want to hand her back to me?" Andrea asked Kenny.

"What?" he responded, realizing he'd gotten comfortable walking with the baby in his arms, but now thinking she really might detonate or something. "Oh, yeah, sure."

Andrea put JoJo on her shoulders and held her hands. The baby squealed in delight. Her father was so tall that it was JoJo's favorite thing when Jeff put her on top of the world. The much shorter Andrea remained an acceptable option.

After a few steps, Kenny said, "How do you do it?"

"I don't know," she replied. "Just do."

"But it's not what you love," he said. "I mean, I know you love *them*, but—"

"It is what it is," she interrupted, not wanting to dig too much deeper than that.

"I'm terrified of meeting Sitara's parents," he said. "I'm even more terrified of having her meet my mother."

"I get that," she said. "Not about your mom—I mean, just in general. Now, picture Sitara meeting your mother when she's four months pregnant. That was me."

Kenny laughed. "What a nightmare."

"Total nightmare," Andrea added.

"This whole relationship thing feels so . . ."

"Terrifying?"

"No," he replied. "I mean, yeah, but what I was going to say was: unnecessary. Why do we bother? Can you tell me one thing that makes it worth it?"

Sarah and Sadie squealed in delight. Hearing them, JoJo reacted by kicking her stubby heels into Andrea's collarbone and squealing, too.

"On a good day," Andrea replied, "they make it worth it."

They walked several paces before Kenny said, "How many good days do you get?"

She smiled but said nothing, which was answer enough in itself.

"You going to talk to Jeff?" he asked.

"Been figuring out the strategy this entire time," she said.

"What are you going to do if he is doing something wrong?"

"Depends."

"On what?"

"How many witnesses are around when he admits it," Andrea said.

24

SHORT on time to make dinner, Andrea cobbled together quesadil-las using frozen vegetables and leftovers. She only had half a jar of salsa, a quarter bag of shredded cheddar, and zero fucks to give. She was too anxious about her impending conversation with Jeff to worry about dinner. She could have been subconsciously making a bad din-ner to set up her excuse to run out and get ice cream as amends, but that wouldn't explain her routine of making bad dinners on a nor-mal day.

"Sorry dinner was crappy, but how about if we all go get Bent Spoon as my apology?"

The kids cheered. JoJo joined in, even though she had devoured her dinner of Gerber macaroni and cheese.

"Really?" asked Jeff. "Into Princeton on a Monday night?"

"C'mon, Monday is our only night without some kind of activity going on for them," she said. "Let's go! Half hour. Maybe they'll have that ricotta pistachio you like so much."

Jeff felt the pull of the ricotta pistachio.

"If they do, can you bring it back?" he weaseled.

"If I bring it back, it'll be half-melted and you'll make a boo-boo face," she said.

The kids laughed at that.

"You do make a boo-boo face, Dad," Ruth said.

Andrea might have to start paying her oldest daughter an assistant's salary.

"Okay, let's go," Jeff said.

The kids applauded. JoJo, on a seven-second reality delay, clapped, too, missing her hands with every other attempt.

THEY FOUND A parking space in Palmer Square. Eli and Ruth opened the stroller as Andrea took JoJo out of the car. Jeff fumbled with the parking app on his phone.

Set across from the Princeton campus off Nassau Street, the square was an open-area mall with several high-end clothing and white-privilege knickknack stores, and several dine-in and takeout restaurants. It had been built in 1938 in a colonial revival style to complement the architecture of the university campus and create a central hub for the town's traffic flow and commerce. It was considered an act of urban renewal, though people now, as much as then, conveniently ignored the fact that its construction had led to the displacement of the African American community that had lived on a street that would no longer exist. But ultimately, who could be concerned by such things a century later, when good chocolates from Thomas Sweet and fine dresses from Zoë could be had?

Bent Spoon was an uncomfortably small ice cream shop with an eclectic neo-hippie vibe that offered even more eclectic ice cream flavors. The store faced the Palmer Square green, an open space with a few huge pine trees, tables for sitting, and just enough grass to let little kids run around. The green abutted the historic Nassau Inn, which was Princeton's only full-service hotel.

All in all, it was quite the idyllic setting in which to accuse your husband of graft.

Getting the ice cream was an ordeal, as Andrea had known it would be. Between the cramped space while ordering and the menu variety, she dealt with more noise and questions than she needed. JoJo was the easy one because she couldn't read and didn't know any better: Madagascar vanilla bean. Jeff and Eli both went with the NJ ricotta pistachio. Andrea knew it wasn't Eli's favorite, but he was in a phase where he desperately wanted to please his father. The dumb kid. Ruth and Sarah agreed to go splitsies, sharing dark chocolate mint cookie and Greek yogurt with candied walnuts. Sadie got NJ blueberry mascarpone, or as Ruth called it, blueberry Al Capone. Andrea and Jeff didn't ask how she even knew who Al Capone was, but Andrea took an inner pride that she did.

They sat at two empty tables on the green. It was a Monday night in September, so there was less "civilian" traffic. Students passed them by without a second glance. Just a larger-than-average family out for ice cream. Nothing to see here, thought Andrea. No murderers being hunted down or lying, thieving husbands being interrogated.

The kids wolfed down their ice cream and asked if they could run around the green. Andrea told them only if they kept an eye on JoJo. Ruth took the baby from Andrea's lap.

"Gross! She has ice cream all over her face," her daughter said.

"So do you," said Andrea. "Shut up and go play."

Jeff kept an eye on the kids as he ate his ice cream.

"You want any?" he offered.

"I do, but no thanks," she replied. "I don't want to risk my membership card with the Cellulitists."

"You don't?" he said, smiling.

"I had a talk with Kenny this afternoon," she said, ambushing him just as he'd gotten complacent. "Some things he told me got me a little worried."

"About Molly?"

"About you," she said.

"Me?" He reacted with a smile on his face that she realized she could take as either incredulity or guile. "Did I kill Derek now?"

"About some business arrangements you were involved in," she said. "With him."

"What?" he said.

"You and Derek. And Martin. Involved in something that could be shady?"

"I'm not in business with Derek," he replied.

She wondered how carefully he was parsing his words. How carefully he *had been* parsing his words.

"Present tense, sure, because he's dead," she said coldly. "I've been thinking about something you said."

"What?"

She considered their conversation from a few days ago in an entirely new context:

I got a secondary assignment. It's the good team. It's generated more money than I expected, but it's probably going to be over pretty soon.

Why?

The project hit a dead end.

"You said 'the good team,' but you meant it as in Derek Goode," she said softly.

He laughed and it sounded genuine, not condescending.

"Andie, honestly, that's kind of crazy, conspiracy-theory thinking," he said. "I mean, I wish I could be so clever, but you know I'm not."

"Except . . . for when you are," she said.

A flash crossed his eyes—defiance, indifference, fear, or all at the same time? His fingers loosened their grip on his small plastic spoon. The opposite of what someone who was guilty would do. He slowly, casually had another spoonful of ice cream. The opposite of what someone who was guilty would do. He ate the remainder of his cup, even down to scraping the melted remnants at the bottom, without saying a word in his own defense. The opposite of what someone who was guilty would do.

She waited, until he finally said, "Andie, after everything we've been through, how stupid would I have to be to do anything illegal?"

When Jeff had originally confessed his financial crimes to her, he hadn't been repentant or remorseful. He had been annoyed, frustrated that he had been caught, but not truly embarrassed by what he had done. He had rationalized his actions because they had generated exponentially greater returns for everyone involved. Until they hadn't, and that was when he had gotten caught.

When the market took a dip in 2012, Jeff had predicted it, planned for it, and used it as his bait to lure clients to move their funds to the wealth management company he was starting. He had made his first million by age twenty-five, as he'd promised Andrea he would when they'd met in college.

They had an apartment in Jersey City for the first two years of their marriage, but after Eli was born, it had become too cramped. So, a new baby, a new company—creatively named Stern Wealth Management— and a move to a new house had all happened at the same time. Since Jeff set up shop in Princeton, she reluctantly returned to West Windsor, the town where she had spent her teenage years. They settled into a house that was ridiculously larger than they needed, but—as if she hadn't had enough warning signs through the early years of their relationship—Jeff had assured her that a bigger house meant they could have more kids. And he had guaranteed they'd have five times as much money before he turned thirty.

By the time he turned thirty, their assets were five times what they had been, just as he had promised. She never questioned the fact that the math hadn't made much sense. They had five times more, though the market hadn't performed five times better.

She hadn't questioned it, because she hadn't wanted to know the answer.

It made no sense to her that he had been so greedy, had risked so much of what they had. But secretly, in her heart, in her mind, with every embarrassed look from people at school who knew, people on the sidelines of soccer games who whispered, during every second of every day for those two years, Andrea had been thinking: You never let me be who I wanted to be so that you could do this? So that you could become this? Turn us into this?

Coming out of her reverie, she said, "We have a source that you, Martin, and Derek discussed the idea of doing something together."

"A source? Really? *We*. You and Lee? Working together?" he replied, getting more annoyed as he went along.

"We're just asking questions," she said.

"Toward what end, Andie?"

"I'm trying to determine if Molly killed Derek," Andrea replied. "So that's the ultimate end, but to get there, I need motive. Sex is always a motive in a marriage, but so is money."

"They've certainly been motives in our marriage," he muttered.

She wasn't sure how to take that. They hadn't had sex in over a year. She had politely rejected any of his half-interested attempts until he agreed to get a vasectomy, which he had refused to do.

During an uncomfortable silence, she weighed a variety of things she could say. She decided to simply go with what she *should* say. "If you're doing anything illegal again, Jeff, anything that hurts our family, I'll divorce you."

"Because a divorce wouldn't hurt our family?" he said. He walked over to a trash bin and threw in his ice cream cup. He watched the kids playing tag with Josephine, who showed incredible gumption in straining to chase after her older siblings at a scooch crawl. Jeff was an oddity. He was gentle with the kids, and caring, but he spent very little time with them. He had his own pressures, she knew, but in the eternal tug-of-war between spouses who worked and those who stayed home, each side thought the other had it easier.

Andrea was never jealous or resentful that Jeff had an office to commute to, adults to interact with, or concrete to walk on, she was just jealous and resentful that she didn't.

All couples should trade places for a month and walk a mile, she thought.

But none of that had anything really to do with the fundamental flaw in their natures. The brilliant, deductive Andrea had spent their entire marriage failing to solve the mystery of herself and avoiding the responsibility of her nature, while the brilliant, inductive Jeff had spent it avoiding the nature of his responsibilities.

She really didn't want to trade places with him.

Jeff didn't face her when he finally replied, "Everything I do is for the security of this family. I'm not going to jeopardize that again."

Just like Molly, Jeff had answered every one of her questions, but he hadn't *really* answered them at all.

Maybe some things just were what they were. Maybe one plus one just equaled two.

Almost no husbands committed, much less lied about illegal financial activities after they'd already been caught having lied and committed financial illegalities.

Almost no wives killed their husbands when their husbands had already been diagnosed with a potentially fatal heart disease.

But Andrea knew there was a variable to those equations that made the human mind impossible for math to predict.

Some husbands *did* lie.

Some wives *did* kill.

Jeff called for the kids to gather up and call it a night. Time to get home, take baths, and finish homework. He asked Ruth and Eli to help

Josephine. The kids all giggled as JoJo walked like a drunken John Wayne with her oldest siblings holding her hands to help her stay erect.

Andrea watched, wanting to smile, but feeling like she was going to cry.

Sometimes, the problems didn't have a solution.

Sometimes, in a marriage, one plus one didn't equal a couple.

25

TUESDAY morning found Kenny looking over Sitara's shoulder, glazed eyes staring at another round of variations of the first cut on his interview with the killer of Satku Sasmal. Kenny was exhausted by the editing process. He lacked the patience it took to differentiate between choosing a tic of the lip or a blink of an eye. Editing worked the canvas with a fine, delicate brush. He preferred the measured madness of a van Gogh.

Kenny was also distracted because Jimmy and Shelby were performing a soft surveillance on Darrah Smalls. He preferred to be a gumshoe out in the concrete jungle, cigarette in his mouth and a smoking gun in his hand. He didn't want the cigarette to be smoking because he hated the smell.

"I think the left hand looks more nervous," said Sitara. "He's tapping faster."

"Yeah," Kenny said absently, but in his mind, gumshoe Kenny had just kicked a door down to find Derek and Darrah in flagrante delicto. She tried to cover herself up with Derek's navy blue worsted wool suit jacket, but she failed, revealing a tantalizing hint of cleavage.

Gumshoe Kenny said, "I always recommend zoot suits to cover both hoots, doll."

"Kenny!" Derek shouted.

But it was Sitara who had said it, while smacking him in the back of the head to emphasize her point. "Are you with me? I'm going to lock 02:59."

Kenny looked at the screen. Sitara was a good producer, he thought, but maybe a great producer would have made sure her cameraman, who happened to be Jimmy for that session, had caught a sequence of their interviewee's restless leg syndrome throughout the entire conversation. Interspersing a shot like that in conjunction with the finger tapping would have maximized the dramatic tension.

Kenny had always loved writing, and even though this was really his first experience in documentary film, he wondered if he would ever be happy if he couldn't direct.

He knew that Sitara pushed him to focus because this was part of the process he wasn't interested in. In the time they had worked together, she had immersed him in all aspects of production. Kenny didn't know if that was because Sitara wanted them to have common ground or so that he could see how hard her work was and how hard she worked, or if she saw potential in him that he preferred not to see in himself.

He knew the pieces of the Kenny puzzle were all there, but they were still scattered. Like any puzzle, Kenny was a compilation of pieces that might eventually come together to make a beautiful finished image, but he feared she wouldn't give him the time it would take to put them together.

She was a year older than he was and probably ten years more mature. She had her own apartment, albeit in Queens and not Brooklyn, where she wanted to be. And yes, until this past year, her parents had helped her out every month with the rent. But in her defense, she had been paying off her student loans and each year their assistance had consistently decreased. She had grown up. He knew he was still growing up.

"You really want to go with Jimmy and Shelby and play private detective, don't you?" she said.

"I most certainly do, boss!" he replied with exaggerated enthusiasm.

She gave him a flash drive and smiled. "Sorry, you can't. We have to get through the Eversham and Appelhans interviews by the end of the day. Run through them both and give me your shot preferences."

Kenny sank just a bit in his chair. He really was in a relationship if he kept expecting Lucy not to pull the football away, only to watch her pull it away again as he fell.

He plugged the drive into his laptop and wondered if at that very moment Jimmy and Shelby were putting a cleavage-thrusting Darrah Smalls under the hot lights.

At 6:45 a.m. Darrah Smalls left her apartment in Jackson Heights and rode the F train into Manhattan.

At 7:10 a.m., she bought an Aloha Açaí bowl from Juice Generation in Times Square.

At 7:17 a.m., she bought a double espresso macchiato from Manhattan Espresso Café.

At 7:23 a.m., she entered the lobby of her building.

At 10:44 a.m., Shelby Taylor was so sick of hearing Jimmy Chaney ask her what they should do next that she demanded he leave their stakeout spot, which was a much cooler way of saying to leave their fire hydrant.

Chagrined, Jimmy shuffled away. He perked up when he saw a bagel shop a block away. He ordered a cinnamon raisin with honey walnut cream cheese and a coffee—his fourth of the morning—and sat down at a counter that looked out onto Madison Avenue.

He texted Shelby: call me if she comes out
She texted back: no

> **JIMMY:** c'mon

> **SHELBY:** I didn't want you with me in the first place.
> She can make you.

> **JIMMY:** i am pretty unforgetable

> **SHELBY:** your an idiot and you spelled unforgettable
> wrong go back to the office

> **JIMMY:** and do wat

> **SHELBY:** what you usually do

> **JIMMY:** i have no idea what that is

> **SHELBY:** no kidding

He shrugged, took a bite of his bagel, and started playing Bubble Cloud.

MEANWHILE, SHELBY WAITED by the fire hydrant across the street from Darrah's building. She could stand on a Manhattan street all day and not get bored. She thought Charleston and Boston had offered an eclectic look at the human race, but nothing could hold a candle to New York City.

Her back hurt from the standing, as did the mostly psychosomatic pinch of her abdomen from where she'd been shot. This was the best and the worst for her. On the job and surrounded by a sea of people she could dissect, but alone with her thoughts.

Shelby waited for an hour before Darrah Smalls emerged from the building. Darrah walked downtown to Fifty-first Street and made a right, heading west. Shelby followed from a safe distance as her target entered the Duane Reade pharmacy near the corner of Sixth Avenue.

There was an alcove between the Duane Reade and a Chase Bank with a revolving door leading into a narrow office building. She had a plan, but would need to time it right. She heard the door to the Duane Reade open two times. Spinning the revolving door for effect, she walked out onto the sidewalk, pretending to be engrossed in her phone. Both times she saw that it wasn't Darrah.

The third time was the charm. Shelby spun the door and walked recklessly onto the sidewalk, staring at her phone. Darrah, carrying a small bag, tried to avoid Shelby, who plowed right into her, hard. The Duane Reade bag was knocked out of her hand.

Shelby's phone clattered on the sidewalk closer to Darrah, while Darrah's bag had fallen closer to Shelby. The ex-cop put on her sweetest Southern tourist voice as she bent down to get Darrah's bag. "Ah'm so sorry, sweetie, that was totally mah fault."

Frustrated, Darrah bent over to get Shelby's phone.

As Shelby stood up, she purposely grabbed the plastic bag from the wrong end, causing the paper prescription bag inside it to spill out.

The paper bag had the script stapled to it.

"Oh, ah'm so clumsy, ah don't belong anywhere above the Mason-Dixon Line."

"It's okay," Darrah said, though her glare said it was anything but.

Shelby struggled to insert the paper bag into the bunched plastic bag, ensuring herself enough time to get a good look at the label.

"It's fine," said Darrah. "Here's your phone. The screen is cracked."

"Oh, no," Shelby said, when she really meant: *Fuck, that wasn't part of the plan.* "Here's your bag, ah'm sorry. Ah can't believe ah broke mah phone. They cost an' arm an' a leg to replace."

"Yeah, lady, I'm from the city, so the broken-bottle con isn't going to work on me," said Darrah. "Have a good day."

Darrah started to walk away. Shelby dropped the exaggerated accent. "The con wasn't about the phone."

That piqued Darrah's confrontational nature. She stopped, a sly smile on her face. The lawyer enjoyed a concrete catfight as much as a courtroom battle. Shelby liked her.

"You know who else has syphilis?" Shelby said. "Molly Goode. That's a fucking coincidence."

"I don't know what you're talking about," said Darrah.

"Molly can't take penicillin, though. She's allergic," said Shelby. "But the script in your bag was for Bicillin L-A and that's a penicillin G benzathine used to treat syphilis."

"Who are you?" Darrah asked.

"Someone working to get to the truth," Shelby replied.

"Insurance agents? I talked to you already," said Darrah.

"Not an insurance agent."

"Then you're working with that idiot messenger boy, who is working with that prick reporter?" said Darrah, gaining the measure of her opposition. "I have nothing to say."

"I understand why you wouldn't," Shelby said. "I'm sure no one in your law firm would want to know you gave Derek syphilis while you were having an affair."

Darrah whirled in anger. "He didn't get it from me, I got it from him! I hooked up with him one time in the office and that was it. He had coke even though he knew he wasn't supposed to be doing it. He played the 'I could die at any minute' card, and we just won a nice settlement for our client, so we did it."

"Only that one time?" Shelby asked.

"You want to find out who gave him the syph, try checking out one of his stripper friends he's always fucking."

Darrah walked away again, and this time Shelby let her. She looked at her cracked screen. It still worked, but the cracks across it were bad. She called Jimmy.

"Meet at the subway station. She's on Fifty-first, so make sure she doesn't see you."

He said, "You spelled *you're* wrong earlie—"

Shelby hung up before Jimmy could finish his point or ask a million questions.

MINUTES LATER, HE was waiting by the entrance. "Did you get anything?"

"She has syphilis," said Shelby. "She said she got it from him."

"And where did he get it from? Molly?" asked Jimmy.

"See, you're thinking the right way, but it gets more interesting," said Shelby. "Darrah said Derek caught it from the strippers he bangs."

Jimmy whistled, a wide splash of teeth spread across his face. "Thank God there are strippers involved!"

26

"OF course there are strippers involved," Andrea sighed. Sathwika was on the Bluetooth as Andrea drove with JoJo to meet the non-murdering members of the Cellulitists for lunch.

"I think it makes it even more interesting," Sathwika said, sounding hollow through the speakers.

"I'm glad you're having fun with my misery," Andrea said.

"I'm sorry, I know," her friend said. "You called to prep your thoughts for meeting with Crystal and Brianne. How can I help?"

"You only know them from what I've told you," Andrea said. "And I have my biases on the subject, so at this point, filtering me out of it, would you go hard or soft?"

"I'd go soft," said Sathwika.

"That was quick. Why?"

"They suspect nothing yet, and may know nothing," said Sathwika. "In crisis management, when you're in an early phase of the inquiry, you can't let subjects that you need to provide you important context think they're a part of the problem."

"Because they think they're being accused of the wrongdoing that you're trying to uncover?"

"Exactly, and they get defensive or evasive," Sathwika said. "By going soft, you make them a part of your own curiosity. You're validating that it's okay for them to question if Molly did anything wrong, not interrogating them because they're protecting her."

"Got it," said Andrea.

"You're going to do the exact opposite of what I just said, right?"

"We'll see how it goes," said Andrea. "Call you later."

She pulled the Odyssey into the Mercer Mall parking lot and drove over the drudgery of multiple speed bumps until she found a spot near Zoës Kitchen. Once again, Brianne and Crystal had arrived before her and claimed an outdoor table on the patio sitting area with a gorgeous view overlooking the parking lot across from Nordstrom Rack.

They had texted Andrea before she'd even left the house and gotten her order, so a nice 270-calorie Greek salad was waiting for her on the table, alongside a can of Spindrift watermelon sparkling water and a plastic cup filled with ice.

"We just sat down," said Crystal. JoJo caught a glimpse of her white teeth and the sheen of her shellacked hair in the midday sun and became mesmerized. Crystal happily took the baby from Andrea and got her settled into the high chair by the table. "Hello, Josephine, you keep getting bigger! Yes, you do!"

"Sorry I'm late," Andrea said. "A bunch of shit hit the proverbial fan."

"What happened?" asked Crystal, but she said it playfully to the baby.

"I don't know if I should talk about it," said Andrea. "It involves Molly and Derek."

"What?" asked Brianne.

Andrea hesitated, pretending to weigh whether she should talk or not.

Then, feigning reluctance, she said, "Kenny got an anonymous call after Derek died. The caller said they thought Molly had killed her husband."

She tried to keep an eye on both Crystal and Brianne at the same time. They reacted exactly the same way: exaggerated surprise. The problem was, Andrea couldn't tell if either was faking it or if that was just their usual response to pretty much everything from murder investigations to coupon circulars from Bed Bath & Beyond.

"Josephine, tell your mommy that is so, so crazy! Derek had a heart condition," said Crystal as JoJo giggled.

"And he was likely to die soon, I know," Andrea said. "But *soon* is a relative term, Crystal, to someone who is in an untenable situation."

"What do you mean?" asked Brianne timidly.

"What do you know about their marriage?" asked Andrea. "How many affairs was Derek having? How many did he have in the past? What kind of shady business was he involved in?"

The two women exchanged uncomfortable glances. They each knew what they knew, and they each knew that the other knew something, but they didn't know what the other knew. Andrea waited, feeling her patience for the soft approach dwindling faster than even she had anticipated.

"The cold sore on Molly's lip?" said Andrea. "Molly has syphilis. She got an STD from Derek. His associate at the firm also got it from Derek. And Derek got it from a stripper that he slept with."

Brianne looked away from them, her fork uselessly flicking at the edges of her salad.

"Did you know?" Andrea asked her.

"Yes," Brianne said softly. "I knew."

Andrea turned to Crystal. "Derek, Martin, and Jeff were involved in a shady business deal. I don't know the details, but Wendell was asked to be a part of it last year. Did you know about that?"

Crystal confidently, proudly responded, "Wendell told me the day they approached him. But he also told me he had no interest in getting involved, and that was that."

Andrea looked to Brianne. "But Martin went along?"

She nodded her head slowly. "I don't know the details."

"And do you know if Jeff is involved?" asked Andrea. She regretted taking her eye off the prize, which was Molly and Derek.

"You don't know?" Brianne asked, expressing surprise and judgment at the same time.

"He says he's not," said Andrea, going for broke. "But we all know there is precedent for him lying to me."

"So, since you can't trust your husband, you don't trust us?" said Crystal, cutting to the chase and to the core.

"It's not that I don't trust the two of you, Crystal," said Andrea. "It's that maybe the two of you shouldn't trust Molly."

"She's never lied to us," said Crystal.

"How can you be sure of that?" asked Andrea. "What do you *really* know? What do you know of her past before she married Derek? Or her family? Or who she was in college? Look at what you didn't know about me!"

That even shut Crystal up.

"Give me a reason to get off this train I'm on," said Andrea. "Because after this last year, you know I won't stop."

"No matter who you run over?" asked Brianne, followed by, "What about Henry and Brett?"

"Maybe you should ask Molly that question," Andrea said, avoiding having to answer it. "I won't stop until I find the evidence that proves I'm right."

"Or proves you're wrong?" muttered Brianne.

Andrea smiled. "But that won't happen, will it?" She chewed on a forkful of Greek salad. "Because both of you know things about Molly that make you suspect things about Molly."

Brianne bussed her tray. She walked back and sat down. Crystal pushed Cheerios out of JoJo's reach, then moved them back, making the baby laugh uproariously. Her infectious fun was incongruous to their bitter silence.

After a few more casual bites of salad, Andrea finally said, "You don't have to tell me what you don't want me to know about yourselves or your husbands. I don't care unless it pertains to Derek's death. But if you tell me what you know about Molly, I'm all ears."

Crystal continued to play with JoJo, pretending she hadn't heard a thing Andrea had said, but in a playful tone to keep the baby interested, she said, "Molly hated her family. She thought they were inbred and jealous of her. She's never returned home once since her parents' funeral."

"They died in a car crash?" asked Andrea.

"While she was in college," said Brianne.

"And her relationship with her siblings?"

"Nonexistent," said Crystal. "Listen, we know Molly can be a bit aloof."

"Cold," interjected Brianne.

"Like an ice cube," agreed Crystal. "She worked in Philly after graduating college. After meeting Derek at a conference, she took a job in Manhattan to be able to see him more often. It's not really that suspicious, is it?"

"No, of course not," said Andrea, throwing them a bone to let them think she could be reasonable about this. "But, we look for patterns of behavior. How they form and sever relationships. Things like that."

"This isn't just about the call you said Kenny Lee got," Brianne said.

Tiptoe around it or stomp all over the minefield like an ape? Andrea chose to stomp.

"I think Molly exacerbated Derek's heart condition in some manner and that led to his heart attack. Derek was having multiple affairs, doing drugs, struggling to advance at work, getting involved in some kind of illegal business scam, and she'd had enough. I also think Derek was hitting her—"

"I don't think Derek would do that," Brianne said.

"She always wears long-sleeve shirts," said Andrea. "Always. And if either of you say her fair Irish skin, I'll hit you in the heads with my salad bowl. There was some kind of physical activity in that marriage, whether consensual or not, I don't know."

Neither responded. Andrea continued, "Put yourselves in my shoes. Think for a minute as if you were me. Possible physical abuse. Probable financial misdeeds. Proven affairs outside the marriage. And you're Molly, you rationalize all that in a nice neat bow by thinking to yourself, 'Well, he was going to die soon anyway.'"

Crystal let it sink in. Andrea knew she had created reasonable doubt in her favor.

Brianne didn't give much away. Her friend's thoughts, usually so random and scattered, seemed to have been corralled behind a very well-guarded white picket fence. She softly said, "In a manner, you said."

"In *some* manner, I said," Andrea replied.

"What does that mean?"

"A chemical agent, a prescription drug . . . something."

"But you don't know," said Brianne.

"No."

"Wouldn't one of those postmortem medical things have been done?" asked Crystal, in her singsong voice for JoJo that now just sounded purposefully annoying.

"An autopsy," said Andrea. "And . . . normally it would have been."

"But?"

Andrea hated to admit how easily she had been played. "But I asked the police not to and they asked the medical examiner."

"Because Molly asked you to ask them?" said Crystal.

Andrea nodded.

"But why would she have done that?" Crystal asked. "Unless she thought the autopsy would have found something?"

"What are we supposed to do now?" Brianne asked.

"Tell me the truth about what you know," Andrea said. "Anything could be a clue."

"Molly did cocaine for years when she was working for Wells Fargo," Crystal blurted. "She said she slept with her boss to get a promotion and it was the most cost-efficient forty-five seconds of her life. She was bisexual until she met Derek. And maybe afterwards, too. She got fall-down drunk at her parents' funeral and her siblings are still mad at her for it. The boys are terrified of her. She doesn't hit them, but she is super strict and they feel they can never do anything right. Derek always protected them from her. She thinks Brett is gay. Or is going to be gay. Or is gay, it's not a decision you make, right? And she thinks you think you're better than us, Andie."

Andrea and Brianne both just stared after Crystal's diatribe.

JoJo started laughing, reaching for Crystal's lower lip.

"I'm sorry," she said. "That was so rude. She told me all of that in confidence."

"Wow," muttered Brianne. "She said she told me all the same things in confidence, too."

Brianne and Crystal started laughing.

Andrea didn't laugh along with them. She couldn't let this become playful, or let them think that this absolved them in any way for the things they weren't saying. And she was certain there were things both still weren't saying.

She stood up, picking JoJo out of her high chair.

"You're both hiding things from me," she said bluntly.

"We're not," Crystal protested, though Andrea noted Brianne said nothing.

Andrea continued, "And you're doing it for one of three reasons: you think Molly is innocent and she didn't do anything; you think you're protecting your husbands; or you're protecting yourselves because anything I find out may incriminate either one of you."

"That's not fair," snapped Crystal. "You asked us to meet you for lunch and you attack us?"

"This isn't an attack, Crystal," Andrea said pointedly. "This is a fair and friendly warning. If you don't heed the warning, then you will see the attack."

"Like you calling us Cellulitists?" Crystal asked.

"What?"

"Your name for us," Crystal said. "Kenny Lee told Wendell and he told me."

Of course he did, thought Andrea. She didn't need this distraction.

"It's nothing, Crystal," said Andrea. "It's just my stupid Queens insecurity, that's all. That kind of sarcasm is how I protect myself from getting hurt."

Andrea started to walk away with JoJo when Brianne found her voice and said, "What if there's a fourth reason you're not thinking about?"

Andrea stopped in the lane between the restaurant and the parking lot.

"What's that, Bri?" she asked.

"Maybe we—I—maybe we want to protect you," she said.

"Really?"

"Maybe we don't want you and your kids hurt if Jeff gets in trouble again," she said.

Andrea nodded. "Fair enough. But if it's a choice between letting Molly get away with murder and Jeff getting punished for crimes he committed, then it's no choice at all."

She walked away. Looking over Andrea's shoulder, JoJo cooed and made stretchy hands toward Crystal, who was waving, near tears.

Andrea stopped once more, blurting out loudly, "And I want to call her JoJo, not fucking Josephine, so try to respect that!"

JoJo started to cry at her mother's anger.

Andrea turned toward her car, but still heard Crystal say to Brianne, "I think that baby likes me more than she does Andie."

"Pretty shitty choice either way," Brianne mumbled.

ANDREA DROVE HOME, full of piss, vinegar, and salad. She took Route 1 instead of the local roads so she could unleash her frustration on the accelerator. Since the Odyssey could barely crack fifty miles per hour, the desired effect felt anticlimactic. JoJo hadn't stopped crying. Andrea turned right, onto Princeton-Hightstown Road.

Lunch hadn't gone as she'd hoped, but at least the Cellulitists were now all on notice.

JoJo grunted in agreement. Or she had to take a poop.

The baby turned bright red and released a load into her diaper. It immediately made the inside of the Odyssey smell like a barn.

"Son of a bitch, JoJo, c'mon!" she said. "You're not the one who ate the feta cheese!"

JoJo laughed.

Andrea cracked open the windows and let the late-September air whistle through. The humidity of the previous week had broken and it was finally starting to feel like fall. She loved autumn; the drying and dying of the leaves, to her, had always meant the opportunity for renewal. There was something buzzing inside her. She had felt it for months. An impending sense of freedom and of new possibilities. The old was withering and dying, with renewal on the horizon.

She knew now that proving Molly had killed Derek would rupture her relationship with her friends and seriously impact her husband and her family.

"So what if it does?" Andrea muttered.

27

*C*LOSING in on eleven p.m. on Tuesday night, Kenny, Jimmy, and Shelby went to Elegance Gentlemen's Club on the Upper West Side of Manhattan. Kenny could count on one hand how many times he'd been to a strip joint. Jimmy required many extra hands just to throw around the bills that Kenny had provided him.

Derek's credit card expenses had led them to this location in search of the dancer Derek Goode had been sleeping with. Kenny put a cap of $472 to get the information they were looking for. Jimmy had waved, tossed, and tucked seventy-two singles and gotten absolutely no useful information out of it. He was happy to report, though, that Destiny, Fusion, Shaniqua, Barbarella, and Silky all thought he was super hot.

Shelby had told Kenny to let Jimmy have the Washingtons, because he couldn't be trusted with the Jacksons. Kenny was confused—and embarrassed—that she knew how to work the dancers better than he ever could. All Shelby had said was, "After my divorce, I was pretty keen on trying new things."

She had let that hang in the air for their puerile imaginations to percolate.

After some small talk that cost Kenny only a hundred dollars, Shelby secured a private dance with their person of interest, Genesis Jones. Jimmy and Kenny wanted to go with them, but Shelby held them back. She returned twenty minutes later, two hundred dollars lighter, but with information that was worth its weight in gold.

"It was Genesis," Shelby said. "Derek paid for the Ultimate Elegance Experience package a few times over the last six months. She says the bastard didn't get the STD from her, she got it from him."

"Why won't anyone take responsibility for being the STD carrier?" Kenny muttered.

"Here's where my quality time with Genesis gets more interesting," Shelby said.

"I honestly can't imagine this getting much more interesting than how interesting I'm imagining it had already been," said Jimmy.

"Keep it in your dreams, big boy," Shelby said. "Derek did cocaine with Genesis at least five times."

"Confirmation," said Kenny. "What else did you find out?"

"The insurance agents were already here," said Shelby. "Genesis told them about Derek's drug use."

"THEY DON'T WANT to pay out on the insurance policy," Kenny said as he bounced JoJo on his knees. Dozens of geese floated in the pond behind Andrea's house. Between her bouncing giggles, JoJo tried to emulate their squawks. He added, "She's going to learn goose before she learns English."

"We don't learn enough languages in this country, Li Jie," Andrea muttered, using the Chinese name only Kenny's mother used—and only used when she was deriding him. Which, Kenny thought, had occurred far less often after he'd banked the Putnam and Netflix advances.

"So, the problem as I see it is—" Kenny started to say.

"If Derek was running around doing cocaine, and that is what led to his heart attack—"

"Then Molly didn't kill her husband," Kenny finished for her.

"How reliable is this dancer?" Andrea asked.

"As reliable as anyone who calls herself Genesis Jones could be," Kenny replied.

"Is that her stage name or her real name?" Andrea asked.

Kenny stopped bouncing JoJo for a second. "Shit. I have no idea."

"You never thought to ask?"

"I wasn't the one who talked to her!" he said. "Shelby Taylor did."

"The former cop didn't get a real name?"

"Maybe she was enjoying the private dance too much to ask?"

"Seriously?"

"Could Genesis Jones even *be* someone's real name?" an exasperated Kenny replied.

"If it was a stage name, why would she include a last name?" Andrea asked.

The unanswerable questions in this investigation were expanding exponentially, Kenny thought. JoJo made more squawking sounds and wriggled her butt for attention. Kenny obliged and continued bouncing.

Andrea stood at the deck rail looking out over the man-made pond. It was fed by a creek that had been partially dammed a century earlier by the farmer who had owned the land. Other than the noise from the geese, it was idyllic.

A gunshot retort echoed through the air.

And other than the gun club on the other side of the pond, it was idyllic.

The Patriots Rifle Range was hidden from view of the houses behind a long thicket of woods, but the houses weren't shielded from the sounds of the outdoor shooting range. This club member came every

Wednesday at noon to hone his skills and safeguard the town from all threats to the Second Amendment.

The Patriots Rifle Range had been there for over sixty years. Very few of its members were even West Windsor residents, but that didn't stop them from enthusiastically challenging every leaf blower and lawn mower for the town's coveted—and highly competitive—award of "most obnoxious suburban obstacle to peace and quiet."

Kenny said nothing to Andrea, letting her process this death blow to her case. It had been *their* case until last night, when Kenny had lost faith in it. He had gotten involved because he was desperate to chase a dessert he didn't need in lieu of the meal he already had on his plate.

And maybe, Kenny thought, as he looked into the miraculous spark of life in the baby's gleeful eyes, he wanted to sabotage his life as much as Andrea did hers.

Both of them were so afraid that settling in meant giving up. Settling in, settling down, becoming comfortable and happy with their place meant they had become comfortable with themselves.

Kenny knew that both of them were terrified of being comfortable in their own skins.

Another gunshot echoed.

"Fuck," Andrea said.

"Quarter in the swear jar," Kenny absently said.

"Fuck the swear jar," Andrea muttered. Her hand tapped the rail nervously, but in a discernible rhythm. Kenny suspected it was a timing mechanism for her, a way of measuring the gears that were grinding in her brain. He'd never seen her do that before, though he suspected it was something she preferred others not see. She added, "And fuck Molly Goode."

"You're ready to give up?" he asked, hoping she would say both yes and no.

"Fuck Molly Goode," Andrea said again.

"Feels like we're going over ground we've already covered," Kenny muttered.

He was tired. Since he and Jimmy had missed the last New Jersey Transit train home the previous night, Kenny had sprung for an Uber and they hadn't gotten home until almost four a.m. He'd been woken up at eight thirty by a call from Sitara, curious if he would be coming into the office, because Jimmy and Shelby were both already there.

"Teacher's pets," he muttered and hung up, falling back asleep for another hour.

During the Uber ride home, buzzed from the three watered-down bourbons he had milked, Kenny had talked with Jimmy about life and love. His friend was so free and casual about both that Kenny marveled at his seeming indifference to the burden of responsibilities and expectations that were placed on everyone who had just turned thirty.

If they weren't married yet, there was something wrong with them.

If they were married, but didn't have kids yet, there was something wrong with them.

If they had kids, but didn't have a mortgage yet, there was something wrong with them.

If they had a mortgage, but didn't have a prestigious pre-K sorted out yet, there was something wrong with them.

If they had a prestigious pre-K sorted out, but didn't have a college fund established yet, there was something wrong with them.

For millennials, the word *yet* was both a lure and a cudgel.

He thought Andrea wasn't going to accept the death of her case. Kenny could admit he'd gotten involved in this for all the wrong reasons, so that made it easier to admit it was over.

"Better now than if we'd gone further down the road," he said aloud, surprised he'd said it at all, much less in a baby voice while speaking to JoJo. What was it about babies, he wondered.

"Further down the road might have gotten us closer to our destination," she said.

"Or further away from the simple truth," he said, still speaking in JoJo talk.

"You're ready to drop this?" she asked.

"Even if you gathered a mountain of evidence, cocaine in Derek's system when he had a heart condition is going to be reasonable doubt to any reasonable jury."

"I know," she said.

Kenny stood up, holding JoJo out. "What do you want me to do with this?"

Andrea gestured to the portable playpen that was opened up on the deck. He put JoJo inside. The baby wobbled on her legs a bit before dropping to her ass. At first, she struggled to stand up again, but then she was distracted by the geometric blocks lying in the pen and she started playing with them.

Andrea's cell phone rang. She screened the call. She answered.

"Guess what I have in my hands?" Detective Rossi asked.

"A request from Derek Goode's insurance company for an exhumation of his corpse and a toxicology examination of the remains," she said.

Frustrated he couldn't say, "I told you so," Rossi said, "Shit, how did you know?"

Andrea didn't respond.

"I'll let you know what we find out," he said.

Rossi hung up. Andrea put the phone down.

"They will find cocaine in his system," she said. "And Molly skates."

Kenny shrugged his shoulders and left, walking down the deck and around the side of the house. Andrea looked out over the pond, wondering how she had gotten this so wrong.

MIDDAY on Thursday, Brianne Singer was the last to arrive for lunch. The hostess at Mediterra in Princeton walked her over to the outdoor table where Molly Goode and Crystal Burns waited. Andrea had not been invited, at Molly's request, though the others hadn't complained. Brianne sat down at the table arranged in the corner of the tented sitting area facing Hulfish Street and the back entrance to Palmer Square.

It was a beautiful, sunny day; the air was crisp and the breeze light. A busboy immediately filled Brianne's glass with water. Crystal had a mineral water and Molly was on her second cosmo.

"It's going to be that kind of a lunch?" asked Brianne.

"It was that kind of a breakfast," Molly replied. Brianne could tell she was fighting against the alcohol that was already in her system. She hoped her friend wouldn't drink much more, since Molly tended to get meaner the more she drank.

"What did they say when they called you?" asked Brianne.

Crystal gave her the letter that was on the table. "Molly let me read this because you were running late."

Brianne thought, Yes, Crystal, you always know everything first. She looked at the letter. It was an official request from the Hanscomb Insurance Company to the Mercer County medical examiner that Derek Goode be exhumed for a toxicology report. The police had to formally pass the request to Molly, because the decision to accept or deny the request was hers.

"It's horrible, isn't it?" Crystal said.

"They want to avoid paying out the life insurance," Molly added.

"But don't they need a reason of some kind?" Brianne asked.

"They have three million reasons," Molly slurred slightly.

Crystal googled some information on her phone and said, "I think you can say no."

"Yes," Molly said. "But if I refuse their request, they can claim I violated the terms of our policy, and if I do allow them to exhume Derek, I risk that he violated the policy."

Crystal felt nothing but sympathy for Molly's situation. She wanted to believe her friend was an innocent victim, so she did.

Brianne felt nothing but uncertainty about it. She wanted to believe her friend, but she knew she couldn't.

"Isn't it odd the police didn't do an exam when Derek died?" Brianne probed.

"Andrea has quite the influence on them," Molly said, smoothly taking the last sip of her drink and then wiggling her glass in the air until she caught the waiter's attention. "Does she have the same with the two of you?"

Crystal and Brianne didn't know how to respond.

"Surely, she has discussed all this with you," Molly said.

They hemmed and hawed.

"It's quite all right," Molly continued. "She was rather direct in asking me and I was equally direct in answering her. Why would I kill Derek?"

She picked up the letter that had been left on the table and waved it. "Depending on what they find after they dig my husband up, he either died of natural causes, or he died of self-inflicted natural causes."

"What are you going to do then?" Crystal asked.

A baby at a table right next to theirs started to cry. The mother sat alone with her child. She was Indian, or Pakistani; none of them knew how to tell the difference. The woman picked the boy up from his travel seat, which had been resting atop a high chair. The boy looked positively gelatinous. The mother, thin with very piercing brown eyes, seemed a little embarrassed, but as she put the baby against her chest and burped him, she strove for defiant.

Eyes turned back as the waiter deposited another cosmopolitan on the table for Molly. She took a leisurely sip. "Well, I have an appointment at the police station with that swarthy little Detective Rossi and his brutish companion at three o'clock."

That surprised the others. Brianne said, "Today? That's in two hours. Are you sure you should be drinking before going to meet them?"

"Darling, I think I should be drinking so that I *can* go meet them," Molly cooed. She smiled, then took another relaxed sip of her supportive pink concoction.

AT THREE O'CLOCK that afternoon, Molly walked through the front entrance of the police station. From behind the security glass, Sgt. Templeton announced her arrival and buzzed her in. She was led through the rows of cubicles in the open office space to a larger cubicle that contained two desks and two extra chairs. Detectives Rossi and Garmin stood up to greet her.

"I have a room reserved," Rossi said as he picked up a folder from his desk and gestured to an open door along a wall.

They entered the conference room, where two other men stood up to greet her. The shorter man was Caucasian, midforties, doughy, with hair sweat-slicked to one side, the other African American, large but firmer, likely the same age, also with a receding hairline. Both men might as well have worn name tags that read "Insurance Agent."

Rossi introduced them: Lawrence "Call me Larry" Miller and Harold "Call me Harry" Walters. Each professed their sincerest condolences for Molly's loss as they were seconds away from demanding she dig her husband's body out of the ground so she could lose some more.

"Mrs. Goode," Larry said, "we regret making this request of you."

"But, in seeking resolution for your husband's life insurance policy, several questions were raised," Harry interjected.

They ping-ponged off each other, two heads rattling off one long, run-on sentence. Molly lost interest less than halfway through. The cosmos, on top of the two drinks she'd had that morning, had taken their toll and she had a splitting headache. Finally, she said, "Boys, let's stop with the extreme oozing of sincerity and concern. I'm too tired, and frankly, have drank too much today to appreciate your efforts."

The men all glanced at each other uncomfortably.

"Let's cut to the chase. If you dig Derek up and he has drugs in his system, then he was in breach of his policy," she said. "And if I don't let you dig him up, then I forfeit the policy."

Larry and Harry reluctantly nodded.

"Do you have any reason to believe your husband had been doing drugs, Mrs. Goode?" asked Garmin.

"No, Detective Simian—I mean Garmin." She abruptly corrected herself, covering her mouth with her hands, but it wasn't enough to stifle the release of a giggle. Composing herself, Molly said, "No, I don't. But Derek's job required him to entertain in the city a lot. He did drink."

Then, turning to Larry and Harry: "Which wasn't against the insurance policy."

Then, turning back to Rossi and Garmin, she lied: "Did he do anything more than drink? Not to the best of my knowledge. Not since college. Well, a little weed when we were first married, but nothing since the kids were born. Except a drink here or there or everywhere."

She turned back to Harry and Larry again: "Still, not a violation of the policy."

Part of Rossi thought she was playing them all. Coy, innocent, hurt, slandered, angry, and righteous all at the same time. And she was doing it well. Maybe Andrea was right?

Molly absently rummaged through her purse. "Where do I sign?" she said abruptly.

The men were a little tentative. They had expected more of a fight.

"I have nothing to hide," she said. "If I lose out on the insurance policy, then I lose out on the insurance policy. It wouldn't be the worst thing my husband has ever done to me. I mean, three million dollars would certainly rank right up there, but at least he was sweet enough to leave me four years on the mortgage, thirty-one thousand a year in property taxes, and two college educations to pay off."

She pulled out a pen and gave the men a sweet "fuck you" smile.

Rossi removed a document from his folder. Like Olympic-level synchronized swimmers, Larry and Harry took turns deftly removing separate papers from the one folder they'd placed on the desk. Molly held her Montegrappa Fortuna Mosaico pen and signed her name several times. She returned the pen to her purse.

"Let me know the time of the exhumation," she said. "I would like to be there to monitor the activity."

"You have to be there, ma'am," said Rossi. "And we will let you know once it's scheduled."

Molly firmly shook everyone's hands and left.

AT FOUR FIFTEEN that afternoon, Vince Rossi met with Andrea and Sathwika at the Starbucks in MarketFair Mall. Because it was after school, the women had dragged several of their brood along. Sadie chased Sathwika's eldest son, Divam, around the mall as both tried—and failed—to keep up with Sarah. Sitting within a group of tables inside the coffee shop's mall storefront, Andrea struggled with JoJo, who wanted to join the scampering kids, while Aditya rested in his mother's arms.

Sathwika related, almost word for word, what Molly, Crystal, and Brianne had talked about during lunch at Mediterra. From her adjoining table, she had heard everything they had discussed and, even though she hadn't been recording the conversation, relayed it back with perfect recall.

Earlier, Andrea had received a text from Brianne apologizing that she hadn't been invited to lunch. Andrea learned when and where, then responded politely: It's okay. Molly will tell you I already confronted her.

Since Andrea had wanted eyes and ears on the scene, she had called Sathwika.

Sathwika's takeaway was that Molly had been so dismissively casual about Andrea's accusations, she had convinced Crystal and Brianne there was no substance to them.

What Sathwika and Rossi didn't know was that Brianne, certainly, and Crystal, possibly, had a vested interest in believing Molly because it meant protecting their own husbands. Andrea wasn't quite ready to share that with them yet. Dragging Rossi and Sathwika into Jeff's possible illegal activities seemed unwise at the moment.

"Molly presented herself as very aware of her situation and very comfortable in her narrative," Sathwika said. "She's the ultimate conundrum for people like us: you can't tell if she's telling the truth or if she believes the lie so strongly that it becomes the truth."

"Having just spent half an hour with her, I agree with your assessment," said Rossi. "But you're not even covering the worst aspect to all of that."

"What's that?" asked Sathwika.

"That if people like us can't tell for sure if she's lying, then a jury never will," said Andrea.

Rossi took a sip of his black coffee. He scowled. He hated Starbucks. He said, "Molly was surprisingly relaxed at the prospect of forfeiting the policy. Could the money really not matter to her?"

Andrea shrugged and said, "When will the exhumation take place?"

"There's urgency to get this done," Rossi said, "so probably sometime early next week."

"Can I be there?" asked Andrea.

"You most certainly cannot," said Rossi.

"Can a member of the fourth estate be there?" asked Sathwika.

"Shit," said Rossi. "Please, no. . . ."

29

K ENNY sauntered across the grounds of the Dutch Neck church cemetery with inappropriate glee. It was Wednesday at eight fifteen a.m. Even though they'd had several days to prepare for him, Rossi and Garmin were in no mood for Kenny's antics.

"Hi, Detectives." He waved to them.

Molly Goode stood off to one side of the exhumation crew hired to remove the casket from the ground. A heavyset woman in her late forties with salt-and-pepper hair and a dour demeanor watched over the backhoe as it dug into the soil. Larry and Harry oversaw the operation.

The woman approached Kenny. "I'm Diane Kerwin, the cemetery director for the church."

"I'm Kenneth Lee," he replied, and then, still not having gotten permission from his former editor to use them as the paper of record, added, "I'm with the *Princeton Post*."

"I don't understand," she said.

"I don't understand what you don't understand," he replied.

"Why you're here?"

"To report on the exhumation of Derek Goode," he said. "I mean, you didn't think I was doing a 'Tombstones of West Windsor' article, did you? But come to think of it, that could be kind of cool, too."

"Why would you want to do a story about that?" she said.

"The tombstones? I guess it's interesting, seeing the old family names and how they inform the current—"

"I meant about the exhumation!" she said more loudly.

Rossi and Garmin exchanged a glance. Garmin muttered, "FuckingKennyLee."

"Oh, I'm sorry," Kenny said. The grin on his face managed to be acidic and innocent at the same time. "Derek. Sure. Well, a forty-year-old man dies of a heart attack and a few weeks later his body is being exhumed, it raises some questions. And you might not know this about me, which I'd be a little surprised and disappointed if you didn't, but I tend to be a bit of a nuisance when there are questions looking for answers."

"But how did you find out about—" Diane started, but Molly interrupted her.

"Mr. Lee was informed by a close friend of mine who, apparently, has decided she does not want to be a close friend of mine any longer," Molly said.

Kenny smiled. "Molly. Nice to see you again, though I'm sorry it's under such difficult circumstances."

"No comment," Molly said.

"About the circumstances being difficult?" Kenny asked.

"No comment," she repeated.

"Okay, I'll just watch," he said. "And maybe take some pictures."

"You will do no such thing," said Diane.

"I'm pretty sure it's not illegal," said Kenny. "Detectives, is it illegal?"

Rossi and Garmin shook their heads. Reluctantly. FuckingKennyLee.

"But it is indecent," said Diane.

The grinding noise from the yellow-orange Caterpillar backhoe loader forced them to raise their voices over the sound of digging.

"I would have to take your word on it, Diane," Kenny said. "I'm not that well versed on the topic. For example, is it decent to try and scam an insurance company into paying out on a policy when you know you're in violation of it?"

That perked the ears of Larry and Harry.

"I'm sure those two fine gentlemen find that indecent," Kenny continued.

Diane Kerwin shuffled uncomfortably. She looked to Molly for guidance.

"Is it decent to get away with murder?" Kenny continued. "I mean, I'm confident Vinnie and Charlie find that indecent. Are we still on a first-name basis, guys? We were last year. Anyway, I don't know how Molly feels about any of this on account of her no comments. How about it, Molly, is it indecent to get away with murder?"

"That's enough, Lee," said Garmin as he moved his massive body between the reporter and the women.

Putting his hands up in surrender, Kenny retreated a few steps.

Once the digging ended, the loader backed up with annoying beeping sounds and two workers jumped down into the hole. They arranged the harness and chains under the coffin so it could be lifted.

Rossi casually worked his way over to Kenny.

"She doesn't have enough," Rossi said softly.

"She doesn't have anything," Kenny said.

"But you do?" he asked.

"The possibilities percolate, Vinnie," Kenny replied.

"You really should call me Detective," Rossi said.

After an extended silence, Rossi said, "What do you have?"

"Business that might be shady business," Kenny said. "Shady business that could provide motive."

Rossi pointed at Larry and Harry. "There's your motive right there, don't you think?"

"The insurance policy?" asked Kenny. "Yeah, normally, that would be a pretty good motive."

"But you're implying not in this case?" Rossi said.

The workers hopped out of the open grave and secured the four chains to the backhoe's bucket. They gave the operator a thumbs-up and he lifted the stick until the chains formed a taut pyramid.

"I imply nothing," said Kenny. "I'm agreeing with you that three mil is a pretty good motive."

Rossi nodded. The Caterpillar operator slowly raised the backhoe's boom and the coffin emerged from the ground. It sloughed off dirt in a drift of dust. Molly made a mild show of discomfort. Diane placed a hand on her shoulder.

The coffin was lowered to a transom carrier. The workers brushed off excess dirt from the coffin, then, along with Harry and Larry, they lifted it and slid it into the back of a van. It would be taken to a medical examiner hired by the insurance company to perform an independent autopsy.

Harry and Larry walked to the women, bearing a clipboard and wearing their sincerest of sincere faces. Both women signed several forms in several places. Harry and Larry gestured with the clipboard to Garmin and Rossi. They pointed at each other, then reluctantly Garmin shrugged. He stepped forward, took the pen from the insurance boys, and signed the forms.

The workers left the plot open, the dirt that had been removed set aside, away from other burial plots. Harry and Larry left in the van. The workers moved the backhoe loader to the trailer that was parked in the lot on the side of the church's nursery school.

Molly thanked the detectives and left. Diane Kerwin trailed her, a few paces behind.

Kenny looked at the empty hole in the ground.

He thought of his father, who had been cremated, his ashes spread in the ocean waves of Cape May, where he had loved to vacation.

He thought of his mother. Would his father have killed her if he could have gotten away with it? Doubtful. He loved her and was willing to be deferential to her, which she demanded as a condition of that love. Would his mom have killed him if she could? Why would she have bothered? His mother had already killed his spirit, so what benefit could she have gained from killing the body?

"What are you thinking, Lee?" Garmin asked, breaking a several-minute silence.

Kenny looked around. The cemetery had cleared out except for the three of them.

"I'm thinking we're missing something," he muttered.

Garmin snorted. "I think you're missing everything, because there's nothing there."

"Charlie has a crush on Mrs. Goode." Rossi smiled as Garmin playfully pushed him. Rossi didn't smile often. Kenny found it creepy. Turning to Kenny, he continued, "You know Andrea has bounced around multiple motives already. Physical abuse, money, adultery. I mean, it could be a combination of all of that, sure, but . . ."

"But you're thinking the same thing I am," Kenny said. "None of those things would probably have bothered this woman in the slightest."

"Yeah," Rossi said.

"So . . . ?" asked Garmin, hating Kenny's guts but reluctantly intrigued by the way his mind worked.

"So, what if she's hiding something else?" Kenny asked.

IT took the independent lab hired by Hanscomb Insurance a week to
provide its examiner's findings. Detectives Rossi and Garmin rifled
through the report: traces of cocaine were found in the urine samples
drawn from the bladder, connoting short-term use; traces of cocaine
were found in hair follicles, connoting long-term use.

Chief Preet Anand waved them into his office. They handed him
the report like chastened puppies. He flipped through it, frowned, and
said, "It's on me."

"We vouched for Andrea, Chief," Rossi said. "We should have required the ME to perform an autopsy."

"Since the township is absorbing the cost of the exhumation, the
insurance company hasn't made a big issue of it," Anand said. "So, at
most, it'll just require a few forkfuls of humble pie when budget time
comes around."

"And Molly Goode?" asked Garmin.

"She doesn't have much of a leg to stand on," Anand said. "She
asked Andrea Stern to ask us to skip the postmortem. No, it just calls
into question any future dealings with Mrs. Stern and jumping through
the hoops of her hunches."

"She still thinks Molly Goode had something to do with this," Rossi said. "The reporter does, too."

"The reporter?" questioned Anand. "The annoying one from the Sasmal case?"

"Kenny Lee," Garmin confirmed.

Anand laughed. "I'll try not to let his threats give me a brown star cluster."

Rossi and Garmin had quickly gotten used to Anand's preference for military slang. He did it, they had come to realize, as a reflexive use of language and a not-so-subtle reminder that he thought himself immune to the petty politics of the job. If you'd shot someone and been shot in the Middle East, very little that happened in a New Jersey suburb was going to faze you.

"Andrea asked if we could notify her when the report came in," Rossi said.

"Absolutely not," Anand said. "We follow procedure. We notify Mrs. Goode, arrange a meeting with her and with the Hanscomb agents present. The sooner the better, by the way. After that, if you're gossiping over coffee or drinks, it's on your time and on your dime."

Rossi and Garmin nodded, took the report folder back, and left the office.

HOURS LATER, Molly Goode sat alongside Larry and Harry and Vince and Charlie in the only conference room available to them on short notice, which was the smallest in the station. It was uncomfortably cramped as Larry and Harry presented the news to Molly. They were sympathetic, since they had to assume she had nothing to do with Derek's activities and indeed was being harmed by things her husband had done.

"Do I have any recourse for appeal?" she asked.

The men exchanged glances.

Larry said, "You can hire an independent lab and perform a new examination, Mrs. Goode, but you would have to pay for that, and for the transport of your husband's body."

"Mrs. Goode, I don't think you'll get a different result," said Garmin. "I'm sorry."

"So . . . ?" she asked, sadly, letting them plunge the knife into the poor widow's back.

Larry and Harry each waited for the other to say it. No matter how long they'd been doing this, which was a pathetically long time for both of them, this was the hardest part of the job. Harry thought it was probably his turn, which meant Larry would pay for their next lunch.

"Mrs. Goode, I'm sorry," Harry said. "Your husband was in violation of Code 15.4 of his policy indicating the use of medically prohibited substances, thereby canceling the obligations of the Hanscomb Insurance Company toward the fulfilment of the policy's monetary obligations."

She held herself in reserve for several seconds, then choked back tears. Garmin reached over to place a hand on her back and she brushed it off with anger. Then, softly, "I'm sorry, Detective. I'm just . . ." She let it trail, her hand balled into a fist. She quivered slightly from anger.

"It's understandable, Mrs. Goode," said Harry. "And we're sorry this is the result of your husband's activities."

A single tear came down her cheek.

"I haven't worked in ten years," she said. "But now . . ."

Garmin slid the tissue box in front of her. She took one and dabbed at the tear.

"Never mind," she said. "I'm sorry. It's unseemly. I live a life of ridiculous luxury compared to most. I have the means to overcome this."

She composed herself quickly. Reaching into her purse, she looked to the insurance agents.

"What else do I need to do?" she asked. "Sign any forms?"

Larry slid the paperwork in front of her. Sticky tabs indicated the places she needed to sign.

Harry gathered the paperwork. "Your husband's casket is scheduled to be reinterred tomorrow morning at ten if you would like to be present."

She let out a sound that was half cackle, half choking. "I think I'll pass on that."

With perfunctory shaking of hands and repeated regrets, Larry and Harry left.

"Is there anything else I need to sign for you, Detectives?" she asked. "A promise that I won't sue the department for not performing an autopsy?"

"No, Mrs. Goode," Rossi said.

She stood up and shook their hands, thanking them for their patience and understanding.

As she reached the open door to leave, Rossi said, "Mrs. Goode, did you ask Andrea to get us to forgo an autopsy because you knew this would happen?"

She stood in the doorway for several seconds, an odd look on her face that Rossi had trouble reading. Several years' worth of frustration and recrimination, happiness and anger, hope and, ultimately, unfulfilled possibility all crossed her usually stoic face within those seconds.

"Derek was ultimately a very immature and a very selfish man, Detective," she said. "Maybe I was always too serious and that's what led him to overcompensate. I don't want to put all of the responsibility on him. Marriage is . . . well, it's marriage."

Molly Goode left without having really answered the question.

Garmin gathered the paperwork and left the office as Rossi made a call on his cell phone.

Andrea answered. "Did you get the report?"

"Recent and prolonged use," said Rossi. "Officially deemed a fatal coronary caused by excessive use of drugs."

He heard her sigh over the phone. He hated when she sighed. It was one of the few childish affectations she had, but he also knew that meant she was either frustrated, disappointed, or, worse, thinking something through.

Or even worse, he corrected himself, all three combined.

He suspected this was an "even worse" scenario.

"She just sacrificed three million dollars," she said.

"Sacrificed? No, it was taken away from her," he replied.

"What if Molly had been willing to sacrifice the money in order to get away with murder?" Andrea asked.

"Then I'd say she really wanted to see this guy dead more than you thought," he said.

"What if Molly had spent a lot longer than we thought planning the murder of a husband who was going to die sooner rather than later?" Andrea said. "What if the leads we've chased were part of a plan she had put in place—including asking me to get you to bypass the autopsy—because she knew it would lead to the moment you just had with her? Walking out of the police station, forever absolved of his murder because of what his death cost her?"

"So, you have no evidence that she killed him, but you plan to prove she did it by showing she planted evidence to prove that she didn't kill him, all as a way of covering up that she actually did kill him?" Rossi asked.

"That's exactly right," she said.

"And that's exactly crazy," he replied.

"But I'm not crazy, Vince," Andrea said.

"No," he reluctantly agreed.

"And neither is Molly. The total opposite, in fact. She plans and organizes to exacting, meticulous degree."

"But even if you were able to prove she prearranged her own alibi, you'll still have to find evidence that she actually did it," Rossi said.

"Totally doable," she said. He could practically hear the sly, mischievous smile spreading on her face.

As much as Andrea wanted justice, she liked having found an interesting sparring partner.

PART THREE

In Slickness and in Wealth

31

SHE is out of her mind!" Kenny said as he ended his call with Andrea. He turned to Sitara, Shelby, and Jimmy, who were at their desks working. Except for Jimmy, who was at his desk not working. Unless conducting an SFW Google Images search of Lupita Nyong'o was his assignment for the day.

"The housewife detective just told you they found cocaine in Derek Goode's system?" Shelby said without having heard Andrea's side of the conversation.

"And Molly Goode lost three million dollars," Sitara said.

"That's a hell of an alibi," Shelby replied.

"Hell of an alibi," Sitara agreed, staring at Kenny as she said it. "Except the housewife detective doesn't think it is."

Kenny put his hands up defensively. "Hey, I said she was out of her mind, didn't I?"

"But when you say it, it sounds like you're excited," Sitara said.

"It does," Jimmy chimed in.

"Peanut gallery, shut up," Kenny said.

"Is that a racist thing?" Jimmy asked.

"I think it is," Sitara said.

"I'm not sure," Shelby said. "And I come from a long line of racists, too."

"They were the cheap seats in vaudeville shows," Kenny said. "I opt for class-based slur, not race-based. But can all of you shut up now? Andrea thinks everything we found out about Molly and Derek were things Molly planned and planted for us to find. And, as an aside, isn't Shelby's use of the word *housewife* as a pejorative also inappropriate?"

"It was," Shelby said. "But not racist."

"I couldn't get away with using it," Jimmy chimed in. "And I'm not even sure what pejorative means."

"So, to prove Molly Goode killed her husband, we have to prove she created an elaborate plan over months—or even years—involving at least a half dozen other people, so that at some point she could be absolved of inducing the heart attack that killed her husband, who was going to die of a heart attack anyway?" Sitara said.

"While at the same time, knowingly kissing three mil bye-bye," Shelby added.

"When no one but Andrea ever had any real suspicion that Molly had killed her husband to begin with?" Sitara also added.

"Sounds hinky," Jimmy said, looking up from his pictures of Lupita Nyong'o.

"It would be pretty fucking incredible if Molly did do that, though," Kenny said, smiling.

"It really would," agreed Jimmy.

"Only one way to find out for sure," said Kenny.

"You're both idiots," Sitara said. After a minute, she added, "Just for the sake of argument, what if you're asking the wrong questions? What if you shouldn't be asking if Andrea is crazy—"

"Probably a given at this point," muttered Shelby.

"—or asking how Molly Goode could have woven such a ridiculous plan?" Sitara continued. "What you should really be asking is: What kind of person would think that way? What kind of person spends such a substantial chunk of her married life planning to kill her husband?"

GOOD TIMING, KENNY *thought as he was being driven home from what should have been the best day of his life. On the day that Walter O'Malley resigned as governor of New Jersey after a two-year investigation into his illicit sexual activities, embezzlement, and fraud, twenty-four-year-old Pulitzer Prize–winning journalist Kenneth Lee found out his father had Stage 3 cancer of the liver.*

Kenny had managed to get through a dozen local and national media requests for interviews by balancing his emotions in the tried-and-true fashion taught him by his parents: by having no emotions about it at all.

In the backseat of the car driving him home, he had called his dad twice and his brother, Cary, once. Neither answered.

Forty minutes later, Kenny entered his house on King Haven Court in Plainsboro through the garage. He noticed the sheets in the downstairs guest bedroom were rumpled. He poked his head into the empty room. There was a tissue box on the night table. A pair of his mother's panties and her bra had landed on the floor beneath the window. When he turned to leave, he came face-to-face with his mother, who was completely stunned to see him.

Blaire's thick dark hair, with carefully selected streaks of gray running through the sides, was wildly disheveled. Her dress was wrinkled and had been haphazardly thrown on. She wasn't wearing shoes, which was the norm for their house, but she also wasn't wearing pantyhose, which was odd for her. And he knew she wasn't wearing underwear, because they were on the floor of the guest bedroom. She had always been an incredibly attractive woman, but just now Kenny was terrified to even contemplate that she looked downright hot.

Every instinct he had screamed to pretend nothing was going on. He ignored those instincts.

"Where is he?" Kenny asked.

"He left," she said. "Luckily, before you arrived."

"I meant Dad!" he shouted.

"He had an appointment with Dr. Chen," she said calmly.

"And you didn't go with him?"

"I also had an appointment."

"Obviously," he said as he left the room.

"I meant a house viewing," she called after him as he went upstairs.

Fifteen minutes later, he heard her shower running.

Then he heard his father come home.

As he entered the kitchen, Kenny said, "Dad, I'm sorry."

They shared an awkward hug.

"I will fight this," his dad said. Kenny sensed little confidence in the words.

"Did you feel anything was wrong?" he asked. He got two bowls and forks out.

"I felt some symptoms, but I didn't know what it was," his dad said.

"For how long?"

"I mentioned it to your mother occasionally, but you know how she is about getting sick."

"Sure," Kenny said. "Same way she is about anything she considers a sign of weakness."

It took his father three years to die from the cancer.

In their last conversation, he said to Kenny, "Take care of your mother, Li Jie."

Kenny asked, "Why, Dad? She never took care of you."

His frail, withered hand clutched Kenny's as tightly as it could. The grip had all the strength of a crumpled piece of paper. "Don't blame people for what they can't be."

KENNY STOOD IN the empty conference room, looking out the large windows across to the NYU dorm. One kid could be seen doing yoga in his dorm room; others were doing schoolwork. A girl blithely walked through her room in a bra and jeans looking for a clean top among a pile of clothes. He barely noticed any of it. He was thinking about his mother and father. And Molly and Derek, and Andrea and Jeff and, ultimately, himself and Sitara.

Did marriage inevitably decay into disenchantment and frustration? A gradual abandonment of freedom? Surely, marriages could continue to be meaningful, thriving partnerships. He'd seen several on TV.

Did Blaire think she'd earned the right to treat his father like shit because his weakness warranted it? William's ways had ground her to the very nerve. For her, unforgiving strength was a sign of character. That her husband had contracted a fatal illness was an assault on everything she believed.

Kenny watched Sitara run through editing choices with Jimmy and Shelby. He wondered how long it would be before either one of them started to feel alone in the union.

He was a reporter. She was a documentarian. Their very existence was about digging through dirt to uncover every inner truth to be found. How many decades sifting through a person's thoughts, beliefs, and predilections before finding out there was nothing left to excavate from the hole? How many years did you still have left together after that, wondering if maybe you had dug your own spiritual grave?

Kenny shuddered. He suddenly felt sympathy for Molly Goode.

32

*I*T wasn't Andrea's imagination that Kenny had ended their conversation abruptly. He wasn't the type to feign interest, so when he had hung up before she'd finished saying, "Let's check back in with each other before the end of the week," it had left her wondering if perhaps Kenny wouldn't be checking back in with her before the end of the week.

She hated to admit it, but she couldn't investigate Molly's complex deception without Kenny and his coworkers. They had access to New York City that she lacked. Andrea was playing the game with one hand tied behind her back. Game? No, more like a battle. Where only one side was armed. Would she have to go it alone?

Her insecurities kicked in. What was it about her that alienated people? She knew she was arrogant, sarcastic, and judgmental, but was that reason for people to be so wary around her?

Tito Envaquera had named her Insight, because Andrea Abelman could see right into you. In a world where everyone demanded to be seen, she was shunned because she could see through you. She knew you. It had kept people away from her all through high school, even when she was going out with the perpetually popular Cary Lee. Before she met Jeff, her only real friend in college had been her roommate, Zhi Ruo Gwan.

And Andrea had gotten her killed.

Maybe people had a valid reason to be afraid of her.

HER MOOD IN the car as they drove down the turnpike was palpable. Because they were looking at houses in the Princeton area, Jeff had suggested visiting Andrea's parents while they were in West Windsor. And before Andrea could say, "No fucking fuckity-fuck way," he told her he had already reached out to them to let them know they were coming.

She was restless, feeling Elijah kick in her belly. She didn't like the name, but she'd gotten to name Ruth, so it had been Jeff's turn.

"I'm sorry you're so mad," Jeff said. "I shouldn't have called them without asking you, but Andie, they've barely seen Ruth since she was born."

"The minute they say anything stupid, we're out."

Jeff thought they wouldn't be there very long.

After seeing several ridiculously large mansions, they drove to her old house in Berrien City. Andrea hadn't been back in a long time.

Jeff drove past the train station. They turned onto the block where Andrea had lived from seventh grade until she left for Columbia. Berrien City was a small community of single-family homes that had been built after World War I. The variety of houses along Berrien and Scott Avenues alternated between beautifully quaint and slightly dilapidated.

Andrea's house had always been one of the dilapidated ones. It still was.

They pulled into the narrow, chewed-up driveway. The front lawn was a patchwork of weeds. The house needed a power-washing. The shutters on her old bedroom window were still askew, one clinging by a single rusted screw.

They parked behind her parents' 1996 Ford Focus. Its undercarriage was still held up by bungee cords. To their credit, those cords had been performing their job for over ten years.

"Wow," Jeff muttered, looking around the property. He knocked on the door.

They heard three locks being undone. Andrea knew that wasn't her parents' judicious respect for security, it was paranoia. The door opened. Bernice Abelman forced a smile. Jeff kissed her hello. She gave Andrea a perfunctory glance and, in a genuine moment of unvarnished regret, turned her attention to Ruth. "Oh my god, look at her. Look at her."

Jacob made his way over to the small living room at the front of the house. He wasn't even sixty yet, but he moved with pronounced creakiness. "Hello, hello," he said.

He shook Jeff's hand and then ogled Andrea's very pregnant belly. "Look at you," he said to Andrea, then to Ruth, "And look at you!"

And with that, their interaction with their first grandchild seemed to have come to an end.

Andrea took in her old house. There were several boxes splayed across the uncomfortably cramped first floor, which comprised little more than the living room, a small table area outside the small open kitchen, a small closet, and a small door to the small cellar. Upstairs were a master bedroom, the bedroom she had grown up in, and the single bathroom in the house.

It had always amazed Andrea that her parents had never aspired to more. Not even that they hadn't wanted more for her, but even selfishly for themselves. The stray boxes had been a fixture her entire life, but this was different. They weren't filled with merchandise her father was trying to sell, but packed with her parents' things.

"What's going on?" she asked.

Jacob and Bernice exchanged glances. Andrea knew the look. It meant: How much should we tell her?

Bernice said, "Your father and I are moving to Florida."

"I got a territory lining up that's going to be really good for us," said Jacob.

Andrea cringed on the inside and numbly nodded her head on the outside. "Territory" meant: new scam. "Good for us" meant: getting out one step ahead of whoever I owe money to.

She wanted to get the hell out of there. Ruth trolled around the house and Andrea honestly worried she would contract some sort of flesh-eating virus.

"Where in Florida?" Jeff asked.

Jacob was flummoxed by the simple question. He looked to Bernice. She said, "Ponte Vedra. Or Moon Lake. Maybe Combee Settlement. We haven't decided yet."

They were running away again, Andrea thought. But what could her father have been trafficking in that would warrant needing to flee?

Curiously trying to peek into an open box, Ruth accidentally pulled it to the floor, spilling a stack of folded clothes on the carpet.

"Don't do that!" Bernice shouted with a ferocity far out of proportion to the act.

Ruth started to cry.

Andrea reached over to hold her toddler.

"You can't coddle them all the time," Jacob said.

"How about some of the time, Dad?" Andrea snapped. "Can you hug them once in a while and acknowledge they made a mistake without crushing their spirit?"

"Oh, there she goes," Bernice said with a dismissive wave of her hand.

"Bernice," Jeff said, trying to defuse the sudden tension.

"No, she's right, Jeff," Andrea said, raising her voice through Ruth's crying, well aware she wasn't doing much to soothe her daughter, either. "Here I go again. How about after your brother dies in your arms on a city street at eleven in the morning and your parents don't come to the police precinct to get you until eight at night? How about a hug then?"

What did you do, Andrea?

Those had been her father's first words to her when he had gotten her the day Isaac had died. Andrea had been sitting in the station house for hours wearing a 112th Precinct T-shirt that was too large for her. They had taken the bloodstained shirt she had been wearing when Isaac was stabbed.

"Oh, with the drama!" Bernice exclaimed. "That was a lifetime ago! Get over it!"

Andrea wanted to explode, but Jeff's hand, which had been on her thigh, tightened slightly, just enough to calm her down. She bit her lip and tended to Ruth, brushing the girl's thick dark-brown hair back off her neck and kissing her on the cheek. She whispered something into Ruth's ear. Her daughter, face still buried in Andrea's collarbone, nodded vigorously. Andrea kissed her again.

"You know what, guys?" she said calmly. "You're right. It is too much drama. Every time we see each other, it's just too much. And that's on me, I admit it. I haven't gotten over Isaac's death."

"You know why he was killed, Andrea," Jacob said. "You've always known."

"I've always known that you blamed me for it," she said.

They had always been afraid to talk about Isaac's death. Not because the subject hurt them. It wasn't until that moment that Andrea realized why they had always hated her.

Because they feared her.

As they drove away, Andrea honestly didn't know if she'd ever see them again, and she couldn't muster a reason to care. Inwardly, she thanked her parents for having taught her the most valuable lesson she could ever hope to learn in life: to always give people a reason to be afraid of her.

JOJO CAWED IN her baby talk, which had just started to struggle to form coherent words. Andrea went back into the house and lifted the baby out of the playpen. "You're not afraid of Mommy, are you? No, you're not."

She looked at her phone. Normally by noon on any given weekday, Andrea would have had a dozen or more group texts from the Cellulitists. This morning there were none. They were shutting her out. Her friends were angry or afraid to talk to her. She needed someone who believed in her.

She swiped through her contact list. She dreaded dialing the number.

Ramon Mercado answered before the first ring had ended. "Andie, this is a nice surprise."

"Hi, Ramon," she said tentatively to the FBI agent who should have been the man she had spent her life with.

"You wouldn't believe how boring the last month has been," he said. "Tell me you need help with something."

Andrea smiled.

33

JOJO screamed for the first half hour of the drive. She finally fell asleep somewhere around exit 13. Andrea wished she could join her, though falling asleep at the wheel on the New Jersey Turnpike could prove problematic. As always, the thought of Ramon had her in knots.

Ramon and his wife had their first child in February. He'd sent pictures and they'd talked. She then saw him early in the summer during the Sasmal trial. When she was in college, they had loved each other, but getting pregnant with Ruth and then marrying Jeff had put a crimp in their budding relationship. Over the past year, Andrea had reconciled her feelings about the life they never shared, so why was she nervous about seeing him again?

She was buzzed in through the security gate at the FBI building in Newark. Ramon met her in the lobby. As they rode the elevator up, he reintroduced himself to JoJo, who took to him immediately. Smart girl. The baby reached out for him and he looked to Andrea for permission. She let JoJo slide out of her hands and into his arms. JoJo pressed her head against his chest. Smarter girl.

"You look tired," she said.

"Benito still isn't sleeping through the night," he said. "Is that normal?"

"Every baby is different," Andie said. "It took Eli and Sarah a year. Benito will get there. How has Maria been handling everything?"

"Postpartum, angry at me because I'm not home enough," he said. "And she has a right to be, because we've had a bank fraud case that's been dragging for months. With the kinds of cases I keep catching, I feel like we could use twenty more experienced accountants and a lot less field agents around here."

"Feh," Andrea grunted.

"Tens of thousands of documents to sift through and political pressure to go easy on the target."

"Double feh," she said. JoJo tried to mimic her mother. They laughed.

They reached his floor. Andrea greeted several of the agents she had briefly worked alongside last year. Nakala Rogers gave her a big hug. Ramon led Andrea to a small conference room. He sat JoJo on his lap. "I'll leave you with both hands free in case this requires trademark Andie Abelman Queens hand gestures," he said with a smile.

"Probably just this one," she said, smiling back as she raised her middle fingers on both hands. He laughed and covered JoJo's eyes. "No histrionics today," she promised. "In fact, I need you to tell me if I have anything at all or if I'm crazy."

"The floor is yours," he said.

She proceeded to relate the events of the past few weeks. Listening intently the entire time, Ramon played peekaboo with JoJo. Andrea waited patiently as he mulled it over.

"You're crazy," he finally said. Waiting for her disappointed reaction, he followed with, "But you might have something."

"I don't understand," she said.

He stood up, his crisp button-down shirt clinging to his tight body. Four months into being a father and Ramon still had abs of steel. That wouldn't last. She used to have breasts that defied gravity, and now they were so low to the ground as to provoke depravity.

Pacing slowly around the room and dipping JoJo up and down to giggling caws, Ramon said, "Let's operate under the assumption that Molly Goode has known of your past for a year, but maybe longer, and she's been planning to kill her husband that entire time, or longer."

"So, any decisions she made about the murder would have taken into account that I would get involved," Andrea said.

"And anyone smart enough to do that would be smart enough to realize an inescapable truth," Ramon said.

"And what's that?"

"That you would figure it all out," Ramon said. "That no matter how smart she was, you would be smarter in figuring it out."

"You think she planned on getting caught?"

"No, I'm suggesting she planned on getting away with it," Ramon said. "But that required you suspecting her of the crime and, ulti-mately, amassing enough evidence to arrest her for it."

"That's what I've been thinking, that she planted all the evidence we found," said Andrea.

"Some of it she might have planted, but she likely used things that were already happening to her advantage," Ramon said. He dipped JoJo all the way down to his feet and quickly rushed her back over his head.

"Let's break this down," he said, handing JoJo back to the seated Andrea. The baby was less than thrilled by that result.

Ramon took a marker to the whiteboard that lined one wall. At the top, he wrote Molly's name. Beneath it to the left, he wrote Andrea's, and to the right, he wrote Derek's.

Under Derek, he wrote "Heart Condition."

Ramon continued to talk as he broke down a flow chart. "Okay, instead of thinking of building a case against her, let's deconstruct everything you would normally do, because she planned for that. So, I'm Molly and I know Derek has a heart condition that could be easily triggered and he is either (a) using cocaine behind my back or (b) I'm giving him cocaine."

"Without his knowledge?" she asked.

"Mixed in his food, on his toothpaste, in his milk," said Ramon. "If he was using cocaine, then were there witnesses? You say yes, there were. Fine. Deconstruct that. Are we sure they are telling the truth?"

"Why would they lie?"

"Because if Molly had an elaborate plan to outfox you, then planting witnesses to Derek's cocaine use would be an elaborate move," he said. "Conversely, say that Molly knew Derek was doing cocaine and offered potential witnesses money to verify what he was already doing and admit that to the insurance investigators."

Andrea provided a few more details about the people involved. Ramon continued to build the chart. She wasn't thrilled he had put her at the top of the chart as one of the people Molly was manipulating, but she couldn't deny it, either.

Ramon continued, "Molly had to combine what she knew Derek was already doing—business scams, affairs, drugs—with her expectation that you would be investigating her."

Andrea wondered if she should tell Ramon about Jeff's involvement. She stayed quiet.

"From Kenny's conversations with the law firm, we have witnesses to the trifecta: the cocaine use, the affairs, and the business fraud," Ramon said. "And as usual, when not discussing a serial killer, it boils down to: Who made the money?"

"Hard to reconcile that when Molly sacrificed her insurance policy," Andrea said.

"What if she sacrificed a bishop to save her queen?" he said. "What if Molly willingly walked away from three million—"

Andrea completed the sentence aloud along with Ramon: "Because she knew she had access to more money than she was sacrificing."

Ramon smiled.

She fell in love with him all over again and didn't care to chide herself about it.

"The business scam accumulated enough money that she could pay off the witnesses, pay off the accomplices, and still walk away with more than the insurance policy would have given her," Andrea said.

"Always follow the money."

She trailed off, her thought incomplete, as Ramon wrote one final, bolder line at the bottom of the board:

Where is the money?

She stood up and handed JoJo off to him casually. He blew a raspberry into the baby's belly to make her laugh. This should have been them all along, she thought absently. The two of them could have eliminated all crime on the planet and still had time for takeout sushi dinner.

Except Ramon didn't like sushi.

Okay, she thought, he was perfect, but not everyone was *perfect* perfect.

Andrea took in the whiteboard.

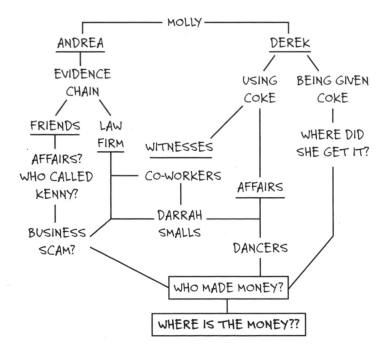

She absorbed it: the connections, the possibilities, and the uncertainty of it all.

With her eyes closed, she traced her hand from the bottom of the chart and slowly ran her fingers upward. She had to deconstruct the lies.

Molly paid the dancers to give Derek cocaine, or he did it willingly while they watched.

Darrah didn't have an affair with Derek, but Molly paid her to say she had.

She also didn't have an STD, but was getting the antibiotics as a cover.

But Molly did have a cold sore. Could she have given it to herself? Could she have acquired an STD from a different source? That seemed like an overcomplication. Like Ramon said, some things Molly manipulated, others had to have been opportunities presented to her that she used to her advantage.

Were Derek's coworkers lying about the side scam? No. That part had to be real, because Derek's Medicare scam was the nest egg Molly planned to loot in order to justify sacrificing the insurance payout.

And how much more did the Cellulitists know? Had Crystal or Brianne been the one who called Kenny to tip him off? And was that part of Molly's plan all along?

Ultimately, it all traced back to Molly.

Why did she want Derek dead? And how did she plan to get away with the money? How much had she promised to pay the people she needed to help create her elaborate fiction? Or had they already been paid?

She looked at the bottom of the board:

Who made the money?
Where is the money?

Andrea knew the answers would be found in one place. The place she really didn't want to go: her husband.

"What're you thinking?" asked the man she wished had been her husband.

Whether I should tell you about Jeff being heavily involved in Derek Goode's fraud, she didn't say out loud.

If she told Ramon, he would provide invaluable insight into how she should approach the issue, but the interstate Medicare fraud would force him to get the FBI involved.

If she told him, she would be confirming the mistake she had made years ago when she chose to marry Jeff. Ramon had offered to support her and help raise her child. It was a ridiculously immature, if meaningfully romantic, notion. At the time, they had known each other for less than a year. He had recently been engaged. They felt the same way about each other, but had never acted on those feelings. She wished they had.

Andrea had accepted a long time ago that she had made the wrong choice.

Realizing Ramon had waited long enough for a response that he had become uncomfortable, she said, "I'm stuck on the money."

"Well, sure you would be," he replied casually, "considering you know that Jeff is involved."

She shouldn't have been surprised, but she still was.

Ramon seemed slightly offended by that, but willing to forgive her arrogance because he had always found it incredibly interesting.

"I don't know how deeply he's involved," she said.

"I figured as much," he said. "Because if you did know for sure, then you would have told me, because it would constitute a federal crime."

He started erasing the whiteboard. "I also figured you didn't need to take a picture?"

"No," she replied. The chart was seared in her mind.

"If you do get proof of Jeff's involvement in such a crime, you should feel safe calling me about it," he said.

"There is no one I would rather report my husband's potential second criminal case to than you, Ramon," she said, going for humor but finding only sadness.

"Who made the money? Where is the money? Find those and you will unravel Molly's web."

"Assuming there is a web."

"We both know there is," Ramon said, once again making her feel validated in the simplest, most meaningful way he could.

"Yes, we do," she muttered.

He walked over to her and plucked JoJo from her lap. Slinging the baby onto one arm, he gently held Andrea's hand and tugged until she stood. Off her curious look, he hugged her. His arm felt like corded steel. His back felt like she was running her fingers over wave-worn stone. All in all, hugging him was like holding a cloud made of granite.

She wanted to cry.

She wanted to live.

Ramon's brown eyes locked with hers. He said, "You can tell me anything. No judgments. No fears. Okay?"

She nodded her head, refusing to say anything for fear of her voice cracking.

She wondered if Maria Mercado knew she was the luckiest woman on earth.

RAMON WALKED ANDREA out to the parking lot. He helped her put JoJo into the Odyssey and gave the baby a big wet kiss on top of her head.

They hugged goodbye, awkwardly kissing each other on the cheek.

As she got in the car, he said, "Andie, you can't just focus on proving Molly's guilt. You have to think beyond that, the way she has. Namely, her expectation that she was going to get away with it. So, then, what is Molly's plan for her getaway? And how can you get there before she does?"

34

As time allowed on Thursday and Friday, Kenny, Jimmy, and Shelby dug deeper into Derek Goode's client list. They also obtained the resident lists of Martin Singer's senior living facilities and the accounts Jeff Stern worked with at Merrill. The latter was made more challenging because Jeff was barred from trading, which meant they had to see if the team he worked for had made any excessive profit from the sale of stocks affiliated with industries Martin Singer was involved with.

ON FRIDAY NIGHT, Kenny and Sitara sat on a bench in Madison Square Park eating Shake Shack and reviewing what they had learned.

"Martin Singer provides the names of real people, whose documents Derek duplicated to turn into fake accounts to bill Medicare for false services," he said, laying out the flow of the scheme.

"Then Jeff Stern used those fake identities to make trades, in essence laundering the money from the false medical services through the market and back into a legitimate account," Sitara continued. "And you're saying the money in that new account would be enough to justify Molly killing her husband, who is integral to the continued operation of the account, while at the same time sacrificing an insurance policy worth three million dollars?"

"I don't know," Kenny stammered. "I mean, I don't know the amount they have in the account, but I also don't think Derek was necessary to keep it going. Once the false documents were created, the lawyer's job was pretty much done."

"Well, you still have a lot of questions to answer," she said.

"But you think there are questions that could be asked?"

"Better for you," she said, dragging a fry slowly through the ketchup glob on the opened wrapper she used as a plate. Reluctantly, almost to the fringe of seductively. "I think there are questions that *should* be asked."

AT NINE THE next morning, Kenny parked at the Mercer Oaks golf club off Village Road West. The two-story white structure saw robust Saturday morning activity as golfers took advantage of the crisp fall day. Knowing he needed to work hard to fit in, Kenny had worn a long-sleeve pink polo shirt and khakis. The only way he could have improved on his infiltration of the six-figure-salary club would have been to own plaid pants. Still, he felt ready to assimilate with the natives in the wild.

He wore a brown Princeton cap. Though it was ill-becoming of any self-loathing Rutgers man, Kenny had used the cap to troll for stories among the Princeton elite. He checked himself out in his car window. He smiled. He looked almost Caucasian. He ambled his way inside. He had confirmed Martin and Jeff had booked an eight thirty a.m. tee time on the East Course, which meant by nine they'd he hitting the third hole. He casually strolled through the clubhouse and crossed the greens of the second and third holes.

Trying to differentiate one suburban golfer from another was challenging because they all looked alike to Kenny. He looked for a very tall white guy partnered with a very short white guy.

Withstanding the withering glares at his green-crossing faux pas, he waved sheepishly as he interrupted some of the other white guys. He wondered if their frustrations were over his actions or his epicanthal folds, then decided to split the difference and assume it was both. Kenny's parents had spent their entire lives trying to get into clubs like this one. Not literally the club he walked through, but metaphorically. Growing up, Kenny had watched them, always knowing that they might be allowed to join but they'd never really be *members*.

Each and every one of these guys could legitimately be considered an upstanding citizen of their communities. They did charitable work, donated to causes, went to church or synagogue as often as was necessary, pretended to help with household chores, struggled as much as everyone else to help their kids with schoolwork that was already beyond anything they had learned, and they all tended to have very frame-worthy families.

Just like Molly and Derek Goode.

Kenny caught sight of Jeff and Martin making their way to the fifth hole.

Wondering how to handle the interaction, he approached the two men from behind. He had done a decent job of bracing Wendell Burns on the train, but even then his heart hadn't been in it. He needed to commit, and the only way to do that was to be offensive.

Or go on the offensive; he always mixed those two up.

"I recommend a five iron," he said.

They turned. Jeff's face showed a trace of concern. He still unfairly blamed Kenny for having dragged Andrea into the Sasmal murder. He regained control of himself and snidely replied, "Why do I get the feeling you're not a golfer?"

"At Jenkinson's Boardwalk, I putted the colored ball into the alligator's mouth and watched it come out of his butt," Kenny said. Then looking to Martin, "Hi, Martin. We haven't met. Kenneth Lee."

Martin turned to Jeff. "The reporter?"

"I'm standing right here, Martin," Kenny said. "You can ask me. Yes, the reporter."

"You know who I am?" Martin asked.

"I've just said your name twice, Martin," Kenny responded. "Whoops, three times."

"From the outfit, I assume you conned your way through the clubhouse?" Jeff said.

"Apparently, all assholes are allowed," Kenny said.

"Did Andie send you?" Jeff asked as he continued walking to the next tee. Martin, uncertain, followed.

"She did not," replied Kenny. "And she'd be pissed if she knew I was here."

"She usually doesn't need a reason to be pissed," Jeff replied.

"What's going on?" asked Martin. His neck had started to hurt from swiveling back and forth between the two men.

"I'm glad you asked, Marty," said Kenny. "Jeff, why don't you tell Marty why I'm here."

"He's here to bust our balls and waste our time," said Jeff as he took out his driver.

"It is refreshing to see you without Andie around so all that macho can come out as you hit a little ball with your skinny club while wearing plaid pants and a visor."

Setting his ball on the tee, Jeff calmly looked back at Kenny. "I'll tell you the same thing I told her: nothing to see here."

Kenny noted Martin's obvious discomfort, so he decided to use his wedge. Or should that have been his driver? He said, "Yes, Marty, I know about your little Medicare scam."

Martin tried to hide his panic.

Kenny continued, "I know about the proxy accounts Derek set up. Next step is finding out who Jeff used to make the trades for him."

That forced Jeff to stop halfway through his swing, scraping his club against the grass and knocking the ball three yards off the tee.

"We'll give you a mulligan on that one," Kenny said. "Right, Marty?"

Martin nodded vigorously.

"Are you allowed to talk, Marty?" asked Kenny.

Martin nodded again, but this time he wasn't selling it.

"Between you and Wendell, it's like marriage slowly eats away at your vocal cords."

Jeff retrieved his ball. He was trying to keep his cool.

"Yes, boys, I talked to Wendell," Kenny said. "But don't worry, he didn't have much to say, because he was smart enough to stay clear of all your illegal bullshit."

"Supposing there was any truth to anything you're insinuating," said Jeff. "What incentive would we have to talk?"

"Well, for Marty the Mute, I'm assuming the sheer joy of finding out he *can* talk would be reason enough," said Kenny. "But for you, Jeffrey? I don't know. Maybe the chance to stay out of jail for the *second* time in your life? Maybe the chance to preserve your marriage? Assuming you even care about that."

Jeff, not in the least a violent person, tried to use the elongated excessiveness of his six-foot-five-inch height to intimidate Kenny. "Haven't you fucked up my life enough?"

"If you mean by helping your wife fulfill the calling she should have always followed and getting several criminals and one murderer behind bars, then yes, Jeff, I have fucked up your life enough over the last year," Kenny said. And before Jeff could respond, he continued, "And for the record, at five foot three inches tall, your wife intimidates me in ways you couldn't even come close to matching."

Martin got in between the two men. "Guys, c'mon."

Kenny stepped back. Since he was in much better shape now, he was certain he could outrun them both.

"You've been running a Medicare fraud scheme," he said. "Once I define the details—and guys, I *will* define them—I'll have the motive for why Molly Goode killed her husband. She's who we're after. You can either be the means to help us get her or collateral damage. Choice is yours."

He started to walk away.

"What choice would that be?" asked Jeff.

Kenny ignored him and locked eyes with Martin. "Come clean now and be guilty of fraud. Or come clean after you've been arrested and be guilty of fraud and accessory to murder."

He didn't expect the timid man to break in front of his accomplice, but he did want to plant the seed for it. He handed Martin one of his business cards. "That's for you, Marty. Jeff already knows how to get in touch with me. One way or the other, I'll be hearing from you both."

Kenny tipped his cap to both men and trudged back across the greens with a giant grin on his face.

LESS THAN AN hour later, Jeff Stern surprised Andrea at Sarah's soccer game. Stunned to see her father, Sadie attacked his leg. JoJo crawled over to attack the other one.

"Everything okay?" Andrea asked.

"Marty hurt his wrist, so we called it a morning," Jeff said.

"I have another chair in the car," she said.

He sat down on the grass next to her and kept play-wrestling with the kids. "No worries."

They watched Sarah score two goals in the span of about three minutes.

"She's too good," he muttered.

"Calculating how much money we'll save if she gets a Division 1 scholarship?" she said.

"We should be so lucky," he said.

He seemed pensive. He wasn't great at hiding his emotions. Certainly not nearly as good as he was at lying about them.

"Martin didn't hurt his wrist," she said.

"No," he replied. "No, he didn't. Although the way he swings off the tee, it's a miracle he doesn't dislocate every joint in his body."

He silently watched the game for a few minutes, a soft glow of true pride on his face as his daughter completely dominated all the other children on the field. It couldn't have been genetic, since neither of them was particularly athletic. When she wasn't pregnant, Andrea was at least coordinated and had extremely fast reflexes. She retained many of the physical remnants of her grifter past.

Andrea knew what her husband was thinking: It was a miracle they could make these things. Together. But Jeff didn't know what she was thinking: it was a shame they disrespected that miracle by being such poor parents.

She hadn't set out to be a bad parent, but Andrea thought she was.

"What's wrong?" she asked.

"You lied to me," he said.

That got Sadie's attention. Jeff had to understand she was old enough now to pick up on everything.

"Sadie, let Daddy put you and JoJo on the blanket," Andie said. "Play with your sister a bit."

Andrea strolled away from the row of parents on the sideline. Jeff joined her.

"I did what now?" she said.

"At Bent Spoon, you asked if I was involved in anything with Derek," he said. "I said no."

"And since Derek was exhumed and cocaine was found in his

system, have I said or done anything that would lead you to believe I didn't believe you?" she asked.

He had no answer for that because he didn't know she was bluffing, so instead he said, "Kenny Lee interrupted us at Mercer Oaks this morning."

"He did *what* now?" she asked, and Jeff sensed that volcanic Queens temper waiting to erupt. He was glad it wanted to erupt at Kenny Lee and not him.

"He said he's been digging into Derek's affairs," Jeff said.

She put her hands up. "Last time I talked to Kenny, I said the only way Molly could have killed Derek is if she had constructed a ridiculously complex web of planted witnesses, informants, and evidence. He told me I was crazy and that was that."

"If it's not for you, then why is he bothering?"

"I don't know," she said. "Unless he found something. *Were* you lying to me?"

"No," he lied with convincing emphasis. "Are you lying to me now?"

"No," she lied with convincing calm.

ON Monday morning, Andrea and Sathwika drove to Intercourse, Pennsylvania, to see Molly Goode's brother and sister. Having reached a cruising speed of seventy miles per hour without shaking the Odyssey apart, they sped along Interstate 276.

They approached the Plymouth Meeting exit. After protesting through the entire drive, JoJo and Aditya had fallen asleep ten minutes earlier. Sathwika and Andrea finally had the chance to talk.

"The town they live in is actually called Intercourse?" Sathwika asked.

"Everything we have to talk about and that's what you land on?"

"When the opportunity presents to land on Intercourse, ride it out," she said.

"Oh God, fine, get it out of your system," Andrea laughed. "There was originally a racetrack nearby called Entercourse. Other sources say it was named that because two highways crossed each other, which is why the town was first called Cross Keys. That evolved into Intercourse. Or it's just that *intercourse* was an English term for social interaction."

"All of it a very polite way to avoid calling it Fucking, Pennsylvania," said Sathwika.

"Anyone from New Jersey calls everything on this side of the Delaware River Fucking Pennsylvania," Andrea replied.

"I've never gone this far past Philadelphia," said Sathwika. "Are people with my shade of brown skin allowed out here?"

"I honestly have no clue," said Andrea. "I haven't spent much time in places where your shade of brown is an issue."

"You really are a creature of New York and New Jersey," she said.

"I prefer just New York," said Andrea with a smile. "And just the real city at that, not including Staten Island."

They got off the interstate at King of Prussia and continued southwest on Route 202. Traffic slowed as they passed their first Amish family in a horse and buggy riding the shoulder of the road.

Andrea glanced at Sathwika, who just laughed. "Surreal."

"Watch an old movie called *Witness* with Harrison Ford," Andrea said. "They filmed parts of it here."

"Okay, run through what you're expecting to get out of this," Sathwika said.

"I need to know why there's such a separation between the siblings," Andrea said. "Just based on the interaction I saw, they're hiding something."

They drove through the small town. It was a quaint mixture of Amish tourism, farm equipment stores, flannel, and horse crap. After a few turns, they reached Holly Drive, where the Parkers lived. Technically, the small, neat red-brick ranch with a one-car garage was in the neighboring town of Gordonville. The house had been built in the sixties, and the Parkers had done an excellent job of maintaining it. There were two cars in the driveway, but there was enough room for Andrea to park the minivan behind them.

They woke the babies while transferring their car seats onto their strollers. JoJo cried out of frustration, and Aditya decided to copy her. "I should have taken you up on the offer to have your in-laws watch them," Andrea muttered. "I didn't want to burden them with this Tasmanian Devil." Off Sathwika's confused look, she added, "Looney Tunes. He's a character that's like a manic tornado."

"Samar and Esha would have managed," said Sathwika. "Probably."

They strolled the kids for a few blocks to calm them. The air had a crispness to it and a faint smell of mulch. When the children calmed down, they returned to the Parker home. As they removed the carrier seats and folded up the strollers, Andrea knocked on the white front door. It was quickly opened by Jack Parker.

"Mr. Parker, thank you for seeing us," said Andrea. "I know we only met briefly, so I appreciate you accommodating this intrusion."

"You think Molly had something to do with Derek's death?" Jack said before they'd even entered the house. "Wouldn't surprise us in the least."

Andrea and Sathwika exchanged surprised looks.

Even JoJo and Aditya stared at each other.

Maureen Parker brought in a pot of coffee, and a tea for Sathwika. She served them as they sat around a worn kitchen table. The babies were on a play mat they'd spread in the living room. Andrea knew that JoJo was going to explore. The house was about as childproof as an automobile assembly line, but she accepted they were in a situation where obtaining valuable information might necessitate the sacrifice of her child.

"Maureen," Andrea started, "at the memorial service, you said Molly had 'so much to be private about.'"

"Did I?" Maureen asked. "Maybe I did. It's the first time we'd seen her in several years. The boys had gotten so big."

"But the younger one," said Jack conspiratorially. "Maybe a little light in the loafers?"

"Jack," Maureen chided.

"I don't mean nothing by it," he said.

"Of course you don't," Sathwika said quickly, preventing Andrea from saying something sarcastic.

"Maureen, what does Molly have to hide?" Andrea continued.

The siblings exchanged uncomfortable glances.

"We have no proof," said Jack.

"But we have our suspicions," Maureen said, finishing Jack's sentence.

Two lonely siblings who only had each other and were practically of one mind. Andrea thought about Isaac and wondered what her relationship with her brother would have been like if he'd lived.

Noticing Andrea's mind had wandered, Sathwika jumped in. "Often, when something hasn't been said out loud for a long time, it's better to just say it. Like ripping a Band-Aid off."

"When Molly was in college, she went to Penn State," said Maureen. "We didn't get to go to college, but she was the youngest, so . . ."

"Spoiled brat," muttered Jack.

"During her junior year, our father lost his job at the furniture plant outside of Lancaster," Maureen continued. "He was paying part of Molly's expenses. She had student loans, but she'd lost one of the grants because her grades had slipped, so she wasn't going to be able to pay for her senior year."

Jack decided to get to the point quickly. "She found a way to pay for it."

"Our parents had a car accident the week Molly came home for spring break her junior year," Maureen said. "On their way into town, they drove off the road at the intersection of Route 772 and Centerville Road. They hit a tree. The police couldn't determine a cause for the accident."

"Tree's still there," said Jack. "You can still find little bits of glass in the weeds around it."

"You think Molly tampered with their car?" Andrea asked.

Jack laughed. It was guttural and mean-spirited. "We think Molly tampered with *them*!"

"Drugged them?" Andrea said. The threads were coming together in her mind.

"We have no proof," said Maureen. "But Dad was complaining about not feeling right for a couple days. Dizzy. Really tired."

"Only him?" Sathwika asked.

"She knew what she was doing," said Jack. "Our father never let our mother drive. Lord knows she wanted to, since he drove like he was twenty minutes late to wherever he was going."

Andrea had to get up to retrieve JoJo, who had crawl-walked her way into the kitchen area. Aditya remained hopelessly fascinated by the flat-white ceiling paint above him. Andrea wondered when she was going to get the nerve to have a very frank discussion with her friend about properly evaluating her son's developmental issues.

Bouncing JoJo in her arms, she said, "You think Molly gave your father a drug that impaired him?"

"That would presume she could anticipate that he would be driving," Sathwika said.

"Wednesday morning was when Dad deposited his unemployment check and Mom went food shopping," Maureen said.

"Molly could have predicted what any of us were going to do pretty much down to any goddamned minute of any given day," Jack said.

"But how did she know what drugs to use?" asked Sathwika.

Jack growl-laughed again. "Ask her roommate."

"The one who was a pharmacy major," said Maureen.

Sathwika looked to her friend for a response, but Andrea was somewhere else.

JoJo was rolling on the floor of the Parker home, but Andrea was flashing back to her daughter rolling on the bed in Derek and Molly's master bedroom.

Andrea was standing in Molly's master bathroom, looking inside her medicine cabinet. The bottle of ceftriaxone was in her hand. There were pills still in it. How many pills?

Take one pill per day. Would Molly need a refill soon?

The date on the prescription: September 6.

The name of the pharmacy: CVS. The location was a blur.

The name of the pharmacist? She frowned in frustration. It was also too blurry.

She snapped out of her panoramic immersion.

"Do you remember her roommate's name?" asked Andrea.

"Something Oriental," said Maureen. "We never met her."

"She didn't come to your parents' funeral?" asked Sathwika, knowing that's the kind of thing she would have expected of herself as a roommate.

Jack shook his head. "It was all Molly could do to make it through the ceremony before she took off back to school. Once she got her money from their life insurance, we didn't see her again until the following holidays."

"She stayed up at school that summer?"

"She had a paid internship in the math department, I remember," said Maureen.

"She got her own off-campus apartment. Finished school," said Jack. "Killing our parents worked out just fine for her."

"And her roommate?" asked Andrea.

"Wasn't her roommate anymore," said Maureen.

ANDREA AND SATHWIKA didn't say much after leaving the Parker house. They waited until they'd gotten out of Intercourse and were cruising with some speed to lull the babies to sleep.

"So, Molly got her roommate to help drug her father and then, fifteen years later, she goes to her again for help to treat an STD?" said Sathwika, working the story through in her head. "But they weren't even roommates after their junior year? Were they even close enough friends for that kind of an ask?"

Andrea said, "She didn't ask."

"Blackmail." Sathwika nodded.

"And Molly didn't go to her just for help in treating the STD," said Andrea. "She went to her for whatever drug she used to kill Derek."

"Can a pharmacist dispense cocaine?"

"Under really strict controls," said Andrea. "They amended the New Jersey Controlled Dangerous Substances Law in 2019."

"I was hoping to get a prescription," Sathwika said.

"You don't?"

"Now? No. But in college?" she said, a mischievous glint in her large brown eyes. "I did everything."

"Except kill your parents," Andrea muttered.

36

As Maureen Parker served coffee and tea to Andrea and Sathwika in Pennsylvania, Kenny, Jimmy, and Shelby took advantage of a morning free from Sitara's bemused glares and made cold calls to the residents of Martin Singer's assisted living facilities.

On the whiteboard in the conference room, they had broken down Derek Goode's Medicare fraud scheme:

Martin Singer provides names/ID info of residents at his facilities to: _____

Derek Goode creates false records/duplicate ID.

Martin pays off doctors/therapists and/or creates false invoices $ for things that were never done.

Martin funnels $ paid out by Medicare/insurance companies to: _____

Jeff Stern uses proxy accounts to wash $

With that to guide them, the calls to the elderly residents quickly became cringe-inducing.

"Investments. Yes. Investments. INVESTMENTS!"

"You don't know? I should talk to your husband? Okay, ma'am, may I speak with him? He's dead? My condolences, ma'am. Oh. It was fourteen years ago?"

"Finances. Your finances. Yes, I know where France is, that's not what I'm asking."

By early afternoon, they had covered more than 70 percent of the residents at four facilities and they'd gotten absolute bubkes for their aggravation. They sat in the conference room eating a late lunch of gyro and falafel that Kenny had Grubhubbed.

"Not a single one of those sweet, annoying people knew anything about any of this," said Jimmy.

"Not even the ones who were able to actually talk to us about their portfolios," Kenny said.

"At least it looks like Goode and his crew weren't swindling the old folks," said Shelby. "Just using their names and personal information."

"Or are they setting them up to get caught holding the bag if they have to make a quick getaway?" said Jimmy.

"I don't think so," said Kenny. "These guys aren't the quick-getaway types. Families, kids in school, mortgages. No, this was a long con."

"That isn't hurting anyone?" asked Jimmy.

"It's hurting the taxpayers, which I presume you're one?" Shelby said. "If you even know enough to file taxes."

"I know enough to file taxes," Jimmy said.

"When's the last time you filed them?" Shelby asked.

"I know enough to know they're *supposed* to be filed," Jimmy said.

"We have to get the SEC records for any exchanges in the names of these residents," Kenny said. "That's almost impossible."

Shelby put down her falafel gyro and picked up her phone. She dialed as she chewed. "Jeremy? Shelby. Drinks tonight? Yeah, maybe. Okay, see you later."

She ended her call and looked at the confused Jimmy and Kenny. "That was Jeremy."

"Yes, it was," said Jimmy.

"He's a former client," she said. "He's also an adviser to the board of the New York Stock Exchange."

"And he'll just let you know what trades Jeff's group has been making in the names of the senior residents?" Kenny asked.

"I caught Jeremy's wife cheating on him," she said. "Since she broke her prenup, I saved him about eighty million dollars. So . . . yes, he will."

WHILE SHELBY WENT out for drinks with Jeremy, Kenny and Jimmy worked through Sitara's return and well into the night. By the time Shelby got back to the office it was almost ten o'clock. She was half-drunk, which for the average person would have been fully drunk three times over.

She tossed a flash drive onto the conference room table.

"Firemen and Wall Street guys are the only people in this city who can almost keep up with me," she replied.

Kenny smiled, but less at her than at the giddy anticipation of opening the drive on his laptop.

"Every investment currently in play for every resident of Singer's facilities," Shelby said. "And every trade conducted by the team Jeff Stern is on at Merrill for the last year."

"How many transactions is that?" asked Sitara.

"Few thousand," said Shelby. "Give or take."

"Give or take what?" asked Jimmy.

"A few thousand," said Shelby.

Jimmy and Sitara both rose from the table at the same time and said good night. They left the conference room and started packing their things.

Kenny and Shelby watched them the entire time without saying anything, waiting for them to stop the gag and come back to the conference room.

In nearly perfect synchronous timing, they each flipped their backpacks over their shoulders, waved back to the conference room, and left.

"They're not coming back, are they?" Kenny finally said.

"Nope," said Shelby.

"Are you leaving, too?"

She thought long and hard about it. The thinking hurt her brain.

Shelby plopped down heavily into a chair and said, "Fuck it, let's do this."

Several folders opened on Kenny's laptop screen. Each folder contained hundreds of reports.

They worked for the next eight hours organizing any information that linked Jeff Stern's group trades to Martin Singer's resident list in a meticulous, organized manner.

By hour four, both had started to suspect the same thing, but didn't voice it out loud. By hour six Kenny voiced it. By hour eight, with the sun starting to rise, Shelby agreed with him.

"There's nothing here," she said.

"No, there's everything here," he said, closing his laptop. Without removing the drive, he carried it to his desk and tucked it into his backpack.

"Where are you going?" Shelby asked.

"To see a friend."

"Do you realize it's not even seven in the morning?"

"He'll be in the office by the time I get there," said Kenny. Picking up his phone, he dialed. "Andie? I know it's early. I'm still in the city.

THE SELF-MADE WIDOW 267

I've been working all night. No, it's not to talk about me bracing Jeff at the golf course. I can't believe you didn't call me about that already. No, I can't hear about your drive to Pennsyltucky. I'm just calling to warn you that I'm on my way to see Jeff to publicly embarrass him in the middle of his office."

There was silence on the phone for several seconds.

From the conference room, an exhausted Shelby watched with bemused anticipation.

"Andie, are you there?"

All Andrea said was, "What do you have?"

"It's what I don't have that matters," he said.

"What don't you have?" she asked.

"Who is trading for him," he said. "Someone is using the residents as proxies for the account, but we can't find the account because it's not being run through Jeff's group at Merrill."

"You're sure about all of this?" she asked.

"I'm sure about most of it," he said sheepishly.

"You're threatening his job based on 'most'?"

"You would, if you were me," he said.

Silence again for several seconds.

She hung up.

He understood why Andrea didn't want to agree with him, implying approval, or disagree, implying she thought he was wrong. She knew he wasn't wrong, and saying nothing gave her plausible deniability if Jeff confronted her about it later. Probably let her internalize her anger rather than throw it on Kenny, too.

He made another call with his phone on speaker.

"Albert?" he said to his groggy agent, who'd been woken up. "Yes, I know what time it is. Why does everyone keep asking me if I know what time it is? I need you to set a meeting up for me, ASAP. Forwarding you the number. Yeah, the Merrill Lynch Wealth Management offices at 75 Rock. The Berkson-Sheuh Group. Yes, a Jew and a

Chinaman, thank you for that. Yes, I know we're both Asian so that doesn't make it offensive. Yes, I can see they also have a Stern Group among their advisers, and yes, it's ironic that we know a Jeff Stern. It's even more ironic after I tell you that Jeff works there, too, but he's not in the Stern Group, he's in the Berkson-Sheuh Group."

The lightbulb must have gone on over Albert's head as he let out a lingering, "Oh."

"I need an appointment with either Berkson or Sheuh," Kenny continued. "Tell them I'm looking for financial advice on a story I'm working on. Yes, all of that is true. Am I *looking* to cause trouble? No, not looking. But I can't guarantee trouble won't be caused. Fine. Thank you."

BY SEVEN FIFTEEN, without so much as a coffee to fuel him since four a.m., Kenny emerged from the M train station at 75 Rockefeller Plaza. He texted Albert: What do you have?

> ALBERT: 7:15 a.m. w/ Fred Berkson. He'll be mad to find out you're using him.
>
> KENNY: How do you know I'm using him?
>
> ALBERT: Why does a scorpion sting?

Kenny put his phone back into his sports coat pocket, not sure if he should be proud or offended. He muttered, "It's in his nature."

What did that say about him? Many would say it was a compliment. That he was willing to do what was necessary to do what was right; to do his job no matter what it cost him. Or cost others. Luckily for his skills at rationalizing, he could fairly claim that in his career, it had cost him as much as if not more than others.

The elevator doors opened into the main offices. Kenny had convinced himself he was ruining his friend's life because the job had to get done. Justice. Avenging the dead. And all that crap.

He was led toward Fred Berkson's office by the receptionist. Kenny looked across the cubicle farm in search of Jeff Stern. The walls weren't high enough to contain Jeff's giraffe-like height, so Kenny spotted his head peeking over his cubicle cage. As if what he had been reduced to wasn't enough of a daily embarrassment for Jeff, that had to be rubbing salt into the wound.

Kenny stopped long enough for the receptionist to realize he was no longer trailing her.

"Mr. Lee?" she said. "Mr. Berkson's office is this way."

"Is that Jeff Stern?" he said loudly.

She looked toward Jeff's exposed forehead and hair. "You know Jeff?" she asked. He noted she didn't call him Mr. Stern, which she reserved for the important people.

"Jeff?" Kenny called out with enough volume to get several people with their faces glued to their overnight reports to look up. He kicked it up a few notches, shouting, "JEFF STERN!"

Kenny could see Jeff's forehead tilt slightly, like a confused dog's. He stood up and saw Kenny. Everyone could see Jeff standing and looking at him. And since everyone was watching, it was time for Kenny to be Kenny.

"Jeff Stern! Holy shit! I thought that was your forehead!"

For justice and the dead.

Then he realized he'd forgotten to video the encounter.

"One second," he mumbled, a little embarrassed as he set down his backpack and pulled out his selfie stick. "I should've been prepared. Scout's motto. I wasn't even a Boy Scout."

He assembled the selfie stick and lifted it to record the reactions around the office. It was hard for Kenny to read Jeff's expression. Maybe it was the distance between them, or maybe it was that one of

Jeff's eyes looked panicked while the other looked homicidal. It gave him a Bill the Cat quality from the old *Bloom County* strip.

"What an absolute coincidence that I made an appointment with Fred to discuss how unlicensed traders might use licensed proxies to run illicit accounts," Kenny said. "It's for an investigation I'm conducting on Medicare fraud."

It was impossible for anyone not to have heard him. He looked around to ensure he was the center of attention and continued, "Hi, everybody. Sorry for interrupting your morning. I'm not, really. My name is Kenny Lee. I'm a reporter. You might have read the book *Suburban Secrets*? Gonna be a documentary series on Netflix soon. You're on camera right now for a new documentary I'm working on, currently called TBD, which I admit needs a new name. If you don't want to be seen on camera, just put a piece of black construction paper in front of your faces to save me the expense in postproduction, thanks. If you normally have a blurry face, you should be fine. This is an important scene for the documentary, because it's where one of our bad guys is openly called to task about their role in the evil suburban wife's murderous Machiavellian scheme."

He turned to face Jeff.

Everyone else turned to face Jeff, except a woman sitting outside Fred Berkson's office, who turned to pick up her phone. Probably calling security. Kenny had to cut to the chase.

"I only really have one question for Jeff Stern," Kenny called out. "Since you were smart enough to keep your coworkers out of your illicit Medicare fraud accounts, I want to know who you're working with."

"Son of a bitch," Jeff snarled as he marched down the aisle toward him. Kenny never considered Jeff to be the violent type, but the closer he got, the more Kenny thought he was about to get hit. The choice was to protect himself or to keep the camera locked on Jeff's face.

Kenny decided to take one for the team.

He heard someone shout, "Jeff, don't!"

And then Kenny was punched in the face hard enough to knock him into a cubicle wall and down to the carpet. He tried to hold on to the stick, but it caught under his body as he fell, snapping at the joint and causing his phone to bounce on the floor.

"Fucking asshole!" Jeff shouted as he lifted his elongated leg and spastically stepped on the phone. Kenny was thrilled that it had fallen faceup, which meant Jeff's incoming foot would be caught in glorious splendor on video.

Two of Jeff's coworkers dragged him away.

Kenny gathered himself. He realized he had blood on his lip, and his eye felt gummy. To his surprise, the phone screen hadn't cracked. And his face didn't really hurt much. Jeff was a schlub, so the punch had lacked leverage.

A woman bent over Kenny to help him up. "Are you okay?"

Barely registering that she was really attractive, Kenny turned the camera on himself and said, "How do I look? I haven't been hit since college."

"You're bleeding," she said.

"Cool, right?" he said as he raised the broken selfie stick over his head toward Jeff as his frat-boy coworkers continued to hold on to him. "I understand I just disrupted your workplace and I apologize. Most of you probably haven't even had your second cup of coffee yet, but your coworker, Jeff Stern, is involved in Medicare fraud, and if any of you have information about this, or more importantly, who Jeff might be using as his proxy, you can DM me on Twitter @PulitzerKenLee."

Security arrived. Kenny appreciated that they didn't manhandle him while escorting him out, but he made sure to turn the phone on them so they knew they were on camera.

He walked between them, turning to say, "That's @PulitzerKen-Lee. Like the prize. It's a bit pretentious, but it's also true, so you know I'm legit."

As he reached the lobby to the elevators, he heard Fred Berkson gruffly call out, "Stern! In my office now!"

Kenny smiled.

For justice and to avenge the dead.

And for getting it all on camera, too.

AS KENNY EMERGED from the Fourteenth Street M-line station, his phone pinged. He had a DM notification on Twitter. He opened up the message: Gabriel Pettigrew.

It had come from @LegalBeagle with a picture of a dog on it. Kenny doubted the dog had its own account, but it was Twitter, so he couldn't completely rule it out, either. Except he'd seen a picture of that dog on the desk of the woman who had helped him up.

"Gotcha," he muttered.

Kenny got coffee for everyone. Only Sitara was at the office.

"You're early," she said.

"You have no idea," he replied, dropping his bag on his chair.

"And you're wearing the same clothes you wore yesterday," she said. "You didn't . . . ?"

He handed Sitara his phone.

"That's the name of the person Jeff Stern is using to make his proxy trades," he said.

"You stayed up all night to figure this out?" she asked, surprised and more than a little impressed.

"Shelby and I did," he said. "Only to realize we had nothing. Whatever was being done was outside of the Merrill group Jeff works with."

"You went over there and caused a scene?"

"I went over there and caused a scene."

"And someone from the office sent you an anonymous message?"

"And someone from the office sent me an anonymous message," he repeated. "Except not so anonymous, since I know who it was. A bit of a Good Samaritan with a body on her that would make even the Bad Samaritans blush."

"Forgive me if I don't know the Bible that well," she said.

"I'm not trying to make you jealous, I'm just trying to subtly point out that when you do decide to dump me, I'll have a very voluptuous option available to me in the financial sector."

"That was subtle?" Sitara said while typing. "Got him. Gabriel Pettigrew. Worked for Merrill for four years."

"He left six months after Jeff started," Kenny said, looking over her shoulder. "Just enough time to gain the measure of a like-minded stock cheat."

"This is moving fast," said Sitara. "What now?"

"Now, I sit in my chair, I drink my coffee, and I pray the caffeine keeps me awake," he said, sitting down.

He was asleep within five minutes.

Sitara smiled.

He started snoring within ten.

Sitara thought how much happier she was likely to be if she remained single.

37

WHILE Kenny snored away in the office, Sitara sat in the conference room with the door closed and called Andrea. She felt awkward being the one to tell Andrea what they had uncovered, but it was important for her to know before she heard a skewed version of the story from her husband.

"I'm sorry to be the one to break this news," Sitara said. "I'm sorry there's even news to break."

"I appreciate it," Andrea said. "I prefer the truth, even when I don't like it. Was Kenny too scared to call me?"

"He's too asleep right now."

"Sometimes, he does surprise you," Andrea said softly.

"It is worth it?" Sitara asked, surprising herself.

"Excuse me?"

"Is he worth it?" she asked. "Are the pleasant surprises and his selfish passion worth the effort to penetrate the shields he puts up? Or the way he uses that ridiculous arrogance to cover up his massive insecurity?"

"Wow." Andrea whistled. "Um. Sitara, I don't mean to dodge the question, but, shit, look at me. Look at my husband. Look at the choices

I've made. Who the fuck am I to pass judgment on anyone's relationship?"

"Experience matters a lot to me," Sitara said. "And you're someone who is on the brink of making better choices."

After an uncomfortably long pause that likely answered the question for Sitara, Andrea said, "I don't know. I really don't. The potential is there, but Kenny comes from a damaged family, Sitara. Manipulation, degradation, a lack of empathy. They were terrified of showing their emotions. Kenny was more like his dad, but he thought he had to be like his mom to get by. He was always a really sweet kid, but then . . ."

"You hurt him?" asked Sitara.

"I guess I did," Andrea admitted.

"I know the story, Andrea, and I know absolutely none of it was your fault," she said. "It was just a prepubescent dick twiddle."

"*Eew.*"

Sitara laughed. "Oh, ugh, I'm sorry. That sounded awful. I meant pubescent fantasy."

The moment ended for both of them. Andrea reluctantly came back to reality. She asked, "What's next for this Gabriel Pettigrew connection?"

"I'm the only one here and I'm too close to locking a presentation cut of *Suburban Secrets* for my bosses to do anything today," Sitara said. "But if Shelby or Jimmy come back, I'll get them on it. Well, Shelby anyway."

They said their goodbyes. Andrea had three hours before she was going to meet Crystal for lunch. She picked up JoJo with one hand and called Sathwika with the other.

Her friend was on a stakeout.

Sathwika answered as Andrea made her way to the basement. "Hey, what's the update?" Realizing she had no free hands to turn on the lights, she bobbed JoJo up and down until the baby's beefy feet swiped the light switch.

Sathwika was parked outside Molly's house. Aditya was asleep in the backseat. "She went to YogaSoul at eight. Class is until nine. I'll check in after."

Andrea hung up, wondering why Jeff hadn't called her to complain about Kenny's office assault. He had to know the noose was tightening. She hated to think in those terms, but it was the truth. She expected he would try something. Or would he call someone who might. Or Molly?

Andrea set JoJo down on the carpeted floor.

"Go to town," she muttered.

She accessed Jeff's computer using the new password he had updated two weeks earlier thinking she hadn't known. She searched for Pettigrew's name or trading activity. After nearly an hour, Andrea found nothing. Sathwika texted that Molly was home. Andrea asked her if she could wait to see if Molly made another move.

Sathwika texted back: I have 3 bottles of formula, 3 diapers, and a Kit Kat bar. I'm good for the long haul.

Andrea smiled. She opened Jeff's desk drawer and found four USB drives. Over the next thirty minutes, she went through all of them, looking for possible aliases or anagrams, wasting her time, and getting mad at herself for thinking Jeff would be clever enough for aliases and anagrams.

"Then again," she said to JoJo, "Daddy was smart enough to make Mommy look like an idiot twice now."

JoJo gurgled and it distinctly sounded like she said, "Dada."

It figured that would be the baby's first word. She watched JoJo crawl around.

"Fuck you," Andrea muttered. "Let's not speak of this to anyone."

JoJo clearly replied, "Dada."

Distracting Andrea from her desire to punt the baby, Sathwika texted again: Molly left house I'm in hot pursuit.

"Everyone is having an interesting morning except me," she said to JoJo.

JoJo said, "Dada."

■ ■ ■

ON HER WAY to lunch at school, Ruth received a text from Unknown Name/Unknown Number: Tell your mother to stop or Henry will find out what you're doing.

Her natural instinct was to look around to see if it had come from anyone around her. Of course, it hadn't. Who could know she had been prying into Henry's life? Then she realized it instantly: Molly had spyware on Henry's phone. She had either seen their text exchanges or, more likely if Henry had deleted his texts before his mother had a chance to pry, Molly probably had an app like Decipher, WebWatcher, or mSpy to monitor his activity.

She entered the cafeteria and spotted Henry sitting with his friends. As she headed toward him, building a full head of steam, she got another text: Don't talk to Henry about this. Just tell your mother to stop. If you tell Henry, you're going to get hurt.

She stopped at a nearly empty table. Amy Xu sat by herself on the corner.

"Fuckity fuck," Ruth muttered.

"What is it?" asked Amy.

Ruth waited several seconds, looking around the cafeteria, scanning the faces of the clueless students. She sat down across from Amy.

"I don't know," she said, but even Amy, whose only friends were numbers, not people, could tell that Ruth was scared.

WANTING TO GET the bad taste of their last lunch out of the way, Andrea arranged to pick up salads at City Streets Bar and Grill and meet Crystal at Sayen House and Gardens in neighboring Hamilton Township. The thirty-acre parcel of land had been purchased by Frederick Sayen, whose family had a rubber mill in Hamilton. He'd been a gardener and world traveler, so he surrounded his home with plants and flowers he'd collected during his excursions. Andrea had only been there once before. That was a few years ago, on the day she'd learned she was pregnant with Sadie.

Sarcastically, Andrea thought that the serenity of the gardens may have been the only thing that had prevented her from killing herself that day, or, to be accurate to her mood at the time, from killing Jeff.

She parked at the narrow lot off Hughes Drive and strolled JoJo along the sidewalk until she'd reached the diagonal walking path at the street corner. It led to the white gazebo where she said she'd meet Crystal.

She received a text from Sathwika: **Molly getting off the parkway.**

Where was Molly going that required taking the Garden State Parkway?

Crystal was waiting for her inside the gazebo. She waved enthusiastically when she saw JoJo. Realizing she was supposed to still be angry at Andrea, she stopped. Upon seeing Crystal, JoJo enthusiastically bounced in her stroller seat and Crystal's Herculean self-control quickly melted. She clapped, smiling broadly, and cooed to the baby.

Crystal took JoJo out of the stroller. Andrea arranged their salads on the gazebo bench. "Thanks for meeting me," she said. "I know our last lunch was a little rough."

"I'm sorry, too," Crystal said, maybe not having picked up that Andrea hadn't actually apologized for anything. "I'm glad that horrible autopsy put all of this behind us."

"That's the thing, Crystal," Andrea said through a bite of salad. "It hasn't."

"You're still mad at us?" asked Crystal.

"No, you don't understand," Andrea replied. "The autopsy result was part of Molly's plan."

Crystal looked at her friend as if she were a pimple about to pop, equal parts fascination and disgust. Was she really so lost that she had to desperately create this fantasy life to keep herself happy? And what kind of life was that, suspecting your friends of murder?

"You were smart to not get involved in anything Derek was proposing," Andrea said. "Jeff and Martin weren't so smart."

"Wendell was suspicious," Crystal said, quickly lured by the bait Andrea had dropped.

Andrea broke down everything she suspected that Molly had done not only in preparation for killing Derek, but in anticipation that Andrea and Kenny would be investigating her.

During the discussion, Andrea received another text from Sathwika: Molly parked on Maplewood Avenue near train station.

Maplewood.

"What was that?" asked Crystal, but Andrea didn't hear her.

She was somewhere else.

She stood in Molly Goode's master bathroom, the bottle of ceftriaxone in her hand. Previously, when she had gone back to that moment, the label had been blurred beyond recognition. The letters, gauzy in her memory, now gained definition. Like an optometrist flipping the lens of a phoropter in search of clarity, Andrea could see the letters taking form.

❤ CVS pharmacy
157 Maplewood Ave.
Maplewood NJ

One pill a day. There had been less than a month's worth of pills in the container. There was one refill available. Andrea tried to remember the RPh line on the label indicating the registered pharmacist's name. It started with a J, but it was still too blurry in her mind.

She snapped out of her reverie and asked, "Did Molly ever talk to you about her days in college?"

Taken aback by the abrupt non sequitur, but always happy to talk, Crystal said, "I know she went to Penn State. She had to be an excellent student to keep her grants since money was so hard to come by for her family. She got her first job in Philly after school. Not much else."

"She never told you that her parents died when she was in school?"

"Oh, yes, of course, she did, I'm sorry," said Crystal.

"Did Molly ever talk about her roommates in college?"

"She mentioned living alone in an apartment her senior year."

There was the trap Andrea wanted.

"If money was so hard to come by for her family, how could she afford to live off campus her senior year, much less in her own apartment without roommates?" asked Andrea.

"Oh, I don't know," said Crystal.

She was finishing her salad as Andrea said, "Want to walk JoJo around the garden?"

"Sure," Crystal said, beaming.

They each held one of JoJo's hands. The baby staggered like a drunk between them as they walked the narrow gravel paths of the lush garden. Andrea pushed the stroller with her right hand and let the distraction JoJo posed lull Crystal into a false sense of relaxation.

"Did you know during her junior year, Molly lost her scholarship grants because her grades had dipped?" Andrea said.

"She never mentioned that."

"And her dad had lost his job so they weren't going to be able to afford the tuition, room, and board for her senior year," Andrea said.

Crystal shook her head.

They walked several yards farther before the question dawned on Crystal. "How did Molly afford her senior year, then?"

"She killed her parents," Andrea blurted out.

Crystal was so startled that she almost yanked JoJo off the ground in response.

"What?"

"It was a car accident," Andrea said. "The week Molly was home for spring break. The culmination of a running argument about their money problems."

"That's a coincidence," said Crystal.

"The settlement Molly got from the life insurance covered her senior year and the cost of an apartment," said Andrea. "So, that's a very fortunate coincidence for her."

"I mean, it sounds suspicious, but—"

"Did you know that Molly's roommate her sophomore and junior year was a pharmacy major?" Andrea interrupted.

That also caught Crystal off guard. "No, I didn't. . . ."

"And that her roommate didn't go to the parents' funeral?"

"Oh, but they were kids then. . . ."

"And they didn't room together Molly's senior year?"

Crystal had no response.

Andrea received a text.

> **SATHWIKA:** Molly went into a CVS. Got something from the pharmacist.
>
> **SATHWIKA:** They're talking now.
>
> **SATHWIKA:** Tense!

Andrea texted back: Is the pharmacist Asian?

> **SATHWIKA:** Yes.
>
> **ANDREA:** Does her name start with a J?

"I'm sorry," she said to Crystal. "Distracted."

"Did her brother and sister tell you this?" asked Crystal.

"Before I even asked, Crys," Andrea replied. "I met with them just to get some background on Molly's childhood, what her family life was like, stuff like that."

They strolled past a row of azaleas that were showing their subdued colors for the fall. Andrea let her friend process everything, then said, "It's time to tell me what you know."

Crystal finally talked.

She talked about Wendell's doubts regarding the Goodes' finances. He'd heard through mutual friends at work that Derek's position at his law firm had seriously deteriorated over the past year and he'd never make partner.

Crystal said that Molly had drunk too much at lunch last summer and admitted she wore long sleeves to cover up bruises Derek had left on her. Crystal had asked if he'd been hitting her and all Molly had said was, "He can get rough."

She related that Molly had two cell phones because Derek was obsessive about tracking hers through his GeoLocator. One time, Molly had accidentally called Crystal from the burner phone, which was the only reason she'd admitted it.

Andrea thought some of that to be outright lies on Molly's part to sow doubt about Derek. Henry had told Ruth that Molly was the one obsessed with knowing everyone's locations, and that fit her profile far more than it did Derek's. If he'd had a burner phone, it was likely to talk to any women he was having affairs with, or to speak with clients off the record.

"Hold on one second," she said to Crystal.

Andrea texted Ruth.

> **ANDREA:** Ask Henry if he can geolocate his mom.
>
> **RUTH:** were in class
>
> **ANDREA:** Investigators have to risk detention!
>
> **RUTH:** I have to tell you something
>
> **ANDREA:** sorry, not right now. Time crunch. Need to know where Molly is ASAP!

Crystal pointed out the humongous koi in the pond to JoJo, whose entire body shook in excitement when she saw the fish. Andrea hated to like Crystal, and liked to hate her, but of all the Cellulitists, Crystal was the only one who was at least true to herself. Unfortunately, that usually meant she was a pain in the ass, but there was sincerity and a relentless positivity even to that.

Andrea's text notification hummed.

> **RUTH:** henry said shes home
>
> **ANDREA:** Okay, thanks. What did you want to ask?
>
> **RUTH:** Nothing. TTYL

Andrea quickly scrolled her favorites list and forwarded Molly's number to Sathwika.

> **ANDREA:** If you are still in CVS, call this number
>
> **SATHWIKA:** what if she answers?
>
> **ANDREA:** I don't think she will, but just hang up.

Thirty excruciating seconds later, Sathwika texted: No ring.

Molly used a burner phone to travel to see the pharmacist because she didn't want Derek to know where she'd been going.

Then another text from Sathwika: BTW, pharm name is Joyce Li.

That opened up a world of other possibilities. She texted Kenny: Can Shelby get EZpass info on Derek and Molly?

She put her phone away in the diaper bag, her adrenaline flowing. This wasn't too much happening too quickly, this was just all the pieces falling into place at once. Molly's college roommate had given her the drugs she had used to impair her parents and whatever she had used to push Derek's heart toward failure. Had the pharmacist given her the cocaine or had Molly known Derek was regularly using and taken advantage of that?

Andrea leaned toward the latter on that one.

She sauntered over to the pond and joined Crystal and JoJo. The baby was still enraptured by the koi swimming near the muddy lip of the water looking for food.

"Sorry about that," she said. "Look at her face lighting up."

"Josephine is precious," said Crystal. "I'm sorry, I meant JoJo."

It seemed visibly painful for Crystal to use the nickname. "It's okay," said Andrea. "I'm sorry I was such an ass about it. I think it's become a me-versus-Jeff thing."

Crystal nodded in understanding. "I guess a lot becomes a wife-versus-husband thing."

"Not for you and Wendell," Andrea said quickly, meaning it as more than a prompt to keep Crystal talking.

"No, I guess not," she said. "I mean, we argue, Andie, plenty. I don't know if you've heard this, but I can be a bit overbearing."

She smiled so that Andrea would know she was in on the joke. Crystal was so insecure about herself that self-deprecation was rarely on her playlist.

"Yeah, Jeff and I haven't been good in . . ." Andrea hesitated, wanting to say "forever," but instead, she simply said, "In a while."

"I know," Crystal said. "And I don't think Molly and Derek were either."

"But you were willing to defend her until today?"

"There's a difference between having problems in your marriage and killing your husband," she said. It was ridiculous she even had to say it.

"But now you think it's possible?" Andrea asked.

"I do," Crystal replied.

"Good, because the way today has been going, by dinnertime, we're going to upgrade that from possible to probable," Andrea said.

. . .

ON THE WAY home, Andrea called Sathwika for an update, but there was no answer. She sent a voice text. No response. By the time she scraped the undercarriage of the Odyssey on her driveway apron, JoJo had fallen asleep and Andrea had grown worried.

Had Molly recognized Sathwika in the CVS? This would have been the third time Molly would have had a "casual" encounter with her friend. Between the path at the Plainsboro Preserve, lunch at Mediterra, and now the CVS—in Maplewood, of all places—not even Molly could be so stupid as to think it coincidence, or so arrogant as to think all brown people looked alike, could she? The latter, definitely, Andrea thought.

She gingerly removed JoJo from her car seat without waking her and carried her inside. She laid the baby down in the playpen and called Sathwika's in-laws. They had not heard from her since that morning.

It simply wasn't in Molly's profile to hurt Sathwika. She might have assaulted her verbally, but not physically. But for a second, Andrea doubted herself. What if she had been wrong about Molly all along? Not whether she could kill her husband, but whether she could kill anyone who proved an impediment to getting what she wanted? If she had killed her own parents, Andrea's initial estimations of her friend had already proven too lenient. And what if that leniency had endangered Sathwika?

It wasn't until after Andrea had picked up Sadie from preschool that Sathwika finally called.

"Sorry, my phone died and I forgot to bring my cord in the car," she said.

"Yeah, but you remembered to bring a Kit Kat bar?" Andrea said with great relief.

"Priorities," Sathwika replied. "By the way, your six texts and five voice mails were very sweet. And it's nice to see the more concerned you get, the filthier your mouth gets."

"Fuck you," Andrea said. "Did anything else happen?"

"Molly and Joyce argued off to the side of the pharmacy counter for almost five minutes," said Sathwika. "It got to the point where two customers waiting had to interrupt them so they could be attended."

"Please tell me you heard some of what they were arguing about?" asked Andrea.

"No," Sathwika said, though Andrea could practically picture her friend's beaming smile through the phone. "I could hear everything they were arguing about."

WHILE Andrea was inexorably tugging Crystal Burns to her side of the "friends with murder benefits" argument, Ruth Stern sat at a lunch table in a daze, not realizing she had failed to answer multiple requests about her well-being from Amy Xu.

Ruth tried not to panic. What would her mother do? She thought the problem through and it helped tamp down her fear.

What was Molly worried about Henry telling her?

She could walk right up to him right now and ask him. In front of everyone if she wanted to make a scene, or later, in private. But either way, Ruth didn't think it would gain her anything. Henry was caught in the middle. Asking him about it would only put him in an even more compromising position. His father was dead. His mother may have killed him. His father had been the family peacemaker and now Henry only had the source of his family's tension—his mother—filling the totality of that void.

How would making Henry further fear or hate his mother help in any way?

It wouldn't, Ruth thought.

"Ruth?" Amy asked, this time literally waving her hand in front of her friend's face.

"I'm sorry," stammered Ruth. "I just got a text that scared me a little. I was trying to figure out who it came from."

"What do you mean, scary?" asked Amy, who rarely received texts from anyone of any kind.

"Kind of threatening me," said Ruth, knowing she couldn't reveal too much, but needing some kind of support. "But it's probably nothing. Just one of the boys pulling a gag on me."

"Yeah, that's probably it," Amy agreed. "I wish the boys would pull a gag on me."

"No, you don't," Ruth muttered, once again getting lost in a wave of panic. The only way to know if this was a threat from Molly would be for her mother to figure it out, but she wasn't sure she wanted to tell her.

She looked at Henry, who sat several tables away as something Akush Modhi said made him laugh. She hadn't seen him laugh in days. He was so cute; his smile was contagious. But it was fleeting, as guilt quickly shadowed his face.

She knew that eventually, inevitably, her mother's suspicions about Molly Goode would end up hurting Henry and Brett the most. She didn't want to be placed in a position where she'd be responsible for adding to any of that pain, but here she was. It wasn't Ruth's fault that Henry's mother had chosen to threaten her, but that didn't mean he should bear the burden of his mother's actions. Kids had to suffer for the mistakes of their parents just as much as parents had to suffer for the mistakes of their kids.

Henry needed less of this bullshit, Ruth thought, not more.

She stood up, thanking Amy for the shoulder to lean on. She left the cafeteria. She wouldn't tell Henry that his mother was threatening her, but she'd be damned if she'd let Molly Goode get away with it. In that regard, Ruth's sense of justice was very much like her mother's. And now she had resolved to get home so that she could tell Andrea and see her wrath released.

■ ■ ■

"THAT GODDAMN BITCH!" Andrea snarled.

Her first instinct was to get in the Odyssey and drive it right through Molly's living room bay windows. She went as far as to snatch the keys from the kitchen island where she'd left them. Andrea enjoyed the idea of the mess a drive-through would make, with the added bonus that Molly might be sterilizing the grand piano and get run over as well.

That would solve a whole lot of her problems, but Andrea knew it wouldn't do a thing to help prove Molly was a murderer. The only thing that would do that, Andrea realized, was doing the hardest thing imaginable when dealing with a threat to her daughter: nothing.

"Quarter in the swear jar!" Sadie exclaimed from the family room.

Lowering her voice, Andrea said to Ruth, "Let me see your phone."

Reluctantly—because what teenager wanted their mother to look through their phone?—Ruth handed it to Andrea. She made it painfully clear that she wasn't reading any of the texts other than those from Unknown Name/Unknown Number.

"I think Mrs. Goode did it," Ruth said.

"Why?"

"Because she was afraid Henry might tell me something?"

"You think Henry knows something?"

"No, not about what she had done, Mom," Ruth said. "But about what she was going to do?"

Andrea nodded, handing the phone back to her daughter. Ruth was already seeing this the same way Ramon had. Andrea had to stop fixating on finding definitive proof that Molly had murdered Derek—although it was still necessary—and start focusing more on how Molly planned to get away with that murder. Though she was a slave to her own twisted genius, Andrea had to accept that the best chance of catching Molly would be letting her escape.

39

KENNY woke up from his office nap around eleven. Jimmy and Shelby arrived at the offices by noon. Sitara told them they could focus on the Goode case all day. Kenny was glad she was on board. Because he was an imbecile, he took that to mean he and Sitara could have a future together. He thought a relationship was all about his partner sharing his goals, whose metrics had been clearly established that morning as: truth, justice, and the American way.

Sitara told him that while he was napping, she'd called Andrea about his visit to Jeff's office and learning about Pettigrew.

"You think I should call her?" asked Kenny. "See if it blew up?"

"She is having lunch with Crystal Burns to get more information about Molly. Check in with her later," Sitara said. Hitching a thumb toward Jimmy and Shelby, she added, "You have to organize their plan of attack."

In the conference room, Kenny related what had happened that morning to the others. He showed them a close-up of his swollen lip to confirm that fisticuffs had been involved.

"You said he punched you once," Jimmy said.

"He did."

"Then it wasn't fisticuffs, plural," Jimmy said. "It was fisticuff, singular."

"In other words, one punch is all it took," Shelby added.

"First of all," Kenny said, "there is no such word as fisticuff. It's always plural by definition. And second of all, I wasn't there to fight, I was there to provoke. Mission accomplished."

"One punch from a guy that looks like a bean sprout mated with an uncooked sausage," Jimmy said.

"Shut up," Kenny said as he went to the whiteboard. "They know we're onto them, so we have to move fast."

"They only know we're onto them because you felt like getting punched in the face," Shelby said.

"I didn't feel like—" he stopped himself. They were just having fun at his expense. "We have three avenues to deconstruct."

On the whiteboard, he wrote:

Cocaine/Affairs/STDs = Darrah Smalls/Genesis Jones

Proxy Clients/Medicare Fraud = Gabriel Pettigrew

E-ZPass/Phone Geolocation = Molly

"Dibs on Darrah and Genesis," Jimmy said quickly.

"Maybe I should take the women?" Shelby said. "Only 'cause Jimmy's gonna fuck it up."

"I know, but I need you on the E-ZPass," Kenny said. "We can't get access to that kind of information like you can."

"Easiest way would be to get a warrant for it," said Shelby.

"Based on the evidence we have, I don't think the West Windsor police would ask a judge for a warrant," Kenny said. "So, you're gonna have to find someone to get drunk with again."

She got up from the table and casually said, "I can make a couple calls."

Once she left the room, Jimmy said, "I'm not sure if I love her or hate her."

"Why does it have to be a binary choice?" Kenny asked. "Okay, back to Darrah and Genesis—"

"Speaking of love," Jimmy interrupted.

"Yeah, here's my suggestion," Kenny continued. "Don't go at them like a walking erection."

Jimmy said, "I'll have you know that I was planning to approach Darrah out of genuine concern. If Molly's scam is coming apart, she stands to get in trouble. As a lawyer, she knows it would be in her best interests to get ahead of the shitstorm that's coming."

"That's good, actually," said Kenny. "Okay, yeah. You'll catch her as she's leaving work?"

"Wait until she gets on the subway," Jimmy said. "No easy way for her to get out and she probably won't want to make a scene."

"What about Genesis?"

"Well, you're going to the ATM and take out a few hundred bucks and then hand that money over to me and that should be enough," Jimmy replied.

"Okay. Shit, this is costing me. Wow, that sounds like it might work," Kenny said, sounding more surprised than he'd probably intended. "I get Pettigrew. I'm going to crash his office later this afternoon."

BY FOUR IN the afternoon, Jimmy had left for the Finch, Conover & Stanton law offices and Shelby had spent two hours in the conference room with the door closed. Kenny had spent the afternoon breaking down his questions for Pettigrew and drinking a lot of coffee.

A little after four, as he was getting ready to head downtown, Andrea called. She told him about her trip to Pennsylvania, followed by her lunch with Crystal, and Sathwika's adventure at CVS.

Kenny was floored. He said, "Run through what Sathwika heard again."

"Molly and Joyce Li were arguing about the antibiotics. Molly needed two different prescriptions filled, one of ceftriaxone and one of penicillin. Joyce said—and Sathwika quoted her—'Haven't I done enough for you?' To which Molly replied, 'And you know what I can do to you.'"

Their discussion was interrupted by Shelby's loud shout from behind the closed door to the conference room. "Butter my ass and call me a biscuit!"

"What the hell was that?" asked Andrea.

Kenny said, "Shelby was looking into the E-ZPass and burner phones, so in South Carolina, that must translate to good news."

Shelby rushed to the printer, which had started to warm up.

"What do you have?" Kenny asked. Then he added, "I'm on the phone with Andie. Putting her on speaker."

The printer hummed. Three pages printed out. Shelby grabbed them from the output tray and said, "Molly has three E-ZPasses."

"And she only has two cars," Andrea said.

"Bingo. And one of them is registered to a business."

"And Molly doesn't have a business," Andrea said.

"Bingo," said Shelby. "But the business account E-ZPass bills are sent to a PO box at the West Windsor post office."

"Which means Molly didn't want Derek keeping track of her movements during the day," Andrea said.

"And there are plenty of reasons why," Shelby said, flapping the papers in her hand. "Maybe you'd like to know a few places she's visited? Exit 143A on the Garden State Parkway three times in the last four months."

"That's Maplewood, where the CVS pharmacy is," Kenny said.

"Exit 144 on the parkway twice," said Andrea.

"That's South Orange," Kenny said.

"Hold on," Andrea interrupted. They could hear her fingers stabbing at a keyboard. "Joyce Li lives at an apartment complex on 153 Valley Street, in South Orange."

"Who is Joyce Li?" asked Shelby.

"The pharmacist who was Molly's roommate in college," said Kenny. "C'mon, Shelby, keep up."

"Shelby, ignore him," said Andrea through the speaker.

"Ah always do," muttered Shelby.

"Almost twenty years ago, this roommate gave Molly the drugs she used to kill her parents," Andrea said.

"See, now this is getting good," said Sitara. And off Kenny's look, she added, "Good enough that we might have a second season of *Suburban Secrets* here."

Much to everyone's surprise, Kenny said, "I love you, baby!"

They were all taken aback by it. Even he felt thrown off by the spontaneity. Through the speaker, Andrea said, "I can only imagine the awkward silence over there, but Kenny's absolutely horrific timing notwithstanding, what else do you have, Shelby?"

"Turnpike tolls on weekday mornings and early afternoons in July and August that coincide with the locations of all four of Martin Singer's assisted living facilities," Shelby said.

"Molly found out about Derek's fraud scheme," Kenny stated as much as asked. "And she was pressuring Martin for details?"

"Planning how to access the money after she killed Derek," said Andrea.

"And one last one," said Shelby. "Exit 14C off the turnpike on September 19 at 10:15 a.m. Followed by entry into the Holland Tunnel at 10:43 a.m."

"That was after the funeral," said Andrea. "I was having lunch with the Cellulitists, but Molly declined our invite."

"Because she was visiting Gabriel Pettigrew at his office in Lower Manhattan," said Kenny.

"To consolidate control of the account?" asked Sitara.

"I'll find out in just a bit," Kenny said. "What's next for you, Andrea?"

"Sathwika and I are going to talk to Joyce in the next day or two, try to get her to come clean on what happened to Molly's parents, as well as Derek," Andrea said.

"Okay, we're looking to take down the alibi witnesses like Derek's associate and his stripper girlfriend," said Kenny.

"And I'm done for the day after having kicked all kinds of ass," Shelby said with a smile.

"You sure did," Andrea said. "Can't wait to meet you in person. Kenny, can you take me off speaker?"

Kenny did, cradling the phone to his ear. He asked, "What's up?"

40

JIMMY Chaney followed Darrah Smalls from her building to the F train platform at Rockefeller Center without being seen. He'd gotten a slew of text updates from Kenny, so he had more ammunition to approach Darrah with. She boarded a crowded subway and he slid in two doors down from her. He wedged himself among the rush-hour commuters.

He slowly wormed his way toward where Darrah was standing. A slight exodus of people at the Lexington Avenue–Sixty-third Street station gave him more room to maneuver. He deftly slid his way right next to her as a push of Queens-bound commuters rolled into the car.

It took her a second to recognize him. He smiled broadly. She did not.

"What a coincidence," he said.

"Fuck me," she said.

"I'd love to, but I'm worried we're getting to the point where it's gonna have to be during conjugal visits," he said.

"What the hell do you want?" Darrah said, looking too tired to have much fight in her.

"I wanted to warn you," he said.

"Warn me?"

"We're getting closer to proving Molly killed Derek," he said plainly. "We also know she was planning all along for us to investigate her."

"She was worried about *you*, was she?" Darrah asked.

"Nah, man, she don't even know who I am," he said. "But she knows who Andie Stern is. And she knows who Kenny Lee is. And I guarantee you, she was worried about Andie, at least."

"And you think . . . what . . . ?" she asked, fishing as much as offering an opening for compromise.

"Molly planned for her alibis," he said. "She planned for Derek's cocaine use and for his affairs. She knew the insurance policy would slip through her fingers. She planned for that, too."

Darrah didn't say anything.

"But you know all this because she planned for you, too," said Jimmy.

Darrah remained quiet.

"How much did Molly Goode offer you?"

Darrah didn't respond.

Jimmy smiled, nodding. "Okay, that's one way to play it."

The subway stopped at the Queensbridge station and a throng of people got off. Seats had become available. This was Darrah's chance to move away from him. If she did, Jimmy knew he had lost her.

She didn't move.

She softened and slumped slightly, losing some of her bravado.

"It's coming apart, Darrah," he said.

"Cops?"

"Not yet," Jimmy said. "But since it's interstate fraud an' shit like that, it'll probably all go straight to the FBI. Did I mention Andie and an FBI agent from Newark are super sweet on each other?"

He hoped mentioning the FBI would escalate the threat Darrah felt.

■ ■ ■

DARRAH SMALLS WEIGHED how much she should say to this strange man. He had a sweetness to him, but she wondered if it was less out of innate goodness and more as a means to achieve an end. She suspected his cocky charm worked just fine in coaxing random women into sex, but here, now, he was using it to get her to trust him. And was that because he really wanted to protect her or just to get a confession out of her? Darrah had fought her entire life to avoid weakness and the entreaties of men making promises they would never keep.

But she had also made choices in the past six months that she deeply regretted.

For her, the conflict was not between accepting Jimmy's lifeline and fighting the truth, it was in knowing that if she gave voice to those truths, she would be exposing her own weakness. She had worked her ass off for twenty years and she was only thirty years old. This wasn't fair. None of any of it was fair. Molly Goode had offered her a shortcut. All it had taken was prostituting herself, both body and soul.

"Your stop is coming up," he said, surprising her. "Last chance, Darrah. The choice you make affects the rest of your life."

They reached the Jackson Heights station.

As the doors slid open, she said, "Come get a drink with me."

Darrah thought that possibly for the first time in his life, Jimmy Chaney wouldn't be getting a drink with a beautiful woman with the intention of scoring, but for the sake of helping her.

KENNY SAT AT a small blue table outside Adventure Cafe as people filed out of the Yard, the Delancey Street building where Gabriel Pettigrew had office space. A few times he held his phone up to compare the picture he'd downloaded with some of the well-groomed, well-manicured, well-educated, well-dressed frat boys who emerged from the building, only to see they weren't his target. It was stunning how many of them looked alike.

A little after six, his boy came out. Pettigrew was well over six feet tall. He wore a perfectly tailored suit, silk shirt, and eight-hundred-dollar Zilli glasses, which probably weren't even prescription lenses.

"Mr. Pettigrew," Kenny said, standing up so that he directly blocked him on the sidewalk. "Kenneth Lee, *Princeton Post*. I'd like to ask you a few questions about Derek Goode."

"I'm late for something," Pettigrew said, trying to brush by Kenny. "Set up an appointment with my secretary."

"You don't have a secretary, Mr. Pettigrew," Kenny said, stopping Gabriel in his tracks. "You have a desk in a co-op workshare, and no judgment, I just don't want you blowing smoke up my ass like I don't know what's what."

Rather than intimidating Pettigrew, that amused him, which intimidated Kenny a bit.

"How well did you know Derek?" Kenny asked.

"If you know 'what's what' then why would you even have to ask?" Pettigrew said.

"Let's walk," said Kenny. "Just two Phi Epsilon buds having a casual conversation."

"I was in Sigma Ep," Pettigrew said.

"Po-tay-toh, po-tah-toh," said Kenny. "I always found frat brothers to be total douches anyway."

"If you're here, and you know I was . . . acquainted . . . with Derek," Pettigrew said, choosing his words carefully, "then you know how deeply sorry I am about his untimely death."

"I can tell you're still in mourning, Gabe," Kenny said. "Can I call you Gabe?" Pettigrew didn't reply. Kenny continued, "Molly Goode came to see you after her husband passed away."

Pettigrew grunted.

"We called the Yard," Kenny continued. "She checked in at the security desk at 11:03 a.m. She signed in to see you. You let her in. Got a grunt for me now, Gabe?"

Pettigrew weighed how much Kenny really had on him versus how much was just casting bait. He answered, "Must not have been that important if I barely remember it."

"Or maybe it was just so emasculating that you don't want to talk about it," Kenny said.

"Emasculating?"

"Yes, Gabe. To deprive a male of his role or identity; to make someone or something weaker or less effective."

"Fuck you, man," he said.

"Did she at least leave you with one testicle?" Kenny said, that buzz in his brain telling him that was probably the one that went too far.

Pettigrew grabbed him by the shoulder. He didn't let go of Kenny's shirt. "What kind of fucking reporter are you?"

Kenny tried to dislodge Pettigrew's hand, but his grip was like a vise. "You are creasing the sports coat," he said.

"I'm sure JCPenney still has them in stock," Gabriel said, letting go.

"Oh, a class joke. How classy," Kenny said. "Especially from the man using old people to run a Medicare scam."

Pettigrew backed up a step. He stood at the corner of Delancey and Ludlow. He stared at the Duane Reade to his right, the Bank of America on the corner in front of him, and the six lanes of clogged traffic to his left. He had no way out.

After an agonizing minute of silence, Pettigrew said, "Jeff came to me with Derek's plan. It was smooth. Smart. I told Jeff I could work it."

"And work it you did," Kenny said.

"We had a good run," Pettigrew continued.

"How good?"

"By Labor Day we had nine in the account."

"Nine?"

Pettigrew looked at Kenny the way a master chef might look at the newly promoted assistant grill manager of a Burger King.

"Million."

"*Nine million?*" Kenny said, louder than he had meant to.

"No one was getting hurt," he said.

"Derek got hurt," Kenny said.

"He had a heart thing," Pettigrew said. "Shit, he told me he was running the scam to set up his family in case he died."

Kenny had a sarcastic response but kept it to himself. Don't derail someone when they're in the middle of confessing. And don't derail someone when you were about to prove they threatened a minor.

He texted Andrea: Now.

Within seconds, a phone in Pettigrew's suit pocket vibrated. He reached in and absently removed an iPhone. Realizing it wasn't that phone, he hesitated.

"It's the burner phone inside your other pocket," Kenny said.

Pettigrew said nothing.

Kenny texted Andrea again: It was him.

"Threatening a minor, Gabriel?" Kenny said. "That is incredibly weak."

"I was only trying to scare her to stop gossiping," Pettigrew said.

"Which you would have known nothing about, much less had her number, unless you'd gotten both from Molly," Kenny said. "Why did she care enough to try and scare a sixth grader?"

"Distraction," Pettigrew answered. "She gave me the number and that was all she said."

Pettigrew knew he was completely caught.

"C'mon, I live in SoHo," he said. "I wasn't going to drive to New Jersey to hurt some kid."

"But scaring them is okay?" Kenny jabbed. "Good to know where you draw the line, Gabe."

"What do I do now?"

"You cooperate with the FBI," Kenny said.

"I can do that."

"And I strongly recommend you don't touch the account after today."

"Too late for that," said Pettigrew.

"What do you mean?" Kenny asked.

41

*A*FTER what had been an incredibly hectic Tuesday, getting stuck on the parkway for over half an hour on Wednesday morning had made things feel numbingly anticlimactic. Headaches notwithstanding, the wait had given Andrea and Sathwika a chance to talk through yesterday's events and plan for their impending confrontation.

Sathwika was still upset about Ruth having been threatened, but she knew Andrea was kicking herself about it enough.

"I'm the one who involved her," said Andrea. "Even though the texts were just meant to scare her, it's still infuriating."

"And?"

"And I have to fight against every instinct telling me to put a gun to Molly's head to get her to talk," Andrea said.

Finally, one lane opened up and traffic inched forward at a crawl.

Ten minutes later, they approached Joyce Li's apartment building at 153 Valley Street in South Orange. The Third & Valley complex was a red-brick four-story building. The ground floor was used for retail space. They had called the CVS in Maplewood and learned that today was Joyce's only day off.

They buzzed her apartment. She answered through the intercom.

"Joyce Li, my name is Andrea Stern," she said, parsing her words carefully to avoid complications down the road. Without a private investigator license Andrea had to walk a fine line. Any confession Joyce made now could later be claimed to have been coerced or given under false pretenses if Andrea led her to think she was acting in an official capacity. "I am here with my associate Sathwika Duvvuri. We'd like to talk to you about your relationship with Molly Goode."

A second's hesitation, a tentative answer. "I don't know anyone by that name," Joyce said.

"Ms. Li, we know that's not true," said Andrea. "We know you were roommates with Molly Parker at Penn State your sophomore and junior years, and we know you recently saw her at the pharmacy where you work in Maplewood."

A longer hesitation.

The door buzzer sounded to let them in.

Joyce Li met them at the landing of the stairs leading to her second-floor apartment, watching as they lugged the portable car seats with their sleeping babies. The pharmacist was shorter even than Andrea, with close-cropped hair and very tired eyes. She was slightly overweight, dressed in plaid pajama bottoms and a gray Penn State hoodie. She watched them mount the steps with a wary, defensive glare, but something else, too. It was a look Andrea had seen often in the eyes of people who had been caught: a combination of defeat and relief.

"What do you know?" she asked, not prepared to let them into her apartment.

"Do you really want to do this out here?" Andrea asked.

Joyce relented and let them in. Her small apartment was sloppy, signs of someone who was severely overworked and unhappy.

"I know you," she said to Andrea as they walked inside.

"You do?"

"From the news," the pharmacist said. "The murders? In the same town where Molly lives."

Andrea nodded in acknowledgment.

"I was in the pharmacy when Molly picked up her prescriptions," Sathwika said. "I overheard your argument, Ms. Li."

"We also talked to Molly's brother and sister in Pennsylvania," Andrea said.

"Her parents," Joyce said softly enough they could barely hear it.

"Why did you do it?" asked Andrea.

"I didn't know at first, I swear," she said. "Molly said her father was having trouble sleeping and needed muscle relaxants because his back was hurting him. I gave her, like, ten Halcion tablets."

"And when you heard her parents died in a car accident?" Andrea probed.

"I asked Molly how she gave them to her father," Joyce said. "She said just at night before he went to bed for a few days."

"She lied to you," said Sathwika.

"I didn't know, I wasn't sure then," said Joyce.

"You still haven't answered my question," Andrea said.

"I told you."

"No, you told me why Molly asked you, not why you were willing to steal from the university pharmacy and risk getting caught, maybe kicked out of school," Andrea said.

Joyce didn't say anything.

"We're not interested in your secrets other than how they pertain to proving Molly's guilt in the murder of her husband," Andrea said.

Still nothing.

"Whatever blackmail Molly has on you," Andrea said coldly, "you have to ask yourself one question: Is it worse than being arrested as an accomplice to murder?"

Joyce broke. "I'm not protecting myself, I'm protecting my parents.

They're illegal immigrants. I am, too. We came here when I was two years old."

"Molly knew and threatened to expose you?" Sathwika said sympathetically.

"All of the documents I'd used to get into college were forged," said Joyce. "Scholarship grants I got, student loans, everything would have been jeopardized."

"Even after Molly's parents died, you didn't see that as an opportunity to fight back?" asked Sathwika. Andrea let her play good cop.

"No," said Joyce.

"Because she would have twisted it?" Sathwika asked.

Joyce's attention was only on Sathwika now. "She would have blamed me for it somehow—and my parents would still be outed."

"That's awful you were in that situation," said Sathwika, reaching over to place a comforting hand on Joyce's, whose hands were clenched in a tight ball by her knees.

"I couldn't live with her after that," said Joyce. "I could barely live with myself. I hadn't talked to her since the end of our junior year until she walked into my pharmacy a few months ago."

"When?" asked Andrea, surprised by that timeline.

"In late July," Joyce said. "She needed an antibiotic and she couldn't take penicillin."

"And why would she drive an hour to get that from you instead of her own pharmacy?" asked Sathwika.

"Because she didn't have a prescription from a doctor," said Joyce. "She was embarrassed and angry at her husband for giving her an STD and she forced me to dispense them to her."

Andrea and Sathwika exchanged glances. They were both piecing together in their minds which strands of Molly's web were lies and which were truths that she used to spin the lies. As Andrea suspected, Molly had contracted the STD by accident. Derek had gotten it from outside sexual contact; he had then spread it to at least three other women: Darrah Smalls, Molly, and the recipient of the second prescription Molly had procured from Joyce. Andrea felt confident she knew who that third person was.

"Did she ask you for cocaine?" Andrea asked.

Joyce seemed confused by that, which only served to make Andrea more of the enemy in the pharmacist's mind. Sathwika quickly jumped in. "We know pharmacists are rarely allowed to prescribe cocaine, but hospitals can prescribe topical solutions, right?"

"Sure, I guess; it's not commonly used anymore," said Joyce. "But I just don't understand."

"Due to Derek's suspicious behavior prior to his heart attack," Andrea said, "an autopsy was performed. Enough cocaine was found in Derek's system that it was deemed a contributing factor to his death."

"I did not give Molly cocaine," Joyce said. Andrea knew a truth could also be used to cover up a lie.

"But you gave her *something*?" Andrea asked.

Joyce fought back tears. She nodded. Sathwika held Joyce's hands again.

Andrea tensed, knowing this was the moment of truth, and was annoyed that this was when JoJo had chosen to stir. She didn't need the baby to distract Joyce. The pharmacist seemed ready to talk, nervous, terrified, actually. Andrea expected a torrential confession to erupt out of the woman's mouth.

Joyce only needed to say one word.

BEFORE LEAVING, ANDREA and Sathwika told the pharmacist they would try to minimize her complicity, but it would be difficult. They recommended she look for a lawyer for both herself and her parents. They also promised they would give her fair warning before confronting Molly about the accusations or bringing the West Windsor police or the FBI onto the case.

Sathwika thanked Joyce for her courage. Andrea didn't have that kindness in her. She didn't think of Joyce as a victim so much as a pawn. And she had played enough chess growing up as part of her training to know that pawns were nothing more than useful tools, capable of great moments, but more often than not, simply fodder too weak to stand on their own.

They ate lunch and packed the kids back into the van for their next stop, in Chester Township. The gods of Jersey traffic willing, the drive to the Mountainside Senior Care Facility, owned by Martin Singer's family, would take forty-five minutes. The family's four facilities were in close enough range that even if Martin weren't working out of the site in Chester, which he usually did, they could still drive to the other locations to find him.

They turned off Route 206 South and up a winding drive. Andrea wondered if every one of these senior facilities hired the same architect. It was a three-story brick complex with cedar-vinyl siding made to resemble a series of fused townhomes on the outside. They entered the large foyer facing a grand staircase that went up to the second floor with stairs at either side that went down to the pool and gym area.

Andrea and Sathwika pushed their strollers to the front desk.

"Hi, we were hoping to speak with Martin Singer," Andrea said.

"Do you have an appointment?" asked the woman behind the counter.

"No, but if you tell him he was recommended to us by Gabriel Pettigrew, I'm sure he'll want to see us." Andrea smiled.

The woman picked up her phone handset and dialed an extension.

Within seconds, the office door behind her swung open far more forcefully than had likely been intended, and a panicked Martin Singer faced them.

"Andrea?" he said, his voice managing to sound soft and loud, surprised and terrified all at the same time.

"Let's talk," Andrea said.

Martin looked at his lobby manager and then at Andrea. He might have been timid, but he wasn't a fool. He nodded. "Let's go outside for a walk."

And avoid any internal security systems, Andrea thought. She reached into her bag to turn on her phone's Voice Memos app, emerging with a pacifier for JoJo to cover her move.

Outside, the sidewalk circling the entirety of the property couldn't accommodate three people with two strollers walking side by side. After Sathwika introduced herself to Martin, she took a position behind them as they all walked.

"How much do you think we know?" Andrea asked.

Martin didn't say anything.

"The answer is, we know enough," Andrea said.

He didn't respond. Trying to manipulate a confession out of someone who didn't talk would be challenging.

"Kenny might have mentioned to you on the golf course a few days ago that the sooner you come clean and fill in those gaps, the better it'll be for you in the long run," she said.

"What did Jeff say?" asked Martin.

"Jeff hasn't been given the options I'm giving you," Andrea replied. "Not yet, anyway."

Martin seemed to want to respond quickly to that, but he wasn't the kind of person who spoke without first chewing on the words through the nervous grinding of his teeth for several seconds. Finally, he said, "What options are you giving to me?"

Andrea made an impulsive decision born out of frustration at the husbands in all their lives, rather than for the sake of the flow of the interrogation. "Say what were you going to say."

He shook his head nervously. "Nothing."

Andrea was going to push, but behind them, Sathwika said, "I can't imagine how hard this is, Martin. I wouldn't want my husband to have to make these kinds of decisions. Whatever you did, I'm sure you thought you were just helping your family."

Andrea should have taken it as a clear signal from Sathwika that she needed to be less forceful in her approach. But her friend knew her well enough to know how futile that signal would be.

"You were this close to showing some balls, Martin," Andrea said. She could practically feel Sathwika's full-body cringe behind her. "You were so close to speaking your mind, but you can't do it, can you?"

He said nothing.

"Keeping it all bottled inside can't be good for your blood pressure," she continued. "I can't believe your family was originally from Staten Island and this is how you turned out."

"Maybe it's because my family is from Staten Island that I turned out like this," he said.

"Props to you then, Martin," she said. "But that means you should know what it takes to be a survivor. In a marriage where you barely have a voice, in a job where you have no passion, I get why you listened to Derek's pitch. Was it just the money, or the chance to be your own man, have your own secrets, feel some excitement, maybe some fear . . . ?"

When Martin didn't immediately respond, Andrea reached into her bag and sent a pocket text to Sathwika telling her not to talk. Her friend still couldn't get over how Andrea managed to do that without looking at the keypad. They came around full circle to the main doors. Andrea knew it was now or never.

"I thought it was a good idea," Martin finally said. "It was supposed to be low-key, just build up an account little by little to help with things . . . mortgage, the college tuitions."

He paused. Sensing they might lose him, Sathwika said, "Andrea said you have triplets. I worry how I'll pay for college and my three are spread out. I can't imagine three at the same time."

Martin laughed. It came out like a panicked exhalation. "Jeff pushed it," he said, his anger growing and directed toward Andrea. "Pushed to do more, faster. Him and Pettigrew basically took over the whole thing."

Andrea wasn't sure how to respond to that. Was Martin purposefully trying to throw her off? They didn't get it, she thought, or they didn't want to get it. None of them did—not Jeff or Martin, Brianne or Crystal; maybe not even Sathwika totally understood. Andrea no longer cared who got hurt if it meant stopping a killer from getting away. She had wasted too much of her life already to worry anymore about the bad choices other people made.

Even if they were people in her life. *Especially* if they were people in her life, she thought.

This was going to hurt her family and friends. And Andrea didn't give two shits anymore.

"You fucking come clean now, Martin," she said angrily. "Right. Fucking. Now. Or Jeff gets the chance for the deal my friends at the FBI will offer."

"You've told the FBI?" Martin asked, stunned, hurt, and terrified.

"Now or never, Martin," she said.

It was now.

Martin started talking.

42

A FEW hours later, Andrea and Jeff maintained a cold détente as they ate dinner and then avoided each other as they helped the kids with their homework. When Andrea went to check on Ruth around ten p.m., her daughter asked her if everything was going to be okay.

"I don't know," Andrea said. "We know who texted you. You were never in any real danger, honey, but I'm sorry they scared you."

"Was it Mrs. Goode?" she asked.

"It was someone working with her," Andrea said. "Kenny confronted him in the city and confirmed it was him. The FBI is talking to him now."

"What about Dad?" Ruth said.

"Your father may have been involved in some illegal business," Andrea said.

"Again?" asked Ruth, exasperation and concern in her voice.

Andrea weighed how to answer. She really didn't want to throw Jeff under the bus in front of her kids, but she was done lying to cover for him. "This was different than last time, Ruth. This involved your father's friends getting together to make some bad choices."

"Did he steal from anyone?" she asked.

"No," she said, then elaborated. "Not from people. I'm still putting it all together, Ruth, but it was like sharks stealing from other sharks. The minnows—that's how they think of regular people—they weren't hurt by it."

"Stealing still sucks," she said.

"Yeah, it does."

"Is he going to get in trouble?" Ruth asked.

"I don't know yet," Andrea replied. "We still have to talk about it. I won't lie to you, but I can't tell you everything until we figure it out, okay?"

"Okay," Ruth said.

Before Andrea left her daughter's room, Ruth said, "Oh, Mom, Henry said something today that I thought was weird, then he texted me tonight, too. He said that his mom was super angry."

"Did he say why?"

"Just that she's been pissed off about everything the last few days," Ruth said. "And he said she was taking their luggage out of the basement."

Andrea didn't respond, waiting to see if Ruth could play it through.

"He said it was even weirder because she hadn't put their summer clothes away yet like she usually did."

Andrea nodded.

"Do you think she's leaving?" Ruth asked.

"Or getting ready to in case she thinks she needs to," Andrea said.

Tears welled up in Ruth's eyes. "What happens to them?"

Andrea didn't need any further clarification to understand her daughter's distress. "I don't know, Ruth. I really don't. If Molly runs, she would probably take Henry and Brett with her, I'm sure. If she is arrested, then one of the family relatives would take them in."

"Henry and Brett love their aunt and uncle," she said. "But they live in Chicago."

Andrea said nothing, letting the reality sink in for her daughter.

She patted Ruth's hand and turned to leave. Her departure was interrupted when Ruth bluntly said, "Don't you care, Mom?"

"About Henry and Brett? Of course I do, honey."

"I mean, in general, really," Ruth said. "You go after a killer, but do you ever think about what gets left behind after you catch them?"

"I think about it a lot," Andrea answered so quickly, a part of her wondered if it was true. She waited a bit before continuing. "But I'm not responsible for what's left in the wake of the tornado, Ruth. The tornado is."

That was all. That should be enough, Andrea thought, knowing that it wasn't when the wake included children and family friends. Henry and Brett would be casualties of their mother's arrest, and their father was a casualty of her actions. Of course it wasn't fair they would bear the brunt of something they weren't responsible for, but as trite as it sounded, life wasn't fair. And though it might seem cold or callous, she didn't want to raise her children to expect otherwise.

"You okay?" she asked her daughter.

Ruth nodded, but it wasn't convincing.

Guilty and defiant at the same time, Andrea softly said, "Okay, good night."

She checked in on the other kids, then went downstairs, thinking about what Henry had said. Summer clothes meant warm climate getaway. Was the pressure getting to Molly? The dominos were starting to fall. If what Martin had told her and what Pettigrew had told Kenny was accurate, Molly was sitting on several million dollars. But accessing it or moving it could be a different set of problems for her.

A soft light peeked from under the basement door. Jeff was down in his office. She steeled herself for the conversation she was about to have.

Andrea stood in the open door to his office; his back was to her as he worked on an Excel file.

"You lied to me," he said.

"You lied to me," she said. "Which one of those do you think was worse?"

"Martin won't return my calls or texts."

"Because he decided to tell us the truth," Andrea said. "And he's probably scared of you. Or he feels guilty that he made the smart choice. Probably all of the above."

"It was just money, Andie," Jeff said. "It didn't mean anything."

"Derek wasn't killed *by* the money, Jeff, he was killed *for* it."

He finally turned to face her. "That's clever. But whether Molly killed Derek or not, I had absolutely nothing to do with that and you know it."

"I do," she said. "But you still don't get it. You were doing something wrong—*again*—and you hid it from me—*again*. You risked hurting your family—*again*—and worse, you're the one who pushed everyone else to increase the risk."

He said nothing. He folded his arms as she talked, feigning intransigence even though every word she spoke was the truth.

"And you also refuse to accept that even if you never meant for that to be the outcome, by forcing more money into the account, you gave Molly the financial reason she needed to justify killing Derek."

"What do you plan to do, Andie?" he asked.

"That's not the question you should be asking."

"What is, then?"

"What do *you* plan to do, Jeff?"

43

HE next day, the 9:10 a.m. New Jersey Transit Northeast Corridor express train pulled into New York Penn Station at 10:21 a.m., running only four minutes late. Andrea and Sathwika risked the thrill-a-minute ride known as the platform elevators and wrestled their strollers onto the escalators. They hit the savage streets of Manhattan, ready for action. Much to Sathwika's chagrin, Andrea wanted to walk the twenty-plus blocks down to Union Square.

"No flab means abs," Andrea said.

You could take Andrea out of the Cellulitists but you couldn't take the Cellulitists out of Andrea. The truth, she knew, was much less about her weight and much more about her desire to feel as much of the city as she could. She didn't get into Manhattan often, but the concrete was a colonic cleansing of all things suburban.

After turning right on Broadway to head south to Union Square, Sathwika smiled and said, "You love this way too much."

"I do."

"You look positively . . ." she trailed off, uncertain of the right word.

"Energized," said Andrea.

When they got to Union Square Park, Sathwika wanted to get a tea. Andrea called Kenny and asked if anyone wanted coffee. He texted her their orders, thanking her, and she was mildly amused at the thought of office-Kenny politely gathering everyone's drink orders. She might have been knocked off her feet if she knew he had done it from memory.

Kenny met them at the elevators and walked them through the office to the Muckrakers space. As he made small talk, Andrea and Sathwika knew what each was thinking: this could have been them.

Andrea shrugged it off. It was yesterday's lament. In her mind, she had to start planning for the future. And in many ways, the meeting they were now going to have was the first day of that future.

Kenny did a surprisingly admirable job as a host, making introductions for those who hadn't met. Sathwika knew Sitara and Jimmy, as did Andrea, but they were both happy to meet Shelby face-to-face.

"I'm a fan," Shelby said to Andrea.

"From what I've seen of your work on this, likewise," said Andrea.

Sitara led them all into the large conference room. Andrea asked if she'd be joining them, but Sitara could only stay for the first hour. She had a lunch meeting at the Netflix office to finalize the in-house screening plans for the rough cut of the *Suburban Secrets* series.

Playing nice, Andrea asked if they could get a sneak peek at some point. Sitara surprised her by saying that she fully planned to get Andrea's approval on the final edit before advance screeners were sent out to the press in late January.

That surprised Kenny, too, who said, "Does Andie have contractual approval rights?"

Sitara shoved him lightly into the conference room. "No," she said, "but she does have moral approval rights."

With that, and the babies on their respective mothers' laps, they all settled in.

JoJo couldn't take her eyes off Jimmy, who was sitting across from

Andrea. For that matter, even Aditya seemed to be mesmerized by his gleaming smile.

"They can sit with me," Jimmy said.

Both women immediately took him up on the offer and handed him the babies.

He bounced them both on his piston-like legs. JoJo giggled. Aditya tried to giggle, but mostly just blew spit bubbles.

"You volunteered for diaper duty, too, if one of them goes, right?" Sathwika asked with a giggle.

Andrea wondered if her friend was flirting.

"Hey, I got six nieces and nephews, I can change a diaper in thirty seconds flat," Jimmy said.

"Marry me," Sathwika laughed, erasing any doubt from Andrea's mind.

The others had all sat down, but Sitara remained standing. She would lead the meeting, because she was naturally disposed toward leading. She got them into a productive flow. They separated all of their information—documents, maps, and photos—into two piles at the head of the table. One pile was Molly-related materials, the other pile Derek-related items. They went through them and organized a third pile that contained materials where Molly's and Derek's separate activities overlapped.

Sitara wrote Molly's name in large letters on the top left corner of the wall-length whiteboard, then Derek's name at the far right.

"I gotta go," Sitara said. "You guys have everything you need to make the connections."

With that, she walked out of the conference room.

Andrea watched Sitara get her backpack and coat. She waved and left.

Andrea turned to Kenny and said, "She's your mother."

"That is completely gross," said Kenny.

Jimmy laughed. "I never thought of that! She *is* like your mother!"

Andrea stood up. It was her time to take over. She made a Face-Time call. The others in the room heard the gruff voice on the other end say, "You know I hate these video calls."

She turned the phone to face the conference room.

"Detective Vince Rossi, meet former Charleston police sergeant Shelby Taylor," she said. "You know Kenny, Jimmy, and Sathwika."

Kenny said, "What're you doing?"

Andrea turned the phone to the whiteboard. She talked Rossi through all the evidence they had gathered.

"If that woman really did kill her husband, Andie, I'd be first in line to put the cuffs on her," he growled. "But your case against her for murder remains circumstantial."

"Fine," she said. "I'll bring the financial fraud to Ramon."

"Wait, you can't bring this to anyone yet," Kenny said. "We can't give this away to the authorities until we have more people on camera. We're not private detectives here, Andie. You might think of yourself that way, that's fine, but we're documentarians, which means we have to document."

"Then you're all invited to my house tonight," Andrea said.

"For what?" Shelby asked.

"I'm going to have a few people over after dinner. Just coffee and some dessert canapés," Andrea said.

Shelby turned to Jimmy. "Those are little desserts."

"I know what they are," Jimmy said. He hadn't known what they were.

"Who else is invited?" asked Kenny.

44

"Most of you know Kenny Lee," Andrea said to the group reluctantly collected in her family room. "Crystal and Brianne, you might remember Sathwika. We met at the soccer fields last year. Brianne, you met Jimmy last summer. He works with Kenny now. I'd like to introduce you to Shelby Taylor, who is a private investigator working with the production company making Kenny's documentary for Netflix. She was also a cop for the Charleston police department for many years. We've been working together for the last few weeks trying to find out the truth about Molly and Derek."

Crystal and Wendell Burns shifted anxiously next to each other on the sofa, clasping hands in support against the discomfort they knew was coming. Brianne and Martin Singer sat in end chairs across from each other on opposite sides of the couch, too obvious a metaphor for the gulf between them. And Jeff . . . Jeff looked like he completely understood why Molly might have wanted to kill her spouse.

"Why is he holding a camera?" Wendell asked, pointing to Jimmy. "And why are there two other cameras set up on tripods?"

"Because," said Jeff. "They want to capture the 'gotcha' moment on video."

WHEN JEFF HAD come home from the city half an hour earlier, he asked why there was a van from McCaffrey's supermarket in their driveway.

"Because the person delivering the party treats needed some form of transportation to get here," Andrea said casually, pointing to the delivery person who was arranging the dessert canapés on two platters.

"What party?" he asked.

"Probably I shouldn't call it a party," she said. "It's more of a social gathering."

Jeff looked past the open family room off the kitchen and through the glass French doors leading to the sunroom. Kenny and Shelby sat on the wicker couch. Jimmy stood, setting up a camera tripod.

"What is he doing here and who are the other two?" he asked.

"They're my coworkers," Andrea said. "I thought it would be polite to invite them to our social gathering."

"What social gathering?" Jeff exclaimed, succumbing to the game she was playing.

"I know you hate that on weeknights, but it seemed like the best time to do it."

"Do *what*?"

The doorbell rang.

"That's probably Sathwika," Andrea said, practically skipping to the front door to let her friend in.

She greeted Jeff and he tried to be polite, but the entire situation was too surreal for him.

As Sathwika walked by Jeff toward the family room, he noticed her arm cyst was missing.

"Where's the baby?" he asked.

"My in-laws are watching him," she said.

He looked around. "Where are our kids?"

"I hired a sitting service to take everyone's kids to Chuck E. Cheese," she said. "Dinner, games, until nine o'clock."

"Including Josephine?" he asked.

"No, Sathwika's in-laws are watching her, too," Andrea replied.

"Then what do you mean 'everyone's kids'?" Jeff asked.

And then the doorbell rang again.

NOW, SITTING ON the couch next to Crystal, Jeff fidgeted uneasily. His wife was about to blow up all their lives. He knew he'd made a mistake, but he didn't think it was irreparable. The business plan had been very elegantly constructed. Even his preference for increasing its draw wasn't ill-conceived. They could have comfortably milked it for two or three years, and then closed it all up with ten million apiece and no one would have been the wiser.

If only Molly Goode hadn't been such an utter bitch.

Andrea poured a little wine for her friends and a lot for her frenemies.

"I don't understand why Wendell and I are here," Crystal said. "We didn't do anything wrong."

"You didn't, Crys, but I'll get to that in a minute," Andrea said. She took a sip of wine, then drank the whole glass.

"Okay, it's no secret that I suspected Molly killed Derek," she began. "At first, I had a hard time proving it. Give Molly credit for that. And it shouldn't be a surprise she did a great job of playing all of us in different ways." She looked at Jeff and Martin, then fixed a stare on Brianne. "For a little while, anyway."

Andrea motioned to Shelby, who walked up to her carrying a short stack of folders. Andrea plucked the first one off the top.

"Each folder contains a signed affidavit from a different person attesting to what Molly Goode did in the act of recruiting them—or blackmailing them—to lie and steal for her," Andrea said. "Genesis Jones is a dancer in New York who had frequent sex with Derek. In July, Molly paid her ten thousand dollars to sleep with Derek, procure cocaine, and partake in its use with him. Genesis called an anonymous tip to Derek's insurance company that led the investigators to her, and then she corroborated his cocaine use. Their sexual activity also led to Derek becoming infected with an STD. She denied it at first, but has since admitted she was the cause of transmission. In turn, he infected Molly."

Handing the first folder over to Kenny, Andrea plucked another folder.

"Darrah Smalls is an associate at Derek's firm," she continued. "She was paid two hundred and fifty thousand dollars to have sex with Derek and provide eyewitness accounts of his drug use to the insurance investigators. Fearing more repercussions at work, at first Derek refused her advances, but when she offered him cocaine, they did sleep together."

"But Derek had a heart condition, I don't understand any of this," Wendell said, unsure if he should be addressing his wife, Andrea, the stationary cameras, or Jimmy, who was walking around recording them on a handheld.

"It gets complicated," Kenny said as he took the next folder. "Bill Winthrop. An associate on Derek's team. He helped provide paperwork to create the fake client accounts that were going to be used in the Medicare fraud. He wasn't a part of Molly's original plan, but five thousand dollars was wired last week into his bank account to remain quiet about his role. When we confronted him about this, Bill not only decided jail time was not worth five K, he was highly offended he was offered so little in comparison to Darrah."

Kenny continued, "Gabriel Pettigrew. Former coworker of Jeff's at

Merrill. Fired because, well, as far as we can tell, because he's an ass-hole. Jeff can confirm that, right? Or maybe the fact he threatened your daughter for talking to Henry Goode?"

"What?" snapped Jeff.

"It's taken care of," Andrea snapped harder. "But now you know the kind of partners you chose to work with."

Kenny continued, "Pettigrew laundered the money from the Medi-care account by running it through legitimate stock investments, which Jeff supervised. Gabriel copped to all of it, including the fact that if you check the account now, you might be surprised it's almost entirely drawn down, with just enough left in it to qualify Jeff and Martin for federal racketeering charges."

"What are you talking about?" Jeff said.

"A week after Derek died, Molly withdrew several million dollars out of the account and Gabriel kept his mouth shut because she offered him a skim of one mil," Kenny said.

"Fuck!" Jeff exclaimed. "Fucking bitch!"

"You don't know the half of it, sweetie," Andrea said, as she took the last folder from Shelby. "Joyce Li was Molly's old college room-mate. Now she's a pharmacist. In college, Joyce provided Molly with the benzodiazepines she used to cause her parents' fatal car accident. And a few weeks ago, she provided Molly with insulin. That's what she used to trigger Derek's heart attack. Undetectable after several hours, which is why she didn't want an autopsy performed at the time of death, but was okay with it taking place weeks later."

That caught the Cellulitists off guard.

Andrea strolled toward Brianne. Brianne downed what was left of her second glass. "Joyce Li also gave Molly the antibiotics she needed to treat her syphilis to one other person who was infected by Derek."

Brianne said nothing.

"You made the call to my phone, right?" Kenny said to Brianne. "To warn me about Molly."

"You had a burner phone because Derek gave them to all the women he was having affairs with," Andrea said.

Brianne said nothing.

Martin also remained quiet.

Andrea realized it wasn't because he was timid, or embarrassed, or ashamed.

"You knew?" she asked.

"You *knew* she was having an affair with Derek?" Crystal said. "How didn't I know?"

"Molly found out," Brianne said. "She told Martin to let it keep going or she would tell the police about the insurance fraud."

"She wanted the affair to continue to compromise Derek—and his accomplices," Andrea said.

"Suburban insanity," Shelby said. "Molly didn't need to work too hard to make it seem like she was an innocent surrounded by nutcases."

"She's the nutcase!" Brianne shouted. "The long sleeves to cover her bruises, that's not because Derek was abusive, it's because she forced him into S-and-M sex. She kept all her toys in a locked metal suitcase in her closet."

"Derek told me she was into that, too," Martin said, finally finding his voice.

"Her children were terrified of her," Brianne said. "Those kids have been mentally abused. Derek was the only good thing between them and her!"

"This is crazy," Wendell said.

"All of this is crazy, Wendell!" Martin exclaimed. He grabbed a bottle of wine and drank all of it in a massive, prolonged chug. Everyone stared in silence.

Martin stood up. He staggered slightly. "What's fucking crazy is pretending that this is all that our lives are supposed to be! Fucking go to school and go to college and then get a job, but guess what, you can't even get a job doing what you love. You have to work for your family's fucking senior living facilities. Surrounded all day with dashed dreams and senility and the smell of urine and old people—it's on their clothes, their furniture, everything—why is it on everything they own? How can this be what we've chosen for ourselves? A life of Amazon deliveries with more clothes and more candles and more soaps and more decorative fake flower arrangements for the patio table? Picking colors and patterns for towels and tablecloths and curtains, window treatments, and carpets. Chrome faucets or brushed nickel? Who gives a shit about *any* of that? How is *that* life? How is it living when you see the look every day in your wife's eyes, so bored with you that you can't blame her in the least, because you're so fucking bored with yourself?"

He took a breath, then kept rolling. "And every week you make the grocery shopping list and you complain about fucking Wegmans giving you no room to move your cart in their aisles and putting the price stickers on their fucking cold cuts so you can't open the fucking bag without tearing it! And why do they change where everything is in the store every two weeks? Every two fucking weeks! Why can't they just leave things where they are for one month? The lawn mowing and gutter cleaning and leaf blowing all summer long from eight in the morning until seven at night! And is your landscaping looking better than your neighbor's? Should we power-wash this year or next? It *never* ends! *Never!* How dead do I have to be that when I found out my wife was fucking my friend, I didn't even give a shit? *I just don't care!* I have to steal in order to feel alive, but the fear of getting caught makes me feel dead inside! And Amazon pulls up again with more fucking soaps! *Who the hell needs so many soaps?* Can I just have a bar of soap, please? A regular bar of soap! Why would anyone on the fucking planet want their hands to smell like blueberry cobbler or pumpkin spice cream or cinnamon sugared donut? Who wants their hands to smell like a donut? How the fuck is that soap?"

THE SELF-MADE WIDOW   327

Spent, Martin collapsed on the sofa chair. He still held the empty bottle in his hand. He politely placed it atop a trivet on the coffee table.

"I like that trivet," he mumbled.

No one talked for several seconds. Andrea let the outburst sink in. Martin's diatribe was exactly what she needed to knock the legs out from under anyone there who had been planning to continue fighting the inevitable.

"The reason you are all here," she said, adding with an eye toward Crystal, "including you and Wendell, is to admit to everything you have done and anything Molly has done to compromise you."

Shelby handed out general affidavit statements to Jeff, Martin, Brianne, Wendell, and Crystal.

"Wendell and Crystal are here to sign affidavits as eyewitnesses to everyone's voluntary engagement with the statements," Andrea said. "Sathwika is registered as a notary public in both New York and New Jersey and she'll certify your statements."

"You call it voluntary, but it feels like blackmail," said Jeff.

"You would think that way," Andrea said. "This is a lifeline. For all of you."

"We want Molly for murder and embezzlement," Kenny said. "The only way we get her on the former is if all of you come clean on the latter."

"Will that keep us out of jail?" asked Martin as he looked over the blank form.

"I hope so, Martin. I mean that honestly. I'm sorry you were all sucked into this. Initially, I only wanted to see Molly pay for her crime," Andrea said. "But cooperating now will go a long way in the eyes of state and federal prosecutors."

She could tell from the look in most of their eyes, including her husband's, that they weren't buying her attempt at reconciliation.

Brianne brusquely signed her statement and handed it to Shelby.

She walked over to the sofa chair Martin sat in. He was engrossed in writing his statement. He looked up, tentative.

She reached out her hand to him.

It hung in the air for a moment, but just for a moment.

He held her hand.

Her large brown eyes wet with remorse, Brianne said, "If you want, I can get rosemary mint soap instead."

45

WHEN Andrea called Molly after the weekend, she wondered how her friend would react to seeing the number come up on her caller ID. Andrea knew surprise or anger would be superseded by curiosity.

"Hello, Andrea," she said casually.

Standing on her deck with JoJo lying on a deck chair while she changed the baby's diaper, Andrea calmly spoke into her headphone mic. "Hi, Molly. Thanks for answering."

"We are adversaries, Andrea, not barbarians," she said.

"We have to talk," Andrea said. "Today. Just you and me. You pick the place. Out in public, if you prefer."

"Andrea, you're being deliciously mysterious," Molly said. "Do you really think you have it all figured out?"

"I do," Andrea replied.

"You don't, or I'd be in handcuffs already," Molly said.

"The cuffs are coming, Molly," Andrea said. "My friends in law enforcement don't think enough of you as a criminal mastermind to worry that you'll flee, so they said they'd prefer to cross every *T* first."

Molly chortled. She didn't like being disrespected. She said,

"Before the children are out of school. I'll text you the location fifteen minutes in advance."

Andrea hung up and made another call.

Ramon Mercado didn't answer. She left a voice mail and he called back within minutes.

"This is a risky play," he said.

"You're the one who told me to skate to where the puck is going to be, not to where it's been."

"Andie, you know it's unlikely you'll get her to confess."

They spoke for several more minutes to go over the logistics of what Andrea had planned. Her timing was extremely tight and predicated on getting Molly frustrated or scared enough to reveal information they still needed for an arrest warrant on the murder.

"Molly might be dangerous," he said. "Please be careful."

"Are you kidding me?" Andrea laughed. "I've been waiting a long time to try out the spear-hand technique you taught me."

Ramon laughed. "I hope you have to wait a lot longer."

"You're no fun," she replied, thinking how much fun he really was.

"You're ready for this?" he asked.

"One call to make for another piece of circumstantial evidence that's been nagging me and I'll be ready," she said. They hung up. She looked up the number for the Jos. A. Bank Clothiers in the MarketFair mall and dialed.

THE GROUNDS FOR Sculpture in Hamilton was a twenty-minute drive from West Windsor. Founded by artist Seward Johnson, grandson of the Band-Aid Johnsons, the site was meticulously carved from forty-two acres of industrial wasteland to form an oasis of landscaped walking paths that contained hundreds of outdoor and indoor sculptures.

The stylish Rat's Restaurant also provided access to the grounds, and that's where Molly said they should meet. Andrea had received the text twenty minutes earlier. She found Molly waiting for her at the bar. A cosmo, half-empty—or half-full, depending on your inclination—rested in her hand.

She looked as if Cruella de Vil had been cast in an Irish Spring commercial. Overdressed for the cooler fall day, she wore brown corduroy slacks and a rust-colored funnel-neck coat over a beige cashmere cardigan. A year ago, Andrea would have been jealous of how well put together Molly was, but now she only saw a desperate need to be accepted by the kind of people she expected to find at the Grounds for Sculpture during a weekday lunch.

Andrea wore black Eddie Bauer Storm sneakers, badly worn jeans, and a New York Jets sweatshirt, an outfit chosen purposefully to irritate Molly.

"Nice," Andrea said. "This place is cool. You mentioned it before, but I've never been here."

"I'm not used to seeing you without a child of varying age in your arms," Molly said casually.

"I thought the occasion warranted a sitter," Andrea said.

"Would you like a drink, then walk the grounds?" asked Molly.

"Sure," Andrea said.

Molly sipped the rest of her drink as Andrea downed a whiskey in a quick gulp. "Ready when you are," she said.

Molly smiled, not in a snarky or condescending fashion, but with the relaxed air of someone enjoying herself. "First, the restroom," she said.

"Weak bladder?"

Molly crooked her finger in a "come hither" motion. "I want to check you for recording devices."

It was Andrea's turn to smile. She was enjoying this, too.

The bathroom was empty.

Molly looked through Andrea's shoulder bag. She turned off Andrea's phone, rummaged through a few makeup items, credit cards, loose bills, receipts, coupons, and a tin of mints.

"Why would anyone who has nothing to hide worry if I was recording our conversation?" Andrea asked.

"Off with that horrible sweatshirt," she said.

Andrea lifted it off. "The Jets do suck," she said. "A generational consequence of growing up in Queens."

She stood in front of Molly in her bra.

"Pants, too," Molly said.

"Oh, c'mon, I'm not going to have my crotch wired."

"That's exactly what someone like you would do," Molly said, waiting.

Andrea kicked off her sneakers and took her jeans off.

She stood, exposed in her bra and panties, looking better than she had in over ten years, but knowing she still looked like a steamed gyoza in comparison with Molly. And she decided to own it. A year ago, she would have let the embarrassment and insecurity overwhelm her, leading to anger and self-recrimination.

Now she stood as tall as her five-foot-three-inch body would allow.

Molly walked around her slowly, eyeing her up and down. "You have put in the work, Andrea. Good for you."

Skirting seduction with disrespect, Molly inspected Andrea's bra.

"The only wire that's hiding in there is an underwire," Andrea said. "A lot of it."

Molly ran an index finger under the straps and along the top of the bra.

If she was looking to fluster Andrea, it wouldn't work. Andrea had been there and done that since high school. And if Molly was trying to seduce her, it wouldn't work, since after spitting out five children, the only thing that would get Andrea hot would be Molly in cuffs. Or maybe Ramon putting Molly in cuffs.

"Undergarments are best presented as a set. It really does look better when they match," Molly said. She took a few steps back, indicating the attempt at intimidation was over.

"I tend to put on whatever seems clean," Andrea said as she put on her pants.

They left the bathroom and walked out the French doors off the back of the restaurant. They stood in front of a small fenced-in koi pond that separated the restaurant patio from the grounds. Molly handed her a wristband.

"I bought tickets for both of us," she said.

They crossed a green wooden arched bridge that led them over the pond to the ticket gate, which was dressed up like something out of a kids' fairy tale. Most of the paths were gravel, which crunched under their feet. They walked a few steps and Andrea stopped at the first sculpture she saw. It was made of shiny aluminum.

"Is that, like, a flower?" she asked. "I'm bad with art. I guess I lack imagination."

"Oh, I certainly doubt that," Molly said. "If anything, you have far too active an imagination."

"Is it imagination when what you've imagined is real? Does that make sense?"

"You think you've found the truth you were looking for?" Molly asked.

"Oh, absolutely," Andrea said. "It's why I wanted us to talk. I mean, for your sake, it may be the last chance you'll get."

"Ah, I was hoping for something a little more unpredictable than expecting me to confess," Molly said as she moved on from the *Doubles* sculpture.

"How about you should feel very lucky I don't break your perfectly plastic nose for having someone threaten my daughter?" Andrea said, regretting it the minute her anger overwhelmed her desire to control the conversation.

"I would never threaten Ruth," Molly said, neither denying nor admitting her role.

"I never said you did," Andrea cut in quickly.

"If anyone did that, Andrea, I would certainly hope that harm had not been the intent."

Molly walked away. Andrea waited a few beats to calm down, then followed.

Molly stopped by the *Lakeside Table #1* sculpture, which was literally just a fully dressed table and chair set overlooking the smaller of the Hamilton Lakes that lay to the east of the property. There were three small boats on the lake. As soon as Andrea caught up, Molly quickly moved on. She knew Molly was taking the time to think through her position. Confronting her about the threat to Ruth seemed to have thrown her off.

Molly walked along the lake path, ignoring two men in a canoe who were fishing. She stopped at a bronze and resin statue named *Redon's Fantasy of Venus*. As she admired the work, Andrea came up behind her and softly said, "You can confess, Molly."

"Just between us girls?" asked Molly. "As we're standing in front of a woman emerging out of a clamshell representation of a vagina? Too on the nose, Andie."

"Is there another sculpture you'd prefer to confess in front of?"

Molly laughed and said, "Certainly something less obvious than this. This isn't a female thing, is it? I certainly don't think so."

"In what way do you mean?" Andrea asked.

"Oh, the aggrieved, abused spouse kills her husband in a fit of jealous rage, or a defiant act of self-defense," Molly said. "Far too pedestrian for me. And, I would hope, for you as well."

"I don't think of you as aggrieved or abused."

"No, thank you. Neither do I," she said. "You, on the other hand, are both."

"Am I?"

Molly's laughter was throaty, with a rasp of contempt. It sounded like sandpaper scraping against guitar strings. She said, "You are truly a piece of work. For all you are, you are also so much less."

They walked past a spirally, shiny sculpture that looked like a twisted horn.

"You have made choices of weakness your entire adult life, Andie," Molly said. "Out of fear of yourself, perhaps? By that, I mean, the fear of the burden that your talents must bring."

Andrea casually walked ahead of Molly and took a side path that tucked into a small alcove of sculptures at the end of the small lake. Molly followed her. They stood on an interactive sculpture taken from a Monet painting. The men in the canoe had stopped twenty yards offshore, their fishing lines in the water.

"I didn't mean to offend you," Molly said.

"Of course you did," Andrea replied.

Molly smiled. "Annoy you, possibly, but honestly, not to offend. You choose to diminish yourself, Andie. You let Ruth's birth create the excuse that allowed you to avoid your responsibilities. You let every other child harden the cocoon you'd built around yourself. I know you regret that, because I regret it in my own life. The difference is, you let it make you angry with yourself and I chose to become angry at the world."

"Haven't you always been that way?" Andrea asked.

"I don't know," she answered honestly. "As far back as high school, yes, I'm certain. My mind worked . . . well, let's just say Intercourse wasn't a good fit for me."

Andrea nodded. "That name really is a gift that keeps on giving."

Molly laughed. "It certainly fucked me."

"So, what are you saying? That my choices, my mistakes, would serve as justification for murder?" Andrea asked. "I don't buy that. Not the least of which, Jeff's transgressions don't meet the bar of self-defense."

Molly said nothing.

"And neither did Derek's," Andrea added.

Molly still said nothing.

She turned away from the lake and back to the main path. Andrea followed. The trail wound through rolling knolls of grass. Molly stopped to admire a bronze sculpture called *Trio*. It looked like twisted antlers. It resonated with her. Entwined, uncertain, but still striving to reach skyward.

"How did you feel when you found out about Jeff's fraud a few years ago?" Molly asked.

Andrea walked away from the sculpture and baited Molly to follow, saying, "Furious that he had lied to me."

"But?" Molly asked, taking the bait and walking briskly to catch up with her.

"But mostly mad at myself."

"Because you should have known," Molly said.

Andrea wandered toward an imposing curved sculpture called *Skyhook*. A young blond woman who had been looking at the piece turned at her approach and walked past them. "Are you saying Derek was lying to you? That you didn't know about the affairs, the Medicare fraud scheme?"

"I knew about the affairs," Molly said. "His brilliant white smile and those gleaming blue eyes; it was too easy for him. Life was a cocktail party."

"And what is it to you, Molly?"

She smiled. "A fight. And one that I intend to always win."

"What about the fraud scheme?" Andrea asked. "When did you find out about that?"

Molly said nothing.

"I told you, I came to give you a chance," Andrea said. "Just confess. There were mitigating circumstances. Derek cheated on you, lied about your finances, was committing fraud—and if he physically abused you, if he hurt the kids in any way . . ."

Molly looked over the *Skyhook* sculpture carefully. Made of steel and foam, epoxy, cable, and paint, it looked like a giant letter *S* looped through a pale blue donut. So many sculptures seemed twisted or turned inside out. Two things, once separate, now entwined around each other, retaining aspects of their original selves, coexisting while screaming for independence. Were she and Molly two sides of the same coin? Were their marriages the ultimate human sculpture?

"I have nothing to confess," Molly said.

"Do you really believe that when you say it?" asked Andrea. "Or do you say it to try and convince yourself to believe it?"

Molly shrugged. "I don't need to accommodate my perception that I've done nothing wrong to your perception that I have."

"You coerced your roommate in college to give you the drugs that led to your parents' car accident," Andrea said. "How would you perceive that?"

To Molly's credit, she remained composed.

"The loss of my parents was a tragedy," she said.

"Your brother and sister certainly thought so," Andrea said. "So did Joyce Li."

Panic and anger quickly slid across Molly's cold eyes.

"You remember your old college roommate, right?" said Andrea. "You must, considering you reunited with her this summer."

Molly turned away from the sculpture and walked briskly down the path to buy herself some time. She waited at an intersection. Andrea walked past her and toward a large rectangular fountain. She stopped at a small walking ramp that led to the main sculpture, allowing Molly to catch up.

The Nine Muses comprised several stone sculptures, facing each other on a granite platform in the middle of a fountain in a plaza surrounded by pine trees. An African American woman stood on the other side of the plaza, about thirty yards away, with her back to them, drawing the sculptures in her sketchbook.

"I knew I hated Derek within weeks of having married him," Molly said unexpectedly.

"Why?"

"After returning from our honeymoon," she continued. "With the adrenaline from the wedding, all that stress—do you remember how chaotic that time felt for us?"

"Kind of shotgun in my case," Andrea said. "City hall in Manhattan."

"Anyway, so much stress, and for what?" asked Molly. "Both of us were returning to work the next day, and as I lay in bed, I looked at him with his mouth open, snoring away, and I distinctly remember thinking, 'This is what I'll be looking at for the rest of my life.' Have you ever thought that way?"

"Of course," Andrea replied.

"And then I remember thinking, 'Hopefully his heart goes before my sanity does.'"

"Turned out to be a photo finish," Andrea muttered.

"You know that's not true," Molly said.

"Molly, I think you are the sanest person I know. Which makes what you did all the worse."

"Does it really, though?" Molly asked. "We are very similar in so many ways, Andie. We see things from all angles. We see linear structure for cause and effect, parabolic reciprocity—or perhaps even a Möbius strip—to establish motivation, divine declaration, and, once opportunity presents, to seize the moment for exploitation. We take a bird's-eye view of a map and see it in terms of time, distance, and topography. Frankly, there is no other person I know—or have ever known—who I could have just said all that to who would have understood it."

"I know that Moebius was a French comic book artist," Andrea said.

"Don't belittle yourself, or me, with that kind of flippancy," snapped Molly. "You are so much smarter, so much better than what you have allowed yourself to be. I don't know why. I thought perhaps it was out of some absurd desire to fit in with the idiots, but that kind of false modesty ill-suits you."

"You've done it, too, haven't you?" asked Andrea. "Tried to fit in with the idiots?"

"I have," Molly admitted. "It's exhausting."

"It is," Andrea agreed. "Is this the confession now? Motivation: you hated your husband as a reflection of how much you hated your life. Declaration: the meticulous planning of the crime, to the point of creating false alibi evidence as a means of obscuring the simplicity of the real evidence. And finally, the moment of exploitation: when the money in the Medicare fraud account reached the point where it exceeded the value of Derek's life insurance policy."

"That certainly seems to cover all the bases," Molly said. She moved away from Andrea, past the woman sketching, through a portico lattice tunnel of ivy, and back out onto a path that led to several more sculptures.

Molly stopped by a particularly stark piece that stood apart from the more geometric ebb and flow of the work across the grounds. Called *Skewered*, by sculptor Francisco Leiro, the bronze statue was of a tortured man writhing in agony, impaled by a pike running through the backside and out the mouth.

"Like looking in the mirror?" Andrea said.

"You think I'm caught," Molly said. "But I feel I am so much closer to freedom."

The woman sketching strolled through the ivy tunnel and sat down on a bed of freshly fallen leaves with her back to them. She began to draw a neighboring sculpture with her thick grease pencil.

"You're coming up with a lot of ways to admit you did it without outright saying you did it," Andrea said.

"I am, aren't I?" Molly laughed.

"You won't be laughing when I prove it was premeditated murder," Andrea said.

"As we've established, Andrea, if you could do that, we wouldn't be here right now."

"Even the circumstantial evidence makes you look bad, Molly. Getting your children sized for two suits for each of them to wear to the memorial service and funeral a full *two weeks* before Derek's 'accidental' death looks really tacky."

Though it clearly caught her off guard, Molly quickly recovered and said, "Certainly not as tacky as seeing you do air quotes around the word accidental."

After a few moments of silence, Molly said, "It was my idea."

"What?" asked Andrea, thinking maybe this was going to be it.

"Establishing the Medicare account," she said. "I gave the idea to Derek years ago. Laid it all out for him. More the fool him for having waited so long to act on it, or more the fool me that he did it without telling me?"

It was Andrea's turn to stay quiet. She let Molly's wistful frustration linger.

"How could we allow ourselves to be defined by our husbands, when they are so much less than us?" she finally asked.

"I've been asking myself that for years," Andrea admitted.

"We're very alike, Andie, but there is one major difference between us that I am quite happy about."

"And what's that?"

"Unlike you, I had the strength to do something about my situation," she said.

"Unlike you, I think committing murder is a sign of weakness, not strength," Andrea said.

Molly smiled, and this time it wasn't dripping with disdain. It was sad. "And what is getting away with it to you, then?"

"I have no idea," said Andrea. "I've never let anyone get away."

With that, Molly nodded and left.

She had smartly danced around admitting to her crimes, but had been arrogantly obvious that she had committed them all as well. If it didn't infuriate Andrea so much, she'd have to give credit to her friend for being so good at being such a bitch.

Andrea might not have gotten a confession, but she got enough. She turned to the woman sketching. "Did you get everything?"

FBI agent Nakala Rogers stopped drawing for a second, removed her cap, and smiled. She held up her large grease pencil and separated it from its casing to reveal a microphone recording device. "Got it."

Nakala reached into her light windbreaker and tugged at the communications harness she was wearing. "Rogers checking in. Suspect has left the grounds. How did everyone do?"

At the lakeshore, only one man was now sitting in the canoe, which was beached against the shoreline. His fishing pole resting across his lap, Ramon Mercado checked the miniature boom mic recording device at the end of the pole. "Everything recorded cleanly here. Lou, check in."

FBI agent Louis Galveston, who had been in the canoe with Ramon earlier, had made his way to the recording device embedded in the *Doubles* sculpture, which had been the first one Andrea had stopped at after entering the grounds. "Galveston copy. Recording captured."

Through Nakala's comm link, Andrea heard Ramon call out, "Joe?"

Agent Joe Benitez, an older man who normally was the team's paperwork expert, looked incredibly uncomfortable as he reached behind the naked female statue of *Redon's Fantasy of Venus*. He removed the recording device that had been affixed to her backside. "Benitez copy. Recording captured."

"Heather?" Ramon asked.

Agent Heather Antos, only six months out of Quantico, retrieved the device she had embedded in the *Skyhook* sculpture that she had installed when she saw Andrea walking toward her position. "Antos copy. Recording captured."

As they gathered along the path on the way back to the restaurant, Antos said, "How did you know this would be the location Molly Goode would pick to meet with you, Mrs. Stern?"

Wincing that she would qualify as a "Mrs." to the younger agent, Andrea said, "A few weeks ago, Molly mentioned the grounds as 'a place that speaks to freedom from so much that binds us, physically and spiritually.' And if there is one thing we got from her today it is that she has felt constrained and bound by her life."

"Poor baby," said Joe Benitez.

"What now?" Nakala asked.

Smiling at Ramon, Andrea said, "Now we go where the puck is going to be."

ANDREA pulled into the Montessori parking lot at a rate of speed wholly inappropriate for an airplane approaching a runway, much less a minivan approaching a preschool. Her brakes squealed to a stop. A staff member opened the door and Sadie trudged out. Her daughter's scowl brought Andrea down from the excitement of the afternoon.

"Mom, you're sooooo late!" her daughter chided.

"I know, sorry," Andrea said. "We have to get JoJo at Mrs. Duvvuri's house."

"I'm hungry!" Sadie whined.

"I'll give you ten dollars if you die of starvation before we get home," Andrea said.

"Ten dollars!" Sadie exclaimed, quite excited by the amount. "Hey, wait, I would have to die to get the money?"

"That is what is called an existential crisis, sweetie," Andrea said. They turned down Sathwika's street and she called her friend. "I'm here."

Sathwika came out carrying JoJo. Andrea opened the Odyssey doors. "I got it," she told Andrea as she put the baby into the car seat.

"Hi, Mrs. Duvvuri," Sadie said.

"Hey, messy head!" Sathwika laughed, mussing Sadie's hair. Sadie mussed Sathwika's hair in return. It had become their thing. Andrea loved that they had their thing, but she hated having to brush that thing out of Sadie's hair afterward.

"How did it go?" asked Sathwika.

"Not bad, not great," Andrea said.

"Call me later with all the details," Sathwika replied as she closed the automatic door.

Two hours later, phone propped on the counter and earbuds tucked in place, Andrea FaceTimed Sathwika while they each prepared dinner. Esha was in the background, "consulting" loudly on every cooking choice her daughter-in-law made.

It was annoying, but comical, especially when Ruth casually strolled by, dragging her backpack across the kitchen floor, and said, "I agree. That's too much paprika."

After hanging up, tired and distracted, Andrea burned her hand on the oven rack.

"Fuck!" she shouted.

"Quarter in the swear jar," she heard Sarah and Sadie chime in from somewhere in the bowels of the basement.

Ruth popped her head in from the sunroom. "You okay?"

"Yeah," Andrea sighed as she ran her palm under cold water.

"The top rack on the oven slid again?" Ruth asked.

"Fucking JennAir," Andrea said.

"Another quarter in the swear jar," Ruth said as they heard Sadie and Sarah saying it again.

"Take a fucking dollar out of my fucking purse," Andrea said as she cut the water and looked at the burn, which created a straight pink line across the palm beneath her thumb.

Ruth did take the dollar out and put it in the jar. And she took a ten and palmed it into her pocket.

"Something's wrong," her daughter said. "Wanna talk about it?"

Andrea sighed. "First let me get this casserole in the oven, then you put the ten you pinched back into my bag, and then let's go out to the deck. And if you're nice, maybe one day I'll teach you how to properly palm a bill."

A few minutes later, they sat on the Adirondack chairs on the deck.

"What we talked about a few days ago, it's all going down soon," she said, feeling she could be honest with her oldest.

"Is Dad going to be arrested?"

"Working on that," Andrea said. "Trying to keep him out of jail."

"But you might not be able to?" Ruth said.

Andrea said nothing.

After a few minutes of the brain-grinding sounds of leaf blowers in the distance and the geese honking in the pond, Ruth said, "What can I do?"

"Support your brother and sisters," Andrea said. "Just be there for them."

Andrea noticed Ruth was trying to be very strong, but she had tears in her eyes.

"I don't blame you, Mom," her daughter said, surprising her, since Andrea had never thought she bore any blame. After a pause, Ruth continued, "I mean, I'm not happy about any of it, but you—you're trying to do the right thing. It's not your fault. . . ."

Her first instinct was to say something defensive and sarcastic, but that wasn't what Ruth needed to hear. Instead, though it tasted like ground glass and regret on her tongue, she replied, "I could have chosen to let things go. Just let them be."

After a minute of silence, Ruth said, "No, you couldn't."

And with that, she hugged her mother tightly.

Despite waging a cold war between them, Andrea and Jeff managed to get through dinner, help the kids with their homework, and get them to bed. All along, Andrea kept wondering if it might be the last night they would be able to do that as a family. After Ruth and Eli fell asleep, Andrea was finally able to sit down with her husband to discuss what needed to be done.

He poured himself a full glass of Aviation gin on the rocks and joined her in the sunroom. He closed the French doors behind him to help muffle the inevitable shouts that were going to come. Andrea had her laptop open and Jeff was surprised to see her FaceTiming with his friend and lawyer, Gary Fenton.

"You told him about this?" Jeff asked.

"You should be happy she did," Gary said. His gravelly voice roared like a lion, but he was a pussycat of a man. Gary was a partner at one of Philadelphia's top law firms. He had been friends with Jeff since they attended summer camp in the Catskills when they were younger. "How could you get yourself sucked into something like this after what we went through a few years ago?"

"It's complicated," Jeff said.

Gary waved a stack of papers that Andrea had emailed him earlier. "I read your affidavit," he said. "It doesn't sound complicated at all."

"Whatever," Jeff said. "What's next?"

"Did Pettigrew tell you about Molly removing the money from the account?" Gary asked.

"No," Jeff said.

"Do you have any idea as to where she might have hidden the money?"

"No."

"Well, that doesn't help," Gary said.

"I think I know something Jeff could do that might help his case," Andrea said.

"I'm all for it," Gary said.

With angry reluctance, Jeff said, "What?"

"You haven't earned attitude," Gary snapped. "You get to say, 'Thank you, Andie. What would you like me to do?'"

"I should thank the person responsible for getting me into this mess?" Jeff said.

Andrea didn't care if the liquor had loosened his tongue. She went zero to Queens on him in 2.2 seconds. "Thank yourself then, you fucking child! *You're* the person responsible for getting yourself into this mess, because you're the one who made the choices to lie, and cheat, and steal. You're the one *always* looking for shortcuts. You think patience and hard work makes you a sucker, when what it does is show you have the ability to earn what you get. The fact you put all of us in this situation again—*again*—and can't accept responsibility for it is fucking exhausting. You are fucking exhausting."

Silence hung in the air.

Finally, Gary said, "Jeff, as your lawyer, and one of your oldest friends, I have to agree with everything she said and I have nothing more to add. Andie, let me know how it goes tomorrow."

Andrea ended the FaceTime call.

They said nothing for several more seconds.

He broke the silence. "Earn what you get? Coming from the person who was a thief for the first ten years of her life? You're so self-righteous."

Andrea snorted a breath of disbelief through her nose, then she chuckled. She couldn't even muster it in her to get mad at him again, softly saying, "You're such a fucking idiot."

"Am I?"

"I'd only be self-righteous if my moral superiority were unfounded," she said. "What you intended to say is that I'm so righteous. And that's because I am. And that's because I'm *right*!"

As she left the sunroom, in a voice lacking remorse, but now also lacking anger, Jeff said, "What do you want me to do tomorrow?"

KENNY looked over Sitara's shoulder. It was late and he had wanted to quit hours ago, but she refused to leave until they had finished editing the promo clips.

"Shelby needs to know what train we're going to be on," he said.

"Look at the schedule and tell her an hour later than whatever train you want to be on," she said.

"It's almost ten thirty," he said.

"Yup."

"And if we're all going to have a sleepover at my condo to get a fresh start on tomorrow, part of that fresh start is getting more than two hours' sleep," he said.

"I love it when you get agitated," she said as she calmly continued working.

"Then you must love me all the time," he muttered absently. Then he realized she was looking at him. "What?" he asked.

She spun her chair around and leaned toward him. She kissed him softly on the lips.

"What?" he asked again.

The office was empty. The cleaning crew had finished an hour ago.

Sitara stood up, taking his hand in hers and leading him into the conference room.

She kissed him again.

"What are you doing?" he whispered nervously. "You said you wanted to finish working."

She kissed his neck.

She reached down, lifting his untucked long-sleeve polo shirt over his head.

She ran her fingertips softly against his chest and down across his flat abdomen. For someone who had never been particularly athletic, he had also always been thin and therefore gave off the illusion of being toned.

Her fingers deftly unbuckled his belt and popped his pants open.

"Are we really doing this now?"

She unbuttoned the rest of his fly in a smooth, descending spider crawl of her fingers.

He wondered how Sitara was better at doing that than he was, when they were his pants.

She guided him back until he lay down, naked, on the conference table.

She lifted off her shirt.

Her hand slid up his thighs.

"The college kids will see us," he said.

Sitara was naked now.

"I don't have a condom," he muttered.

She climbed on top of the conference table and guided him inside her.

Eight seconds later, he wondered if he should apologize.

He apologized.

Lying against him, Sitara smiled, saying nothing, but kissing his bare chest.

In his abject embarrassment and frustration, he wondered what she was thinking, and none of it was in the context of his horrific performance. Would he always be like this? Would it always be like *this*? Would she always be the adult? The person having to make all the decisions? The one expected to always be organized, competent, and composed?

Kenny knew he needed to be constantly propped up. Stroked. Supported. Incessantly. Exhaustingly.

Yes, he was fun. He was brash. He flouted authority. He knew those traits excited Sitara because she wished she had more of them in her, but could she accept a relationship where her strengths were the other person's weaknesses? Why was it so hard to find a partner you could share things with equally?

She lifted herself off him. The conference room table was suddenly much colder as she separated from his warm body. As Sitara got dressed, she looked at him. He was watching her, but he was already thinking about tomorrow's arrest of Molly Goode.

Putting her jeans on, Sitara said, "Text Shelby and tell her we'll meet her at Penn Station in forty-five minutes."

He sat up on the edge of the table. "Tara, I'm sorry. I . . ." He paused. He wasn't sure what he was.

She stepped toward him and kissed him softly. "We have work to do," she said.

"Well, that's better than a cigarette," he said sheepishly.

ON THE LATE train to West Windsor, Sitara and Shelby sat in a three-seater with an empty space between them, while Kenny took the window two-seater across the aisle from them. Sitara used the opportunity to show Shelby the edited promo clips to gauge her opinion and avoid him. Kenny stared out the window and worked through his embarrassment.

He had never cared much about sex. As Sitara had taken his clothes off, as she had taken her clothes off, he understood, on an empirical level, that she was really hot and the circumstances should have been incredibly exciting. And all he had been thinking about was how much he wished he could be planning for tomorrow's capture of Molly Goode.

The thirty-second lovemaking marathon—and yes, he knew he was being generous with the time—hadn't even bothered him as much as the incongruity of the entire situation. He could cut the fingers off one hand for the number of times he'd had sex in the past five years and still have two fingers left. So, yes, the forty-second climax bothered him a little. How could he have been expected to last long?

Ultimately, what Kenny felt was both more than embarrassment and less.

He felt indifference.

He was thirty years old and the only meaningful relationship he'd ever had in his life was with the fear of being in a meaningful relationship. He always questioned everyone else's partnerships because it made him feel above their petty lives, petty grievances, petty failures, and petty triumphs. That hypocrisy provided a poor deterrent to the gnawing monster that ate at his very core: that Kenny Lee knew he would always be alone.

Kenny wanted to be normal, but he hated normality.

He understood why Jeff would cheat and scam to pull one over on the system.

He understood why Andrea had come back to life last year while investigating the Sasmal murder.

He even understood why Molly Goode would kill her husband out of both pure arrogance and sheer boredom.

Kenny knew plenty of people who were happily married, but he didn't know a single person in a marriage who was happy.

Of course, that could be mathematically extrapolated to the people he knew who were single as well, but since math wasn't his favorite subject, he preferred to not let that derail his train of thought.

When Kenny pictured life after the release of the book and the documentary, Sitara wasn't in that image. Working on the *next* book was. And the next doc.

And the book after that. And the documentary after that.

He didn't picture a pregnant wife and a white picket fence.

He was only in love with the work.

For a second, Kenny actually thought he was going to cry.

Then he thought about his five minutes of monster sex with Sitara and he felt good about himself again.

48

THE next morning, Molly Goode woke up feeling satisfied that Andrea's attempt to entrap her at the Grounds for Sculpture had failed miserably. Even if things still turned on her, she had her getaway planned and could act on a moment's notice. Either way, she had won. She made breakfast for the boys with a sunnier disposition than she'd displayed in months. They noticed, too.

Brett asked, "Mom, is everything all right?"

She kissed his forehead and said, "Everything is good and it's only going to get better."

Henry looked at her suspiciously, but in his heart, he desperately hoped it was true.

After both boys had left for school, she looked at her day planner. Yoga at eight. Zumba at ten. Pilates at noon. A shower followed by a light lunch, then off to Whole Foods before Brett came home. All in all, a pleasantly mundane, unpretentious start to her true freedom.

As she made a lemon turmeric flush smoothie for breakfast, her cell phone rang. She glanced at the screen and frowned. She answered it on speakerphone.

"What is it, Jeffrey?" she asked.

With extreme agitation in his voice, he said, "I'm being arrested today, Molly!"

"What are you talking about?"

"The FBI arrested Pettigrew last night," Jeff said. "He flipped, Molly. He told them everything!"

A surge of panic flushed through her, then she calmed herself. "He might have told them everything about you, Jeff, but there is nothing to tell about me. I was never involved in whatever Derek was doing with you."

"Except for the money you took out of the account, Molly!" Jeff shouted. "They know you have it!"

She abruptly ended the call. Her hand shook slightly. She clenched it into a fist, digging her fingernails into her palm until it bled. The stinging pain gave her clarity. She breathed deeply four times in a row, holding a fifth for several seconds before releasing it slowly.

She made a call.

"This is Molly Goode. I want it ready to go by ten o'clock," she said. The person on the other end talked. She curtly replied, "Yes, this morning." Pausing again, her tone went from bored to icy fury. "I'm well aware that's in two hours. I paid you a daily stipend for exactly this contingency. You assured me it would be no problem. So, will it be a problem?" She waited again. "Fine. I will be there by ten o'clock."

She stood in the middle of her kitchen. She grabbed a cast-iron skillet from the hanging rack above the island. Screaming, she slammed it down several times with enough ferocity to crack the granite. She stopped and carefully replaced the skillet on the rack hook. That outburst would take five K off the listing price on the house. She straightened up her hair.

"Alexa," she said. "Play the Pretenders. 'Middle of the Road.' Maximum volume."

The sound system exploded with Martin Chambers's smacking drums, followed by the guitar riff from Robbie McIntosh. As Chrissie Hynde's honey-drip "fuck you" vocals slid into the song, Molly had calmed herself.

She made three trips upstairs, bringing down one large, heavy suitcase at a time. She went to the basement and returned carrying a small fireproof safe. The strap she used to attach the safe to the raised roller-case handle matched the plaid design on the luggage. Even when flirting with desperation, one should try to match.

Molly put everything into the hatch of Derek's Land Rover.

Returning to the kitchen, she closed her eyes. She made a mental inventory of any remaining essentials. In the bags were new toiletry kits, clothes, and several flash drives with family photos, important documents, and banking information, and the last of Derek's burner phones she was able to find.

She went upstairs and grabbed two additional small suitcases. One contained ten thousand dollars in cash, the other over fifty thousand dollars in jewelry.

Chrissie's voice purred, slurred, and growled.

As she was growing up, all the albums in Molly's house had belonged to her mother. She had loved bands with female lead singers, like Jefferson Airplane, Heart, the Pretenders, and Blondie. When Molly was younger, she sought out Hole, Garbage, Evanescence, and Paramore. Women who were all righteously and rightfully pissed off about something, but knew how to play the game when they had to. For a moment, she regretted having killed her mother.

The extended musical interlude in the song hit a crescendo. Molly knelt down in front of the master bathroom door. She lined up the door knob with her face. The angle was perfect. She firmly grabbed the door. As coincidence would have it, Chrissie started counting up from one in the lyrics, and on three, Molly swung the door directly into her face.

The impact knocked her backward to the floor. She took a second to catch her breath and lifted herself up. She looked in the mirror. Her right eye was swelling, just as she'd intended. She straightened her hair again.

Molly looked around her bedroom, confident that she'd done all she needed to.

She carried the two bags downstairs. She grabbed the keys to Derek's Land Rover. She took a last look around the kitchen. They had put a lot of work into the house. Spent a lot of money.

Her taste—her impeccable taste—ran through every piece of furniture, every tile, every paint color, and every fabric choice. It had been their house, but it had been built on her choices.

Everything in Molly's life had been built on her choices.

The song ended.

She took it all in. Over ten years of work. Of building a life. Walking past the very spot where they had brought the boys home from the hospital for the first time. Supervising the gardeners as they had planted the arboretum. Arguing with the husband and wife window designers who were so arrogantly certain her preference for a pencil pleat on the sunroom window treatments wouldn't work. Henry trying to do a flip off the couch and getting twelve stitches after hitting his head against the fireplace mantel.

She thought about Derek and the life they had built together in that house.

Molly said, "Alexa, go fuck yourself."

She didn't look in the rearview mirror as she drove away.

Minutes later, she parked in the fire zone in front of Millstone Upper Elementary School and went to the main office. To alleviate the attendance officer's initial shock at seeing her swollen eye, Molly played the injury off as a nasty pickleball accident.

"I need to remove Brett from school and he'll likely be out the rest of the week," Molly said. "His uncle has been in a car accident in Chicago."

Knowing what the family had been through, the attendance officer went to retrieve Brett herself. Molly could see the visibly upset child being led down the hall toward the main entrance area. He looked ready to cry, but then again, she thought, he looked ready to cry at most everything.

He was weak. She had to be strong for him.

"Did something happen to Uncle David?" he asked.

She said, "We have a flight to Chicago at noon out of Newark. We have to get your brother."

"What happened to your eye?"

"Pickleball," Molly said.

She thanked the attendance officer and hustled Brett out to the car. They drove a short distance down the road to Community Middle School, where Henry attended. She told Brett to wait in the car. Her story to this attendance officer was about Aunt Deirdre being in a car accident in Los Angeles and they had to catch a flight out of Philly in three hours. She purposefully gave conflicting stories to sow confusion should people search for them later.

When the woman wouldn't stop staring at her eye, Molly said, "Pickleball."

The woman called Henry on the school intercom. "Henry Goode, please report to the main office," came the crackly voice through the intercom system in Henry's class. "And bring your work, you'll be leaving for the day."

■ ■ ■

IN HIS CLASSROOM, Henry stood up, confused. Ruth, who sat behind, locked eyes with him. He shrugged his shoulders. She was worried. She wasn't sure if she should say anything. She suspected what might be happening, but it would be wrong to tell Henry, wouldn't it?

Her mom had a job to do, and warning Henry that Molly might be getting arrested could jeopardize that. In that instant, two thoughts flashed through Ruth's mind: Does my mother really have a job if she isn't being paid to do it? And: I may never see my friend again.

When Henry reached the door, Ruth suddenly burst out, "Henry, wait!"

She rushed over to him and gave him a tight hug. Through his confusion, she whispered, "I'm sorry."

She turned and quickly shuffled back to her seat, her head down to escape the stares of her classmates and to avoid showing the guilt Henry would have seen in her eyes. She passed his empty desk and reached hers. She heard the classroom door close. Ruth sat down, ignoring the looks being cast at her, and tried not to cry.

WHEN HENRY SAW his mother, he asked what had happened to her eye.

"Pickleball," Molly snapped, tired of the excuse.

In the car, Henry's suspicions grew. "Mom, what's going on?"

"Uncle David was in a car accident," Brett said.

"Wait, Mrs. Cohn said it was Aunt Deirdre. Mom . . . ?" asked Henry.

"They're both fine, boys, I just wanted an easy excuse to get you out of school," Molly said. She continued driving south on Route 1, passing the malls and taking the exit for Interstate 295 North to Interstate 95 South, toward Philadelphia. They rode under the sign. A slight cruel smile sliced through her tension at the thought of no longer having to live in a state where you were expected to drive north to go south.

"Are we flying out of Philly?" Henry asked.

"I thought we were flying out of Newark," Brett said. "That's what Mrs. Abernathy told me when she walked me out of class."

"We're flying out of Trenton," said Molly.

That confused the boys, since their privileged life had made both aware at a young age that Trenton-Mercer Airport didn't fly planes to Chicago or Los Angeles.

"I chartered a jet," Molly said absently.

They didn't quite understand what that meant. Brett asked, "Is that like we get our own plane?"

"Yes," Molly said.

"To go *where*?" Henry asked, but Molly didn't answer.

He pressed, until they reached the exit for the airport, but she ignored him. They pulled into the winding entrance drive and parked the car in the long-term lot, next to the Trenton-Mercer general aviation building.

They removed the large roller suitcases from the trunk.

"This is a lot of luggage," Henry said, suspiciously.

Molly struggled a bit to make sure the safe was properly balanced and the two shoulder bags with the money and jewels were secure over her shoulder. She walked toward the entrance to the building.

Brett said, "Don't we have to pay for parking?"

She waved him off, musing that the credit card machine at the gate likely lacked "forever" as a pay option.

"Why are you bringing a safe?" Henry asked, his doubts now having become borderline panic. "Mom, please tell us what's going on!"

"Henry, stop it! Just stop," Molly said, continuing to walk. "We have to go!"

"Where?" Henry asked again as Brett tried to keep up with his mother.

She kept walking, now several yards farther ahead.

"Mom, I'm not going anywhere until you tell me what's going on," Henry said.

Molly spun around, unable to control her frustration. "Enough!" she said. "Enough! We have to leave now!"

Henry was near tears, and seeing his brother so upset froze Brett to the spot.

Molly softened. She walked back to them. She tried to gently rub their cheeks, but the bags over her arms made her movements awkward. "Your father was involved in illegal business activities, Henry. Simple as that. He did something wrong for the sake of his family, because he was always afraid he could die at any moment. He secretly made a lot of money and now people are trying to take that away from us. I can't let that happen. *We* can't let that happen. Okay?"

Henry processed it. He nodded.

"Where are we going?" Brett asked.

They went through the elite executive check-in process, which at an airport as small as Trenton was still pretty much the same as the accommodations for the steerage passengers on the *Titanic*. TSA agents checked their passports and inquired about the contents of the safe and the bags with the jewelry and money. Molly looked at Brett and Henry. The hard look in her eyes told them that whatever was going to come out of their mother's mouth was going to be a lie and they would have to go along with it.

"As you can plainly see," she said, gesturing to her swollen eye, "my husband is abusive. This morning, he violated his restraining order. I'm leaving for several months until he chooses to get help or agrees to leave us alone. I took what I could carry out of the house. The safe contains legal and financial documents that I need for my protection. I can open it and show them to you."

The two TSA agents consulted. The color of Molly's skin and the size of the bank account needed to have a Falcon 900EX from

Aviation Charters on standby were sufficient to wave her through with a shrug.

"This way," Molly said to the boys.

Outside, the sleek white jet was forty yards away on the tarmac.

"Over there," she said.

"Wow," Brett said.

She was greeted by an African American woman wearing a white blouse with a sky-blue kerchief knotted around her neck. "Mrs. Goode," she said. "Welcome to Aviation Charters. I'll be your service attendant for your flight to Grand Cayman."

Molly brusquely nodded. "We're in a rush. How soon can we take off?"

"As soon as you're on the plane, ma'am," the attendant said as she gestured toward the airstairs. "Leave your luggage on the tarmac and we'll take care of it."

Molly stepped away from the luggage and grabbed the hands of her sons, who flanked her. Brett looked like he was excited to go on an adventure, while Henry remained distrustful and wary. As they climbed the stairs, Molly finally smiled. Each step brought her one step closer to freedom. Once the door to the plane closed, she would feel safe.

She froze when Andrea Stern emerged from inside the plane cabin to block the open door at the top of the steps.

"This thing is absolutely beautiful," Andrea said, smiling. "You should really let the boys take a look inside."

Molly was paralyzed.

"Mom, what's Mrs. Stern doing here?" Brett asked.

Henry said nothing. He knew.

They heard sirens in the distance, getting closer.

"Let the kids see the inside of the plane, Molly," Andrea repeated. "Now."

Molly turned away from the stairs, only to see the flight attendant blocking her path and holding an FBI badge in the air. That was when Molly knew. Her jaw dropped, then tightened to the point you could practically hear the grinding of her teeth through the noise of the resting jet engines. Recognizing the woman, she said, "You were at the Grounds for Sculpture."

Nakala Rogers said, "Let the boys see the inside of the plane, Mrs. Goode. There are people inside who will keep them safe."

The sirens grew louder. Molly saw four FBI cars emerge from behind the plane hangars to their right and encircle the jet. A metallic gray BMW trailed behind the row of cars.

"Boys, go inside and see the plane," Molly said, having the discretion to understand they didn't need to see their mother arrested.

Brett enthusiastically went up the stairs, rushing past Andrea, still unaware of exactly what was happening. Henry protested at first.

"Go, Henry," Molly said. "Help your brother." She fought back a tear. Her voice, always showing the emotional range of stone, cracked slightly as she leaned into her son and whispered, "Help him forever."

Henry climbed the ladder. Andrea reached out a comforting hand, guiding him by the shoulder. She softly said to him, "I'm sorry."

He looked at her coldly, then turned at the top of the steps to look back at his mother.

Molly brushed her windswept hair to the side.

Andrea softly nudged Henry inside. The window shades were all down, so the boys couldn't see outside. She turned back to the stair landing. She looked down on Molly, hearing Brett behind her: "Henry, look at the size of this TV! This is so totally cool!"

On the tarmac, Kenny emerged from his BMW. Jimmy had bolted out of the car before it had even come to a stop. His Sony XD camera captured everything around him. Sitara and Shelby, who had both been in the terminal recording footage of Molly while she was on the TSA line, stood outside the terminal door, still shooting with their phones. They were getting what they wanted. Andrea wished she could feel the same.

Henry slipped by some of the agents inside the plane cabin and tried to get past Andrea to see what was happening, but she stopped him. She held him tight and he didn't resist, looking for comfort in any way he could get it.

"I'm sorry for what she did, Henry," Andrea whispered to him. "And I'm really sorry for what it's done to your life."

"It was more than the money, wasn't it?" Henry asked.

"Yes," Andrea replied. She would have elaborated if he had pressed, but he simply nodded. He knew.

"What happens to us now?" he asked.

"The FBI will take you to their Newark office," she said. "Your uncle David is flying into Newark this afternoon and you'll go with him."

"Can we get stuff out of our house?" he asked.

Andrea said, "Your uncle will do all that with you."

"Will I be able to say goodbye to my friends?"

Knowing it might be a lie, she softly said, "Yes."

Andrea watched Ramon Mercado cuff Molly Goode and read her rights.

It didn't give her the sexual charge she'd expected that it would. None of this did.

Kenny was barraging Molly with questions, which she refused to answer. Andrea knew he would have liked a response, but he was really doing it because the audio would overlay nicely when he edited together the footage of the day's events. Kenny was very skilled at ensuring his flow of questions told the story whether or not answers were given.

Molly looked up at Andrea, whose back was partially turned from her, still holding Henry. He was just far enough inside the cabin that he couldn't see out. Molly nodded with a grim smile. An acknowledgment that Andrea had won.

Kenny repeated, "Did you kill your husband, Mrs. Goode?"

Molly shook her head slightly so the wind blew her hair off her face. Her chiseled features looked great on camera. She smiled. Perfect white teeth. Calmly composed. A glint of arrogance flashed across her eyes.

"Please, go fuck yourself, Mr. Lee," she said.

With that, Molly Goode was led into one of the FBI SUVs.

49

*I*N the days following Molly's arrest, Andrea had to placate Kenny, who complained that his crew hadn't been given better access to the scene. She also had to negotiate with Ramon for the opportunity to present evidence that Molly should also be charged with two murders aside from the embezzlement charges she had been arrested on. Once she convinced Ramon, she then had to cajole West Windsor police chief Preet Anand into hearing that evidence. And she also had to figure out how to keep Jeff and Martin out of jail.

Placating Kenny had been the easy part. She had basically said, "Tough fucking luck. Sorry you didn't get video from inside the plane of two children having their lives torn apart."

Convincing Ramon hadn't proved difficult, either. He didn't want to muddy the very clear chain of evidence they had on the embezzlement charges, but he understood they had to at least consider the murder charges. Out of respect for Andrea, he agreed to have the federal prosecutor meet with the Mercer County prosecutor to discuss her case.

On Friday morning, the day of the release party for Kenny's book, Andrea stood in the large conference room of the West Windsor Police

Department. Sathwika stood to her side, manning the remote for the slide show they had prepared.

The room was full and the table was segregated by affiliation. To her left were Detectives Rossi and Garmin, Police Chief Anand, and the Mercer County prosecutor. Anthony D'Onofrio was in his early fifties and had been with the prosecutor's office for twenty years. He also seemed incredibly uninterested in the politics of pursuing someone on state charges who had already been arrested on federal ones.

To Andrea's right were Ramon and Nakala, along with two assistant US attorneys, a man and a woman both in their thirties, representing the Newark and Trenton vicinages. Andrea was potentially complicating their lives quite a bit, and it showed in their faces. She knew they'd become even more annoyed upon learning the death of Molly's parents would drag Pennsylvania into the case, too.

Sathwika introduced herself and then Andrea, reminding everyone in the room they weren't dealing with just a couple of bored New Jersey housewives, they were dealing with smart and accomplished bored New Jersey housewives.

Andrea took over as a slide of Molly appeared on the screen, taken from the PTA website of Brett's upper elementary school. Andrea started her rundown of the evidence, presented in a PowerPoint slide show with photos and graphics that Sathwika had crafted with incredible polish.

They presented all the players in the case and how the Medicare fraud overlapped with Molly's motives to murder Derek. They held up affidavits signed by several people, including Joyce Li, who attested to having provided Molly with both the drugs she had used to kill her parents years ago and what she used to kill Derek weeks earlier.

"Insulin?" asked Rossi, unexpectedly interrupting her. "She used insulin to cause Derek's heart attack?"

Andrea smiled. "Untraceable. And combined with the cocaine that

Derek was already putting into his system, his congenitally weakened heart couldn't tolerate the added strain."

They all nodded and Andrea knew she had them. They remained silent until she got to the meeting at the Grounds for Sculpture.

Anand interrupted, looking to Ramon and Nakala. "You set up a full-scale outdoor surveillance operation in advance based on a hunch that's where Molly would choose to meet?"

"No," Nakala quickly interjected. "We set it up based on the deductive reasoning of a criminal consultant we've come to trust."

Andrea smiled inside at that. A year ago, she was jealous that Nakala, unmarried with a four-year-old child, was living the life she had been afraid to. Now Andrea was happy to know she had earned the agent's trust, just as Nakala had earned hers.

"We didn't conduct the sting expecting Molly to confess, though we were hoping she might. Mostly, it was to gauge her disposition toward fight or flight," Andrea said. "Molly tipped her hand to flight, which led us to uncover the chartered jet she had on standby at Trenton airport."

"Preferring to catch Molly in the act of trying to escape on an international flight, we contacted the airline and the airport to prepare the trap," Nakala said. "She was arrested for embezzlement, interstate racketeering, and international money laundering."

"But you still want her charged for murder?" asked D'Onofrio.

"This all started because she *is* a murderer," Andrea said. "Molly Goode gave Derek Goode the insulin that led to his heart attack."

D'Onofrio flipped through the file in front of him. "But the body was exhumed and a medical examiner's report found no traces of insulin?"

Andrea said, "They weren't looking for that, they were looking for cocaine, which they found. But even if they *had* been looking for it, by the time the body was exhumed, the traces of insulin that were used would not have been detectable. Molly knew that."

"Still doesn't make sense she would kill him," D'Onofrio said.

Andrea held up her phone and hit play on an audio file. Molly's and Andrea's voices from their walk at the Plainsboro Preserve filled the room.

MOLLY: But let me ask the ace investigator, why kill someone who was going to die eventually anyway?

ANDREA: That word, *eventually*, is quite the complex variable, Molly. Wouldn't you agree?

MOLLY: That is a valid point. Eventually could seem like an eternity to some.

ANDREA: And eternity sure is a long time to wait.

MOLLY: Far too long.

ANDREA: You never answered my question.

MOLLY: Didn't I?

Andrea stopped the tape. "Derek Goode could have died in a week, in a year, possibly even ten years. For someone like Molly—meticulous to the minute in planning and structuring the events of her daily life and that of her children, deeply unhappy with her husband, and unsatisfied with her life—that was a degree of uncertainty she simply couldn't accept."

Everyone took it in. Preet and Ramon thanked the women and jokingly jockeyed for the chance to hire them both as consultants. "Highest bidder usually wins," Sathwika said with a smile. "But in this case, we're willing to consider daycare to offset your incredibly limited budgets."

"Give us all a chance to talk," Preet said.

"We'll get lunch and come back," Andrea said.

"Anyone want us to bring anything back?" Sathwika asked. "Mizu Sushi? My treat."

Everyone placed orders and after they left, Andrea said, "That was two hundred dollars' worth of food you offered to pick up. Shouldn't you have waited at least until they said they'd be willing to charge Molly?"

Sathwika laughed. "It's a down payment."

"On a murder charge?"

"On our new business," Sathwika said.

Andrea smiled.

WHEN THEY RETURNED from lunch, D'Onofrio quickly stated the inevitable: "I'm sorry, Mrs. Stern, Mrs. Duvvuri. This is excellent work. Excellent. But the evidence remains difficult to establish proof in court. If we failed in prosecuting Molly Goode for murder, that could hinder the federal trial. We will present this evidence to the Lancaster County prosecutor in Pennsylvania, but outside of the pharmacist's confession that she gave Molly benzo, proving Molly actually administered them to her father, and that led to the accident, would be very difficult beyond a reasonable doubt. Even without the murder convictions, she's going to spend a minimum of twenty-five years in a federal prison."

"And she'll get away with two murders," Andrea said. Part of her obvious frustration was for show, but they didn't know that. This was what she had expected since the embezzlement scheme had come to light. In fact, not only had she been resigned to this outcome, she had decided to use it as the precursor to what she was actually hoping to get out of the meeting.

Andrea said, "Let's talk about the cooperation that was provided by my husband and Martin Singer."

50

LOOKING over the raw footage from Molly's arrest, Sitara had repeatedly assured Kenny they'd gotten some terrific video, but it hadn't mattered to him. He couldn't stop complaining that they hadn't been granted access inside the plane. After all the work the Muckrakers had done to provide the information the FBI used to arrest Molly, they shouldn't have been shut out that way.

For days, Sitara's response had been, "We knew all along getting a camera inside the plane was dependent on whether Molly brought her kids with her."

For days, Kenny's response had been, "Kids look great when they're watching their mother get arrested."

And it had left Sitara thinking that Kenny would always feel cheated, about anything and everything. The previous night, before today's planned publication-day party for his book, they'd had an argument about it. Sitara had practically begged him to try and enjoy the day without anger, cynicism, or insecurity.

He promised he would.

It wasn't his sincerity she doubted, but his ability to follow through.

∎ ∎ ∎

KENNY HAD A day's worth of promotion in advance of the party that evening, so he didn't get into the office until late afternoon. Seeing Jimmy in a suit and Shelby in a dress was disconcerting, because jeans and T-shirts had been their wardrobe of choice for months. They all looked like they could chew Manhattan in half and still have enough of an appetite to make their way through most of Brooklyn.

Sitara hadn't gotten dressed yet, though she said she'd be ready in plenty of time.

That got Kenny nervous. Based on his experiences with his mother, when Blaire said she'd be ready in plenty of time, that usually meant they would be thirty minutes late. Maybe he was just looking for a reason to get nervous. Either way, by the time Sitara took her dress to the bathroom to change, Kenny's restless leg syndrome had registered five miles walked on his phone app.

After a few minutes of watching Kenny stew, Shelby said, "We're not going to be late."

"And even if we are, so what?" Jimmy said. "It's your book, man, it's your party. You can be as late as you want."

"He's still mad about the airport and he's trying to create a fake reason for being angry now," Sitara said as she emerged from the bathroom. She casually walked down the hall knowing she looked like a knockout and knowing that everyone knew she looked like a knockout.

"We fucking dress up real nice!" Jimmy hooted.

Shelby said, "Let's get drunk and beat the shit out of a bunch of book nerds!"

THAT WEEK, WHEN Kenny Lee had learned that his book was debuting on the *New York Times* nonfiction bestseller list, and his editor and publisher told him they were exercising the contractual option for his next book, he accepted that maybe he had finally redeemed himself. It had taken him years, but he had done it.

He could stop being driven by his failures.

He could stop being so insecure about everything.

For the first time in a long time, Kenny chose to absorb the positivity around him rather than deflect it. All night long, and even during the interviews he'd conducted earlier, he heaped praise on his editor at Putnam, on Andrea, and on the West Windsor detectives, and respect to the families and loved ones of those who had suffered the tragic losses that had resulted in *Suburban Secrets*.

A little after midnight, they all left the drunken remnants of the party together.

Shelby hailed a cab and dragged Jimmy with her. Whatever they were doing, whenever they were doing it, and wherever they chose to do it, Kenny and Sitara had been smart enough not to ask.

They stood outside Gotham Hall on Broadway and Thirty-sixth Street. It was getting cold out. He draped his suit jacket over her shoulders. Traffic zipped by. The city, in that moment, looked like a field of caffeinated fireflies at night.

Kenny looked into Sitara's eyes. She smiled.

"This was a good night," she said. "You did a really good job."

"Move in with me," he said abruptly.

That caught her off guard. She laughed. "I thought you were going to say you wanted to go back to the conference room and give it another try."

"Take a train down to Princeton with me," he said. "Tonight. Spend the weekend, we'll come to work together on Monday and we'll keep doing it every day."

She demurred slightly, now a little concerned. "How much did you drink?"

"Not nearly enough to give me the courage to ask you to marry me, but enough to ask you to move in with me."

"Kenny . . ." she whispered, trailing off.

"Too soon?" he asked. "We work, Tara. You and me, we work."

"We do, Kenny," she said.

"There's a 'but' there," he said, only because it was clear to him there was a "but" coming.

"No," she said.

"We're going to work together for another year, maybe two," Kenny said. "And there will be another book or another documentary and we'll work on that together. *We work together, Sitara.*"

"I know. We do," she said. "But that's work. It's not—"

"I can be better," he said softly, feeling that he was losing the moment. "I've really been trying."

"I know."

"For the last year, even before you met me," he continued, his words starting to run together nervously. "I've been trying. I know I'm not a good person, not yet. But I've really been trying not to be a bad person. I mean, you wouldn't have gone out with a bad person, right?"

She grabbed both his hands in hers and squeezed tightly. "Kenny, stop. Don't. I can do the 'it's not you, it's me,' thing, and in some ways, it *is* that. But it's me *because* of you."

That confused him.

"I can't wait, Kenny."

"I don't understand."

"I'm thirty-one," Sitara said. "Ten years ago, I refused to go along with the arranged marriage that had been expected of me since I was nine. I told my parents I was young and I could wait. Now, I don't feel as young, and I don't want to wait. I can't wait for you to grow up, Kenny."

"But, I—"

She shushed him by kissing him softly, but quickly.

"I can't live my life waiting for you to learn how to live yours," she said.

They stood in silence for several seconds. He wanted to say something, but for the first time in his life, Kenny Lee had nothing to say. The blaring of car horns snapped them out of it.

"I'll see you at work on Monday," she said. "We'll put *Suburban Secrets* to bed and it's going to kick so much ass that Netflix's algorithm will have an orgasm. Then we start working on *Suburban Spouses*."

"*Suburban Spouses*?" he said. "I like that."

"I knew you would," she said. She kissed him on the cheek and turned back toward Herald Square. "My station is this way. I'll see you, Kenny."

He watched Sitara walk away until she was swallowed up by the city.

He should have had more to drink. He rolled the dice and came up craps.

Kenny wondered why the game needed to be played at all. He was pretty sure that he loved her, but what did love have to do with it, when so many other things got in its way? Having put himself out there for Sitara to shoot down, he wondered whether he did it because he had really wanted to, or because that was what society expected of the new and improved, socially acceptable version of Kenny Lee.

Could spending your life alone be any worse than feeling lonely with another person?

Suburban Spouses really did sound good, he thought.

He breathed in the city air, which now had a crisp bite to it that let you know winter was just around the corner. He held it for several seconds.

He released it in a drawn-out exhalation.

To be honest, it felt like a sigh of relief.

AFTER an excruciatingly tense week and weekend in the Stern household, on Monday morning Andrea rushed to get Ruth, Eli, Sarah, and Sadie their breakfasts while Jeff fed JoJo a bottle. Even though they had tried, putting up Halloween decorations and carving pumpkins, the kids could sense their parents' unease. Just the fact that Jeff hadn't gone to work in the morning had thrown them off.

Thinking he might distract everyone from their tension, Eli took exactly the wrong approach and said, "Brett wasn't in school all week. Is everything okay?"

Ruth threw her spoon down, clanging it off her cereal bowl. "You're such an idiot!" she shouted, storming away from the table.

In unplanned synchronous union, Andrea and Jeff exclaimed, "Hey! Ruth!"

They glanced at each other. Taking their current circumstances into account, neither of them knew if they should find the moment endearing or exasperating. Sarah and Sadie took the choice out of their hands by giggling in unison, "Jinx! Jinx! Jinx!"

Andrea cast ice their way and that shut them up.

"What did I say?" asked Eli, so like his father, oblivious to the obvious, much less the subtle.

"Nothing," Andrea said, though what she really wanted to say was, *I wish you could have a fucking clue about what was going on around you, Elijah.*

Andrea followed Ruth upstairs to her room.

"I'm sorry," Ruth said.

"Apologize to Eli later."

"For him being an idiot or for me calling him one?" Ruth asked.

"Probably the second one," Andrea said. She sat down on the bed next to her daughter, who fumbled to pretend that she was realigning things in her backpack. "I'm sorry, too."

"They're not coming back, are they?" Ruth whispered.

"Henry and Brett are going to live with their uncle David's family in Chicago," Andrea said. "I think they'll be happy there."

"It sucks."

"It does."

"And you said she's not even being arrested for murder?"

"No," Andrea admitted.

"So, you couldn't prove she did it?"

Andrea stubbornly said, "We provided enough evidence that could have led to charges being filed."

"Could have, but didn't."

"Sometimes, it gets tricky, Ruth," Andrea said. "The prosecutors felt they had a much better chance of getting convictions against Molly on other charges. So she will be going to jail."

"And Dad?" Ruth asked.

"We hope to figure that out this morning," Andrea said. "I'm sorry about Henry."

"You knew this was going to happen," Ruth said.

"I did."

"And you don't care?"

"I care a lot," Andrea said.

"But you care about justice more?"

Andrea didn't say anything.

"More than me, or Eli and Sarah and Sadie and JoJo?" Ruth asked. "Even more than Dad?"

Andrea wasn't sure what to say. The truth was far too complicated a mix of grays to boil it down to such black-and-white absolutes. Pressed on her conflicted morality, she went to her natural default: sarcasm.

"I absolutely don't care about justice more than you and Sarah," she said, smiling. "JoJo is still TBD."

Ruth laughed. "God, you're such a bitch."

Andrea might have been taken aback by her daughter talking to her that way, but she accepted it in the manner in which Ruth had intended it. The entitled suburban Jersey brat had unleashed a little bit of the Queens that was in her genes.

"No jokes, Mom," Ruth pushed. "Is the truth worth ruining our family over?"

"No, it's not," Andrea replied. "But maybe it's worth it if it makes our family stronger."

"Will it?" Ruth asked, her eyes suddenly those of a three-year-old begging for comfort.

Andrea had no answer.

AFTER THE KIDS had left for school, Andrea and Jeff dropped JoJo off with Sathwika. Jeff waited in the car as Andrea stood on the porch. JoJo played with Sathwika's hair as her friend asked, "How are you guys doing?"

"Not good," Andrea answered honestly.

"They're going to charge him?" she asked, surprised.

"No, not that," Andrea said. "I expect they're going to plead it down to fines and suspensions in return for full cooperation against Molly and the return of all the remaining money they stole. Luckily, none of it had been spent except for some of what Molly had taken out."

"So, not good between the two of you?" Sathwika said. "Do you want me to take the kids out trick-or-treating later?"

"No. I don't know. Thanks. I can't believe they scheduled this for Halloween. I'll talk to you later. Thanks." Andrea looked back at the car. Jeff was clearly impatient behind the steering wheel.

She looked back at her friend, whose luminous eyes offered nothing but sympathy and support.

"I'm sorry," Sathwika said, hugging Andrea.

"I don't think I am," Andrea said, turning to leave.

ANDREA AND JEFF met Gary Fenton outside the entrance to the FBI building in Newark. Martin and Brianne Singer were already inside and waiting in the lobby. It was the first time Andrea had seen Brianne since her affair with Derek had been exposed the previous week. It was also the first time they'd seen Martin.

Martin and Jeff had agreed to let Gary represent both of them so that they could simplify the process through which they could come to an agreement with the feds. After they were buzzed in, they rode the elevator up in silence. As the doors opened and the elevator emptied, Andrea gently grabbed Brianne's arm and let the men go by. As the others walked to the receptionist, Andrea said, "Bri, I'm sorry it turned out this way."

"It didn't 'turn out this way,' Andrea," Brianne snapped with more venom than Andrea had ever seen in her. "You made all of it happen. You could've done fifty things to make it turn out differently, but you chose the one way that ensured it would turn out *exactly* this way."

Andrea didn't have a response.

Brianne snatched her arm back, adding, "Forgive me if I don't accept your apology and fuck you for being who you are."

Taken aback, but unwilling to let her friend—*former friend, now*—write her own version of the truth, Andrea said, "Brianne, that's fair enough, but while you're looking for people to blame, don't forget: I'm not the one who chose to kill her husband. I'm not the one who chose to manipulate my husband's friends into committing fraud, and I am absolutely not the one who was sleeping with my friend's husband out of sheer boredom."

Brianne fought back tears and tried very hard to play it tough. She straightened up, stiffened her resolve, wiped the tears from her eyes, and said, "Like you said, fair enough. We know where we stand."

She joined Martin, putting her arm through his. They all stood and waited in silence to be let into the offices.

Rocking on his heels, awkwardly, Gary said, "Is anyone going to dress up for Halloween?"

THE MEETING ITSELF was deathly dull and painful for Andrea. Sitting with Ramon and Nakala, she had to endure watching her husband wilt before the evidence presented by the same Newark assistant US attorney who had attended the West Windsor meeting. At first, Jeff acted brusquely, but slowly, his arrogance melted as his options dwindled.

For his part, Martin numbly, and quite meekly, accepted his punishment. His family's assisted living facilities would face heavy fines, which could be paid off through their ongoing operation and/or sale of the properties. Martin would be prevented from accepting any profit from their ongoing operation and/or sale. He would be permanently barred from applying for a certificate of administration for any such future work at both state and federal levels. He was being permanently excised from an industry that he had never wanted to be a part of.

Finished with their case, Martin and Andrea thanked Gary and the feds, then left. There was no telling what Martin would do next, or if the Singers could overcome their marital issues, but at the very least, Andrea thought—rationalized, really—they would be getting a fresh start.

Because this was Jeff's second offense, his negotiations were more complicated. The prosecutor was looking to neuter any and all future involvement Jeff might have with the financial sector. Permanent disbarment by the Securities and Exchange Commission would prevent Jeff from trading in the market for the rest of his life. He had to rescind all future rights to be a certified public accountant, which would prevent him from filing in the name of personal or corporate clients. This would effectively strangle his access to higher levels of income.

Gary fought back against each and every penalty, but kept losing. It's not that his arguments weren't sound or well presented, it's that he was making them in service of a client who had burned his last bridge. Andrea didn't say a word during the entire meeting. There were points where she could have defended her husband, but she never did.

Toward the end of the meeting, as the papers were presented to him and the inevitability of his castration dawned on him, Jeff said, "What if I don't sign? What if I fight it?"

The assistant US attorney said, "Mr. Stern, you're welcome to do that, but even taking your late cooperation into account, the evidence gathered against you by your wife and Kenneth Lee tells me you'd be spending the next several years of your life in a country club prison."

Jeff looked at Gary, who nodded in agreement.

He looked at Andrea with selfish fury.

Jeff Stern signed the agreement.

The assistant US attorney and Nakala Rogers left.

Andrea, Jeff, Gary, and Ramon remained. Andrea realized this was the first time Jeff and Ramon had seen each other since she had been in college. Their brief meetings back during the Morana investigation had been strained, to say the least, considering Jeff thought Ramon was going to get his girlfriend killed or, worse, into bed, though not necessarily in that order.

Gary said, "My client will be available for any and all of the FBI's needs, Agent Mercado."

Andrea locked eyes with Gary and cast her glance to the door, indicating he should leave. Normally lacking the ability to pick up on social cues, Gary got that one. "Excuse me for a second, I have to make a call outside."

When he left the room, Andrea said, "Ramon, we really want to thank you for helping us."

"Do you both really want that, Andie?" Ramon asked, surprising her with a release of frustration that he had clearly been suppressing, maybe as far back as the Morana case. "Because I can't tell if Jeff really wants to thank me."

"For what?" Jeff said. "Ruining my life?"

Ramon laughed. It was the sound of a man who was used to guilty people saying stupid things. "You haven't needed any help doing that for as long as I've known you, Jeff."

"Are we off the record here?" Jeff asked. "Because I want to make sure I can speak freely and not be charged with damaging the precious toenails of a federal agent."

"Guys, stop," Andrea said.

"Say whatever you want to say, Jeff," Ramon answered. "But know that it'll be coming back at you twice as hard."

"You're not better than me," Jeff said. "You're all just as corrupt, just as willing to cut corners to get what you want. That's all I did. I cut some corners. No one got hurt. And I did it for my family."

"You are so full of shit, it's incredible," Ramon said. "You're a weak, insecure man who lacks the strength to do the right thing for the right reasons. You don't deserve her."

"Oh, is that what it boils down to for you?" Jeff snapped. "I should have figured. You always wanted to get into her pants!"

"Jeff!" Andrea said, mortified.

"Hope you have better luck with that than I have lately," he said to Ramon.

"Out, now!" Andrea said, pushing Jeff to the door. She held a hand up to Ramon. "Don't say another word!"

He really wanted to.

"Not another word!" Andrea snapped. As Jeff stormed out of the room, she softened slightly and added, "Let me know how it goes with Molly's arraignment."

Ramon nodded, but true to the commands of the woman he once loved, and possibly might always love, he didn't say another word.

They met Gary by the elevators and he had the same uncomfortable look he'd had in the lobby earlier. Nervously rocking on his feet, he said, "That went really well, I think."

ON THE DRIVE back to West Windsor, Jeff and Andrea barely spoke. She watched the passing of the exits on the turnpike as if each one indicated an opportunity lost. Chance after chance to get off the road she was trapped on. She didn't know where the exit would take her, but wistfully she wondered what kind of an adventure each might bring. Except for exit 10. She knew that one would take her to the Menlo Park and Woodbridge malls, which might have been fun for the afternoon.

Certainly more fun than what she knew was in store for her.

They picked up JoJo from Sathwika's. The most Andrea could give her friend by way of details was, "I'll talk to you later."

At home, Andrea warmed up a bottle as Jeff changed out of his suit. He came downstairs and she said, "Sadie has to be picked up in an hour."

"Okay," he muttered, looking in the fridge for something to eat.

"Does that give us enough time to talk?"

"About what?" he replied, truly dumbfounded by the notion that they might have anything left to talk about.

She snorted. She knew Jeff hated when she did that, thinking it was rude. It really was a reflexive response she'd inherited from her parents, but since Andrea knew her parents were rude, she had to concede that one.

"What do you want to talk about, Andie?" he asked. "About how we're going to split the kids for trick-or-treating? Or maybe about how I'm out of a job now? How we might have to sell the house? About how we might have to dip into the college funds we set up for all the kids just to be able to afford not being able to afford their college tuitions? Or maybe talk about how you plan to get a job to help offset the expenses, but we'll have to use your salary to pay for the childcare we'll need while you're working?"

"That's the first and last bullet in your arsenal, Jeff?" she asked. "The money?"

"Money is the only thing that matters in this world," he replied, raising his voice. "Anything else you get is the result of money!"

"Who are you mad at, Jeff?" she asked.

He hesitated.

"No holding back," she said. "No holding it in. Who are you mad at?"

He slammed the refrigerator door. "I'm mad at you!" he shouted. It was loud enough to scare JoJo, who started crying. It only made Jeff raise his voice more. "Who the fuck else should I be mad at?"

She didn't say anything.

"I'm mad at your bitterness towards me," he said. "That you blame me for the fact you didn't become an FBI agent. You blame me for all the bad choices you made. You are so arrogant and conceited that you can't even look in the mirror and admit you were right by my side with every pregnancy. Right by my side with every piece of furniture we picked out. Right by my side when we had to sell the old house and move here."

Jeff paused, waiting for a response. Not getting one, he continued, "You were mad at me for years because you didn't see my stock fraud happening right under your nose. You're mad at me now that you didn't see the scheme I was running with the guys. This isn't about me. You stopped caring about me—stopped loving me—a long time ago. This is about you. It's always been about you, Andie. Always!"

"How can you say that?" she interrupted. "Until last year, *nothing* has been about me! Your job, our children, your crimes, our concessions. Where is the word *me* in there?"

"It's been about always wanting what you didn't have," he said. "You didn't want to have one kid so young, much less five kids by now, but you never *once* did anything to prevent yourself from getting pregnant. But blame that on me, too, since I refused to get a vasectomy or wear a condom—but that's okay, whatever it takes for you to be able to blame me, fine."

JoJo was still crying. He raised his voice even more to be heard over the din.

"You know everyone *so* well, their hopes and dreams, their accomplishments and regrets, you know the darkest secrets they hide inside," he said. "What did you tell me they called you when you were a kid? With that street trash gang in Queens? Insight, they called you? Yeah, that's you. You can see through everyone as if they were made of glass, Andie, but what's reflected back at you when you look?"

Andrea stood up, trying to get JoJo to stop crying. She walked around the kitchen and slowly bounced her.

"I'll tell you what you see, Andie," he continued. "A grifter. A thief. A con man. Because that's what you were; it's what you still are. In your blood. No better than your parents. Now you just steal people's souls."

"I do *what*?" she seethed.

"Without all these trappings you claim to hate *so* much, without the kids, and the house, and the Cellulitists to make fun of, and the husband who is just enough of a dick that you can justify playing the 'poor me' card—without all of this, you are *nothing*. That's why last year you practically fucking jumped at the chance to solve a crime. You nearly spat Josephine out on the floor for how fast you jumped, never caring if it might get me or the kids hurt. Never caring that afterwards, everyone in town would stare at us like we were animals at the zoo. And now, with Molly? You fucking went off the reservation looking for trouble where no one else could see any. Then, when you found it, it's all *our* fault that you needed to look for it in the first place? It's just you staring at that reflection, Andie, and hating what you see. Your whole life, so desperate to see something more than a Queens street rat! For all the incredible, amazing things you've done, catching the criminals you've caught, it hasn't made a difference in how you see yourself.

"I'm tired of trying to give you what you refuse to give yourself, Andie," Jeff finished. "I'm tired of trying to give you peace of mind."

Saying nothing, she bobbed JoJo into the sunroom and looked out the large windows to their backyard. Some geese floated in the pond. The leaves were coming down like snow now. Another fall, another winter, another spring, another summer. All of it, year in and year out, starting to pass by like gauzed lightning.

Soon, Ruth would be in high school. Eli in middle school. Sarah in upper elementary. Sadie in elementary. JoJo in preschool. There would be countless PTA events, science fairs, Halloween costumes, and pretending to be religious for Chanukah, and Passover, and Yom Kippur. There would be more soccer, and lacrosse, and basketball, and softball, though probably not softball because it bored the shit out of the kids today. And double all that for Sarah, who would make every travel team she tried out for.

There were so many exits on the turnpike. Each of them, any of them, *all* of them could take Andrea on an unexpected side journey. Who knew what she might find in Jersey City, or Newark, or even

Manhattan? Life had become cemented for so many of them based on their responsibility to those exits. Everything between getting on the turnpike and getting off was just buzzing cars and anger.

The lawn mowing would never end.

The leaf blowing would never end.

The snowplowing would never end.

If she hated the suburbs, why had she agreed to live in them?

If she hated having so many kids, why did she love them all so much, except maybe for Eli and Sadie, with JoJo TBD?

If she hated Jeff, why did she stay with him?

Andrea was so terrified of changing her life because in many ways, Jeff was right. She was a gray blob in that reflection. She was an unformed person. She was thirty-four years old and she hadn't lived yet.

She had gotten her brother killed, but she hadn't honored his life.

She had caught three killers, but she hadn't honored their victims' deaths.

She was terrified of finding out who she was without the cold comfort that had come from the things she despised about herself.

If not now, when was she ever going to take the chance?

If not now, *was* she ever going to take the chance?

Led by one hearty soul, the geese in the pond took off, flying up above the yard, circling around, and then heading northeast toward the farm fields to graze before sunset.

JoJo stopped crying.

Andrea turned to Jeff, who was still standing in the family room, his purposeful silence now goading her for a response. So many things she could say. She could berate him for his entitlement or his lack of accountability and responsibility. She could criticize him for his selfishness and narcissism. For his lack of curiosity about people, and his lack of interest in wanting to learn about them. She could ridicule him for liking the Mets and the Jets, but that seemed redundant. So many things she could say, but Andrea found herself having no desire to say any of them.

She looked at her husband, whom she had known since he was barely more than a boy. This flawed partner and flawed provider. Jeff was right in that she had stopped loving him long ago. But what did she really know about love, anyway?

Andrea thought of Kenny and Sitara. Poor Kenny, who completely lacked an understanding of why that relationship wasn't going to work. Was it a general male trait to be so blind to their own inadequacies, or just the men she knew?

She thought of Brianne and Martin, tragically mired in their mutual boredom. Neither was a bad person, they had just allowed themselves to become inured to life. Each had fallen prey to different kinds of seduction to offset what they were missing in their marriage. Andrea really did hope they could reclaim their lives.

She thought of Crystal and Wendell Burns, so comfortable in their relationship and their routine. Andrea had belittled that, but it was only because she was so envious of it. There was a lot to be said for comfort and security in a relationship. Sarcasm aside, Andrea was happy that Crystal and Wendell, the human equivalents of a splinter in your shoe and human paste, could find happiness together.

She thought of the Cellulitists and knew she could live the rest of her life without any of them.

Then she thought of Sathwika, and realized she couldn't imagine living life without her. They would have a future together, no matter what the next sixty seconds would bring. For the first time in her life, Andrea had found a friend. Now it was up to her to figure out how to be one in return.

Lastly, Andrea thought of her parents. Her bitter, shrill, unhappy parents. Always looking for a shortcut, always trying to evade and avoid the truth. Many years ago, she had promised herself that she would never accept living life like they had, and yet, in many ways, she had. Maybe Jeff's harsh assessment hadn't been that far off. The only way to get beyond that was to accept the truth about herself and speak to it from this moment forward.

Andrea looked at Jeff.

He saw the fear in her eyes.

For a second, she knew that he relished it.

That fear meant she would surrender.

Again.

She kissed JoJo on the forehead softly, letting her lips linger. That new-baby smell was fading, but it was still there. She relished it for a moment. This would be her last baby, so she should appreciate it while she could.

Mired in unhappiness for so long, she hadn't appreciated enough of the good things in her life. Starting, first and foremost, with herself. That had to change. The time for surrendering to her unhappiness had to be over.

And all she needed to do was take that first step.

The hardest step, she thought.

She certainly hoped there wouldn't be any harder than this.

Andrea looked up at Jeff. So much she could say, but the only words that came out of her mouth were, "I want a divorce."

ACKNOWLEDGMENTS

Thanks to Howard Alter for financial feedback, Bruce Fenton for legal feedback, and Janet Costa for pharmaceutical feedback. Any of the many mistakes made are purely from my flawed fictionalization of their advice.

Thanks to Hayley and Eric Eden and Aurelia Lambert for their thoughts on the manuscript in progress.

Thanks to Daniel Berkowitz of AuthorPop for having designed my author website (www.fabiannicieza.com). Go sign up for my newsletter now and maybe I'll have finally done a second one by the time this sees print (I'm really bad about that Interwebs stuff!).

Thanks to Simon Pulman, Novika Ishar, Golda Calonge, and Will Bersani of Cowan, DeBaets, Abrahams & Sheppard LLP for protecting my furiously selfish needs.

Thanks to Albert Lee, Mary Pender, Meredith Miller, and Lily Dolin of United Talent Agency, and Katrina Escadero, for creating opportunities that fuel my furiously selfish needs.

Huge thanks to my editorial team at Putnam: Mark Tavani, without whom this book would have no title, much less any qualitative merit you might find; Danielle Dietrich, Kristen Bianco, Sydney Cohen, and Emily Mlynek for helping get the word out; Christopher Lin and Jim Tierney for the great cover design and Kristin del Rosario for the great interior design; and the muckety-mucks, Director of Publicity

Alexis Welby, Associate Publisher Ashley McClay, Publisher Sally Kim, and President Ivan Held, without one and all of whom this book would not exist.

And always the most important thanks of all to my family—Tracey, Madison, and Jesse, my sister-in-law Christine, my brother, Mariano, my sister-in-law Marie, and my nieces, Katie and Annemarie.